R

Lazarus, Texas

Nathan Barber

For Christy, Noah and Emma

Death reveals that the world is not as it should be but that it stands in
need of redemption.
Dietrich Bonhoeffer

PROLOGUE

The buzzer shrieked as the final second vanished from the clock on the scoreboard far overhead. The Lady Tigers collapsed on the floor, exhausted from their Herculean effort. Suddenly, they became aware of the pandemonium around them.

The Lazarus fans poured out of the stands and onto the floor. With their mouths agape and their hands on their heads, the girls from Groom watched the Lady Longhorns pile on their big post player, still sprawled on the floor from the final play. They watched in awe as the Lazarus fans pushed their way past security and surrounded the Lady Longhorns on the court.

Seemingly the entire town of Lazarus danced and cheered and embraced the girls. High overhead, a voice over the loudspeakers urged fans to please clear the floor, please clear the floor.

Coach Lewis waded into the fray. He knew his girls were somewhere in the middle of the chaos but he couldn't get to them. People ran to him, patted him on the back, rubbed his head, embraced him, and said, "That was unbelievable, Coach." The fans pulled him this way and that and hugged and congratulated him. He was sure he'd appreciate it all later but he wanted to get to his girls. Finally, with the fans around him cheering uncontrollably, he broke through the jubilant mass of bodies and found his girls piled on top of one another on the floor. They were laughing and crying and hugging one another.

Exhausted, he sank to the floor to just watch, soak it all in, and commit this scene to memory...

CHAPTER I

The well-dressed visitor pushed open the creaky glass door, and the hot light of the late-morning sun poured into the hallway. The visitor stood with the door half open and felt the blast of cool air rush past him and out into the relentless August heat. From behind him through the open door, the sunlight created an alabaster glow that illuminated the freshly-waxed tile floor. The reflected light revealed before him numerous plaques, framed photos and bulletin boards full of tacked papers and news clippings on the wall to his left, and to his right a beautiful, tall trophy case stretching the length of the hallway. He stepped inside, let the tinted glass door close behind him and paused a moment to allow his eyes to adjust to the relative lowlight of the hallway; the only light in the hall came from a single doorway down the hall on the left and from the small bulbs glowing inside the trophy case to his right.

With an attaché case in one hand, the young man walked slowly toward the shaft of light emptying from the doorway ahead of him into the hall. As he walked, he ran his fingertips along the glass of the magnificent trophy case and surveyed its contents. Inside stood countless trophies of all sizes, most topped with small gold football players, each striking a football pose of one sort or another. Also filling the sacred space sat football helmets scribbled with scores of illegible signatures, footballs decorated in the same manner, varsity letters, vintage red and white letterman jackets, red and white megaphones, and more. On the back of the trophy case behind the assorted memorabilia

3

hung countless framed photos of both teams and individual players. Finally, nestled in between the more prominent pieces of memorabilia and hardware sat several odd bits of nostalgia including several pairs of game-worn cleats, a cowbell painted red, and several small squares of sod.

It's now or never, he thought to himself as he paused momentarily just outside the doorway and took one final, deep breath. He glanced at his watch, tousled his hair a bit and stepped into what he hoped would be the first chapter of the rest of his life.

"Well, hi, Mr. Lewis," came a twangy, west-Texas voice from behind a computer monitor on a desk. Mr. Lewis hardly looked old enough to be addressed as "mister."

"You must be Gladys," he replied, a little surprised. "How'd you know I'm Gabe Lewis?"

"Well, sugar, you told me on the phone yesterday you'd be arriving promptly at 11:00. Besides, we're not expecting anyone else to roll in here in a suit any time soon."

He glanced up at the clock hanging behind the secretary and watched the second hand and the minute hand glide simultaneously over the twelve.

"I reminded Mr. Haskins about you yesterday. He and Coach Cannon had a meeting this morning but they should be back just any time now. You just have a seat and make yourself comfortable."

Mr. Lewis sat down on the edge of the black vinyl chair next to the water cooler and looked around the tiny waiting room, noting the cinder block walls painted red and white, the framed number 83 football jersey hanging on the wall across from him and the Lazarus Longhorns football team photo and schedule poster hanging on the front of the secretary's desk. He grabbed the last tissue from the box on the cracked vinyl seat next to him, wiped the beads of sweat from his forehead and reminded himself to stay calm and confident.

"Ma'am, do you know if the position is still available?" he asked, more out of nervousness than anything; he felt pretty sure they hadn't given away the position in the last twenty-four hours.

"Girls basketball? Oh, yeah, sugar. Still open. Hope it works out for you," she answered before returning to whatever task occupied her behind the desk, leaving the two once again in uncomfortable silence.

After several silent minutes, the sounds of metal-bottomed shoes and deep, booming voices echoed down the hallway and into the waiting room. Through the door a moment later stomped two tall men of athletic build, each wearing a sweaty golf shirt, tight blue jeans, well-worn golf shoes coated in red dust, and a sweat-stained red baseball cap. Without acknowledging either person in the reception area, the two headed straight for the door at the back of the room well behind the secretary's desk, the door beneath the sign that read "PRINCIPAL." The first of the two flipped on the light in the office and the second slammed the door behind them.

The secretary picked up the receiver of her phone, punched a few digits and then turned her back to her guest. With one hand she covered the phone and whispered into the receiver. She nodded silently a few times then turned back to address the visitor from behind her computer monitor.

"Well, Mr. Haskins is back from his, uh, meeting," Gladys said as if she'd been caught telling a little white lie, "and he'll be happy to see you now. You can just go right on in, honey."

Mr. Lewis stood and dabbed his forehead once more with the dingy, already-damp tissue he'd been holding in his hand. *Get focused, Gabe, get focused.*

As he knocked on the door to the office, a voice called from inside, "Come on in, son."

Suddenly feeling a little overdressed, Gabe entered the office to find an older gentleman of ruddy complexion, perhaps in his late fifties or early sixties, leaned back in a red leather swivel chair, feet up on the desk. On the desk sat a nameplate that read "Calvin Haskins, Principal." The red-faced fellow waved Gabe into the office with one hand and, using his other, swabbed the sweat from his forehead with a red and white golf towel.

He dropped the soggy towel on the desk and extended his hand, "Gabe Lewis, Calvin Haskins. Good God, son, you must be burnin' up in that suit. Take your jacket off."

"I'm fine, thank you, sir. I appreciate you..."

"Suit yourself," interrupted Haskins.

Haskins' golfing partner chuckled as he wiped the sweat drops from his face with his shirt sleeve. "Good one, Haskins!"

The stuffy little office had little or no circulation and smelled of a strange combination of sweat, deodorant, old leather and just-in-from-the-heat-of-the-day body odor.

"Mr. Lewis, this is Coach Tommy Cannon, our football coach and athletic director. I've asked him to join us today, you know, you being here about a coaching job. That's as much his jurisdiction as it is mine, I reckon."

"Yes, sir," Gabe Lewis acknowledged cordially. "As I was saying, I really appreciate you having me in today to discuss the possibility of working here at your outstanding school."

As Gabe spoke, he felt himself beginning to sweat through his jacket under his arms and down the middle of his back. He prayed the two wouldn't notice the sweat betraying his nervous state.

Cannon, the younger of the two administrators by fifteen years or so, bent down and untied his golf shoes. Principal Haskins shuffled the papers on his desk looking for something that, judging by the look on his face, had been somewhere in the mess at some point recently. Behind Haskins' desk rose a wall covered with dozens of wooden plaques with inscriptions on brass plates, maybe a hundred newspaper clippings now yellowed with age, a dozen team photos of football squads and an eight-by-ten framed picture featuring a younger version of himself holding a sign that read "State Champs, Again." As Gabe waited for some kind of response from one of the two, he surveyed the wall of nostalgia that reminded him of the trophy case outside.

"Son, did you bring your résumé with you? I swear I had it here a few days ago," Haskins said without looking up from his search.

Gabe opened his attaché case and produced two copies of his résumé printed on fine linen paper. He stood to hand one to Mr. Haskins and then stretched out his hand to offer the other to Coach Cannon. Cannon, though, was changing his socks and didn't see Gabe's offering. Gabe shrugged a little, sighed and set the document on the seat next to the muscular Cannon. Pushing fifty, Cannon's physique was still relatively impressive, except for the significant beer belly that hung over his tight-waisted jeans.

"OK, I remember seeing this. OK, let's see. Alright... OK..." Haskins browsed the biographical information on the pages in his hand. "Assistant coach where?"

"At a private school in Houston. I helped out there with the girls' program while I worked on my master's across town. We did very well, actually, even against some of the bigger public..."

Haskins didn't let him finish. "Undergrad in English and Literature to go along with a master's in philosophy? What are you gonna do with that fancy degree way out here, son?" Haskins asked rhetorically as he continued to scan the papers. "Tell me about this 0-1 head coaching record of yours."

Gabe wiped his head again. "I coached one varsity game after my head coach was hospitalized briefly for chest pains."

"How'd you do? Was it close?" Cannon chimed in.

"We lost by one in overtime to a pretty salty team from Waco. We had the game plan and the girls knew what to do. I think we just didn't have it that night."

"That's a long way from Houston, son. What were you doing playing a team from so far away?"

"Unfortunately for us it was the second round of the playoffs," he explained as he hung his head a bit so as not to make eye contact while confessing his inadequacy.

Cannon chuckled and added, "At least you have playoff experience, now, right? That's, uh, very honest of you to put that on your resumé."

Somehow Gabe failed to find the humor in Coach Cannon's remark.

"Tommy, anything you need to ask Gabe here?"

"Why in the world are you way out here in west Texas looking for a job so late in the game? You know, we start school next week."

"Yes, sir, I know. To answer your question, I've learned an incredible amount about coaching and about basketball philosophy working with Coach Edison the last few years in Houston. I'm confident I have the knowledge and the experience I need to step into a program like this one and turn it around. We did it in Houston; I can do it here, too. As for why I'm in west Texas looking... honestly, I haven't had any offers anywhere else yet. A few interviews but no offers. The job market's pretty tough right now when you have zero years of experience. I saw this posted online..."

"You're a pretty honest fella, huh?" Haskins interjected.

"Honesty is better than all policy, or at least that's what Immanuel Kant said."

Cannon shrugged his shoulders, cocked his head and gave a befuddled look first to Gabe then to Haskins.

"Listen, Gabe, can you swing back by here after lunch? Say, about 12:30 or so? I need to visit with Coach here and we'll look at your résumé again. Will that be OK?"

"Sure. I did have a few questions for you, too, though," Gabe added, trying to keep the meeting from disbanding so quickly. "Don't we need to talk about coaching philosophy and my ideas for taking the program to the next level? Should we go over those now or..."

Haskins stood from behind his desk and walked around to Gabe. He patted Gabe on the back and opened the office door for him.

"Gladys, Gabe's going to be back in a little while, so make sure you're still around."

"OK, Mr. Haskins," Gladys answered from inside an office supply closet next door to Haskins' office. Then to Gabe, Gladys called out, "See you after lunch, honey."

Somewhat bewildered and more than a little frustrated, Gabe Lewis exited the waiting room, meandered down the hall and wandered out into the sweltering heat to look for lunch.

"What do you think, Tommy?"

"I told you not to make him drive all the way out here. He'll do. You know that. Besides, you see anybody else in line for an interview?"

"You know good and well we had to at least make sure he doesn't seem like some kind of pervert or deadbeat. Besides, seems like an eager beaver to me. Get 'em while they're young and train 'em up right. That's what I always say."

Cannon reached over and grabbed Gabe's bio from the chair. He looked over the résumé once more then flipped the papers into Haskins' waste basket.

"It just really doesn't matter. It's girls basketball we're talking about. It ain't football, Haskins."

"What do the girls look like for this season anyway? As bad as last year?"

"What do they always look like? I think they have one senior wanting to play. No size. The girls that are gonna play are average at best. Heck, we'll be lucky to have enough kids out there to put a team on the court and still have a few left over for the bench. What've we got to lose here? He's got a pulse and he's not a creep. If you can use him in a classroom somewhere then he'll be fine. He can't do any damage in the gym because those poor girls don't have a snowball's chance to do anything anyway."

"You're right - he'll do. Besides, we can get him cheap. Alright, it's settled then." Haskins jumped up from behind his desk and rubbed his hands together. "OK, next order of business. I believe, if my memory is correct, it's your turn to buy. I think I hear a Blue Plate Special and a cold Lone Star beer calling my name."

"Yep, it's settled. Let's go get that Blue Plate," said Cannon as they walked out through the waiting room. "Do me a favor, though, Haskins. I need to run to Lubbock this afternoon and pick up some equipment and check on the new uniforms. Can we wrap things up pretty quick after lunch? As long as I can get out of town by 2:00 I'll be fine."

"Won't take long at all," Haskins said and slapped his pal on the back.

Still in their golf shirts and Wrangler jeans, but now in cowboy boots instead of golf shoes, they walked down the hall toward the parking lot. Just past the water fountain, they paused at the trophy case and stared at the football trophy inscribed with "State Champions - 1983." Cannon looked at Haskins and nodded with a sense of deep satisfaction. Haskins clapped Cannon on the back and laughed.

"Greatest day of my life. Period."

"No doubt about it, Tommy," Haskins affirmed as they pushed open the door at the end of the hallway and headed for lunch.

———

The green road sign on westbound Ranch Road 145 read "Lazarus, Texas - Pop. 877." In the state of Texas, Austin, Houston, Dallas, Fort Worth and San Antonio rank as the most important, most influential and most famous Texas cities; all other cities and towns in Texas fall in line somewhere behind these. Far, far down the list, but not quite at the bottom, is Lazarus. Chances are no one outside of Texas had ever heard of Lazarus before the year Gabe Lewis arrived. In fact, hardly anyone in Texas and perhaps only a very few people in west Texas had ever heard of Lazarus until then. To be sure, Lazarus is nowhere to be found on the vast majority of maps, including Texas maps. To say Lazarus is situated south of Friona and north of Muleshoe usually doesn't help people locate Lazarus on a map. Nor does it help to say Lazarus can be found southeast of Bovina and northwest of Dodd.

An hour and a half northwest of Lubbock and an hour and a half southwest of Amarillo, in that gray area between where the Texas panhandle ends and west-Texas begins, Lazarus grew out of the wasteland of Bethany County just after the turn of the twentieth century. J. C. Lazarus and a small group of investors purchased a number of thousand-acre tracts of land on which to graze their cattle. The land was "a bargain" according to Mr. Lazarus and with good reason. With virtually no supply of water, no trees for shade and nothing but wind-scorched dust-producing red dirt for miles in every direction, Bethany County could support only the hardiest animals and vegetation. Texas longhorns were suited perfectly for this environment and Lazarus brought them in to be the very heart of his town.

Shortly after the purchase of the land, Lazarus and his cohorts plowed and leveled a half-mile strip of land and called it Main Street.

At the northern-most end of Main Street on the east side of the street, Lazarus set aside an acre of land upon which to construct the courthouse. On the southern-most end of Main Street, but on the west side, Lazarus built a large brick building in which he located the general store, the post office and a real estate office. Typical of a small Texas town, the walls on the ends of the building were a deep red brick, and storefronts with large windows adorned the front, which faced Main Street. From one end of the structure to the other, a customer could stroll under a wood-shingled awning along a porch of wood slats.

Though occupied now by Mary's Kitchen, Billy's Barber shop, an attorney's office, a doctor's office, the Take One video store and Lester's Liquor Store, the original building still stands. The awning is a little worn and some of the original shingles have been replaced; the decking along the storefronts is dusty and worn but still in great condition. No hitchposts remain in front of the stores and offices but it would be easy to imagine thirsty horses tied to them nearly a century ago. The original bricks on the back and ends of the building remain remarkably intact. Now faded from age and exposure to the unforgiving west-Texas elements, the lettering, hand-painted by Mr. Lazarus himself on the southernmost brick wall of the Bethany County landmark, can still be recognized: "Welcome to Lazarus - We hope you'll stay a while."

And "stay a while" is just what people did. Although people didn't flock to the isolated, upstart cowtown, those who did venture westward to hang their own shingles in Lazarus generally stayed in Lazarus. By the 1920s, Lazarus, Texas peaked somewhere near a thousand residents, according to the best recollections of the old timers. As the years went by, though, people for whatever reason stopped moving to Lazarus and the population stabilized after the Great Depression. Those who moved to town married, had families and made for themselves modest, comfortable livings working the land or working in the few businesses that Lazarus could support. Their families did the same. The next generation married, had families and made their own livings in Lazarus. Almost without exception, those who were born in Lazarus grew up there, worked there until their tired bodies could work no more, and then died and were buried in Lazarus Cemetery behind the Bethany County courthouse.

Over the years, Lazarus sent its share of favorite sons off to the Great War, World War II, Korea, Vietnam, the Falklands, the Gulf War and then to Afghanistan and Iraq. The town prayed hard for each of its sons who took up arms for his country and, just like each time before, the sons returned home to heroes' welcomes, fanfare and even the occasional parade. Into the melee of each armed conflict Lazarus sent one or more of its own. By the grace of God, though, as the old timers will tell you, the sons returned home with ne'er a scratch nor a blister nor any wound other than an aching in their hearts for those soldiers around them who had given their lives.

The old timers of Lazarus still talk of the deep religious character of the town and how that had always spared Lazarus the suffering and pain so often felt by other people in other places. The newspaper archives of the Bethany Herald tell no stories of deadly epidemics in Lazarus, no tales of deadly twisters or floods, no deadly car crashes, no accidents at the feed mill, no murders, no suicides, no tragedy. As in any other town, death and dying were part of life in Lazarus, but it seemed almost as if the Angel of Death visited only those in Lazarus already on their deathbeds and never before. Over the years, the people of Lazarus had taken this grace for granted.

People simply lived their simple, ordinary lives the way their parents and grandparents had. The people of Lazarus grew content and never developed a sense of adventure, curiosity or desire to explore the world that lay beyond the limits of Bethany County. Those few who did brave the wilds of community colleges or universities of Lubbock, Amarillo or even Clovis, which lay just across the New Mexico border only a few miles west of Lazarus, always made their way back home to learn the family trade, accept a managerial training position at the mill or teach in Lazarus schools. This feeling of contentment, unintentionally bred into the generations of offspring of Lazarus, brought with it skepticism toward anything perceived as out of the ordinary, risky, or heaven forbid, ambitious; the only risk-taking in Lazarus occurred on the gridiron. Living in Lazarus in recent decades required very little risk of those who homesteaded there and that was, perhaps, the single most appealing aspect of life in Lazarus for those who called Lazarus home.

Population 877, thought Gabe Lewis, who found himself at once completely out of his element so far north and west in his own state. *Far cry from Houston.*

The aspiring young basketball coach wisely drove in from Houston the day before his interview and spent the night in the only lodging in Lazarus, the Motel 6 on Ranch Road 145 on the outskirts of the town. He was counting on this interview to pay off so, against the advice of his friends and family, he'd loaded all his belongings in his Blazer; Gabe had no intentions of returning to Houston. For the entire drive from Lubbock north and west toward Lazarus, the horizon dazzled with a sunset not often seen over the high-rise office buildings and apartments of Houston. With neither buildings nor trees to block the view of the horizon, the sunset of a million shades of pink and orange, complete with brush-stroked clouds, gave Gabe a clearer understanding of why visitors to Texas leave believing things really are bigger here.

The day before his interview with the principal, Gabe arrived in Lazarus just as the sun dropped completely below the horizon and secured his room for the night at the mostly vacant, second-rate motel. Without even changing his clothes, he immediately carried several boxes of books and video tapes up two flights of stairs to his motel room. As he repeatedly ascended and descended the stairs, he noticed two things in particular: the hot, dry wind that blew incessantly carrying with it tiny grains of red dirt and the foul stench of a skunk hanging in the air despite the wind.

As if he were preparing for a playoff game with a last-minute midnight session of game tape after weeks of mental preparation, the twenty-something watched a few minutes of basketball instructional videos to keep the finer points of the game fresh in his mind. After a shower in sulphur-scented well water, quite a departure from the highly-chlorinated water back in Houston, Gabe browsed some of his favorite passages in well-worn books by Coach K, Pat Summitt, John Wooden and other coaching greats. With a wealth of basketball knowledge floating around in his mind, Gabe lay his head on the hard, flat pillow and fell asleep as he played out in his mind the perfect interview.

Well-rested despite sleeping in unfamiliar surroundings, Gabe awoke early the next morning to the wake-up call from the front desk. As he sat pensively on the edge of his bed two minutes later, the alarm clock shrieked a backup wake-up call. This was the day he had been looking forward to for a long time. His gut told him this was going to be a good day. *The power of positive thinking*, he said to himself over and over.

After showering for the second time in twelve hours, he dressed himself in the mirror hung on the back of the motel door. He wore the only suit he had, a slick gray suit his parents bought for him when he graduated from college a few years earlier. His red tie, his "power tie," coordinated well with the gray fabric of the jacket and pants, he figured, and gave him a look of maturity and, perhaps, authority. Also, he figured a red tie might earn him some much-needed bonus points in the interview since the school colors of Lazarus were red and white. Against the advice of his parents, Gabe declined a trim, let alone a haircut, before he left the city. His shaggy yet stylish blond hair occasionally confused "adults" and led them to believe he was a high school student or a college freshman at most, a fact he in turn enjoyed and despised.

His appointment wasn't until 11:00 so he had a few idle hours during which he could relax. A big believer in eating a hearty breakfast on game day, Gabe set out to find some coffee and some breakfast food. Certain he wanted breakfast neither from the shelves of the nearby Chevron service station nor from the "As advertised - free breakfast bar" of the Motel 6, Gabe asked the motel clerk for directions to a good place to eat a real breakfast. He climbed in his dust-covered Blazer and drove less than a minute to Mary's Kitchen, a quaint diner located in what appeared to be the oldest and most historic building in town and the only place in Lazarus that served real food for breakfast.

After a quiet and reflective breakfast of coffee, eggs, bacon and toast, Gabe returned to his motel room to get mentally prepared for the interview. Fifteen minutes before his interview was scheduled to begin, he returned to his SUV and drove the short distance to the Lazarus High School administration building. He arrived a full twelve minutes early, so he waited in the comfort of his vehicle until 10:55 a.m. He timed his attack so he would be in the office exactly at 11:00 as he had been instructed.

Despite being impeccably on time, the 11:00 meeting with the principal and the athletic director didn't pan out exactly as he had pictured in his mind the night before. Nevertheless, they asked him to return after lunch for a second interview, a callback of sorts, he supposed. Not wanting to be late for the meeting after lunch, Gabe drove to the Dairy Queen he passed on the way into town the night before and ordered a burger, all the way, fries and a Diet Dr. Pepper. Every town in Texas has either a Dairy Queen or a Sonic - it's required by law. After scarfing down the value meal, he returned to the administration building where, again, he sat temporarily shielded from the unforgiving heat in his SUV and began his third reading of *Sacred Hoops* by Phil Jackson. Exactly as he had done earlier in the day, Gabe Lewis made his way back inside and down the hall for his afternoon meeting. Again, he arrived precisely on time.

Still dressed in his gray suit, white shirt and red tie, Gabe fidgeted in his seat as he rehearsed in his mind the things he figured he needed to say to secure this position, his first real job. For the entire 617 miles from Houston to Lazarus in his blue Chevy Blazer, Gabe thought of a response to any and every question he imagined Haskins and Cannon possibly could ask. He was as prepared as he could be for anything Haskins might throw at him. Educational philosophy, classroom discipline strategy, career goals. Gabe had those topics covered. He thought about X's and O's, motivational strategies, offenses and defenses. He had the basketball details covered, too. Now he had only to recall the things he'd worked out in his mind during the drive from Houston and to answer with confidence.

Gabe also had rehearsed an exhaustive list of questions for Haskins and for the A.D. What's the record of the program over the last five years? ten years? Why is the position available? What's included in the job description for this position? What are the expectations going to be in terms of win-loss ratio? How will success be measured in the program? Which is more important: wins and losses or a classy program? He was ready to make an impression now since he hadn't been given the opportunity in the first meeting.

"Honey, they'll be back pretty soon," Gladys said confidently at 1:00, thirty minutes after he'd arrived at the pre-arranged time.

The second hand seemed to slow down and the temperature in the building seemed to rise minute by minute. The sweat began seeping through his gray coat again as he waited in the heat.

Finally, at 1:25, Haskins and Cannon strolled in through the reception area and into his office. Ten minutes later, Gladys' phone buzzed. After about five seconds on the phone, Gladys, once again without looking out from behind the monitor, motioned for Gabe to go on in to Haskins' office. Gabe stood, stretched his arms and, at the last second, noticed a drop of mustard staring back at him from the middle of his tie. The mustard, now congealed on the silk tie, looked like a bad tie tack. He sighed, buttoned his coat trying to conceal the condiment stain, and headed into Haskins' office to wow the old timer and the athletic director and earn the job for which he had driven more than 600 miles out of civilization and into the middle of nowhere.

"Mr. Lewis, Coach Cannon has to take care of some important errands in Lubbock here pretty soon so our session's gonna be real quick this afternoon. I hope that's OK."

"Yes, sir."

"So, you looking to stay here a while or just use us as a stepping stone to something bigger somewhere else like our last coach did?"

"Mr. Haskins, I'd like to build something here," he said as he stood spontaneously and looked at both men before him. "I'd like to build a program here, put this program on the map. From the looks of the things on the wall behind you, you did the same thing once with the football team."

"Twice, actually," Haskins replied as his chest swelled a little. "The first time was in '65 and the second was in '83. You know, Tommy here was my go-to guy in that '83 season. He was one heck of a quarterback, I tell you. Fastest white kid I ever saw. And strong, mercy was he strong."

Coach Cannon crossed his arms and smiled with a sense of pride and satisfaction as he leaned against the wall.

"What you're doing now, Mr. Haskins, is exactly what I want to be able to do ten years down the road. I want to look back with pride and reminisce about the great teams, the great players, the great seasons. Mr. Haskins, Coach Cannon, give me a chance and I can do that here. I know I can."

Haskins chuckled as he stood up and walked past Gabe and into the waiting room. He reappeared a moment later with a file folder full of papers in his hand. He flipped open the folder and pulled from it a few papers on which he scribbled once he returned to his chair behind his desk. When he finished writing, he stood and reached for Gabe's hand.

"Coach Lewis," Haskins began, "welcome to Lazarus."

Coach Gabe Lewis shook Haskins' hand, signed the contract without hesitation and then shook Cannon's hand. The new coach was so excited he hardly could contain his enthusiasm.

"Swing by this Friday and we'll get you squared away on your classes, your practice schedule, and all that good stuff. You got a place to stay 'til then?"

"Not yet but you can bet I'll find one," answered the most excited young coach in the entire Texas panhandle. "See you gentlemen Friday."

Coach Lewis clutched his copy of his contract in one hand, grabbed his attaché case with the other and danced out into the reception area where Gladys sat now pounding away at the computer.

"Congratulations, honey. See you in a few days," Gladys called out as Coach Lewis disappeared into the hallway.

The power of positive thinking, Gabe thought again to himself as he walked out, smiling, contract in hand. Giddy with excitement, Coach Lewis almost laughed out loud but restrained his exuberance and limited himself to a Cheshire Cat grin. At the end of the hall the newest employee of Lazarus Independent School District opened the door and headed out into the heat of the midday sun. As the oppressive heat created a ripple effect in the air above the pavement of the parking lot, three large figures climbed out of an extended cab Ford F-350 heavy duty pickup. The three apparitions made their way through the parking lot toward the building.

"Excuse me," said the smallest of the three figures, a sturdy man in work clothes. "You work here?"

Yes, yes I do, thank you very much, Coach Lewis thought to himself. He really wanted to say that aloud. "Yes, sir, I sure do. What can I do for you this afternoon?"

"I'm looking for the school office, to get these two registered for classes before the school year gets started."

"Yes, sir. Right through this door," he said as he pointed, "down the hall, then the door at the end on the left."

As the three headed inside, Coach Lewis stood for a moment in the parking lot and took in his surroundings before climbing into his vehicle and heading off to find a place to live.

Still inside the high school office, Cannon looked at Haskins in near disbelief and grinned. "You know, he's such a nice guy. It almost ain't right to let him have that job. He has no idea what he just got himself into."

"No, sir. No idea at all, Tommy," the principal agreed as he shook his head and stared down at his boots. "It may get deep around here real quick. I hope that kid's got him a good pair of boots. On second thought, I bet you a hundred dollars that kid ain't never owned a pair of boots in his life."

"Yea, you can say that again. Oh, well," exhaled Cannon. As he left Haskins in his office, he said, "I need to grab my purchase order then I'm headed to Lubbock. See you tomorrow."

Cannon turned and went to Gladys' file cabinet. He rifled through the folders for several minutes desperately searching for the elusive purchase order that was his ticket to brand new football uniforms. Unexpectedly, an unfamiliar voice from across the waiting room peaked his curiosity.

"Is this the high school office?" asked the stranger.

"Why, yes it is. What can I do for you, sir?" Gladys responded from behind her computer.

"My name is Samuel Colter. We're moving in from Amarillo this week and I need to see about getting my twins signed up for school. Y'all start next week, right?"

"Yes, sir, we sure do. Is this one yours?"

"Yes, ma'am, this is Corey. I think Sam ran off to look at the gym."

Coach Cannon straightened up and turned around to assess the newcomers. Before him stood a robust, blue-collar man with the kind of strong, healthy build only a hardworking fellow can come by through a rare combination of good genes and a lifetime of working with his hands. The man held a cowboy hat in one hand. His rolled up denim sleeves revealed rugged forearms and strong, thick wrists. Standing next to him was a strapping, husky young man, maybe three or four inches better than six feet. His neck must have measured nineteen inches around and his shirt sleeves were just about to lose their grip on his biceps. His sandy-brown hair hung down over his forehead and just a little into his eyes. Cannon nodded to the man then made his way across the lobby toward the big, strapping boy.

"Don't just stand there, son. Say hello to the man."

"Hi. Corey Colter," he said as Coach Cannon approached with an outstretched hand.

"Tommy Cannon, head football coach."

"Then I guess we'll get to know each other pretty good, Coach, since I'm hoping I can play for you guys this season," Corey said.

As Cannon drooled over the gift dropped at his feet by the football gods, Principal Haskins emerged from his office to discover the source of all the commotion.

"Welcome to Lazarus," Haskins said. As he spoke, he finally got around to shaking Samuel's hand then returned his gaze to Corey.

Still in disbelief of his good fortune and still shaking Corey's powerful hand, Coach Cannon wondered out loud, "Is Sam the same size as you?"

"Near about."

Coach Cannon, his heart racing the way it does in the waning seconds of a close game, continued, "Sam play football?"

Mr. Colter looked first at Corey then at Coach Cannon and nodded his head. "Probably could."

Almost as if on cue, Sam Colter appeared in the doorway to the office reception area. Corey was absolutely right - Sam was just as tall as Corey though neither as thick nor as bulky. Cannon, Haskins and even Gladys were fixated on Sam. No one in the room moved. No one blinked. No one said a word. No one even drew a breath.

Mr. Colter continued, "Sam, well... she prefers hoops to football."

CHAPTER II

"Hey, Patton, good to see you, buddy. How's your summer been?"

"Summer's been great, Calvin. Just got back from Vegas for my twentieth with Elaine."

"Has it been that long now?"

"Yep. Twenty years. I guess that means you've been principal now, what, like thirty?"

Calvin Haskins rubbed his forehead in disbelief. "Yea, I guess so. Time flies, huh?"

"Sometimes it does and sometimes it just drags on and on," replied Patton McArthur.

Twenty years ago, Patton McArthur coached and taught across the New Mexico border at Clovis High School. At the time, he was just the assistant boys basketball coach and a high school biology teacher. At a teachers' summer conference in Las Vegas, Patton McArthur met Elaine Bishop in a buffet line at the Stardust Hotel and Casino. Three days and one torrid affair later, Patton and Elaine skipped the convention's keynote address and got married in a wedding chapel across town. McArthur, so crazy in love with his new bride, resigned from Clovis and moved to Lazarus to be with Elaine, the science teacher for Lazarus Elementary and Lazarus Middle. McArthur spent a year working the graveyard shift at the feed mill and helping out as the assistant coach with the boys basketball team for no pay before the science teacher at Lazarus High School finally retired. Haskins

25

immediately hired McArthur to teach and to be the assistant boys basketball coach. A few years later, the head coach retired and McArthur was promoted. Haskins and McArthur had been fishing, drinking, skeet-shooting, card-playing and golfing buddies ever since.

"I appreciate you coming in tonight to visit with me, Coach," Haskins began as he flagged a waitress. "What are you having? The usual?"

"You know me too well."

The waitress, who looked more like someone's kindly and beloved grandmother, brought over two waters, two long neck beers and a basket of chips. "How're you boys doing tonight? Mr. Haskins, we have the okra tonight. You want that with your chicken fried steak special? How 'bout you General? Okra, too, or just the mashed potatoes and green beans."

"Sure, Martha, we'll have the fried okra," Haskins said as he removed the cap from his bottle.

Martha had owned and operated Mary's Kitchen for as long as anyone can remember. Her older sister by nearly twenty years, Mary, opened the place in 1945 after her husband had returned from Europe. At the time, Martha was just a child. Martha grew up in the diner, having been raised by her sister rather than by her parents. From the time she was old enough to drop out of school and work full time, Martha waited tables at Mary's Kitchen. She took over when her sister lost interest in the business and decided to spend time at home gardening and raising African violets with her husband. After more than a few years of comfortable retirement living, Mary and her husband both passed leaving the place to Martha.

"Martha, you've gotta be getting too old to be waiting tables these days," joked Coach McArthur.

"You're pushing your luck, General. You know there isn't anything I'd rather do here than wait tables. How else would I get to keep such good company? You gonna come visit me in the kitchen or back in the office while I do the books? I didn't think so."

Martha was a people person. She didn't want any part of cooking, cleaning or taking care of the paperwork. Instead, Martha insisted on being around the customers so she could get to know them. Those in Lazarus who had never been to Mary's Kitchen could be counted on one hand and Martha knew all her customers. A cynic might suggest Martha just wanted an angle on everyone in town so as to keep the tips rolling in, but Martha was as genuine as they come in Lazarus or anywhere else, for that matter.

Martha took their orders and turned them over to the short-order cook in the kitchen.

"So what's going on, Calvin?" the General asked.

"We hired a girls coach today."

"Another one? Five in five years, huh? Who'd you find this time?"

"Kid out of Houston. Has assistant coaching experience there. Not really any head coaching experience. A real go-getter, though."

The General shifted in his seat and sighed, "A go-getter? I'm getting too old to have to deal with these high-energy, idealistic types. Come on, Calvin. You're just creating headaches for both of us."

"You do realize we start school next week and we were still short one teacher and one head coach. We were out of options. Besides, he's so wet behind the ears that he'll do whatever we ask him to. No problems, I assure you."

By no means was this the first time these two had done business in Mary's Kitchen. In fact, countless business meetings in Lazarus had occurred in Mary's Kitchen over the years, not only between these two pals but also between other influential people of Lazarus. Bank loans and divorce papers frequently changed hands across the tables between the red vinyl booth seating. For Haskins and McArthur, the booth of choice was the booth in the far corner of the diner, the farthest booth from both the entrance to the diner as well as from the entrance to the kitchen. From this booth, Haskins could keep tabs on who came and went from Mary's. This booth had the best location also because it saw the least amount of traffic and passersby, thus making the booth the most conducive for productive, if not clandestine, business meetings.

"I don't want no headaches, Calvin. I'm serious."

Haskins tipped up his bottle and consumed half its contents in three big swigs. He set the bottle down on the table, leaned in and looked his buddy in the eye.

"Here's the deal. You can keep your normal schedule. You'll have the gym every Monday, Wednesday and Friday just like always. The new is gonna wear off this thing for him pretty darn quick, so all that energy he has now ain't gonna last long."

"Fair enough. As long as I have your word on this."

The two were so engaged at this point that they no longer paid attention to the other patrons of Mary's Kitchen. They focused entirely on the issue of Gabe Lewis.

"You have my word. And don't worry about the budget either," Haskins continued in a reassuring tone. "He's coming in so late in the game that he won't have any idea where the budget goes, who gets what, who gets how much, and what have you. I'm pretty sure we have enough balls and uniforms left over from the last few years that he won't need anything. If he asks, just tell him the budget's already been used up."

"Sorry to interrupt, boys," said Martha as she served the county's biggest, and best, chicken fried steak smothered in white gravy, mashed potatoes on the side, also smothered in white gravy, fried okra and two great big pieces of Texas toast. "Ya'll just holler if you need some fresh bottles or if you're ready for some coffee."

Over the years Martha had overheard many conversations that surely never were meant for her to hear, but she rarely involved herself in the conversations between patrons. She just eavesdropped and gleaned useful tidbits here and there.

"She's priceless, huh?"

"Yep, one of a kind," agreed Patton. "So you don't expect any trouble with this kid, huh? That's good."

"Young and impressionable, far as I can tell. Make sure you give him the lecture, let him know how things work around here. Any pipe dreams he has, snuff 'em out quick. Take him out for lunch on Friday and charge it to the school."

"Friday it is."

Talk turned from business to details of McArthur's trip to Vegas, including a complete account of all the money he lost at the craps tables, the blackjack tables, the roulette tables and the slots. Bite by bite the artery-clogging dinners disappeared and so did the bottles of beer. Martha kept the beers coming to loosen the boys up and to prime them for a big tip at the end of the meal.

"How 'bout some coffee and pie? We have apple pie and I think we have some chocolate pie left, too," said Martha, still up-selling, looking to score a tip of the five-to-six dollar variety.

Haskins drew a deep breath and exhaled as if to free some room in the waist of his pants for dessert. He shifted his attention to the display case along the wall between the kitchen entrance and the cash register hoping that a glimpse of one of the two pies would help him decide whether or not to indulge in the simple pleasure that was Mary's Kitchen's award-winning pies. As his eyes scanned the patrons on the way to the display case where Martha kept the pies, Haskins saw a fresh, familiar face.

"I'll be darned, Coach," Haskins said, pointing to a table across the diner occupied by one shaggy-haired young man. "That's the kid right there; that's Gabe Lewis. Want to meet him?"

"I'll pass, Calvin. I'd hate to get too friendly with him now only to have to lay down the law on Friday." McArthur turned to Martha, "You know, I think I'll pass on the coffee and pie, too. Just leave me the check, Martha." He turned back to his boss, "The longer I'm gone the more details I have to give Elaine. You know, Calvin?"

"Well, in that case, I guess I'll pass, too, Martha. Leave me my check and I'll get outta here."

Coach McArthur dropped a couple of bills, shook Haskins' hand and winked goodbye to Martha. He walked right past Gabe and stared over his shoulder at the book Gabe had on the table. The General shook his head, looked back at Haskins and shook his head again as if to say, "I don't know about this." The General turned quickly and headed home to try to explain to Elaine why dinner required him to be gone so long. Haskins, in absolutely no hurry, dropped a twenty and some ones on the table, wished Martha a good evening then made his rounds through the diner shaking hands and patting backs.

Just as Martha had planned, her boys, partially out of generosity and partly due to slight inebriation, left sizable tips on the table next to the dozen or so empty bottles, the plates smeared with congealed gravy and the greasy napkins. Martha pocketed the tips, some of which got reported to the IRS, but most of which went in a jar labeled "college fund" in her cupboard at home. She bussed the table then returned to the kitchen. A moment later, Martha went to the front window and unplugged the neon "OPEN" sign. The regulars knew this was Martha's polite way of telling people she was tired and ready to go home. Within minutes, nearly everyone in Mary's Kitchen had paid for their meals and gone on their way. The only people left in the diner once the regulars cleared out were a young girl with a toddler and Gabe Lewis.

"She's getting so big," Martha said to the girl as she made googly eyes at the toddler and touched her finger to the baby's nose. "Time sure goes by fast, don't it? Sounds so cliché and corny but, by God, it's the darn truth."

"Yes, ma'am, it does. Hard to believe she's walking pretty good now, and even trying to do some talking." She rubbed the child's blond hair and kissed her cheek.

"It wasn't so long ago I was saying the same thing about you and your sister." Martha untied her apron and sat down next to the girl. She turned and looked over her shoulder at Gabe sitting across the room. "See that fella over there reading his book?"

"Yeah. Never seen him before, though. You know who he is?"

"Sure do. That's your new coach. Coach Lewis."

"Well, he's sure cuter than any coach we've had here in a while, but he sticks out like a sore thumb. I'm pretty sure he ain't from around here. What do you think?"

"About him being cute?"

"No," she retorted as she rolled her eyes. "What do you think? From around here or not? Think he'll be OK here?"

"We'll have to see, won't we," Martha said as she stood up and grabbed her apron. "I tell you what I do think. You should take yourself over there and introduce yourself."

Coach Lewis finished reading Phil Jackson's *Sacred Hoops* in his motel room and decided he should revisit the diner where he ate breakfast and get some dinner. Breakfast that morning was outstanding, much like he remembered breakfast from childhood when he would spend weekends with his grandparents out in the country, far away from the big city. He supposed dinner would probably be about the same quality as his breakfast, so he walked from his motel to Mary's Kitchen to sample the best, if not the only, dinner cuisine Lazarus had to offer.

No longer dressed in his suit, not only because of the heat but also because he thought he drew entirely too much attention to himself in it, Gabe trekked to Mary's Kitchen wearing an Abercrombie and Fitch t-shirt, khaki cargo shorts and flip flops. He honestly believed he would be totally inconspicuous dressed this way in Lazarus, Texas. Tucked under his arm was one of his favorite books, John Fitzsimmons

Mahoney's *The Tao of the Jump Shot*. He had read this one three times already and was anxious to get into it again.

Once he reached the diner, he noticed the terrific smell of the place. The aroma of the diner was that of cooking grease, grease used to cook fries and onion rings, used to fry chicken fried steak, steak fingers, chicken tenders and whatever other fried foods Mary's had to offer. The smell was so thick it hung in the nostrils and clung to the clothes of all who dined there. Even though Gabe hailed from Houston, he was no stranger to down-home, hole in the wall cooking. He enjoyed eating at places like Mary's Kitchen. He believed places like Mary's went a long way toward defining the culture, the very essence, of the city or town where it's located.

"How 'bout this booth right over here?" asked the waitress, an older woman whose name tag simply said "Mary's." She handed him a laminated menu that clearly had been printed on cheap paper using a cheap home printer.

"Thank you very much," he said politely. "This will be just fine. Could I start with a Diet Dr. Pepper, please?"

"Comin' right up, darling." She disappeared into the kitchen.

Gabe Lewis hadn't noticed at breakfast what a fascinating place Mary's Kitchen was. The red vinyl booths and red chairs, if it weren't for the worn spots on the vinyl, looked fresh off of a time machine from the 1950s. The display case against the wall displayed beautiful pies just like in an old fashioned grocery store or delicatessen. On the wall behind the cash register hung faded autographed 8 x 10 photos of Willie Nelson, Pat Green, Johnny Cash, Patsy Cline and a few others Gabe didn't recognize, including a few who looked like genuine rodeo cowboys.

"Here's your Diet DP," said the waitress. "You ready to order?"

"Let's go with a cheeseburger and seasoned fries," he answered. He pointed to the pictures on the wall behind the register. "All those guys came through here?"

"Sure did. Some more recently than others, though. Most of them on their way into or out of Lubbock or Amarillo."

"Fascinating."

"Really or are you just being polite?"

"No, really. I think it's really interesting. I think the fact that all those guys ate here kind of defines what this place is. Don't you?"

"You know, I never thought about it like that but you're absolutely right, darling."

They exchanged smiles briefly.

"I'm Gabe Lewis. Are you Mary?"

"No, I'm Martha. Nice to meet you, Gabe Lewis. Let me go get that order in for you. Should be about ten minutes. You just holler if you need me."

Gabe pulled out his book and started reading. Every few pages, he stopped and looked around at the other patrons. Part of him hoped he would go unnoticed and part of him hoped people would see him and wonder who he was. Nobody he saw was looking back at him. He didn't realize, though, that everyone in Mary's Kitchen had already noticed him and knew instantly he was not from Lazarus. He also didn't realize that nobody in Mary's Kitchen cared who he was. About twenty or so pages into his book, his food arrived.

"Like I said, just holler if you need me," Martha said with a smile.

Gabe ate and read at the same time. He took a bite then read, took a bite then read. After a while, Martha refilled his drink and he didn't even notice because he was so engrossed in his book. When he ran out of burger and fries, Martha was at his table almost immediately.

"How 'bout some pie and coffee to top off that meal tonight? We've got apple pie and chocolate pie and regular and decaf."

"Sold. Let's try some apple pie and coffee, two creams, two sugars. Thanks."

"Vanilla ice cream on top of that pie?"

"Whew," he exhaled. "Sure. Why not? Let's go for it."

Martha brought the heaping dessert and coffee and set them down in front of him.

"So, I heard you're gonna be the new girls basketball coach."

Hey, she knows who I am! This is going to be so fun! He nodded. "Yes, ma'am. Signed the contract today. How'd you know?"

Martha pointed to the back corner of the diner at Principal Haskins and another man that Gabe had never seen before. "Like I said, I heard it."

"Oh," he said as turned back around. "Who's that with Mr. Haskins?"

"That's Patton McArthur, also known as The General. Mostly because of his name but they say he has quite a temper, too."

"Who is he?"

"He's the boys basketball coach. I'll come back and we'll visit a little bit later," she said as she cleared the dirty dishes from his table. "Enjoy that pie and ice cream."

Gabe took his time with the pie and coffee. As with his meal, he read and ate, read and ate. When he reached the bottom of his coffee he still had another bite or two of pie left on his plate. He looked up to wave at Martha and noticed that he was almost alone in the diner, save a young girl and a small child. The neon sign no longer was illuminated and Martha was just sitting and visiting with the girl. Martha stood and picked up the child as the girl slid out her side of the booth and made her way over to the booth where Gabe sat alone with his book.

"Excuse me," the girl said with a bashful smile, afraid she was interrupting, "are you the new basketball coach?"

"I sure am. I'm Coach Lewis. Do you play ball?"

"Yes, sir. My name's Autumn Griffin. I've played since I was in the 7th grade," she answered bashfully. "Can I sit down for a minute? I just wanted to come say 'Hi.'"

Coach Lewis had seen enough basketball players in his time to know that Autumn might play basketball, but she was no basketball player. He could tell right away that, despite her thin-to-average frame, she had not been blessed with a muscular, athletic build. More cute than anything else, she made him think that if he'd been ten years younger, he'd have been quite taken with her. Autumn had her dirty-blond hair pulled back in a pony tail that hung just at her shoulders. Her kind, hazel eyes sparkled even in the dim light of the diner. Autumn tried in vain to restrain her smile but her lips would have none of that. Coach Lewis could tell in no time that she was a genuine, down-to-earth kid. Player or not, she'd be great to have around.

"Sure. Have a seat."

"So, how'd you end up here?"

"Well," he began, somewhat surprised by Autumn's directness, "I found the job posted online, I called the principal..."

"Actually, Coach," she interrupted, "I meant *why* are you here, in Lazarus?"

"This seemed to me like a pretty good situation, a place where I could come in and build something. Besides, there was a coach that needed a team and a team that needed a coach. Seemed like a natural fit."

"Really..." Autumn seemed skeptical. "You know anything about us?"

"Is there anything I *should* know about you?"

"Well, we're terrible. Have been for a long time."

"Then I guess it's time to change that, don't you think?"

The young coach exuded a confidence that was instantly contagious.

"Yes, sir," affirmed Autumn with a smile. "It'll be good not to be bad my senior year."

"It's good not to be bad any year."

She noticed the book lying face down on the table. "What are you reading?"

He picked up the book and handed it to her. "It's called *The Tao of the Jump Shot.* Ever seen it before?"

"No, sir. What's it about?"

"It takes principles of Taoism and applies those principles..."

Autumn interrupted. "OK, you're in Lazarus, Texas, Coach Lewis. What is that?"

"Taoism? A very old Chinese philosophy, or religion depending on who you ask. Ring a bell at all?"

"Lazarus, remember?"

"Right. Well, the whole point of it is to find harmony and balance, like there is in nature."

Autumn gave him a blank stare. "Still not following you."

37

"OK, look at the picture on the cover. That's called Yin Yang. It represents a perfect balance between the masculine and feminine in the universe. See," he said as he pointed to the image with his finger, "there's a perfect circle with two identical parts. Same shape, same amount of black and white. Perfect balance. Still with me?"

"So far."

"The whole point of Taoism is to find the Tao, or the way. That's a state of being where one just *is*. Ideally, there's no effort to *be*, one just *is*."

"I think I get what you're saying but what in the world does that have to do with basketball and jump shots?"

"The idea is that the perfect jump shot occurs when there's no effort to make the jump shot happen. The perfect jump shot just *is*."

"I'm sorry. You lost me again."

"The point is that the perfect shot is one that you just do without even thinking about it. OK, you drive yet?"

"Yes, sir."

"Can you drive a stick?"

"Sure can."

"If you get in your car or truck and it's pitch black, would you have to think through all the steps in order to get your key in the ignition? When you're driving a stick, do you think, really actually think, about all the steps involved, which gear you're in and so forth?"

"No, sir. I just do it. I've done it so many times that my hand just knows where to go and what to do. Same thing with driving a stick, I guess."

"See? There you go," he said with a smile. "Now you're starting to get it. If you watch film of the great pure shooters, people like Mark

Price, Calvin Murphy, Larry Bird, Jeff Hornacek, whether they realized it or not, they understood the Tao of the jump shot, or the free throw or whatever shot they took. They didn't have to think about the mechanics of the shot, they didn't have to think about elbows in, they didn't have to think about the release point, the follow through, or anything else. They could just catch and shoot the effortless shot. Granted, they had to practice it thousands and thousands of times, but once they found the Tao, well, the rest is history."

Autumn was blown away. By this time, Martha and the child had joined the two and Martha, too, was in awe.

"So we should practice shooting, or whatever, until it comes naturally without us having to think through it. We just do it... or rather, it just happens. Right? Don't think about all the steps, just let it happen?"

"Have you read this book?" Coach Lewis responded with a smile, trying to boost her confidence. "That's the whole idea. Makes pretty good sense, doesn't it?"

"Yes, sir. It sure does." After a slight pause, Autumn challenged her new coach. "So, you gonna fix our basketball team with a bunch of Chinese philosophy?"

"Probably not, but we'll have to see."

Martha interrupted. "I hate to break up this little pow-wow, but April is getting really tired and she probably should be gettin' home and gettin' to bed."

Autumn stood up and took the beautiful child into her arms. She grabbed her backpack and headed for the door. As she reached the door she turned back to the two adults. "See you on Monday during athletics. Have a good weekend, Coach." She walked out the door and past the front window then u-turned and re-entered the diner. "Hey, Coach. Welcome to Lazarus." She smiled and left for the evening.

"She seems like a nice kid," he observed out loud. "It'll be fun getting to know her."

"She's a wonderful kid. You'll enjoy being around her. Everyone does. A gentle spirit, that one. She and her sister live with me. My granddaughters," Martha said as she cleared Gabe's table into a bus bin. "Tell you what, Mr. Lewis. This one's on the house tonight. Swing by here sometime this weekend and we'll have that visit."

"That's very kind of you. Thanks for dinner tonight, by the way. I ate too much, but it was terrific."

"You can't eat here every night or you'll gain fifty pounds before the season starts. Understand?"

"Yes, ma'am," he said with a big smile. "I guess I'll be getting home, or to the motel rather. I have plenty to do tomorrow so I'll need to get some sleep tonight. See you this weekend, Martha."

Martha waved goodnight and Gabe headed back to his motel. Satisfied by the meal and excited about his future, he felt like he was in the right place. Martha shook her head and sighed.

"Who was that?" called a girl's voice from the kitchen.

"That was Autumn's new basketball coach," Martha answered.

"Well, what do you think?" called the voice again.

Martha threw her towel into the bus bin with the dirty dishes and sat down in the booth. Coach Lewis had forgotten his book on the table. She picked it up and put it in the front flap of her apron.

"Well, Summer," said Martha as she stood again and headed to the kitchen and flipped off the lights in the dining room, "I think he's way too good for Lazarus."

40

CHAPTER III

Friday nights in Lazarus were reserved for sporting events. During the winter months Friday night meant basketball games. The people of Lazarus patiently endured basketball season but only because basketball was generally accepted as the best, most efficient way to keep the boys in shape until football practices began again in the spring. Make no mistake: plenty of Lazarus fans attended the games, but never was there excessive excitement about Friday nights in the winter months, except when talk in the stands centered on how the boys really looked to be in shape or this boy or that seemed to be a step quicker than he was on the gridiron. However, during the fall, Friday nights brought a buzz and a magical atmosphere to Lazarus, and to towns large and small all over Texas.

In Lazarus, as in many other Texas towns of the same approximate population, the high school student body never has been large enough to support a full football squad. Though times were much better these days, many a season came and went back in the lean years when Lazarus could field only nine or ten high school boys, not even the eleven required to play in traditional football games. The alternative to the traditional game of eleven-man football is one of the most exciting sports that no one knows about: six-man football. With scores frequently in the sixties and seventies per team, six-man football boasts wide-open offenses, long runs, deep bombs and little or no defense to speak of. It is this electrifying version of Texas' favorite sport that miraculously draws many hundreds of fans, from Lazarus alone, to the quaint west Texas football stadiums each Friday night to live and die with the Lazarus Longhorns.

As do most small Texas towns, Lazarus has had a longstanding fascination with and an incredible emotional investment in football. The men of Lazarus all donned the spikes and pads and took to the gridiron once a week in the prime of their youth. The diner, the barber shop, the gas station and the churches to this day remain havens for discussions about the great moments in Lazarus football: the 99-yard kickoff return against Nazareth for the district title as time expired in the final game of the '52 season, the Statue of Liberty play against Dimmitt that earned the Longhorns their first ever undefeated regular season in '64 and the state championship seasons of '65 and '83. The players and coaches of the two championship seasons still are revered in Bethany County as demigods and are venerated in public forums on a regular basis. Regardless of what evidence the record books may offer to the contrary, the championship years aside, the men of Lazarus still speak of the esteemed football tradition and long for the days when they laced up their spikes and charged the field to the roars of the throngs of rabid Longhorn fans.

The women, too, have fond memories of their Friday nights in Lazarus as vivacious young girls on the verge of womanhood. The women rarely have any recollection of the scores of the important games, the length of this run or that, the number of interceptions made against this team or that. Rather, what the Lazarus women remember most is the emotional roller coaster that went along with letter jackets, promise rings, homecoming dances and the occasional post-game moonlit drives with their beaus to the water tower or to the drive-in theater just twenty minutes north of town in Friona.

Because of the Longhorns' storied past, perhaps recreated somewhat larger than life by those still consumed by thoughts of their glory days, Longhorn Stadium, located just off Ranch Road 145 behind Lazarus High School, fills to capacity for every home game more consistently than the First Church of Bethany on Easter Sunday. No matter the weather, the Longhorn faithful make their way to Longhorn Stadium for each home game to pay homage not only to those who wear the red and white currently but also to those who have gone before them on the gridiron. Neither rain nor snow nor wind nor ice can keep the fans from the bleachers. The same goes for games on the road. The distances from Lazarus to other high school stadiums never has been a deterrent for those loyal to the Longhorns, those who religiously make their pilgrimages to the far-off battlefields of Groom, Hedley, Turkey Valley, Kress, Silverton and Cotton Center whenever the Longhorns travel.

Friday nights during the fall are indeed reserved for the boys of Lazarus High School. The last Friday night before the school year, however, has always been reserved for a different group of boys and a game of a different sort: backyard football at the home of one of the Lazarus High School football coaches. This year's game would be played at Coach McArthur's house. The participants in the not-so-high-stakes game were not the chiseled, farm-raised, fit young men of Lazarus but rather the Lazarus High School and Lazarus Middle School coaches. Most of the players of the back-to-school games of the last few decades boasted bum ankles, trick knees and other assorted battle wounds collected, at least according to those who bore the wounds, on the gridiron. The players, with few exceptions, all played for the Longhorns once, though some more recently than others. Those who played on the last Friday night of the summer each year were mostly coaches but a few select non-coaches were allowed to participate. Non-coaches though they were, these exceptions to the rule had been good players in their day, and were still part of the network of good ol' boys in Lazarus.

"Now what I want to know is why you didn't get us some better weather for the weekend, Haskins," griped the General about the triple-digit temperature. "After all, I'm hosting this thing. The least you could have done was get us some cooler weather."

"Hey, I brought the beer," answered Haskins as he lifted his can of Milwaukee's Best and laughed.

About seven o'clock in the evening, the sun still shone brightly over the horizon and the hot wind still blew across the barren red dirt of Bethany County and across the backyard full of brown, sun-dried Bermuda grass. The cheap stereo on the back porch, set to loop, played the "Urban Cowboy" soundtrack over and over again. Undeterred by the heat, the good ol' boys of Lazarus lounged in the General's backyard in folding chairs borrowed from the high school cafeteria. They had been arriving since about four o'clock and had been drinking since about five after four. Next to the covered porch, just a short toss from the grill, sat a giant green garbage can and it was filling up quickly with aluminum cans.

"Don't know about you guys but I'm ready to get this show on the road," said Coach Cannon to anyone who would listen.

"The party or the season?" asked Haskins.

"Well, both, but I was talking mostly about the season. We should be contenders this year and if that Colter kid can contribute then God knows what we'll do when we hit our stride."

"Too bad you didn't get *two* Colter kids!" joked McArthur. "Heard about that shocker! Lazarus goes fifteen years with no transfers, we finally get two and one of 'em's a damn girl! What are the odds of that?"

All the coaches laughed out loud, even those that didn't hear the conversation but didn't want to be left out of the fun.

"That Lewis kid lucked out, that's for sure." Haskins crushed his empty can on his thigh and tossed it toward the garbage can. "Too bad that's not going to be enough to help those girls do squat." The can rimmed out and landed under the grill. "Coach, you did invite Lewis didn't you?"

Coach McArthur pulled another cold one from the cooler and tossed it over to Haskins. "Yep, he said he'd be here." He turned to a weathered old guy in a rocker sitting near the stereo. "Bill, he's got lots of energy. You're gonna have to help keep him out of trouble."

Bill Merrick taught social studies at the middle school and needed just a few years to begin drawing retirement. Bill moonlighted as a basketball official in the 1970s and 1980s. When Bill's knees gave out on him, Haskins gave him a stipend to be the assistant coach for the girls basketball team at the high school. Although Bill believed he knew more about basketball than anyone else in the county, he never had any ambition, never caused any trouble and never asked for anything other than to be left alone. The only thing Bill cared about was getting in his years so he could retire, lease an RV and drive across the Old South touring Civil War battlefields. When the bell rang at the end of each

45

school day, Bill raced the kids out of the parking lot. During the season, Bill loitered at the gym and gave the appearance of being busy while the girls practiced, largely on their own. For the last fifteen minutes of practice each day, Bill paced the baseline, tapped his foot and generally looked annoyed and ready to leave.

"You guys hired a go-getter, huh? You know I ain't got the get-up-and-go anymore to keep up with these energetic types."

The motley, slightly inebriated bunch laughed unsympathetically at his plight.

Coach Cannon interrupted the laughter. "Y'all know, Jasperson'll be all excited about this guy, thinkin' his kid's gonna play ball in college one day now that we got us a new coach."

"I heard my name over there," said the voice nearest the grill. "Quit talking about me when I ain't around!"

Rick Jasperson played football at Lazarus under then-Coach Haskins and earned All-District honors his junior and senior years. His daughter, Mary Jo, would be a sophomore at Lazarus. Both Mary Jo and her father believed she would be the first player from Lazarus to play professional sports. Both overestimated her potential more than just a little.

"Calm down, Rick. We're not really talking about you. When are those burgers gonna be ready?" McArthur called back across the way.

Jasperson set down his grilling utensils, picked up his beer and headed back to where the rest of the men had congregated on and around the porch. By this time, there were eleven coaches and former players relaxing around the porch. Haskins' wife and McArthur's wife were both inside preparing the rest of the food for their boys. They knew to stay inside because this was "the men's time" and to come out only to deliver more food.

Haskins' wife stepped outside and the voices quieted. "Neill is on the phone for you. He says it's important that he speak to you right away."

Haskins finished his beer, threw the can in the general direction of the garbage can and headed inside. The rest of the guys couldn't imagine why the superintendent would be interrupting the traditional coaches' get-together. After several minutes Haskins emerged from McArthur's kitchen with a consternated look on his face.

"Neill just told me that Summer Griffin will be returning to school on Monday."

No one but Cannon spoke. "The other Griffin kid's coming back? You're serious?"

Haskins took a serious tone. "Yep. Monday. Just like that."

"What prompted this?" asked Coach Cannon. "I haven't heard anything about this. I can't have that kind of distraction during the season. You know what happens when these boys quit thinking with their heads and..."

"Listen." The principal interrupted and addressed the group with animated hand gestures. "We're kind of over a barrel here, fellas. Seems we don't really have any ground to stand on here. I think it's best we just drop it, OK?"

Every small town has scandal and Lazarus, through the years, had plenty of its own. Summer Griffin happened to be the latest scandal in Lazarus and had been for a couple years now. Everyone on the porch wanted to know more but no one was bold enough to keep prodding Haskins for information. Something completely out of the ordinary must have happened for Summer to be returning to school at Lazarus. A few more beers and perhaps somebody would be uninhibited enough to broach the subject again. On the other hand, Haskins didn't take a serious tone like this often.

As the sun started to set on west Texas and the pink clouds over the horizon faded to orange, the familiar aroma of mesquite-grilled burgers and sausages hung in the air around the porch. The number of partiers had grown to thirteen and the group was growing restless. Everyone was ready to eat but they knew they had to play a quick game of football first; it was tradition.

"Hey, Haskins," asked the General, now feeling the buzz of the hot August evening and the cold beer, "when's your boy gonna be here?"

———————

Coach Lewis finished with the copy machine just after four o'clock. He had been so engrossed in what he was doing that he never once noticed Gladys giving him the evil eye from behind her desk. Gladys was the copy machine queen and she ruled her domain with an iron fist from behind her computer monitor. However, she liked the newcomer and hated to spoil his enthusiasm so she didn't interrupt him. She stared at him and started to run him out of the building more than once but she knew he had nowhere else to go so she just let him keep working.

"OK, Gladys, I'm finished now," he said over his shoulder as he hole-punched the last of his stacks of papers. "Sorry to keep you waiting on a Friday afternoon."

"That's OK, hon. I've got no plans other than to go home and watch the soaps I recorded today. Another hot date with a half-gallon of Blue Bell Rocky Road. Typical Friday night in my life, sugar. Hope yours is better than mine."

"That doesn't sound so bad," he answered politely as he tried to make her feel better about her boring existence. "My hot date is with all the coaches over at Coach McArthur's tonight."

"No offense, sugar, but I'll take my ice cream and my soaps. If it gets too hot over there, feel free to swing by my place."

"Thanks for the offer, Gladys." He tried to catch a quick glance but she was leaning down behind her desk sorting some files in a bottom drawer. "You need to get out of here. I've kept you around long enough." He picked up his papers and waited for her to stand up behind her desk.

"I'll lock up, sugar. Go on, I'll be out directly," she said as she waved him out the door. As he headed out into the hall and waved goodbye Gladys hollered to him, "Don't forget what I said!"

What does she mean by that? He shook his head and headed out the door to his Blazer. He dropped his papers in the passenger seat and cranked up the engine. His forehead and back at once broke a sweat when he sat down on the burning vinyl seat. He was only driving a block or two and he knew the AC would never get the car cooled off by then so he rolled down his windows and drove out of the parking lot and down the street to Mary's Kitchen.

Mary had left a message that morning with Gladys asking Gabe to come by after he finished at school. She was making good on her promise to visit with him later. As he parallel parked in the street outside the diner, he noticed the sign in the diner window: Fri. Night

Special - Chicken Tenders or Meatloaf, 2 Veggies, Rolls or Cornbread - $6.99. It was a little early for dinner but he was hungry. Besides, he didn't know what to expect at the coaches' party later: feast or famine. He opened the door of the diner and was greeted by the familiar smell of cooking grease and homemade bread and the soulful sound of Willie Nelson and Ray Charles on the jukebox.

"Hey, Coach, how are you?"

Coach Lewis remembered the friendly, effervescent voice from just a few nights ago.

"Hi, Autumn. I'm alright, how are you? May I sit back there?" He pointed at a booth toward the back of the diner.

"I'm great, Coach," she said without looking back. She motioned for him to follow her back to the corner he requested, "I'll let her know you're here. You want a drink?"

"Sure. How about a Diet Dr. Pepper?"

Martha emerged from the kitchen, made her way across the restaurant and gave the coach a hearty pat on the back. She sat down across from him in the booth and took off her apron.

"Glad you could make it. I guess you're headed out to the game tonight, huh?"

Gabe grabbed a few napkins from the dispenser and wiped his forehead free of sweat. He didn't want to look but he feared he'd sweated through at least his shirt and perhaps, unfortunately, his jeans, too.

"Actually, I was headed out to the coaches' party at Coach McArthur's house tonight. I don't have to be there for a few more hours, though."

"That's what I meant." Seeing that he was a little confused, Martha explained the annual old timers' game.

"That's interesting. A game, huh?" he replied as he shook his head. "They forgot to mention that little detail."

"Well, don't fret about it. They'll all be a little loose so just go with the flow and you'll be fine. Meatloaf or tenders?"

Autumn had returned with his drink and was ready to take his order.

"Let's go with the tenders and surprise me with the vegetables."

"White gravy?"

Coach Lewis wrinkled his brow and dragged a giggle from Autumn. "You know, I never have understood white gravy, so I think I'll pass unless you've got brown. Thanks, Autumn."

Martha smiled as Autumn retuned to the kitchen.

"So, how was your day? Ready for your first day of school on Monday?"

Coach Lewis breathed a heavy sigh and stretched his arms out across the back of the booth. He paused for a few seconds to take in the sounds of the jukebox. He hadn't noticed the music the last time he ate at the diner. Beneath the table he tapped his feet to the rhythm of the blues wailing through the monophonic jukebox speaker. He recognized just by listening that the jukebox was so old that it played 45s and not CDs.

"Well, it was a long day to be honest with you."

"How so?" Martha leaned in a little and tilted her head just a bit to the side. Her face was wrinkled and tired from years of hard work in the diner. Her eyes were warm and they hinted there was much more to this woman than meets the eye.

"Oh, where do I start? I guess it started when I got to school this morning and asked Gladys for the keys to my room. Much to my chagrin, she informed me that I'll be a floater. In other words, I won't have my own room and I'm going to share a few different classrooms with some other teachers. Then she handed me my schedule."

"And?"

The neophyte educator pulled the folded schedule from his back pocket; the paper was damp with perspiration. "First period, twelfth grade study hall. Second period, eleventh grade study hall. Third period, tenth grade study hall. Fourth period, eleventh grade English. Then lunch duty. Fifth period, tenth grade English. Sixth period, conference period. Seventh period, ninth grade English. Every single class is in a different room so I have to haul my things around on this decrepit TV/VCR cart with only three good wheels. One wheel is screwed up because of a piece of gum that's stuck to it. It makes this awful sound as it rolls down the hall and veers off to the left no matter how straight I try to push it."

In a reassuring, motherly tone, Martha tried to make him feel better. "That's not so bad, is it? Didn't you want to teach English?"

"Yes, ma'am, but that isn't even the end of the story." He sat up straight and took a few sips from his drink. "I had a note in my mailbox to see Coach McArthur, the boys basketball coach."

"Oh," Martha said as she drew in a long, measured breath, "I've known Patton for a long time. How'd the visit go?"

The young coach paused for a moment and reflected on the meeting.

Coach McArthur's office was at one end of the gym situated between the visitors' locker rooms. His office contained nothing but an old metal desk with a worn-out vinyl-covered swivel chair behind it. On the walls were a clock, a twelve-month calendar and a poster of Las Vegas. His desk was cluttered but not disheveled. The bare, white-washed cinder blocks were cold and uninviting.

"Come on in, son," he said from his swivel chair as Gabe approached his door. "Sorry I don't have a chair for you. I'm Patton McArthur. Coach Cannon and Mr. Haskins asked me to visit with you before we get started with the school year. Kind of show you the ropes around here, you know?"

"Yes, sir."

McArthur didn't waste any time getting to the point. "OK, son, here's how practices work. We got one gym here and one weight room. The football boys will more than likely be in the weight room a pretty good bit, especially here at the beginning of the year. My boys will practice Monday, Wednesday and Friday in the gym. Your girls can have the gym Tuesday and Thursday."

"And then we switch every other week?" Gabe asked optimistically.

"No, son. That's the schedule. You and the girls gonna have to earn the gym time if you want more. Once the official practice season begins, the boys will practice every day until five o'clock and you can have the gym as long as you want after that every single day, except game days, obviously. Last one in the gym needs to sweep the floor, refill the coolers and lock up. Keep that in mind when you decide how long you want to run your practices."

He sorted through the stacks of papers on his desk and found a manila folder.

"Here's your schedule of games. We didn't get too ambitious with your schedule for this year but you do have a couple of world-beaters on there. With the exception of Sudan, Whiteface and Shallowater, it's pretty much an average schedule 'til you get to district. If you can get an average team together by the time district starts you might can be above .500 going into district. After that, well... everybody has to learn somewhere, son."

"Well, Coach, I'm actually very optimistic..."

"Now I've been here a long time so let me give you two pieces of advice. First, you better know how to play man defense. That's all everyone plays out here. That's all that's worked in the past and that's all these kids know how to play."

"Everyone, huh? Why is that?" Gabe thought he was finally going to be able to discuss Xs and Os with someone else who shared his love of the game.

"Because, son, this is west Texas," McArthur barked as he stood and leaned forward on his desk. "That's what we play out here! If you got half a brain then you'll remember that."

So much for Xs and Os. Gabe took a deep breath and refrained from arguing. "What's the second piece of advice, Coach?"

"Just remember you coach girls."

Gabe was floored. "What's that supposed to mean?" he retorted in a defensive tone.

McArthur ignored the question. He walked from behind his desk and led Gabe out into the gym. He pointed across the length of the gym at a door on the far wall opposite his own and between the home locker rooms.

"That'll be your office, son." The General returned to his office and slammed the door behind him. Gabe headed across the gym floor, his eyes fixated on his office door, when he heard the General's door open again and the General call to him, "By the way, you need to be out at my house tonight for a little get together for all the coaches. Gladys will give you directions - be there about dinner time."

Before Gabe could answer, the office door slammed shut.

Well, I guess I won't be getting any help from him. Undaunted by the unpleasant experience of "visiting" with the General, Coach Lewis continued on toward his office door. He wanted to remain as stoic as possible; although, he actually was giddy about having his own office. As he reached the office door, he imagined a plaque above the door that read "Gabe Lewis, Head Girls Basketball Coach." He imagined his office walls decorated much the way the principal's office was with team photos, trophies, news clippings and framed jerseys. As a smirk appeared on his face, he reached out and turned the knob. He paused for a minute and turned it again.

"Locked! That's about par for the course!" he muttered under his breath.

The golden fried chicken tenders melted in his mouth. Martha didn't say a word; she was a good listener and she knew he just needed to vent to someone patient enough to sit and listen. He sampled the green beans and the mashed potatoes and found them as delectable as the tenders. Whoever had prepared the veggies had been plenty generous with the butter and the salt. Martha smiled at his obvious satisfaction.

"Well, Coach, I guess it hasn't taken you too long to discover Lazarus' dirty little secret."

"That people here don't like outsiders?" he quipped between mouthfuls of mashed potatoes.

"Well, that, too, but it wasn't where I was headed. The one real blemish on this great little town of ours is, well, almost like a disease. Lazarus is a good ol' boys' club, always has been and always will be. Imagine your tree house when you were a little kid with the sign hanging out front that read 'No Girls.' That's Lazarus."

"Why is that?"

"You're a smart boy and I can tell you've read plenty. I don't have to tell you that men have been intimidated and threatened by women since the beginning of time. Why should our little neck of the woods be any different? Men built this town, men have always run this town and that's just the way it is in Lazarus. That's just the way it is lots of places, though. We're not unique. I know that. But it's part of who we are here."

He finished his meal and washed it down with what was left of his drink. He wiped his face with napkin and leaned across the table. He looked Martha directly in the eye.

"Why are you telling me this?"

"You still don't get it, do you? Listen, I know you're ready to charge Hell with a water pistol right now and I think your enthusiasm is just... real endearing."

"But..." He knew the proverbial "but" was just around the corner.

"I know you have all these exciting things planned for the girls and it's just... I don't want you to get your hopes up too high." She stared away, somewhere far away and kept speaking without making eye contact. "The good news for you is that nobody has any expectations of these girls. The bad news is..."

The message was becoming clear.

Coach Lewis finished her sentence. "The bad news is that nobody has any expectations of these girls."

Martha said nothing. Her silence confirmed what the newcomer was beginning to see. All the pieces fit together now. The hasty interview, the cold shoulder from the General, the dilapidated office: Haskins and Cannon didn't care at all who they hired for this job. They didn't care that he had a master's degree. They didn't care that he had worked closely with a successful coach for several years. They didn't care at all, at least not about the girls.

"I didn't even tell you about the office, did I?"

"No." Martha returned her attention to her young friend. "Tell me about the office."

"I finally found the maintenance guy, Dee, and he unlocked my office. What did I find inside?" He threw his hands up and began counting on his fingers, "Brooms, mops, buckets, dirty towels on the floor, a pile of lost and found clothes, a broken swivel chair, a vast assortment of indigenous bugs and spiders. Oh, and three scorpions - one dead and two alive. We didn't have scorpions in Houston. Welcome to Lazarus, huh?"

"Yea, welcome to Lazarus, Coach," Martha chuckled. "Now there's one more thing you gotta understand about the General." Martha leaned in to speak and Gabe leaned in to hear as she lowered her voice. "Football is king in Lazarus. Always has been, always will be. The only thing the General has control over in this town is his gym. And believe me he sees it as *his* gym."

"That certainly helps explain the chip on his shoulder," Gabe observed. "Well, it's not the end of the world, right?"

Martha reached across and took his hand in hers. Gabe noticed she had the same kind eyes as Autumn, only older and wiser. "A wise man once said, 'God will not permit any troubles to come upon us, unless He has a specific plan by which great blessing can come out of the difficulty.'"

"So, Martha, why are you telling me all this?"

"Coach, with the way the hot winds blow across Lazarus all the time, a breath of fresh air will be nice to have around here."

Gabe blushed. He didn't often handle compliments very well. He glanced down at his watch and noted he still had well over an hour left before he needed to be at Coach McArthur's.

"You mind if I stick around and relax a little? I don't have anywhere to be for a while and I'm enjoying your company."

Martha gave him a pat on the hand and smiled.

He hadn't noticed during his conversation but the diner had filled to near capacity and there was a line forming at the cash register. The meatloaf at Mary's Kitchen was second in popularity only to the pies, so hungry people from all over Bethany County made their way into Lazarus for Meatloaf Fridays at Mary's.

"Shouldn't you get back to work? I'll be fine by myself. Your place is getting pretty busy."

"We'll be fine. The nice thing about running a place is that you get to make the rules. I can visit as long as I want. Besides, Autumn could use the extra tips." She waved to Autumn and summoned her to the booth. "Darling, can you bring some pie and a refill for Coach Lewis?"

"Yes, ma'am," she replied obediently but graciously.

He watched her walk across the diner and he wondered why she spent so much time here in the diner with Martha. "So, the other day you mentioned she was going to be one of my players. Forgive me if I'm being too forward but will it really be feasible for her to play basketball, work here and take care of her baby?"

"Actually, Coach, that won't be a problem at all," Martha said with a grin. "April isn't hers. April's her sister's baby, although she's not much of a baby anymore. Autumn just works here over the summer, on the weekends and sometimes after school to help make ends meet."

Coach Lewis's face turned Lazarus Longhorn red. He shook his head slowly and apologetically. "I'm so sorry. I just assumed... That was really stupid of me."

"Don't worry about it. No harm no foul, right? Summer's her sister and she works in my office and keeps my books. She's a pretty gifted mathematician so I let her take care of all my financials."

Autumn returned with the pie and a new Diet Dr. Pepper. She cleared his table and placed the pie and drink carefully in front of her new coach. After smiling politely again at Coach Lewis, she returned to the kitchen with his dirty dishes.

"You see, it gets kind of complicated," Martha continued. "Summer got pregnant when she was in the eleventh grade. She stayed in school without anyone knowing until it was obvious she was pregnant. Some of the parents complained, raised a ruckus. Well,

Principal Haskins felt sorry for her so he let her stay in school until she delivered. That was April 30. She missed the whole last month of her eleventh grade year but she still went back to school on the last three days and passed all her final exams. Then she got a letter over the summer from the school board informing her that she wouldn't be allowed to return for her senior year because she violated the morals clause in the district's student handbook. She should be a freshman in college this year but she doesn't even have her high school diploma yet."

"You've got to be kidding!"

He had never even met Summer and his heart ached for her already.

"Serious as a heart attack."

"And the father?" he asked. Martha just looked at him. "Don't tell me. Let me guess. Nobody said anything at all to him, right? He's still in school."

"Welcome to Lazarus."

The two sat and stared at each other, one frustrated and the other dumbstruck.

"Would she go back to school if she could?"

"She can't."

"Theoretically, if she could, would she go back to school?"

"That's just not an option. We've been talking about studying for the GED now that April's a little older. School's out of the question, I'm afraid. That's been made perfectly clear."

The young idealist remained calm on the outside but his insides churned. He couldn't understand how, in the twenty-first century, this kind of backwards thinking was still being allowed. He liked to think of himself as enlightened and above such archaic misogyny, and he had an idea about how he might help. He sat pensively for a moment then asked to use the phone. With a focused and intense look on his boyish face, Coach Lewis excused himself and went to the telephone behind the cash register.

Martha beckoned Autumn and then sent her for Summer. The two girls returned to the booth where Martha sat intently watching half of what appeared to be a very animated conversation between Coach Lewis and someone on the other end of the phone call.

"Just what is that boy up to?" Martha wondered aloud. The three of them sat and stared for the duration of his conversation. As he hung up the phone and headed back to the booth, the three long-distance eavesdroppers pretended to be engaged in their own conversation.

Coach Lewis slid back into the booth and noticed that Summer had joined them. She looked so much like her sister. Same hazel eyes, same blond hair, same irresistible smile. She looked different, too, though - her face rounder and fuller, more mature, but still quite pretty. Coach Lewis had no difficulty imagining that Summer would have been considered attractive to high school boys before circumstances changed for her. In fact, Summer never shed the extra weight she had gained during her pregnancy - part of the price she paid when she unwittingly sacrificed the last few years of her childhood to become an adult.

"So," he began with his curious and eager audience, "I had an ethics professor in grad school that was a civil liberties attorney. She bragged to us all the time about how she handled dozens of pro bono cases for the ACLU and for individuals and this scenario is right up her alley. Honestly, I think she did that kind of stuff as much for publicity as for anything else, but she always encouraged us to call her if anything interesting came up. She jumped all over this when I explained the situation. To put it nicely, she's a bulldog when it comes to things like this. I would never want to cross her when she gets her mind set on something. I hope you don't mind that I called her."

"I don't want to raise a stink and I sure don't have the money for a lawyer," Summer said.

"Don't worry. Professor Anthony said this one's a no-brainer and probably will take nothing more than a few calls and a few letters on her letterhead. She said she'll be in touch with a few people around here by the end of the day and they, whoever "they" are, shouldn't need much more cajoling when she's done with them. She prides herself on being a 'champion of the downtrodden' and I certainly think you qualify. She's a crusader if ever I saw one. She comes across pretty abrasive sometimes but she's in your corner on this one. By the way, Summer, I saw April when I was here a few days ago. She's beautiful."

"Thanks," she said proudly. "Well, since you made that call, I guess you ought to know that Roy Haskins is the father," Summer said with her head down. "That's Principal Haskins' grandson."

Now you tell me! Coach Lewis reached across the table and grabbed Summer's hand. "Listen, Summer, no one will ever know who made the call and no one in the administration will ever give you any grief again if Professor Anthony comes through for us like she said she would. She's one of a kind. I promise: she'll take care of this for you and you can get on with your life."

"Just like that?"

"Just like that."

"I sure hope you're right," Summer said looking for some kind of reassurance from someone else at the table.

Coach Lewis smiled the reassuring smile Summer needed to see. Inside, though, he hoped he was right, too.

"Well, ladies, I hate to eat and run, but I have to be somewhere before too long. Summer, it was nice to meet you and, hopefully, I'll see you at school on Monday. Autumn, I'll definitely see you Monday. Martha, keep me posted and let me know if you hear from Professor Anthony - I gave her your number here at the diner. She may not even call, but I gave her your number just in case. You guys have a great weekend."

Coach Lewis dropped a five-dollar bill on the table and went to the cash register to pay his bill. As he put his wallet back in his jeans pocket, he turned and smiled back over his shoulder at Martha, Summer and Autumn.

Gabe Lewis suddenly had three fans for life. For the first time in Lazarus' long memory a coach actually showed an interest not only in girls basketball but also in the wellbeing of the girls themselves.

"Breathe deeply, girls, breathe deeply," Martha said. "A breath of fresh air is hard to find around here."

Coach Lewis headed north out of Lazarus proper on County Road 260, a lonesome stretch of west-Texas road on which a traveler can get to either Lubbock or Amarillo. With butterflies in his stomach, he passed the beautiful Bethany County courthouse and the Bethany County cemetery on the northern edge of town and drove along 260 for about two miles just as the directions indicated. He flipped on his left turn signal as the stone entrance gates to Mesquite Branch Estates came into sight. Mesquite Branch was the only "subdivision" in Lazarus. Built in the mid-1980s, these eight modest ranch-style houses were the newest homes in all of Lazarus. At the end of the cul-de-sac sat Patton McArthur's house. On the right side of McArthur's house was Principal Haskins' house. Flying proudly in front of Haskins' house on two tall white flag poles were the American flag and the Texas flag, at exactly the same height. Parked in front of the houses, in the driveways and all around the cul-de-sac were a dozen or so vehicles, mostly trucks.

Coach Lewis parked his Blazer and grabbed the twelve-pack of Diet Dr. Pepper he picked up at Wyatt's Grocery. Dressed in trendy jeans, a polo shirt and stylish leather boat shoes, the young, nervous coach made his way up the drive. As he made his way to the front door he heard the music blaring from behind the house. No one answered the door so he walked tentatively around the house, through the swinging gate of the iron fence and into the backyard.

"There he is," said Haskins as he caught a glimpse of Gabe coming in through the gate.

Gabe looked up to discover a dozen pair of eyes surveying him. He realized instantly he was overdressed. He looked more ready to shop the Galleria than to chum it up with the good ol' boys at a backyard cookout in west Texas. Most of the others there were dressed in faded t-shirts or worn out coaching shirts and tennis shoes. More than half of them wore red polyester-blend coaching shorts, the short tight ones that the rest of the coaching world stopped wearing in the late 1980s save a few old school softball coaches.

"Grab you a beer out of the cooler, son," McArthur said as he walked over to Gabe and put his arm around the newbie. "Guys, this is Gabe Lewis. He's gonna be our girls' coach this year and I'm gonna be showing him the ropes 'til he gets his feet under him around here."

The General seemed entirely too personable considering his tirade earlier in the day.

"No, thanks," Gabe said politely to the General's offer. "I'll just have bottled water if you've got it."

The General took it personally that his guest refused his hospitality, regardless of how shallow and ill-intentioned the hospitality actually was.

"Son, you ain't gonna find no bottled water around here," he snapped back.

Seeing the potential for a confrontation, Coach Cannon wisely interrupted. "Hey, let's get this game going before we run out of daylight."

At this, everyone jumped up and tossed their cans into the nearly-full garbage can. As the group stirred about, Coach Cannon introduced Gabe to everyone, making especially sure Gabe met Bill, his new old assistant coach. To Gabe's surprise, most everyone there was at least congenial; he attributed the congeniality primarily to the alcohol, based on all his prior experiences in Lazarus.

The scene seemed to Gabe to have been plucked from some movie he had seen once. A dozen or so beer-bellied old timers in pseudo-athletic attire, some even sporting fuzzy red headbands, bending and stretching all over the backyard as the sun set behind them.

"The irony," Gabe chuckled under his breath.

Haskins and Cannon numbered the players off one-two-one-two and assigned the players to different teams. Somehow the principal and the other two head coaches landed on the same team. Gabe, of course, found himself on the other team.

"Bill, you playing?" asked Haskins.

"Maybe next year," Bill called back from the rocker on the porch. "Maybe next year" is what Bill said every year.

Once the two teams were in place and the boundaries of the playing field had been delineated with potted plants, watering cans and lawn chairs, the teams marched to opposite ends of the yard.

"Shirts and Skins," yelled Cannon as he removed his shirt to reveal a rather odd sight. His arms, shoulders and chest were firm and well-defined. Beginning just below his pecs, though, his tight, round belly made him look several months pregnant. He had a rather pronounced farmer's tan; his arms, at least to the midpoint of his biceps, were a dark, golden bronze while the rest of his torso, save the back of his neck, was a pale flesh color. "We're Skins!"

One by one the old timers peeled their sweat-stained shirts from their bodies and tossed them to the makeshift sidelines. What they uncovered was a sight Gabe would not soon forget. If they once had been formidable athletes, time had not been kind to these has-beens. Gabe really didn't care to look at Principal Haskins, Coach Cannon, the General or the rest of his new acquaintances as their pasty white, hairy bodies glistened in the waning sunlight. At that moment, Gabe reaffirmed his vow to take care of himself, to eat properly and never to let himself go the way these guys had.

"Here we go," yelled Cannon, the Skins' self-proclaimed team captain as he hurled the ball downfield toward the Shirts.

One of the Shirts called for a fair catch then missed the ball entirely. Gabe knew this was going to be entertaining, judging by the smell of alcohol seeping from the pores of the guys around him. They reeked of beer and they weren't exactly fleet of foot; this would be entertaining indeed. The Shirts lined up and the first play from scrimmage was a long, incomplete pass down the sideline that landed behind the sage bushes near the fence. Each successive play met with similar futility. The Shirts turned the ball over on downs and the cycle continued with the Skins. Possession after possession the two teams traded fumbles, dropped passes, incompletions and turnovers on downs. With each change of possession, the play became more and more rough and the contact increasingly deliberate. Whether his teammates were too tipsy to notice or whether they had done it intentionally, Gabe hadn't touched the ball a single time. Finally, after nearly an hour of sweaty bodies colliding with one another, someone declared the next team that scored would be the winner.

The Skins huddled, drew a play, one that scored a game-winning touchdown back in the day, and headed to the line of scrimmage. Jasperson dropped back, took the long snap and handed off to Cannon. Cannon took two steps toward the sideline and drew the inebriated defense his way. He turned and flipped the ball back to Jasperson, who then threw a bullet down the opposite sideline toward a streaking yet stumbling shirtless receiver. Precisely at the moment the ball was released, Gabe realized that anything he wanted in this game he was going to have to take for himself. Being the only sober player on defense, the twenty-five year old broke on the ball and cleanly intercepted the pass with a magnificent grab. Still dressed in street clothes, Gabe headed back up the sideline. All the Shirts stood and watched as he raced back down the field toward the Skins.

His teammates had explained to him before the game that only girls played touch football so this would be an all-out, full contact game of old fashioned tackle football. He thought about this as he rocketed toward the two lawn chairs at the other end of the yard that marked the end zone. The only obstacles preventing him from scoring the winning touchdown were six angry, hairy-chested, topless men under the influence of Texas heat and alcohol. Jasperson and another Skin whose name escaped Gabe tried to tackle the elusive, yet well-dressed Shirt. However, they tripped over one another before they could get the proper angle to cut him off. Haskins tried next but Gabe planted right and spun left, easily avoiding a tackle by his new boss. Haskins, like the two would-be tacklers before him, found himself watching Gabe's back from the ground. The fourth Skin decided tackling Gabe would be too much effort so he sat down on the lawn and watched the spectacle unfold with his hands in his lap.

The last two defenders were Cannon and McArthur. By this time, the two remaining Skins took a good angle and positioned themselves between the swift and sober ball carrier and the lawn chair goal line. The most cunning of the three footballers effectively still in the game, if only because he was sober, Gabe decided to use the old timers' overactive sweat glands against them. Rather than going around them, Gabe decided to lower his shoulder and squeeze in between the two jiggling, slimy torsos in front of him. Just as planned, Gabe tucked the ball under his arm, lowered his head and shoulders and squirted through. As he emerged on the other side, smeared with other men's sweat, the bellies of the two Skins shook and rippled as they bounced off one another and onto the dry, crunchy grass beneath them. Gabe turned, looked at the eleven other men staring at him in disbelief and dropped the ball in the end zone. No one cheered. No one clapped. No one slapped his butt and said "Good job."

Gabe headed back to the porch with two-dozen or so eyes staring at him. As he stepped onto the porch, he turned back to the eleven stunned competitors. "Shirts win."

CHAPTER IV

The rickety ceiling fan whirred and stirred the hot August air that hung in the girls' locker room. The smell of sweat and the stench of body odor clung to the walls, to the industrial carpet on the floor and to everything in the lockers. As the door flung open, eight exhausted girls filed into the dingy white locker room and sprawled over every inch of the floor. Their bodies ached, their lungs hurt and their eyes stung as the beads of sweat rolled over their eyelids. After a few minutes of lying on the floor feeling sorry for themselves, one of them sat up to start peeling off her shoes and socks.

"Oh my God, I love this feeling!" shouted the newest Lady Longhorn.

The seven other girls groaned in disapproval and a few even threw towels and three-day old socks at Sam.

"What? You won't ever experience the feeling of winning games without the feeling of lactic acid burning holes in your muscles in August."

The lactic acid was indeed burning their muscles, almost to the extent the afternoon heat had burned the backs of their shoulders and necks for three of the five practice sessions of the first week of school. At least a dozen of the eighty toes in the locker room had blisters and nearly all of the one hundred ibuprofen tablets that began the week in the bottle on the sink were long since gone.

"I've never been in so much pain in my entire life," added Nairobi Whitaker as she straightened up and massaged her calves. Nairobi was the one player on the team, and perhaps in the entire county, that could touch the rim; the fact that *her* calves hurt was significant. Her skills didn't match her athleticism, but she was still young.

One by one, the girls dragged their throbbing bodies from the grungy carpet and planted their backsides on the two benches that stretched the length of the lockers along the back wall. The ceiling fan didn't really help the temperature in the locker room, but the girls all looked up at it as if it were giving the gift of cool air.

"Yea, this is the hardest first week of practice we've ever had," Autumn optimistically said with a smile. "Maybe that's a good sign, though! Right?"

Molly Frost and Mary Jo Jasperson were the first to change out of their practice gear and into street clothes. They tossed their dirty clothes into the hamper and headed for the door.

"Seems to me like just a sign of another week of hell when we get back on Monday," Molly retorted. "He won't have a team left if he keeps this up!"

"No kidding! When are we gonna start shooting and working on our offense?" Mary Jo interjected as she gave Molly a high-five. "I did not sign up for track!"

The two outspoken players continued to gripe back and forth as they exited the locker room and headed out of the gym.

Now dressed in street clothes, too, Sam stood and sank her dirty clothes in the hamper with a slow-motion jumper from the corner of the locker room. "I take it you guys aren't used to this, huh?"

"No way, Sam! I went through last preseason," explained Nairobi, "and this is way worse. I'm with Autumn, though. I think it's a good sign. And at least Coach acts like he wants to be here."

"I think he definitely wants to be here," chimed in Brooklynne as she rubbed Autumn's shoulders. "I sure don't know why, though. And I sure wish he'd stop with all that crazy philosophy talk. My brain hurts every day after practice as bad as my muscles."

Brooklynne and Nairobi threw their sweat-soaked things into the hamper and waved to the others as they left for the weekend. Sam said goodbye and hustled out to catch Brooklynne and Nairobi. The only players left in the locker room were Rita Rosales, the only true point guard on the team, Cassie Lassiter, the only freshman girl in school that played basketball, and Autumn. As they finished changing clothes, Rita and Autumn noticed Cassie sitting at the end of the bench still in her red practice jersey and shorts, head in her hands.

"Hey, what's the matter *chica*?" asked Rita.

Just as Nairobi was the lone African-American player, Rita was the lone Hispanic player on the team. Rita, along with Autumn, quickly had established herself as a mother hen, an encourager. As Coach Lewis had explained to her after the second day of practice, this was a great quality for a point guard. Her new coach also had applauded her toughness and tenacity. Her fiery Hispanic family had passed their genes on to Rita and what she lacked in skill she made up for in determination.

"Yea, what's going on Cassie?" Autumn added.

Autumn used her body to slide Cassie down the bench and then sat down beside her; Rita sat down on the other side sandwiching Cassie between her and Autumn. Rita rubbed Cassie's back and Autumn picked Cassie's head up out of her hands.

"Y'all," Cassie stuttered through her tears, "I can't do this."

In a motherly voice, Rita jumped in first. "Sure you can! We'll all get through this, including you, but we're gonna do it together. Remember what coach said? We gotta be like the wolves, *chica!*"

"You made it through this week and it has to be the hardest of the whole season, just because we aren't ready yet, we aren't in shape yet. It'll get better."

"No," Cassie said as the tears streamed down her face and mixed with the sweat. "We didn't run this much the whole year in middle school. I'm not ready for this. Besides, I'm not any good anyway."

Rita stood up behind Cassie and massaged her shoulders as Autumn got down on one knee on the floor in front of Cassie. Autumn took Cassie's hands and squeezed them.

"Tell you what," Autumn began, "you just get changed, wash your face and get out of here. Take the weekend to think about it and make your decision when you're not so emotional. Between the heat and your hormones, now probably isn't the best time to think about doing this all over again starting on Monday."

"Yea, baby," agreed Rita, "just think about it over the weekend. You know, I wanted to quit before, too, but you gotta be strong! Just think about it over the weekend, promise?"

Cassie wiped her face and nodded her head. "Thanks guys," she mumbled. "Y'all are the best. I can't promise I'll come back on Monday but I'll think about it like y'all said."

Rita and Autumn waited for Cassie to finish changing clothes and they walked her out of the gym. Rita and Cassie climbed in the back of Autumn's pick-up and the three headed home for the weekend.

It wasn't unusual for Autumn to give her friends and teammates rides home from practice even though Martha really didn't want her to.

"That truck drinks too much gas for you to be runnin' all over the place with your friends," Martha always said. Autumn did anyway, not to be disobedient but just to be helpful to her friends. She usually saved a few extra dollars in tips every week just for gas money so Martha wouldn't notice how much gas she'd actually used during the week. The rest of the girls looked up to Autumn because of the way she nurtured them and watched out for them. Even Cassie, who had only been around her a short while, already could see why everyone liked and respected Autumn.

After she dropped her friends at their houses out north of town, Autumn headed back along County Road Y to Ranch Road 1172 where she headed south through town along the main drive. Once she reached Ranch Road 145, headed west and was out of Lazarus proper, she stepped on the accelerator to save some time. She usually could drive the two-and-a-half miles from Ranch Road 1172 to Highway 214 in less than two minutes and the rest of the drive home in another two minutes. She was due at Mary's as soon as she could get home, get showered and get back to the diner. Windows down and the radio blaring a Pat Green song on a station out of Amarillo, the two-tone silver and maroon Chevy pick-up raced across the west-Texas landscape. There were no trees to speak of, at least no tall trees, but plenty of sage and brush along the sides of the roads. Other than the occasional trailer or small house just off the road, the view of the horizon stretched for miles virtually unobstructed. She reached Highway 214 in a minute and fifty seconds, as planned, and turned north. As she drove past Foster Farm, Autumn slowed down enough to make the right turn onto the gravel-and-dirt road about a half-mile ahead that led toward the trailer park she called home.

Not long after the rest of the girls headed their separate ways for the weekend, Coach Lewis sat at his desk and reviewed the notes he had taken over the course of the week both during and after practice. He sighed as he contemplated the task ahead of him. He knew he had a few pieces of the puzzle in place, at least in his mind, but the talent level was less than stellar. This was obvious after only two days of practice. He would have to convince everyone on the team to buy into a system in which each player would have a very specific and well-defined role, a role from which she could not vary. The team and the coach hadn't spent enough time together yet for each player's true colors to shine through the beginning-of-the-season veneer that always wears off over time, so he wasn't sure yet how the girls would react to his plan. As he sat lost in thought, imagining every possible lineup that could be created using the eight players he had available, a knock at the door startled him.

"Hey, Coach," said a young, timid voice from behind the partially-closed office door. "Can I come in for a minute?"

"Sure, Summer. Come on in. And leave the door open, if you would."

Summer Griffin opened the door and sat in one of the old chairs across the desk from Coach Lewis.

"How was your first week back? Like riding a bike?" he asked.

"Something like that," she said as she stared at her feet. From what he'd observed so far, Summer tended to be much quieter and more reserved than her sister. "Listen, Coach, I don't really know how you did it but I just wanted to thank you for getting me back in school. And I just wanted to say thanks for letting me do the stats for the team this year. It's gonna be great spending time with the girls all season, and all year with Autumn. Seeing her only after school just isn't the same as being at school with her. Really, this'll be awesome."

"My pleasure. Besides, I'm going to need someone with your number sense on the bench with me. It's tough to call plays, make substitutions, keep track of our fouls and theirs, our rebounds and theirs, field goal percentage. You get the idea. I'll have some stat sheets for you in a week or two and you can start working with them in practice; by the time the season starts, they'll be second nature."

"Anything you say, Coach." Summer stood from her chair and paused for a moment. "Martha's real excited that Autumn and I are gonna graduate together. She's a big fan of yours, you know. Anyway, thanks again, Coach."

———————

The grating buzz of the alarm clock startled Coach Lewis awake not long after the crack of dawn on Monday morning. He didn't sleep well at all Sunday night. The anticipation of the dawn of the new school year kept his mind racing late into the night. Coach Lewis wanted desperately to make a good first impression, not only on his new students but also on his new colleagues. Like an anxious schoolboy, Coach Lewis donned his new khakis, new shoes and new shirt for the first day of school. He hadn't yet unpacked everything he'd brought from Houston – his small, scantily-furnished rental house on the edge of town, which he'd found only the day before, still had stacks of boxes on the floor – but he'd made sure to unpack and iron his clothes. He had laid out his outfit on his sofa Sunday night to save time Monday morning. After a nice breakfast, Coach Lewis gathered his things and headed to Lazarus High School to launch the first day of the rest of his life.

The majority of the school day passed without event, fortunately for Coach Lewis. All day, his mind was focused on one thing and one thing only - the first basketball practice of the year. When he completed the final academic hour of his day, he rushed to his office and changed clothes to get ready for basketball practice. Dressed sharply once again in khaki shorts, a Nike polo-style shirt and black basketball shoes, Coach Lewis set out to find the storage room that housed his girls' practice gear, balls, jump ropes and the like. After interrupting the General and receiving instructions on where to find the girls' equipment storage room, Coach Lewis made his way up the stairs at the end of the gym to a second floor of sorts. At the back of the floor area, which was covered in out-of-date linoleum, stood a door with a busted doorknob. On the door hung a makeshift sign of adhesive letters that read "irls Storag."

He opened the door, reached inside the tiny closet and flipped a switch that did nothing. Ten minutes and a new light bulb later, Coach Lewis stood in the tiny storage closet and inventoried his equipment aloud.

"...six, seven, eight balls. All old, all flat. Five white mesh practice jerseys. Two torn. Three red mesh practice shorts. A box of jump ropes that look like they've never been used."

Visibly dismayed, Coach Lewis hustled down the steps and across the gym floor to the General's office. The General saw Coach Lewis coming and waved him inside.

"Coach McArthur," he said as he exhaled and tried to calm himself. "There seems to be some girls' equipment missing. Is there anywhere else..."

The General leaned back in his chair, kicked his feet onto his desk and interlocked his fingers behind his head. In a slow, deliberate drawl he interrupted. "That's the only place in my gym that there would be any girls' stuff. If we got it, it's in that closet. That's it except for the uniforms; they're locked in a storage unit by the field house so nobody walks off with them."

Coach Lewis understood exactly what the General was saying.

"OK, just checking," he said, if only to placate the perturbed General.

He headed out of the gym toward the field house where he knew Coach Cannon would be preparing for football practice. Coach Lewis walked through the field house toward the athletic director's office; as he made his way through the weightlifting area, some of the football players snickered. He knocked on Cannon's door only to receive a bitter response.

"Can't you see the door's shut?! Give us some damn privacy!"

Coach Lewis crossed his arms and waited outside Cannon's door. As he surveyed the weight racks, and the big, beefy guys who were lifting, he got the sense he wasn't welcome. The sounds of squeaky weight machines and the clanks of steel plates, along with the unmistakable stench of sweaty bodies, filled the spacious room. Several uncomfortable minutes later, Cannon's door opened and a young man emerged wearing the same "Lazarus Football" t-shirt as all the others in the field house.

From inside Coach Cannon's office thundered, "And you better be thinking with your head this year, son, and keep your zipper up! Your junior year's important. You can't afford to screw this up. Stay away from that girl!"

The young man hung his head as he meandered across the field house to the bench press where a few of his smirking buddies waited.

"Roy Haskins! Our boy Roy!" someone heckled from the far side of the field house, somewhere beneath the huge, framed team pictures of the football teams of seasons' past.

Coach Lewis peeked his head around the door frame at Coach Cannon. "Coach, can I see you for a minute?"

"You've got one minute. I have to get these guys going," Cannon said as he thumbed through some papers on his desk. "Go ahead. I'm listening even though I'm not lookin' at you. Go ahead."

"Coach, I was up in the girls' equipment room in the gym a little while ago..."

"Did you see another rat?" he replied without looking up. "Find Dee and he'll take care of it."

"No. No rats. But not much of anything else, either. We're way low on basketballs and we don't even have a full set of practice uniforms."

Coach Cannon stopped fidgeting and looked up at Coach Lewis. "Listen, Coach, the budget is in real bad shape right now and I'm being squeezed from all different directions this year. See, truth is that the girls' program hasn't brought in any revenue in as long as anyone can remember."

"But that's not how finances work in a high school athletic program. I..."

"I'll try to be more clear for you. We have no money in the budget for the girls this year except for tournament fees, transportation fees and officials' fees. That's it. We'll see what we can do next year for you, Coach."

"Except it isn't for me, Coach."

"Uh, huh. Listen, I have practice in ten minutes and your girls'll be out in ten minutes, too. We both need to get back to work. Let's talk about this later."

"Definitely. By the way, have you seen Coach Merrick? It's almost time for practice and I can't seem to find him."

"Bill will get here when he gets here."

Cannon went back to acting busy and no longer acknowledged that Coach Lewis was even in the room.

Coach Lewis sauntered back through the field house and then back to the gym. As he walked, he remembered something that President Franklin Delano Roosevelt once said. *A man shows who he is by what he does with what he has.* With that thought running through his mind, Coach Lewis shrugged off his encounter with Cannon and tried not to worry about his poor equipment. After all, he wouldn't even be in the gym until the following day so, by his estimates, he had another twenty-four hours to devise a practice plan that incorporated no more than eight basketballs. He returned to his office and scribbled a note, which he placed on the door of the girls' locker room: Girls Basketball Report to the Track.

The bell rang and the countdown to Coach Lewis's first practice reached T-minus-five minutes. The young coach stood in the heat of the day on the track infield and stared at his watch. Five minutes later, the girls remained AWOL. He figured the girls would be arriving momentarily so he rehearsed in his mind one last time what he wanted to say to the team. Several minutes after that and still alone on the infield the coach stood drenched in sweat from the 100-degree afternoon sun. Now somewhat agitated, he marched back to the gym to find the girls and to find out why they had not reported to the track as instructed.

He entered the gym to find the General grilling and drilling his boys. Above the gym in the area around the girls' equipment storage room a half-dozen girls leaned over the rail, watching the boys running lines on the court below. He glanced at the girls' locker room door and the sign was gone. Now well past irritated, Coach Lewis jogged up the stairs toward his team.

"Everyone out on the track. Now! Let's go!"

Startled, the girls jumped into action and took off down the stairs and toward the track. Reclining in a chair leaned against the rail was Coach Merrick, still dressed in his school attire.

"What are you doing, Gabe? We never start with a real practice on the first day."

Coach Lewis, in absolute disbelief, stared at the crabby old geezer. He noticed a piece of paper folded up and shoved in Coach Merrick's shirt pocket behind a pocket protector.

"First of all, I think it would be best if you refer to me as 'Coach' in front of the team. OK?"

"Sure... Coach." Merrick was a tired man who looked as though he should have retired several years ago. The lines on his forehead and his coarse white hair gave him a rough, rugged appearance. No one ever mistook him for the grandfatherly, teddy bear type.

"I put a sign on the locker room door just a little while ago. You wouldn't happen to have seen it, would you?"

Merrick reached in his pocket and produced a folded sheet of paper. He handed it to Coach Lewis and quipped, "I took it down. We don't practice on the first day and the girls were confused."

Coach Lewis stood incredulous and at a loss for words. His chin quivered and his heartbeat throbbed in his temples and behind his eyeballs. Rather than say something he might later regret, the rookie turned and double-timed it down the stairs, out of the gym and out to the track where he found the girls sprawled across the infield sunning themselves; Sam was the only one of the girls standing and stretching. Nearly half the pre-season practice period had now been wasted and, by his estimation, the team would need every minute of every practice they could get if they were to be at all competitive.

"Ladies, everyone up. Let's go!" he called as he jogged to where the girls had gathered.

As he approached, he sized up his girls for the first time.

"Let's get a single-file line across here in order of ascending height."

The girls milled about, grinned at each other, giggled some and finally put themselves in some abstract version of a line.

"Ladies, let's get this line straightened up and let me get a look at you guys."

After another minute, the girls managed to get themselves into a line in the order Coach Lewis had instructed. Standing before the young coach were eight girls, three of whom stood about 5'5" while the rest varied in height; Sam was the tallest at 6'3" tall. None of them wore basketball gear except Sam and one other girl. Most wore short shorts and either tight t-shirts or sports bras. One even wore a shirt that read "Softball is life." The cliché *You never get a second chance to make a first impression* came to mind for Coach Lewis as he made mental notes about each of his players.

"How old are you?" asked one of the three shortest players as she twirled her curly blond shoulder-length locks with her hand.

"What's your name?" was his answer.

"Brooklynne Meyers. How old are you?"

"I don't really think that's so important right now, Brooklynne." He made eye contact with each girl as he continued, "Ladies, my name is Coach Gabe Lewis. I know we didn't get started the way we all would have liked to but we won't let that deter us. The first order of business is to get to know everyone's name. So let's start with you, Brooklynne, and we'll move right up the line until we finish with you, Sam. Tell me your name, your grade and the position you feel most comfortable playing."

"Well, you already know my name," said Brooklynne, a short, cute girl who wore plenty of makeup and looked more interested in makeovers than layups. "I'm a junior and I like to play wherever I can shoot 3s."

"I'm Rita Rosales," said the next girl in line, "and I'm a junior point guard."

"They call me MJ but my real name is Mary Jo," the third girl explained with great confidence. Other than Sam, MJ was the only girl dressed like a basketball player with long shorts, a t-shirt and basketball shoes. MJ didn't compare to Nairobi or Sam in height but she was built like a ball player with firm, lean arms and legs and well-defined calf muscles. "I'm your super-soph shooting guard."

The next two players stood perhaps a few inches taller than the first three and one had a familiar face.

"Hi, Coach," said Autumn Griffin. "I'm a senior - finally! And I'm a guard. I'll play wherever you put me, though."

"My name," began the fifth girl before coming to an awkward pause. She stood about the same height as Autumn and weighed some twenty pounds less; she looked baby-faced but also athletic. Despite not being very tall, she had long, lean arms and legs for such a young player. She had her long, dark hair pulled back in a ponytail. As she spoke, she stared at her feet. "My name is Cassie Lassiter and I'm just a freshman. I don't really know what I play. We didn't really have positions last year and I'm not really very good anyway."

Next in line was the stockiest girl of the lot. She stood confidently with her arms crossed and her weight shifted to one hip. Only two players stood taller than her yet she stood only about 5'8" or so. "My name is Molly Frost and I started in the post last year as a sophomore so I guess that makes me a junior post."

"I'm Nairobi, Coach," said the tall, lanky dark-skinned girl with short-cropped hair. She looked intimidating, but her skill did not match her appearance. "I'm a junior and I was the tallest player on the team until Sam showed up. Guess she's got me beat by a couple inches." She smiled as she elbowed Sam in the ribs.

"Hey, Coach," said Sam with an eager smile. At well over six feet tall, Sam towered over virtually everyone else including her coach. She kept her short blond hair pulled back tight against her head with a thin headband. Her arms and legs looked like a boy's well-defined limbs and it didn't take much imagination to deduce she was extremely strong. "Sam Colter, senior, post. Glad to be a Lady Longhorn, Coach."

Coach Lewis went back through the line and named each girl as he pointed with his pen. Much to the surprise of the girls, he remembered each girl's name and class.

"Let's don't beat around the bush here," Coach Lewis said as he crossed his arms. "I understand this program hasn't been very successful the last few years. I believe in being honest, brutally honest if necessary, and I don't like to sugar-coat anything. I expect the same in return. That being said, does anyone have any thoughts on what's happened here the last few years?"

"Coach," Nairobi interjected, "we just aren't any good. No matter how hard we tried not to, we still lost most of our games."

"She's right," added Rita as she kicked at the dust. "We'd always lose, lose, lose. We tried not to but we didn't never seem to get better."

The coach nodded his head. "Well, that tells me quite a bit, actually. It sounds like maybe you guys have been attacking this from the wrong angle. It sounds like you guys have been playing not to lose rather than playing to win. That being said, we're not talking about last year anymore, or any other year, for that matter."

Brooklynne wrinkled her brow.

"In anything you do, ladies, whether it's basketball or something else in your life, you have to put your energy into being successful rather than into avoiding failure."

"What's the difference, Coach?"

"Good question, Cassie. We're about out of time for today so that's your homework for tonight. Think about that tonight and how it applies to what we're going to try to do here. That's going to be important when we sit down to decide on some goals for the season. We'll be in the gym tomorrow so please be sure you dress appropriately, ladies. The entire team should be dressed and ready to go, on the baseline, two minutes after the second bell. Now, everyone in."

He extended his arm and expected that everyone would follow his example. Sam picked up on the cue and put her hand atop his. Autumn did, too, and encouraged everyone else to join in. There in the middle of the track infield of Lazarus High School stood a circle of nine people whose lives were about to change forever.

"Longhorns on three," yelled Coach Lewis. His hand was at the bottom of the stack of hands in the huddle. "One, two three!"

"Longhorns!" they cheered. It wasn't quite delivered with the intensity he'd hoped for but, he figured, he had to start somewhere.

As the second bell rang after school on Tuesday, Coaches Lewis and Merrick stood at center court and watched the clock on the scoreboard tick down from two minutes. One by one the players emerged from the locker room and lined up across the baseline. With just twenty ticks of the clock left, all but two players stood on the baseline ready to go. Sam recognized the look on her coach's face as he watched the final seconds disappear from the scoreboard. Just as the buzzer sounded, the gym door flew open. MJ and Molly waltzed into the gym toward the locker room.

"Ladies," he called to them calmly, "you and your teammates are on the clock."

A few of the players standing on the baseline sighed and shook their heads as they realized what was happening. The two coaches stood in the middle of the basketball court, their eyes fixated on the stopwatch in Coach Merrick's hand. After what seemed like an eternity to the rest of the team, MJ and Molly jogged out of the locker room and lined up alongside their teammates, chatting casually to one another the entire time.

Coach Merrick shrugged his shoulders to the girls as if to avoid accountability for what was about to happen. Calmly, Coach Lewis whispered something in the old coach's ear. Coach Merrick turned and glared at Coach Lewis and then walked out of the gym. Coach Lewis didn't watch him leave. Instead, he walked slowly and deliberately toward the team.

"Three minutes and twenty seconds. That's how late you were. You two cheated your teammates out of nearly three-and-a-half minutes of practice. That time is gone now and we'll never get it back. Do not let that happen again." He walked over to the scorer's table and pushed a few buttons on the keypad that controlled the scoreboard clock.

The players turned their attention from their coach to the scoreboard.

3:20.

"On the whistle, down-and-backs 'til the buzzer."

"Everybody?" asked Brooklynne, who appeared baffled at the coach's instructions.

"Everybody. The actions and decisions of each player affect the entire team. We can't forget that," he explained as he headed back to the scorer's table. The whistle shrieked, the players sprinted toward the opposite baseline and the seconds began to tick away.

For everyone in the gym, time passed slowly. The seconds crawled off the clock and it seemed that Coach Lewis somehow had rigged the clock to count down more slowly than normal. Only ninety seconds into the sprints, some of the girls decreased their speed, grabbed at their sides and wheezed uncomfortably. The coach stopped the clock and blew his whistle. Most stopped dead in their tracks and gasped for air.

"We're all going to get this done, ladies. We're just getting started. No stopping, no walking, no slowing down. Let's go!" he said with a little more volume than before.

He restarted the clock and the girls took off again. Back and forth they ran, some more quickly than others and some with more effort than others, from baseline to baseline until the buzzer sounded.

"Now we can start practice," he said. "Everyone get a spot on the court and face me."

The girls walked with heavy legs to varying places around the court. A few of the girls leaned over and grabbed their shorts, a few put their hands above their heads and a few just held their sides.

"Show of hands. How many of you have seen or read *The Jungle Book?*"

Every player on the floor raised her hand and looked curiously at their new coach.

"That was written a long time ago by a gentleman named Rudyard Kipling. Among other things, he wrote a number of very famous poems. One of my favorite lines from one of his poems says 'The strength of the pack is the wolf and the strength of the wolf is the pack.' I want you to give this some thought during practice today. This will be our theme for the rest of the week. I also want you to think about what in the world that has to do with what we're trying to accomplish here."

The players looked around in amazement. Eyebrows raised and eyes wide, they glared at their new coach then shifted their eyes back to one another. Before they had a chance to get too caught up in their own bewilderment, the coach worked them through a number of footwork drills. The practice intensified as the minutes passed. Defensive slides, defensive slides and more defensive slides. Back and forth across the lanes, up and down the sidelines and zig-zagging back and forth across the court the girls slid in a defensive stance while the coach corrected each girl's posture and footwork as she passed by him on the floor. Within minutes, the lactic acid burned their thighs and buttocks. Just when they thought they would drop to the floor, Coach Lewis moved to a different defensive or footwork drill, then another and then another. By now, Molly, Cassie and Brooklynne were walking through the drills while the rest of the team ran. Coach Lewis calmly watched the social interaction of the girls as some players ran past the ones who were walking. He said nothing. He simply watched. Finally, after an agonizing afternoon, practice drew to a close. Before they broke for the day, they huddled and talked briefly about the "thought for the day" from the day before.

The next day before practice, moved once again to the track outside, Coach Lewis repeated Kipling's line for all to hear and consider while working out. As the sun beat down upon the eight girls and one coach, the team jumped rope, ran sprints of varying distances and somehow mustered scores of crunches and pushups. Just as in the workout of the day before, some of the girls bowed out of the drills. Again, Coach Lewis just watched and made mental notes.

With Thursday's practice once again in the sweltering, un-air conditioned gym, the team focused on defensive drills, footwork and exercises to build strength in their legs. Now two full days removed from the first real workout of the year, every player's body ached from head to toe and every fiber of every player's exhausted body burned the way only overworked muscles can burn. On this day, though, Coach Lewis reminded the team of the Kipling phrase repeatedly. Practice wore on as it had the two days prior.

As the players did their full-court defensive slides, Cassie, the youngest and meekest of the bunch, stumbled backwards and fell flat on the floor. As Autumn approached her fallen teammate, she and Coach Lewis made eye contact for a split second, but a split-second was all it took. Autumn slid past Cassie then stopped. She walked forward to the freshman lying spread-eagle on the floor and lifted her up. As her teammates saw her do this their eyes widened, their heads nodded or their mouths stretched into grins. A few looked across the court to their coach for affirmation and he nodded.

As Brooklynne moved past Coach Lewis, though, she asked, "Am I missing something?" Coach Lewis raised his eyebrows and slowly shook his head.

Practice returned to the track on Friday. For the third consecutive day, the entire team was on time and ready to begin practice as per Monday's instructions. In the searing heat of that Friday afternoon, the coached pushed the girls to their physical and mental limits with cycles of 200-, 400- and 800-meter runs. The conditions were brutal, the girls were physically and mentally exhausted from the week of practice, but Coach Lewis pushed and pushed. With a few girls fighting back tears, Sam and Autumn, the team's only seniors, repeated the immortal words of Kipling to those who wanted desperately to succumb to the heat and the stress, "The strength of the pack is the wolf and the strength of the wolf is the pack." A few responded to this encouragement while MJ and Molly simply ignored them. Finally, the bell rang from the field house signaling the end of the day and, more significantly, the end of the week.

"Ladies, everyone in," called Coach Lewis to his exhausted team. As the team huddled around him he praised his team. "I'm very proud of us. We hung in there and worked hard four consecutive days. If we work this hard all year, our effort won't go unrewarded. We have to be honest with ourselves, though. We aren't in very good shape, we aren't very fast and we don't have much depth because of our numbers. We won't be beating teams with our speed and athleticism, so we'll have to make sure we work harder than everyone else long before we ever set foot on the court for a game."

Coach Lewis extended his arm into the center of the huddle and the girls followed suit, too exhausted to argue or do otherwise.

"Longhorns on three," he cheered for them. "One... two... three!"

The team summoned the last of its energy and managed a mediocre cheer. They broke their huddle and dragged themselves back to the locker room inside the gym. After several minutes, the players intermittently headed home for the weekend. Autumn, Rita and Cassie were the last to leave the gym. Shortly after the girls had begun their weekend, Summer stopped in for a brief visit with Coach Lewis.

Earlier that day during lunch period, Coach Lewis had invited Summer to put her math skills to good use with the basketball team. He explained to her that he needed a reliable statistician if he had any hopes of measuring various elements of the team's progress over the course of the season. Flattered, Summer welcomed the opportunity. Her return to school after giving birth to an illegitimate child had not been an easy task. She knew the administration didn't want her there. She knew the boys from the football team talked about her. She knew the other girls talked about her. The only true friends she had left in the small school were on the basketball team and she was glad to have the chance to spend her time with people who accepted her.

Alone in his office after Summer left, Coach Lewis scribbled for a while on a pad of paper whose pages contained diagrams of basketball courts and lines next to each court for notes. This pad of paper often served as the artist's canvas for Coach Lewis. As he doodled on the pad, Coach Lewis suddenly realized the intensity of the silence in the office and in the gym. He returned his pencil to the basketball-shaped coffee mug on his desk and strolled into the gym.

He stood on the baseline beneath the basket closest to his office. To his left were the stands where he hoped multitudes of people would gather to watch his team. The antique wooden seats were smooth from decades of Longhorn faithful sitting and standing and filing in and out of the rows. They seemed to be original to the old, quaint gymnasium. New, aluminum benches or stadium seats would have been anachronistic in this gym. High above the floor to his right were large windows that hadn't been cleaned in years. They were much too high for anyone to see either in or out and their sole purpose was to allow sunlight to fill the gym each day. For a few moments each evening when the sun strikes the windows at the proper angle, the dirty windows filter the sunlight to create a mystical ambience in the gym. On that Friday evening at the exact time Coach Lewis stood alone beneath the basket, the sun shone softly through the panes and illuminated the red longhorn at center court painted on the hardwood floor as the new basketball coach lost himself in the moment. Tiny particles of dust danced in the sunlight and reduced the glare of the sun's rays to a warm glow. The serenity of the quiet gym rolled over the coach's soul.

Coach Lewis closed his eyes and imagined how the gym must sound on Friday nights with standing-room-only crowds gathered for contests with playoff implications. He imagined the squeaks of twenty basketball shoes on the freshly-waxed hardwood. He heard the pop of the nets as the long-range jump shots reached their targets without even touching iron.

He heard the slamming of the gym door. That cacophonous sound, however, was not part of his Friday afternoon mystical experience. The sound of the slamming door was real, and it preceded the echoing footsteps that were headed his direction. Bill Merrick had returned to the gym and the look on his face indicated he had something to say that either could not or would not wait until Monday.

"Coach Merrick, we've missed you at practice the last few days. Is everything OK?"

The old assistant kept walking toward Coach Lewis until he stood toe to toe with the youngster. Neither blinked and neither flinched.

Coach Lewis broke the silence and spoke first. "Coach?"

"Now you just listen to me, son. I have a few things I need to get off my chest and you'd be wise to hear me out."

"Go ahead, Coach, you have my undivided attention." Coach Lewis's expression remained stoic and his eyes resisted the urge to blink. Inside his young body, though, his heart pounded and his temples throbbed. He gritted his teeth so Merrick wouldn't see his chin quivering.

"I can't come over here every day and watch what you're doing to those girls. They're girls, son; they can't handle the kind of physical treatment you're givin' 'em out there. This isn't a football team."

"Actually, Coach," interrupted the younger, "I believe with all my heart they can do more than what they've done already, more than what they believe they're capable of and obviously more than what you..."

Bill's jaw clinched and as he ground his teeth then he unloaded. "Don't you interrupt me. You're gonna ride those girls and push those girls and for what? You're gonna put them through boot camp and they're still gonna lose twice as many games as they win and then what? What will you have accomplished? Not a damn thing! All that hard work and no results! Truth be told, there's probably a lot more people out there that like basketball more than I do but, believe it or not, I do care about those kids' wellbeing. You're killing those girls for nothing and that's not fair to them. Now you think about whether or not this whole thing is worth all that trouble."

Coach Lewis stared intently at the bitter old man. He took a deep breath and asked his antagonist, "Are you finished, Coach?"

"You bet I'm finished! You're on your own the rest of the way, son. And don't even think about coming back to me to ask for help with scouting reports or anything else." Bill poked his wrinkled, bony finger in Coach Lewis's chest. "If you keep up this foolishness, I hope you don't win a game. Not a game! Maybe that'll prove to you what everybody 'round here already knows! Everybody but you, that is."

The old codger wheeled and stomped across the hardwood toward the door. He kicked the door open and left the gym with the same fury as when he entered.

The tranquility disrupted, Coach Lewis looked back at the waning sunlight as it climbed over the sills and in through the windows. He was reminded of some words of wisdom imparted upon him by his former head coach. *It isn't what happens to you that's important. It's how you react to what happens to you that's important.* Despite his attempt to focus and regain his composure, the moment was gone. The timely glow of the evening sun he had enjoyed so much just minutes ago vanished into the dusk.

CHAPTER V

Every Sunday morning several of the Lady Longhorns gathered on the back row of the First Church of Bethany. Brooklynne, MJ, Molly and Cassie attended First Church and had since they were born. Rita, from a family of devout Roman Catholics of Mexican descent, drove some twenty minutes each week to attend mass in the next town over. Nairobi, Summer and Autumn attended yet another church; none of those three was exactly welcome at First Church for one reason or another. On this particular Sunday morning, Sam and the rest of the Colter family were in attendance at First Church, too. Sam didn't sit on the back row with the rest of the teenagers, though. Her mother and father required the twins to sit alongside them on the front pew. Though Sam couldn't have known, that probably was just as well.

Throughout the pastor's welcome, the prayers, the hymns and the offering, including the extended offertory hymn, the girls remained relatively calm and respectful on the back pew. After the organist finished her musical worship during the offering collection, though, the girls pulled out their paper and pencils and began the traditional Sunday morning gossip exchange. Every Sunday morning in churches across America, teenagers migrate to the pew farthest from the pulpit for one reason and one reason only. Beyond the line of sight of their parents and too far away for the pastor to notice the disrespectful behavior, teenagers pass notes, giggle and churn the rumor mill like there's no tomorrow. This tradition is as old as church-going itself and the girls of the First Church of Bethany were no exception to this standard of Sunday-morning teenage behavior.

The ruffling of pages as the congregation pulled their Bibles from beneath the pews and turned to the appropriate passage, as instructed to by the pastor, camouflaged the sounds of the scribbling of pens and pencils and the tearing of paper. Cassie sat on the end of the pew in the back, right corner of the sanctuary. Next to her sat MJ, then Molly and then Brooklynne about half-way down the pew. Molly held the paper in her lap and the others leaned in to write their messages. MJ leaned in and wrote the first of the morning's messages.

"New girl Sam – down front"

The other three knew Sam was there but they craned their necks anyway to catch a glimpse.

MJ jotted hastily, "Baller!"

Brooklynne pulled the paper toward her and penned, "Gonna take someone's spot!"

After the others read her note, Brooklynne grabbed the paper again and added, "Not mine though!"

Molly grabbed Brooklynne's pen and scratched through Brooklynne's comments then added her own commentary.

"Looks like a boy – gross!"

Each of the four girls on the pew knew Sam was the real deal, a bona fide stud, college material. Each of the girls also knew that for once Brooklynne was, as they say in Lazarus, "right as rain." However, one of the girls was still in denial about the possibility of losing her starting role to Sam. Of the four in the back pew, Molly was the only one who played post and the only one in denial about what Sam's arrival might mean for the Lady Longhorns' starting lineup. She snatched the paper in her hand and crumpled it into a ball. The other three exchanged glances then sat quietly and uncomfortably for the remainder of the sermon.

After the service, the four bolted from the sanctuary and drove to MJ's house for lunch. Over grilled cheese sandwiches, sour cream and onion chips and Cokes, three of the four girls tried to pick up the conversation where it left off in church.

"OK, back to Sam," offered MJ as she tested the waters.

"Yeah," Cassie chimed in, just wanting to be a part of the conversation. She felt lucky to be able to run with the older girls, and rightly so. Her teammates, these three at least plus Autumn, allowed Cassie to run around with them on occasion mostly because they pitied her. Cassie's father was in jail for writing hot checks and had been in and out of the slammer since Cassie was in the fourth grade. Cassie's mother invested no time and energy in Cassie's life and left Cassie to fend for herself most of the time. Her insecurities often were mistaken for whining but the girls, to their credit, usually overlooked that. On the court Cassie had as much potential as any of the other guards, but she didn't know that yet.

"Guys! Sam ain't that good! She's big but you know she's slow! Big as she is, she has to be!" Molly argued. "Besides, I started last year and if coach knows anything about team chemistry he'll leave things alone."

"He's an English teacher not a science teacher," Brooklynne said. The other girls grinned and rolled their eyes. "He does know how to make us sore, though. That's for sure. I can't hardly move and it's been that way all week."

Rick Jasperson moved about the kitchen as if he were busy cleaning the counters and drying the dishes. As he did, he listened to every word the girls said about the new coach, the practices and the new girl, Sam. He added the girls' conversation to the growing dossier of intel MJ had been providing him all week. As the chips and sandwiches disappeared, the conversation grew louder and more emotional. Finally, Rick Jasperson could contain himself no longer.

"Sounds like everybody's gonna be in good shape this year at least. Maybe you girls will finally be able to run and gun a little. MJ, you might get twenty shots a game with a high-powered run and gun offense."

"Offense? What's that? We haven't shot a ball yet!" his daughter declared in disgust. She jumped up from her chair and started shooting mock jump shots around the kitchen table at imaginary hoops hanging high on the kitchen walls. "I'm gonna lose my stroke if we don't start shooting the ball soon."

"Yeah, Mr. J, all we've done so far is defense and running and talking about weird philosophy and literature stuff," Molly added.

Cassie tried again to be one of the girls. "Just running and stuff, and mostly outside, too."

"No offense yet? What's that guy doing? Surely he knows we have to outscore the other team to win," Jasperson added with a sarcastic tone to stir up the girls even more. He spun a kitchen chair around backwards and straddled the chair. He crossed his arms, leaned on the table and rested his chin on his arms. "Sounds like maybe he could use a little help. If he's still doing strange things with you guys in a week, you let me know and I'll offer to help coach you guys. What do you say?"

Rick Jasperson, at least in his own estimation, knew as much about basketball as he did about football, and nobody in Lazarus knew more about football except Tommy Cannon, maybe. Jasperson just knew his daughter had a chance to be a legitimate Division I player despite her lack of size and lack of speed; she'd outgrow those hindrances eventually. The three-point technique he taught MJ, often referred to as the west-Texas push, would allow MJ to shoot her way all the way to a major university, maybe even Tech. If the darn new coach would just let the girls shoot during practice... He'd heard from various sources that Tech, in particular, made the recruitment of small-town girls a real priority. With his help, Jasperson figured, the girls' team might be able to finally turn the corner if they all learned to shoot like MJ. He'd always noticed the flaws in the other girls' skillsets in years past – and how could you not notice, as bad as the other girls were – and this would be his chance to help get the girls headed in the right direction at long last. Furthermore, without serious improvement, the Lady Longhorns would be practically useless to MJ and she might over-exert herself simply because she would have to carry the team and do everything on her own, no matter how big this new kid turned out to be. The team needed him.

Brooklynne, Molly and Cassie looked at each other and shrugged their shoulders. MJ gave her father a high five and pretended to dribble a ball around the kitchen. Brooklynne dumped the rest of her chips on to Molly's plate and tossed her trash in the garbage can. Molly finished her sandwich then took the last bit of Cassie's sandwich right out of the freshman's hands and shoved it into her own grinning mouth. The three stood, waved goodbye to Rick Jasperson and headed to the backyard for a little Sunday afternoon sun worship.

MJ figured she would get plenty of looks at the basket once her dad straightened things out with Coach Lewis. "We'll keep you posted, dad! He'd be crazy not to want your help. You know more about hoops than anyone I know!" MJ high-fived her dad then gave him a double fist bump before heading out to join her teammates, who already were shedding their clothes in the backyard.

————————

Gabe rose early Sunday morning. During his first week in Lazarus he surmised that most of the people in town would be in church on Sunday mornings and that attending church was the right thing to do, especially in a new town; making a good first impression, he believed, would be important to his success in Lazarus. Furthermore, he didn't discount the benefits of having his spiritual and emotional cup refilled.

Based on some things Martha had mentioned, Gabe knew many of the most important and influential people in Lazarus attended the First Church of Bethany, the picturesque little white church in downtown Lazarus surrounded by business establishments. Honest Abe's Used Cars, for example, sat across the street from the church; ironically, though, the Eighth Commandment was lost on Abe despite the close proximity of the car lot to the House of God. Next to the church sat the post office, and directly behind the church, Lester's Liquors. The manager of Lester's, an avid churchgoer himself, always made sure his doors were locked if the church's doors were open; this had been a longstanding arrangement dating back as far as anyone could remember.

Since most of the people Gabe had encountered thus far in his west-Texas odyssey attended the First Church of Bethany, and since he had no desire to sit next to them or even to see them at church, he decided on a different church altogether; after all, Gabe Lewis still felt obligated to be in church on Sunday. Several miles outside of town, even a few miles past Mesquite Branch Estates, rose the rickety steeple of Greater New Life Church, yet another quaint west-Texas church building. The appearance of the crackly white wooden slats on the exterior resembled an antique finish not unlike those sought by trendy big-city shabby-chic designers. The wooden shingles atop the rustic building were bleached by the sun; many were cracked and others even curled up at the ends. Not quite in disrepair, the Greater New Life Church had an endearing quality that, through the years, prompted many passersby to stop their cars on the side of the road and take photos of the old and hitherto insignificant structure.

Earlier in the week, the Griffin girls, at the suggestion of Martha, invited their new coach to their church. He accepted their invitation. True to his word, Gabe rose early to make sure he had plenty of time to get ready and make the drive outside the city limits.

As was his habit, Gabe timed his drive so he would arrive at the church just as the traditional 10:45 a.m. worship service began. As he pulled into the parking lot, though, he noticed the marquee in front of the church: Sunday Morning Worship 10:00. Gabe hated being late; for Gabe Lewis, punctuality was a virtue. He parked his vehicle, jumped out and slammed the door behind him. As his feet hit the dusty gravel beneath him, the haunting soulful music from inside resonated into the parking lot. The piano, the organ and the choir blended together to create a single, powerful gospel instrument whose magic could be heard and felt outside the church nearly as easily as inside. Gabe dashed across the gravel and bounded up the front steps toward the church doors. He grabbed the handle of the church door then paused as the congregation belted the last stanza of the traditional negro spiritual.

As the music and the shuffling and bustling from beyond the door settled, Gabe pulled slowly and gently on the large, iron handle, careful not to draw attention to himself as he entered the building. The decades-old iron hinges, however, decided to announce his arrival to the entire congregation. At once, a congregation of eyes turned to see Gabe standing at the back of the sanctuary, hand still on the door and sheepish smile on his face. He'd always dreamt of being in the spotlight on the stage that was the sideline of the hardwood but at that moment he had never felt so self-conscious. To make matters worse for Gabe, the Reverend Brother Elijah Washington was in rare form.

"Come in out of the heat, brother, and refresh your weary soul with the cooool water that is Jesus!"

For a moment, Gabe wondered if he were in the right place. As the congregation gave a rousing "Amen" to the Reverend Brother Washington's well-intentioned salutation, Gabe nervously scanned the sea of dark skin and bright smiles for a familiar face. After an eternity, Gabe saw Martha, Summer and Autumn peering back at him from the third pew giggling at his embarrassment. Sitting between the two girls was another girl he recognized, Nairobi Whitaker, also snickering. Gabe kept his head down and peered up through his blond locks as he made his way to where the Griffin girls were seated with Martha. He sat down on the hard, wooden pew and glanced around at the rustic, minimalist appearance of the church's interior. There were no fancy pew cushions, no stained glass windows, no ostentatious ornamentation of any kind.

Just as Gabe got seated, Washington raised his arms in dramatic fashion and motioned for his congregation to rise again. The preacher continued without missing a beat.

"Brothers and sisters," whispered the orator from the pulpit, "have you been rebuked?"

From all corners of the congregation, many of whom had their hands in the air, resounded "Amen," "Oh, yes, pastor," and "You're speakin' the truth, brother!"

With his voice elevated slightly, he continued, "Have you been scorned?"

Again, the congregation responded and echoed his increased volume and enthusiasm.

Cloaked in a purple robe, the tall, robust man whose round, bald head glistened with perspiration, grabbed his Bible and shook it as the fire in his eyes began to build. Every word that bellowed from his mouth was deliberate and eloquent, in a west-Texas full-gospel sort of way.

"Don't think, brothers and sisters, for one moment that you're alone in your suffering, in your scorn, in your humiliation. Don't think, my friends that Jesus has asked you to do anything, no, not anything that he hasn't already done."

The pastor's voice was intense and electrifying. As he spoke, the energy in the sanctuary rose to the level of a playoff game in the final seconds of overtime. With his raspy baritone voice and his dramatic enunciation of key words, the pastor elicited spontaneous hand claps, "amens" and raised hands from his brothers and sisters who sat in rapt anticipation on the edges of the old wooden pews.

"Turn with me to the gospel according to Luke, the fourth chapter and the sixteenth verse," he shouted. "Stay with me now." His voice quaked with bravado. "'And he came to Nazareth, where he had been brought up and, as his custom was, he went into the synagogue on the Sabbath day, and stood up to read.' Jesus is in his hometown, people, his hometown!"

He paced back and forth behind the pulpit with enormous, deliberate, heavy, pounding steps as he read. His thick arm held the Bible at eye-level and his eyes remained fixated on the scripture before him in his hand. His eyes widened as he continued.

"Skip down to verse twenty-four, my friends. 'And he said, Verily' Verily! 'I say unto you, No prophet is accepted in his own country.' Are you with me, brothers? Do you see where this is going, my sisters?"

He held his Bible high above his head with his left hand and clinched his right into a fist as he shouted what he read, "'And all they in the synagogue, when they heard these things, were filled with wrath, And rose up, and thrust him out of the city, and led him unto the brow of the hill whereon their city was built, that they might cast him down headlong!'"

"Oh mercy, Lord," shouted a woman from the back. "Scorned and rebuked," shouted another. "Show me th' way through it, Lord," cried yet another of the emotionally-stirred throng.

The Reverend slammed his Bible onto the pulpit and closed his eyes. He paused for a minute and then, with his arms outstretched, his fingers stretched wide and his palms upturned, spoke very softly.

"Picture it if you will, brothers and sisters. Our Lord returns to his hometown, the town where he spent his childhood, where he grew into a man and made many friends. The very people with whom he played games as a child were so blind that they couldn't, no, *wouldn't* see him as the Messiah. These childhood friends, these friends of the family chased our Lord out of the town, out to the hill upon which the town was built." His voice reached a crescendo as he continued. "His folk, his people, his flesh and blood not only scorned him, not only rebuked him, not only rejected him," he said as he raised his arms higher with each phrase, "but they wanted to throw him off a mountain."

The congregation heaved a collective gasp and a man seated behind Gabe stood and shouted, "Preach the truth, brother, preach it to us!" as he waved and pumped his fist in the air.

"Did they?" he asked as he made eye contact with person after person.

"No, preacher," the congregation shouted in unison.

"Did they drive him down to his knees?"

Again, "No, preacher!"

"No! Our Lord was not deterred! Our Lord was *not* deterred!" he cheered with his hands clinched into fists and his arms extended to each side. The veins in his neck bulged from beneath his skin and pulsed with each beat of his heart. "Our Lord Jesus kept his eye on his goal and he kept marching. Undeterred. He marched right through the hostile crowd and eventually on to Calvary so that we, my brothers and sisters, could one day rise up and march to Zion!"

By this time most of the hands in the sanctuary extended upward to Heaven, bodies swayed to and fro and a heavy lady on the front row fainted from the heat and the frenzied state into which she had been stirred either by the Spirit or by the Reverend Brother Washington.

"His own people rejected him and scorned him and mocked him but he was not deterred! With the strength of the Almighty God in Heaven, he persevered and he overcame and he kept marching toward that goal, that prize, that place on another mountain, on Calvary's mountain where he forgave the very people that rejected him and where he saved those same people that rebuked him!"

The rhythmical musicality of Reverend Brother Washington's cadence moved the congregation every time. Martha had promised Gabe, "Nobody can preach like that man."

"Sister Mavis, come forward and lead us in song. And, brothers and sisters, let us sing sooo loud that the saints up on Heaven's heights can hear every word we sing on this blessed morning!"

Goosebumps crawled up and down the necks and backs of the congregated faithful as the organ and the piano and the choir launched into a passionate rendition of "Victory in Jesus" the likes of which Gabe had never heard before. For twenty minutes the body of believers sang and wept and lifted their hands and danced and poured out their souls. When "Victory" finally concluded, Sister Mavis transitioned the choir into another hymn, then another and another. For more than an hour, the Greater New Life Church raised the rafters and shook the windows of that small, west-Texas church. When Mavis finally ran out of energy, the Reverend Brother Washington prayed, invited everyone to Dinner on the Grounds and then prayed again to bless the food. No sooner than he said "Amen," the choir, led once again by a suddenly-rejuvenated Sister Mavis, began the longest arrangement of "Let Us Break Bread Together" ever sung in Bethany County.

Just shy of one o'clock in the afternoon, the brethren of Greater New Life Church adjourned to the church grounds to spend the rest of the afternoon under a rented tent eating, laughing, socializing and enjoying the company of one another despite the sweltering heat and the hot, dust-laden winds blowing in from the panhandle. As Summer and Autumn, with a grinning April in her arms, introduced Gabe to family after family, the sisters beamed with excitement and bragged on their new coach. The two even re-introduced Gabe to Dee, the "maintenance guy," as Gabe once referred to him. Like the last time their paths crossed, Dee greeted Gabe with a grin and quick, upward tilt of his head, sort of the opposite of a nod, Dee's way of saying "Hi," "What's up," or "Good to see you." The girls wanted everyone to meet Gabe and they couldn't have been more proud to show off their new coach. After what seemed a hundred such introductions, Autumn grabbed her coach's arm and dragged him across the grounds to where the Reverend Brother Washington seemed to be holding court beneath the tent.

"Reverend," Autumn said as she tapped him on the shoulder. "Reverend, I want to introduce you to a pretty special visitor. This is our basketball coach, Gabe Lewis. He's new."

As the Reverend extended his large hand toward Gabe he returned Autumn's ear-to-ear smile with a joyful one of his own. No matter where she went or whose company she kept, Autumn's gentle spirit and positivity proved irresistible. The sparkle in her eyes and her west-Texas drawl simply compounded her charm.

"New, huh? Where you from?"

"Houston," Gabe answered as he shook the pastor's large, hot hand.

"A stranger in a strange land… Now, I wonder why the Lord plucked you up out of Houston, and dropped you all the way out here in Lazarus."

The Reverend Brother Washington looked almost into Gabe's soul as he gazed down at him, and Gabe could feel it.

"I'm just here to coach basketball and try to win some games. That's all," Gabe said, still shaking the pastor's now-sweaty hand.

For a moment, the Reverend Brother Washington said nothing, continued shaking Gabe's hand, then released his hand.

"Mm hmm… I see," he finally said. With a smile, he continued, "Then best of luck to you, son. Welcome to Lazarus. You take care of this one now, you hear?"

Autumn dropped her head slightly and to the side just a bit. She pursed her lips and looked back up with just her eyes at the pastor, but her smile refused to be contained. As quickly as she playfully subdued her smile, it returned in all its glory.

The girls' introductions, the welcoming and unassuming smiles, the handshakes and hugs all set Gabe completely at ease. Gabe found judgment in no one's eyes and heard nothing but encouragement from the upturned lips of his many new friends. He observed not only with the way he had been treated but also with the way the congregation treated Autumn and Summer, who gladly handed off little April to anyone who smiled in their direction. The relaxed fellowship reminded him of family reunions at his grandparents' place when he was a child. Despite the obvious differences between Gabe and all-save-three of the other members of Greater New Life Church, Gabe felt unconditionally welcomed for the first time since his arrival in Lazarus.

CHAPTER VI

Coach Cannon slammed the door to the General's office so hard that three plaques and two framed team pictures jumped off their hooks and crashed to the floor. The General spun around and around in the swivel chair behind his desk and pressed his knuckles against his temples. Sitting across the desk from him were Coach Cannon and Principal Haskins; neither said a word. For minutes, three men sat in silence and stewed. Finally, Haskins broke the silence.

"Damn, Patton, what the hell were you thinking?"

Coach Cannon could contain himself no longer either. "How on God's green earth did you think anything good could come of this? What are we supposed to tell parents when they start calling wanting to know if our basketball coach has lost his ever-loving mind? Did you even once think about the consequences of what you were doing?"

The General offered no response. He didn't even make eye contact.

"Patton," Haskins started again, "if you had used your brain for one second you would have known that this was a lose-lose situation. What's gained if things went down the way you planned? Absolutely nothing but some false sense of accomplishment. What if things went horribly wrong? Which apparently they did. And by the way, how did you manage to screw that up? I've been around a long time and seen a lot of things, but come on, Patton!"

Cannon piled on. "That may be the dumbest bet you've ever made. I know you're a gambler but you need to stick to cards and tables. Leave your kids out of your bets from now on! Do I make myself clear?"

Cannon and Haskins folded their arms and looked at each other in disbelief. They shook their heads and sighed. The beleaguered General, feeling now more like a private, stood, took his keys from his pocket and walked between his two superiors toward the door. Without saying a word, the coach walked slowly out of his office toward the gym exit. His slumped shoulders and hanging head said it all.

Haskins looked at Cannon. "We can't exactly undo things, can we?"

"I don't think so. If I could I would but I think he's gonna have to lay in the bed he made on this one. I'm just glad none of my boys were involved in this. I'd kill those knuckleheads..."

"Well, let's go see Lewis and make sure he doesn't get the big head now."

The two frustrated administrators walked the length of the gym toward Coach Lewis's office. Without knocking they walked right in to find a messy desk and an empty chair. Coach Lewis's keys were still on his desk so he hadn't left yet for the weekend. Cannon rifled through the papers scattered on the desk but found nothing of interest, only quick-hitter plays and defensive formations jotted down on dozens of sheets of paper torn out of notebooks. As he finished ruffling the papers, one page caught Cannon's eye. He picked up the sheet that read "TAKE OUT THE GENERAL" across the top and had notes and diagrams below.

"Take a look at this," Cannon said as he handed the page to Haskins. "Looks like our boy did his homework."

Haskins studied the paper briefly and rubbed his forehead with his fingers and his thumb.

"That's how he did it, huh?"

"Apparently so," Cannon answered. "If we can't say anything else about our boy I guess he does his homework. I don't think it would've happened if Patton had his boys from the football team out there, too."

"Agreed. Too late to speculate on that now."

"Well, this is interesting, alright, but I sure can't see this happening when it counts, though? Can you?"

"It better happen when it counts or it's going to be a very long season," popped Coach Lewis as he walked into his office and wedged his way between his two visitors. He grabbed the sheet from Haskins' hand and took refuge behind his desk. "What can I do for you, gentlemen?"

"Don't let this go to your head, son. This ain't the real deal."

Coach Lewis could tell from Haskins' tone that Haskins was deadly serious.

"No, sir. We still have too much work to do to get cocky now. We've only been working a few weeks. I'll let the kids enjoy this for the weekend but we'll be all business on Monday. I promise."

"You planned all along to set him up, didn't you?" Haskins sneered. "What made you think you could beat him?"

"Honestly, guys, I didn't know if we could beat his team or not but we had nothing to lose and everything to gain. You know, sometimes that's not a bad place to be. I watched him practice and I saw how his guys were arrogant just like him. Attitude reflects leadership. Anyway, I knew his kids would be less concerned with basketball fundamentals and more concerned with teaching my girls a lesson. I taught my girls how to play to the boys' weaknesses - their cockiness and the overplaying of every pass - and the girls executed the plan to perfection. And you're probably right, Coach. If the guys from your team were out there filling out his squad, we couldn't have competed with their athleticism. I wouldn't have attempted this if that were the case, though."

Cannon and Haskins looked at Lewis then at each other before turning to walk out of Lewis's office. After they left and after the gym door slammed shut, Coach Lewis collapsed into his chair. He couldn't help but grin at the afternoon's events.

The emotional high from Sunday's service and the time of fellowship afterward resonated with Coach Lewis and he rode the high into Monday. He had a little extra bounce in his step all day long and the students wondered what had happened over the weekend to keep the new guy so chipper. As practice time approached, Coach Lewis thought about the things he wanted the girls to accomplish during the week. He rehearsed in his mind the things he wanted to say, the points he needed to emphasize during the week's practice sessions. He also began to plan for running practices completely on his own now that Bill had bailed on him, not that Bill had been much help the previous week.

Since it was Monday, the Lady Longhorns returned once again to the track for practice. As the team arrived on the track infield to get loosened up, they found Coach Lewis with a box of folders. As they approached he distributed the folders like an evangelist passing out tracts at a mall. On the cover of each folder were the words "LADY

LONGHORN BASKETBALL." The girls were more than a little perplexed.

"Let's go, ladies. Circle up. Everyone should have a notebook. Go ahead and look through it and then we'll get started."

The eight girls flipped curiously through the contents. Inside were pages of lists, quotes, and basketball diagrams. Sam seemed undaunted, but the rest of the girls acted as if they had just been given a text in a foreign language.

Molly thumbed through it, rolled her eyes in her trademark style then crossed her arms.

"We have to learn all this, Coach?" inquired MJ.

"Yea, I don't know if my brain can hold all this information. If I put all this in my brain," Brooklynne added, "I may lose some of my science and math stuff."

Coach Lewis grinned. He couldn't help it. "Ladies, this is your basketball Bible for the next six months. Don't lose it. Bring it to practice every day. Don't lose the pencil in the back, either. You'll need it from time to time to make notes and jot things in the back of your folder, starting today."

The girls practiced selective listening as they continued to fan the pages of the notebooks.

"Turn to the last two pages of the notebook. You should find a 'GOALS' page. Obviously, the pages are still blank because we haven't set our goals yet. We're going to start that process today. As you run through your workouts today, I want you to start thinking about some goals you want to set for yourself and for the team. Everyone understand?"

Some of the girls nodded and a few even acknowledged the instructions with a "Yes, sir." The coach blew the whistle and began the workout. He started the workout slowly then worked up to more intense runs and drills. As the sun beat down and the hot dry air blew across the field, the girls soon realized their coach had turned it up a notch. The soreness that had left some of their muscles and joints over the weekend returned as their legs carried them round and round the track. After only half an hour, Coach Lewis summoned them back to the infield where big red coolers of water awaited them.

"Is it my imagination or are you turning up the heat, Coach?" Rita gasped.

"You could tell, huh?" the coach chuckled. "You know, we *have* to turn it up some. We don't have very many players. That means very little depth. That means more players will have to play extended minutes. That, of course, means we'll have to be in better physical condition than any of our opponents. We may get beat because of any number of reasons but we will not get beat because someone else is in better shape than we are. We have to control the things that we can control. Understand?"

"As much as I hate to say it, I agree, Coach," Nairobi conceded as she was still bent over with her hands on her knees.

"I'm with you, too, Coach," Autumn added, also leaned over resting her weight on her knees.

"Now, about those team goals," the coach said as he made eye contact with each of the girls. "First thing I want you to write in the back of your notebook is what you expect will be different about you as an individual after the season. How do you hope this experience changes you?"

A few of the girls sat down on the dried grass of the infield and scribbled in their notebooks as instructed. A few sat mystified.

"Changes us?" barked Molly. "Why does anything have to change? Why do we have to change? I like me the way I am!"

Coach Lewis looked straight at Molly as he addressed the group. "Why would you choose to participate in something, especially something as tough and challenging as the game of basketball, if it weren't going to change you in some way? Isn't that why we're here? To change something? To get better? To grow?"

Autumn scratched her head. "I never thought about it that way. That's a good point, Coach."

MJ jumped to her feet and went through the motion of a jump shot. "Just as long as my J don't change!"

Coach Lewis failed to find the humor in MJ's remark and glowered her direction. The rest of the team sensed his disapproval. MJ held her follow-through at the end of her imaginary shot then slowly sat back down when she realized nobody except Molly was amused by her antics. For a moment the eight girls sat quietly and most jotted down their thoughts in the notebooks.

"Great. Now let's think about some team goals. Any thoughts?"

"I want to go to the playoffs. I've never missed 'em and I don't plan on breaking that streak my senior year," Sam chimed.

The girls all turned and looked at Sam with disbelief.

Cassie wrinkled her brow and turned to Sam. "Seriously?"

"*Chica*, we ain't never been to no playoffs," Rita snapped.

"There's a first time for everything," Sam replied. "Why not? That's my team goal, Coach. Playoffs!"

Coach Lewis clapped his hands. "I like it! I definitely want us to get to the playoffs, Sam! Good goal!"

"Playoffs!" scoffed Molly. "So what happens when we don't make it? We work all this time then don't reach our goal. Then the whole season is shot. We don't need a goal like that. Maybe a better goal is to not lose more than fifteen games."

Coach Lewis's expression grew serious and for the first time the girls felt his icy stare.

"We must have goals," he explained as he pounded his fist into his hand. "Without goals, we'll be wandering aimlessly through the season. So what if we don't reach the goal. It wouldn't be the end of the world. At the end of the season, if we haven't reached our goal, but we've changed, changed in the way you just wrote in your notebook, then the whole experience will have been worth it. Sometimes, ladies, the journey isn't about the destination. Sometimes the journey is about the journey."

Brooklynne hadn't said a word thus far. At the coach's words, though, she wrinkled her brow, scratched her blond head then raised her hand slowly.

"Yes, Brooklynne?"

"Uh, about this journey... where are we going?"

The coach paused for a moment and then answered with conviction, "We're going somewhere we've never been before."

"That's what I'm talkin' about!" whooped Sam as she leapt to her feet. She helped her teammates up one by one and gathered the girls around her in a huddle for their Longhorn cheer.

As the sweaty girls huddled together, Rita patted Cassie on the back. "Glad you're still hangin' in there, kid. You done good today! You start us off."

The skinny, self-conscious freshman looked up at the girls and the corner of her mouth curled into a half-grin. "Really? Thanks!" She put her hand in first and the rest of the girls put theirs in, one on top of another. Cassie prompted her teammates, "Longhorns on three" and most of the girls responded with genuine enthusiasm. A few, however, still had their own ideas about the season and the coach.

Tuesday's practice brought with it much needed relief from the torturous heat. Even though the Longhorn gym was old and un-air conditioned, the two rickety oscillating fans on each baseline kept the temperature inside around ninety degrees, which, to the girls, seemed like seventy degrees compared to the scorching heat of the west-Texas afternoon sun. Just as he'd done the week before, Coach Lewis ran the team through footwork drills, speed drills, defensive drills and ball-handling drills. The girls handled the drills pretty well until fatigue set in; it being only the second week of practice, fatigue gripped the team after only twenty minutes of the coach's challenging anaerobic drills.

As the girls battled exhaustion and stiff muscles, they struggled to maintain their focus. They dribbled balls off their shoes, their passes either fell short or rainbowed too high, and the girls grew irritable. Coach Lewis recognized the irritability as a sign of physical and mental exhaustion and urged his team to fight through it. In spite of their fatigue, he pushed them harder and harder. Even though the girls felt like they were nearing their physical limits, he knew they could do more, handle more, achieve more.

As Molly struggled through the two-ball speed dribbling drills, her frustration grew until she could contain it no longer. She dribbled the ball in her left hand off her left foot and cursed out loud. Then she picked up the other ball in her right hand and punted it across the gym; the basketball narrowly missed one of the lights suspended from the ceiling of the gym then careened off the wall and landed behind the bleachers.

"I'm a freakin' post! Why do I have to do these ball-handling drills? Shouldn't I be jumping or doing something useful?" Molly exclaimed.

The other girls, surprised by Molly's outburst, stopped dribbling and gawked in disbelief. Basketballs rolled in every direction. Most of the girls knew Molly was a hothead, quick-tempered and not at all bashful, but the new coach hadn't yet seen her temper in all its glory. All eyes turned to Coach Lewis. Everyone in the gym watched to see how he would react. As luck would have it, Principal Haskins had just left the General's office; he had come over to the gym to drop off a fax for the General. The principal shook his head at Molly's tantrum and headed back to his own office across campus thankful he didn't have to deal with her. Coach Lewis spent so much energy trying to remain calm, he never saw Haskins. The coach felt the weight of the girls' stares, though, as he sucked in a breath of the hot, still air and called everyone in to center court. The girls walked in from wherever they were on the court and waited expectantly.

"First, I know you guys are exhausted. I see it on your faces and I can tell by your frustration. You guys have to believe that you can fight through that. Mental mistakes tend to come in bunches late in the game when you're tired, like you are right now. We have to prepare ourselves for those situations."

He looked across the faces of the girls and, remarkably, he still had everyone's attention.

"Now, Molly, imagine we're in the fourth quarter of a big game. You're tired. The whole team's tired. You're getting frustrated because we're on someone else's court and we're getting a big batch of home cooking." Several of the girls grinned at the expression; even though she had no idea what Coach Lewis meant, Brooklynne grinned, too, but only because she didn't want to be left out. "You've been trying to post up all night and you keep getting called for hooking. On the other end, their post is hooking you every trip down. If you have a reaction in the game like the one you just had here, what happens?"

Everyone stood in silence. The team turned to look at Molly but Molly just stared at the floor.

"What happens, Molly?"

"I'll get T'd up? Maybe tossed?"

Her eyes darted back and forth then she lowered her head.

"Exactly. You're tired and frustrated and you have to concentrate even harder to control your emotions when you're tired. Remember, it's not what happens to you that's important. It's how you react to what happens to you. Does that make sense, ladies?"

"Yes, sir," a handful of voices replied.

They broke the huddle and finished practice without further incident. Molly kept her short fuse in check and so did everyone else, even though mentally and physically they were spent. After practice, Sam approached Coach Lewis after the rest of the girls disappeared into the locker room.

"Hey, Coach, can I ask you a question?"

"Sure."

"With all due respect, Coach, are we going back outside tomorrow?"

Coach Lewis hesitated for a moment. Although Sam asked one simple question, she might as well have asked a dozen more. *Why do we have only two days a week inside and the guys have three? Why do we have lousy equipment and the guys don't? Why are we treated like second-class citizens? Why do you let the other coaches treat you like a second-class citizen?* He knew what she was doing. Maybe the team sent her to ask, maybe they didn't. There was no simple answer to the ostensibly simple question; the real answer, though, was complicated.

"Sam, we'll be outside again tomorrow."

Sam already knew the answer to the question. Once Coach Lewis confirmed what she already knew, Sam dropped her shoulders, turned and ambled off toward the locker room.

"However," added the coach in a momentary lapse of reason, "we'll get more time in the gym soon. I promise."

Sam joined her teammates and left Coach Lewis alone in the gym. He went to his office and locked the door behind him. He slipped a Wade Bowen CD in the stereo he brought from home and scanned his library of books. He searched the shelf for inspiration, but to no avail. He closed his eyes for a moment and lost himself in the music. There was nothing like the sound of Texas country to clear his mind. Four songs later he opened his eyes and breathed a sigh of satisfaction. He had a plan. Coach Lewis jumped up, grabbed his keys and headed to the hardware store.

Cassie, the lone freshman, flung open the locker room door and squealed with laughter. Her teammates stared in disapproval. Squealing was for little girls, not high school basketball players and her teammates let her know they wouldn't stand for that kind of juvenile behavior. After her brief reprimand, she waved her arms to get everyone's attention.

"OK, y'all ain't gonna believe what Coach and Summer just did outside for practice today! Get your stuff on quick and come see!"

The Lady Longhorns looked around at one another and, in an instant, made a mad dash for the track infield they had grown to know and hate. As they approached the track, they saw Summer and Coach Lewis gathering up what must have been a dozen or more spray paint cans strewn across the grassy field. The two were red-faced and dripping with sweat. When the girls reached the area where Coach Lewis stood, he extended his arm and made a sweeping motion, palm up, as if to say, "Check this out." The girls stood in disbelief of what lay on the field in front of them. Coach Lewis and Summer had painted a basketball court on the grass. The grass court was complete with lanes, free-throw lines, three-point lines and the works.

"I don't even want to know what's going inside that *loco* head of yours, Coach!" joked Rita.

"Well, guys," Coach Lewis said as he used his shirt sleeve to dry his face, "what do you think? Pretty nice, huh?"

The girls weren't exactly sure how they should react or what they should say.

"OK, let me explain. I have an idea about how to get more time in the gym but we'll need to work on some basketball things while we're outside in order to carry out my plan. Obviously we won't be dribbling but we can sure use this..."

"For passing!" interjected Autumn.

"And transition," added Rita. "Right?"

Coach Lewis smiled and nodded. "You got it."

"And shooting?" MJ asked expectantly.

"No, sorry, not yet." MJ and Molly practiced their pouting faces as he continued. "I won't tell you about my plan yet but, if it works, we'll be back in the gym next Friday. Here's the deal, though. If you want equal gym time then you're going to have to fight for it. Just like in the real world, ladies, if you want equality you better be prepared to fight for it and take it by force. If you aren't prepared to fight for it, then you better be prepared to do without."

MJ made a disgusted face at Molly and thought to herself, *Wait 'til dad hears about this!*

Summer emptied the bag of basketballs and Coach Lewis began practice on the makeshift grass court on the track infield. As the football players passed back and forth outside the fence around the track, they whooped and hollered and made fun of the girls. Redirecting their attention from the heckling back to basketball, Coach Lewis prompted the girls to ignore the boys and focus on the task at hand. Good practice tuning out hecklers and belligerent crowds during away games, he explained. As the practice session unfolded, the coach laid the groundwork for his grand scheme. However, he never fully disclosed the plan to the girls.

The rest of the week went by as had the last: inside on Thursday and outside again on Friday. Once again, the boys, in their pads and helmets, jeered at the girls for practicing on the dried-grass basketball court with spray-painted lines and no goals in the middle of a track infield. Nevertheless, the coach pushed his girls through until the end of the week.

Coach Lewis released his girls early on Friday and the gesture was more than a little well-received by his players. For the remaining few minutes of the practice time, Coach Lewis returned to the gym where the General was drilling his boys on their full-court man press. The aggressive boys overplayed each pass and flew around the court with reckless abandon. He sat, watched, and made mental notes until practice was over.

After the boys finished practice, he asked the General if he could see him in his office for a few minutes. The two head coaches went into the General's office and closed the door behind them. Several minutes later, Coach Lewis emerged with a suspicious smirk. As he walked from one baseline to the other, toward his own office at the far end of the gym, the General's gruff, bellowing laughs spilled out of his office, across the hardwood and followed Coach Lewis the entire length of the court.

Less than two weeks later, things had changed considerably. For this Monday practice, all the girls lined up on the baseline early. The Lady Longhorns had a newfound confidence not only in themselves but also in this crazy new coach, because his crazy plan had worked to perfection. During Friday's practice, only one week after Coach Lewis had scouted the boys and had taken notes on their full-court press, the girls broke the boys' full court press nine times in ten tries, just as Coach Lewis said they would. The girls danced with anticipation, but not because of practice.

The heat of the gym had the girls sweating already, but the girls hardly noticed. As they waited anxiously on the baseline they bounced on their toes. Finally, they got their payoff. The boys' locker room door creaked open and the boys' team plodded along the opposite baseline and out of the gym. Several paces behind the boys walked a somewhat humbled, disgruntled and disheartened General. Though the girls wanted desperately to mock the boys, to cheer and jeer and to rub it in the way the boys certainly would have done to them, Coach Lewis, just moments before, gave the girls his sermon on being cocky and arrogant and how that simply would not be tolerated from a team that hadn't yet accomplished anything really meaningful. Obediently, the girls watched and smiled as the General's despondent troops marched out of sight. When the boys had disappeared from sight, Coach Lewis blew his whistle and circled the girls for the first practice of the new week.

Coach Lewis made eye contact with each of his players and smiled. "The gym is ours every day for the next month until two-hour practices begin. Let's take advantage of the time we have in here. Let's make sure we're a better team at the end of that month. And let's make sure every day that we're a better team at the end of each practice than at the beginning."

The girls nodded in agreement.

"And, by the way," he added, "I'm really proud of you guys."

CHAPTER VII

"You're almost there, Cassie. Keep moving up, hand over hand. Just take it a rung at a time."

"This is the scariest thing I've ever done, Roy. I don't know how I let you talk me in to this."

"Both of you be quiet up there. You're wrecking my concentration," Brooklynne called from below.

"Brooklynne, ignore them and keep climbing," said Logan Russell, Brooklynne's date for the evening and arguably one of the best basketball players in Lazarus. In his own mind, at least, Logan's good looks surpassed all the other Longhorn jocks', even Roy's. Logan didn't bulk up like many of the football players but preferred instead to keep lean and chiseled. His close-trimmed haircut accentuated his lean build. Though his reputation hadn't quite surpassed Roy's, it wasn't for lack of effort.

The crisp October air made the iron ladder cool to the touch and the chilly gusts blowing over the wide-open Bethany County countryside rocked the water tower gently from side to side. The giant red letters on the tank proudly declared "LAZARUS, TEXAS – HOME OF THE LONGHORNS." Roy, Cassie, Logan and Brooklynne certainly would not have been the first Lazarus teenagers to ascend the hundred or so feet up the water tower. As long as the water tower had been in Lazarus, which was probably as long as Lazarus had been in Bethany County, teenagers scaled the tower to court, to count stars and simply to prove that they could. While some daring Lazarus teens, Longhorn football players in particular, considered climbing the tower a rite of passage and a test of manhood, others believed the tower to be the ultimate romantic destination, a place where one's beloved would freely give away her heart, or more.

Logan, wearing his red and white letter jacket, faded jeans, and his favorite cowboy boots, stepped off the ladder and onto the catwalk that circled the tank of the water tower. Brooklynne sidled up next to him and put her arm through his. Her tight blond curls bounced and blew in the breeze. A few steps away, Roy and Cassie sat down on the cold metal grid, Roy first with his legs dangling off the edge then Cassie in front of him with her back pressed against his chest. Roy, like Logan, proudly wore his letter jacket with his jeans and his boots.

The view from a hundred feet above Lazarus caused the four young thrill seekers' hearts to skip beat after beat. Even two hours after the final whistle of the football game, the stadium lights shone bright like an altar fire burning for the football gods while the last of the red taillights trickled out of town. Beyond the city limits and high above the horizon, ten million twinkling stars set the mood for a night none of the four would soon forget.

"Why don't you guys take a hike," Roy said. His straight, brown hair, which hung just below his brow, blew sideways in the breeze.

Logan grabbed Brooklynne's hand and led her along the walkway around the tank and out of sight. As they disappeared around the curve of the tank, Brooklynne looked back over her shoulder at Cassie and winked. Settled comfortably into their seat on the walkway, Roy pulled Cassie in close and put his chin over her shoulder, his mouth next to her ear.

"I'm glad you came up here with me."

Cassie shivered. "This is really nice. I'm glad you asked me."

Cassie lied. Shy, nervous and short on self-esteem, Cassie suddenly found herself far out of her comfort zone. She had no experience with boys and she feared heights more than anything in the world. Cassie had heard stories about Roy Haskins; nevertheless, she craved the attention he had given her recently in the halls and in the parking lot after practices. She needed the affirmation and attention Roy had shown her. He told her she was cute. And when he did, he complimented her girlish face and her long, lean legs, "like a track star but more girly," he said. Roy's reputation combined with his schoolboy charm enthralled her and rendered her powerless. Cassie's timidity and her tendency to blend in, to go unnoticed, kept most boys from noticing how attractive she actually was. Considering the celebrity status Roy had achieved of late, his attention seemed that much more valuable to Cassie. Now perched high above Lazarus and virtually alone, however, she wondered if she might be in over her head.

"I told you it'd be romantic up here."

Roy kissed Cassie's neck just below her ear and Cassie leaned her head back against his shoulder.

"Are you nervous?"

"Maybe a little." Cassie tried to steady her hands.

"Is it being up so high or is it me?"

"Both, I guess." Her hands refused to cooperate.

"Just relax. I'll take care of you."

Roy kissed her neck again and wrapped his left arm around her waist. He slipped his right hand beneath her sweater and placed his large, strong hand flat against her tremulous stomach.

"Shh... It's OK."

Cassie reached back and placed her left hand on the back of Roy's neck. Her right hand she slid along his arm and under the sweater, placing her hand over his and interlocking his fingers with hers; she closed her eyes tight. She tried hard not to think about how high above the ground she sat. As Roy reached and turned her head toward his, his hidden hand slid upward ever so slightly. Cassie let Roy kiss her again, but pulled his hand from beneath her sweater.

"I promise it'll be OK," Roy whispered. "Close your eyes and relax. Try to enjoy being up here."

Roy kissed her harder and returned his hand beneath her sweater. Cassie told him to stop and wriggled in his grasp. When she felt the air beneath her dangling feet, though, she grew still again. Sensing Cassie would not submit, Roy slid back and jumped to his feet. He reached down, dragged Cassie from the edge and leaned her against the tank.

"Wait here," he said. "I'll be right back."

Cassie stared at the stadium lights. As she waited for Roy to return, she slid her fingers down into the metal grid on which she sat and she curled her fingers around the cold metal. The reflection of the stadium lights glistened in each tear that welled up and ran down her cheeks. Without Roy's warmth, she noticed the coolness of the autumn evening, especially with the brisk breeze now blowing in from the north; she'd forgotten how panhandle days could be so warm yet the nights so cool. Cassie breathed in the cool night air then exhaled; she could see her breath in the night backlit by the stadium lights.

Around the curve on the dark side of the tank, two intertwined figures lay on Logan's jacket. Roy smiled and watched the writhing duo in the dark for a moment before calling out to his buddy.

"That's not very nice, Roy. You scared us to death. We could've rolled off here, you know," Brooklynne said.

Logan climbed to his feet and walked with Roy out of sight around the curve of the tank in the opposite direction from which Roy had approached. Brooklynne sat up, pulled her knees to her chest and waited. She shivered in the cool of the night and pulled Logan's letter jacket over her knees and arms. After scanning the dark on either side of her for several minutes, she simply sat and waited, all the while breathing in the scent of Logan and his cologne that clung to his letter jacket.

Time seemed to crawl as Brooklynne sat alone in the darkness. Finally, footsteps approached and a shaky voice called her name.

"Cassie, what are you doing here? Why're you by yourself?"

As Cassie walked closer, Brooklynne could hear her crying.

"Are you crying? Aren't the guys around there on the other side?" she asked. "Seriously, are you crying?"

"I haven't seen Roy in a long time and I haven't seen Logan since you left with him."

Brooklynne stood to her feet, groped in the darkness and grabbed Cassie's trembling hand. Brooklynne now found herself in an awkward situation. Even though they talked at basketball practice, she normally would not have been out socially with Cassie. But being in the company of boys presented an exception to that rule. In their current predicament, though, Brooklynne understood she needed to be there for Cassie, who clearly was out of her league with both the boys and with Brooklynne.

"They're probably clowning with us. I'm sure they're hidin' in the shadows watching us right now."

"Brooklynne, I'm so scared."

"Don't be scared. Hey, let's go scare them. We'll sneak up on 'em. Come on."

Brooklynne pressed her back against the cold tank and pushed Cassie back against the tank, too. Brooklynne didn't provide the comfort Cassie needed, but Cassie had nowhere else to turn. She wiped her eyes, tried to get control of her breathing and followed Brooklynne around the curve of the tank.

"Just like in the cop shows," Brooklynne explained.

Quietly and carefully the girls circumnavigated the tank hand in hand. They moved into the light, back into the shadows and stopped once they reached Logan's jacket exactly where it lay a few minutes earlier. They took a deep, calming breath and decided to split up. They decided they would walk in opposite directions until they met on the other side. If the guys were sneaking behind or ahead of them, one of the two would find the two jerks who must have thought it would be funny to sneak away for a few minutes to compare notes on how the girls kissed. Brooklynne and Cassie smiled tentatively at one another in the darkness and headed in opposite directions. The boys couldn't escape now.

When Brooklynne saw the light of the stadium reflecting off the tower ahead of her, she wondered what she'd find when she entered the glow of the stadium lights. What she found was not what she had hoped.

"This can't be good," Brooklynne said to herself.

On the walkway against the tank, Cassie sat sobbing with her head on her knees. Both knew now what they feared but had refused to say a few minutes earlier. Brooklynne cursed out loud and told Cassie to sit still while she went to get Logan's jacket. As she made her way back toward Cassie, jacket in hand, she searched the ground below for Roy's truck, for any sign of people below. She saw nothing but darkness. She cursed the boys again and sat down next to Cassie.

"Brooklynne, can I borrow your phone?"

"I think I left it in the truck with my purse. Where's yours?"

The look on Cassie's face answered the question. Cassie began to cry uncontrollably and she hit the back of her head on the tank behind her over and over again. Brooklynne grabbed Cassie's shoulders as she knelt carefully in front of her. She wiped Cassie's face with her hands and tried to calm her hysterical, unlikely companion. After thinking to herself, *I can't believe I'm doing this*, Brooklynne leaned in and gave Cassie an awkward hug and a pat on top of her head. She stood up, placed one hand on her hip and the other on the railing around the walkway.

"OK, we got up here. All we gotta do is do it backwards, right?"

Then it happened. An enormous, haunting click echoed across the Bethany County countryside and the stadium lights disappeared from sight. Frigid darkness replaced the glow of the stadium lights. Blackness enveloped the water tower and the girls, both now frozen with fear. With no moon in the Texas sky, the ten million pin pricks in the canopy above Lazarus let in too little light to offer any comfort to the girls let alone sufficient light to descend safely from atop the tower.

"This can't be good," Brooklynne said to herself, out loud this time, though.

Brooklynne sat down next to Cassie who lay curled in a fetal position. Cassie rocked herself back and forth rhythmically and gently, sobbing tears of fear. Brooklynne lay over on top of Cassie and pulled Logan's jacket over the two of them. Brooklynne's eyes filled with tears and her heart filled with panic. The more Brooklynne thought about their dilemma, the more panicked she became. She imagined freezing to death atop the tower only to be found weeks later. She imagined rolling off the walkway and plunging to her death over a hundred feet below. She imagined being struck by lightning as a violent storm blew across west Texas and targeted all the tall, metal structures in Bethany County for lightning strikes. She hoped they'd use a really flattering picture of her, maybe the one from prom last year, when the story broke on the news of the two Lazarus teenagers who froze to death on the water tower.

The panic overwhelmed Brooklynne and she jumped to her feet. At the top of her lungs, Brooklynne shrieked into the night. The blood-curdling screams shocked Cassie, who jumped to her feet, too, piercing the gloomy darkness with desperate cries of her own. The black void surrounding the tower absorbed their screams of terror and the screams went unheard. When finally their throats ached from crying out for help, Brooklynne and Cassie lay down next to one another on the walkway, their lips cracked from windburn and their stomachs wrenched in knots with nausea. They clung to one another trembling and shivering beneath Logan's jacket, beneath the twinkling Texas sky.

Coach Lewis lay in his bed confused by the dream that seemed to prick at his ears. He pulled the covers over his head hoping the rapping would go away and allow him to return to his deep sleep. The rapping grew into a pounding that shook the window to his bedroom. Suddenly he sat straight up in his bed and did his best to knock the cobwebs loose from his head. The rapping and pounding had not been in his dream, but rather seemed to be coming from his front door. He pulled on shorts and a faded Houston Rockets throwback t-shirt, noticed the digital clock that read 3:16 and felt his way through the dark toward the door. He peered through the peephole and saw two people standing in darkness in front of his door. As he opened the door, Sam stumbled into his living room with Martha following close behind; Sam stood red-faced and hysterical looking first at her coach then at Martha. Coach Lewis clicked on a few lights and sat down with them.

The ceiling fan lights overhead revealed a meager, sparsely decorated living room with two wooden chairs and a small sofa. The coffee table in front of the sofa hid beneath stacks of books, a pile of graded papers and empty coffee mugs. In the corner of the room stood a small entertainment center which housed a television, a DVD player and stacks of DVDs. On the wall hung a solitary picture, the team photo of Coach Lewis and the Lady Longhorns taken on picture day at Lazarus High School back in early September.

"Coach, the girls need your help," Martha explained.

"Coach," stammered Sam, "Cassie and Brooklynne are in so much trouble and we didn't know where else to go so we came here and you have to help us, I mean, help them before somebody gets hurt real bad. Autumn's with 'em right now and they're waitin' for us. We gotta go, Coach!"

Still working hard to wake up and make sense of the untimely visit, Coach Lewis rubbed his eyes and concentrated on what Sam was saying. He listened closely as Sam explained that Cassie had made plans to spend the night with Autumn and her. Cassie met them at the football game but disappeared in the chaos as the game ended. They figured she would show up again later so, at Autumn's suggestion, they waited at the stadium for almost an hour after the game. Cassie never reappeared. Figuring she changed her mind about sleeping over, the two girls left in Autumn's truck, got a burger at Dairy Queen then returned to Autumn's house for a night of watching chick flicks and eating ice cream straight out of the carton. As Sam told the story, Martha sat straight on the sofa with her hands on her knees, demure as always. Martha studied Gabe's eyes and face as he concentrated on Sam.

After the first movie, Sam continued, they got a bad feeling about Cassie, butterflies in their stomachs and lumps in their throats. They worried about her being so young and inexperienced and possibly getting into some kind of trouble if she were either somewhere by herself or hanging out with the wrong people. They knew Cassie didn't have enough experience running with older kids to make good decisions. Within the next few minutes, coincidentally, Corey called Sam on her cell to make sure she had arrived safely at Autumn's. Sam told her brother their fears about Cassie, and Corey replayed for Sam the conversations he heard in the locker room after the game. He told Sam how Roy had bragged about his next conquest, Cassie, about the look in his eye when Roy talked about her, and about the chip on Roy's shoulder when he left. Corey also mentioned that Brooklynne might be with Cassie based on what Roy said. For entirely different reasons, Brooklynne never would have been accused of sound judgment either.

Convinced their fears had merit, Autumn decided to wake Martha and the three set out in Autumn's truck to find the girls. The three headed straight to the water tower where they discovered the damsels in distress frozen with terror atop the tower. When the ladies on the ground discovered the two girls high above, Autumn immediately started the long ascent. Over her shoulder she gave Sam and Martha instructions to drive straight to Coach Lewis's house and get help. As Sam and Martha climbed back into the truck, they heard Autumn calling to the girls to be still and that help was on the way.

"So let me get this straight," he said. "The girls are stuck on top of the water tower and you need me to get them down?"

"Exactly," said Sam. "Autumn knew you'd help us."

"And when you got to the tower, only Cassie and Brooklynne were up there, but Autumn is up on the tower now, too?"

"Exactly, and now we have to get there fast to get them down before someone gets hurt."

"Wait a minute, ladies," he said as he looked at Martha. "Why didn't you call the sheriff? Seems like a deputy or maybe the fire department would be better suited for something like this."

Martha spoke for the first time since they sat down inside. "Coach, we don't need trouble with the sheriff. It would be best if his office didn't know about this. It might get complicated if the sheriff's office gets involved."

Coach Lewis let out a sigh as he stood and grabbed his shoes from the empty chair. He laced up his vintage Jordans while Sam and Martha watched. He went to the kitchen and rummaged in a drawer until he produced a flashlight, then he grabbed his keys and wallet and walked back through the living room. On the way to the front door, he grabbed Sam's hand and helped her up, then helped Martha up from the couch. The three piled into the two vehicles out front and drove quickly to the water tower under the cover of a moonless sky.

This is not what I signed up for, he thought as he drove through the early morning darkness. Still sleepy, he rolled down his window to let the fresh air blow against his face. Instead, dust from the truck ahead of him billowed in through the open window. The dust filled his nostrils and made him sneeze and cough. He raised the window and turned the radio up to an uncomfortably-loud level and worked hard to open his eyes completely. Perhaps it was the early hour that kept him in a haze, but the adrenaline had not kicked in yet to jolt him into a state of alertness. As he followed the old truck, his headlights reflected off the dust clouds like high-beam lights in dense fog. Finally after several minutes of fast driving, the two vehicles pulled up beneath the water tower. There were no other vehicles in sight. More importantly, there were no people anywhere in sight, either.

Already dreading the next step, Coach Lewis climbed out of his Blazer and walked beneath the tower, craning his neck upward toward the top. In the darkness, he could see only the outline of the tower and could not make out any details. The ladder to the top seemed to extend from the ground straight up into the night sky. He called out to the girls and they answered with cries of "Oh my God!" and "Please get me down from here!" and "We're fine. Come on up." Martha stood quietly near Autumn's truck and watched as Coach Lewis assessed the situation. Sam wished Coach Lewis "Good luck," patted him twice on the back, then returned to Martha's side.

Coach Lewis held his breath, reached up with one hand, grabbed the rung and pulled himself upward. He had climbed nearly twenty feet off the ground before he allowed himself to breathe again. Hand over hand, one rung at a time, he climbed the ladder toward his stranded girls. The higher he climbed, the tighter his hands gripped the rungs and the longer it took to get each foot off one rung and onto the next. He prayed this would be his only ascent. After an eternity of climbing, he reached the top and pulled himself onto the metal grid where Autumn sat waiting for him.

"That's a long way, huh, Coach?"

He sat next to her and leaned back against the tank. After drawing a lungful of the icy breeze that blew across his face, he smiled and agreed.

"Come on, Coach, they're around this way."

Autumn helped her coach to his feet and they made their way around the tank to where Brooklynne and Cassie sat shivering partly from the damp coolness and partly from fear. Both girls stood slowly and latched onto their coach with vice-like hugs. The embrace showed no signs of ending so Coach Lewis broke the silence.

"Everybody OK?"

Brooklynne spoke first. "Did you bring some help?"

"I am the help."

"I guess you'll have to do," she said through chattering teeth. "What's your plan for getting us down from here?"

"My plan is that we all have to climb down. No one's coming up here to get us down. I'm not sure how we all ended up on this tower at four o'clock in the morning but I'm quite sure we all have to climb down on our own."

If there had been enough light for them to see one another clearly, Brooklynne's face would have displayed the terror in her heart at the thought of climbing back down the ladder in the darkness. Likewise, Cassie's face would have been pale white except for the redness of her puffy eyes. Without hesitation Autumn volunteered to go first. She hugged and kissed her teammates, gave her coach a thumbs up and a smile, then climbed down and out of sight.

Coach Lewis then turned to the girls and explained what they were going to do next. He explained that he would climb down a few rungs, then Cassie would climb down next so he could keep a hand on her to help her feel secure, then Brooklynne would follow. Cassie neither moved nor said a word. Brooklynne, on the other hand, refused to climb down unless he did the same for her. Exhausted and scared to death, Brooklynne started crying and Cassie followed suit. Coach Lewis gritted his teeth, shook his head and ordered Brooklynne to have a seat until he came back for her. Stunned, she sat down as instructed and leaned back against the tank; she huddled inside Logan's jacket for warmth. Coach Lewis took Cassie's hand and led her to the ladder where he began the climb down. Still crying, Cassie eased onto the ladder until she could feel his hand on her back. With each downward step, Coach Lewis told her when to change hands, when to move her foot onto the next rung, all the while maintaining some contact against her back. In any other situation, their close proximity and constant contact would have been beyond uncomfortable and inappropriate, but under the circumstances neither thought about it at all.

After fifteen or twenty minutes of arduous descent, the coach and his players stepped onto *terra firma* where Sam, Autumn and Martha waited to embrace and coddle Cassie. Coach Lewis bent over and leaned on his knees, the ways his players often did in practices, and tried to catch his breath. He rubbed his hands together to work out the soreness and stiffness then turned to face the ladder once more. One final time he climbed to the top of the tower then helped Brooklynne make the treacherous climb down the same way he'd helped Cassie. Exhausted and frazzled, Martha and Autumn took the girls back to their home and Coach Lewis returned to his, where he plopped down on the couch in utter disbelief.

————————

The heat of summer in Bethany County reluctantly faded away week by week as the Longhorn football season marched into autumn. The football frenzy consumed Lazarus and everyone who lived there. Fathers reminded sons of the good old days, spoke with reverence of the all-time great Longhorn players and challenged their sons to match the feats of teams and players of the past. On the last Friday night in August, the Longhorns began the season with high hopes, as they often did, for a district championship, a deep playoff run and perhaps a shot at the Holy Grail of Texas high school football.

After opening the season with a road win over the Antelopes from the tiny town of Whiteface, the Longhorns dropped the home opener against the Aspermont Hornets in front of a standing-room-only crowd. After pounding Whiteface with a steady attack of Roy Haskins at quarterback, Coach Cannon's boys mistakenly believed the Pirates would roll over and submit to the Longhorns. Despite seven touchdown passes by Roy Haskins, the Longhorn defense couldn't stop the Hornets in the fourth quarter. Nevertheless, Longhorn enthusiasts faithfully filled Longhorn Stadium the following week.

The Southland Eagles flew into Longhorn Stadium for the third game of the young season with a 2-0 record and playoff hopes of their own. Roy Haskins gave a repeat performance and singlehandedly clipped the Eagles' wings in front of yet another packed house of frenetic fans. The quarterback with the golden arm dazzled the

Longhorn faithful as well as the scouts from Texas Tech, who came to see if Haskins was as advertised. The scouts were buzzing after the game and were dropping hints to Roy's father about scholarships and playing time in Lubbock. Destiny finally seemed to be smiling on Roy.

Full of swagger after a second victory, the Longhorns hit the road again and traveled to the Panther Pit in Whitharral to tangle with the Proud Panthers. Much to the chagrin of the Longhorn faithful, the Panthers had Roy's number all night and held the blue-chip prospect to a paltry three touchdowns. To add insult to injury, the Panther secondary picked off three of Haskins' passes, a career high for the Longhorn play-caller. In the field house after the game, players pointed fingers, passed blame and took out their frustrations on one another. Sitting at two wins and two losses was not where the Longhorns thought they would be after four games. Coach Cannon, just like the players in so many ways, took out his frustration on his team, and on Roy in particular.

For Cannon, as good as Roy was, Roy would never live up to the legend of his own quarterbacking prowess. There was a part of Cannon that deep down inside secretly hoped Roy Haskins never would surpass his own accomplishments or achieve a more esteemed position in Longhorn lore. Cannon ripped into Roy and the rest of the team with a tirade that peeled the paint off the locker room walls and left the players dejected and demoralized. With powerhouse Groom on the horizon, the Longhorns limped into the following week of practice with little confidence and even less hope.

After an intense week of practice, the Longhorns found themselves in the locker room feeling somewhat reluctant about the showdown with the ferocious Groom Tigers; they listened as Cannon issued warnings and threats before he stormed out of the field house with the rest of the coaches. Before the team could exit, though, Roy Haskins stopped his teammates and poured his heart out to them. He spoke of pride, of playing for one another rather than for the coach, of playing for the name on the front of their uniforms rather than the names on their backs, and of defending their home field. With the entire team on the verge of tears and hopped up on testosterone and adrenaline, Roy Haskins led his team in a charge onto the field just minutes before kickoff.

The Longhorns got off to a quick start against the Tigers by returning the opening kickoff for a touchdown, but the Tigers responded by scoring on their opening drive. The epic battle saw the momentum and the lead change numerous times before the fourth quarter expired. Both teams played to exhaustion and gave all they had. In the end, though, Groom's high-octane offense proved too much for the Longhorn defense to handle. Roy Haskins threw for seven touchdowns and ran for two more in a memorable performance, but even he couldn't match the ten Tiger touchdowns. Despite the loss, the Longhorns headed back to the locker room with heads held high. The team had found the emotional leader they needed in Roy and they were ready to follow him anywhere, into any situation. Cannon, after the game, remained uncharacteristically calm and subdued. He, too, had discovered over the course of the night that Roy had won the allegiance of the team and that rants from the coaches would not be effective so soon after such an emotional performance.

With a new sense of purpose in the days that followed, the Longhorns dedicated themselves to destroying the Amherst Bulldogs at the Doghouse. With no trouble at all, the Longhorns did just that.

Roy's magic arm completed forty-five of fifty-two pass attempts and notched another eight touchdown passes en route to an old fashioned pounding of the Bulldogs. The Longhorns pulled even at three wins and three losses, and more importantly a district record of one win and no losses, with two more easy games ahead before the finale in Motley County. They stood poised perfectly to march into the playoffs, provided they took care of business in the coming weeks.

The momentum from the Amherst game carried Lazarus into their matchup with the Silverton Owls. From the opening drive, Lazarus looked unstoppable. Series after series, Roy drove his team the length of the field and scored at will. Scouts from Oklahoma State, Texas A&M and Baylor now joined the Texas Tech scouts in pursuit of Roy Haskins. By the end of the night, Lazarus had tallied nine touchdowns, seven thrown by Haskins and two others set up by completions from Haskins. As the hype surrounding Roy Haskins swelled in and around west Texas, so did the Longhorns' egos.

Resting comfortably at 4-3 overall and 2-0 in district, the Longhorns allowed their intensity to drop off during the next week's practices despite the intense coaching effort all week long from Cannon and his staff. Even Roy allowed himself to become distracted by dreaming of running a wide-open Division I offense and competing for the Big 12 title. As a result, Lazarus suffered a huge letdown the following Friday night on the road at Cotton Center. Roy tossed six touchdowns, but threw two interceptions as well. Even with the letdown, however, a last-second defensive stand in the red zone secured a three-point win over the Mighty Elks of Cotton Center.

With three district wins, and an overall 5-3 record, Lazarus needed only to handle Motley County at home to earn yet another district championship. Though the Longhorns began the season slowly, Roy's maturity and momentum from the Longhorns' moral victory over Groom catapulted the Longhorns into the limelight. Many Texas football pundits predicted Lazarus to make a deep run and possibly even a semifinals appearance. Having learned from his mistakes the previous week, Roy remained focused and kept his teammates focused, too. The mission all week long was to finish strong and build momentum heading into the playoffs. A win against the high-scoring Motley County Matadors meant a district championship and the chance to host the first round of the playoffs. A loss for Lazarus meant a second-place finish, due to tiebreaker rules set by the district based on total points scored, and a road game for the first round of the playoffs. Roy considered the irony of the Matador/Longhorn matchup and vowed to lead his team to victory no matter the cost.

With the largest crowd in recent memory on hand to enjoy cool weather and a high-powered shootout at Longhorn Stadium, the Lazarus Longhorns took the field in brand new black jerseys rather than the traditional white jerseys. As soon as the crowd noticed the difference, cheers and ovations erupted. An already-electric atmosphere grew even more charged as the kickoff drew near. The hype built up in barber shops and gas stations, in locker rooms and on radio call-in shows around west Texas had everyone in attendance expecting to see something special on that last Friday night of October. Both teams ready for battle, the Matador kicker put the ball in play and the battle ensued.

When the dust settled and the final seconds on the clock vanished from the scoreboard, the Longhorns stood victorious with helmets raised high and tears flowing freely. The fans emptied onto the field to touch the hems of the Longhorns' garments and to take pictures with the players. Behind Roy Haskins' heroic nine-touchdown effort, the Longhorns bested the Matadors by more than a touchdown to claim a district championship despite a difficult start to their season. In the locker room, after the players had made their way off the field through the adoring throng, the atmosphere was no less festive than on the 50-yard line moments after the conclusion of the game.

Coach Cannon and the other coaches delivered a brief and upbeat postgame speech, then turned the players loose to celebrate. The players danced and chanted, they high-fived and slapped butts, they tackled each other and then hit the showers. Then, just like every other Friday night during football season, win or lose, as the guys showered away the sweat and face paint and the grit and grime from the game, the conversation turned quickly to everyone's plans for the rest of the weekend.

One of the players from the back of the locker room shouted above the roar of the two dozen showerheads, "What're you doin' tonight, Roy?"

"Who's it gonna be this weekend?" joked another.

"I'm going out with Mr. Basketball and a couple of girls as soon as I get away from you bunch of punks." Roy stepped out of the shower and moved toward the lockers. As he moved through the locker room, even some of his fellow players couldn't help but notice Roy's chiseled physique as it glistened with droplets of water from the shower. His body, and quite frankly his life, was the envy of all the guys in the room though none ever would admit it.

As the starters finished their showers and dressed at their lockers, the reserves stripped and headed into the showers, hoping there would be hot water left for them. Non-starters almost never got hot water. In fact, a dip in the water's temperature served as the cue for the starters to wrap up and leave the showers. The old-timers all over town still joke about that age-old locker room tradition.

"Still messing with that freshman, Roy?"

"Yea, Bradford, we're still talking. Russell's bringing Brooklynne and we're all headed out. Probably to the water tower. What about y'all?"

"We'll probably drive out to the gravel pit and hang out. Maybe steal a stop sign or two. Something like that. The usual. Nothin' exciting," replied Ben Bradford, the biggest player on the team.

As he sat at his locker and dressed, Corey Colter listened to everything the others said about their plans, plans which did not include him or his sister. Being the new kid in town, Corey Colter rarely received invitations from teammates to hang out, to drive over into New Mexico, to go hunting or fishing, or to do much else of interest. Once or twice he'd been invited to another player's house after a game to play video games; he obliged, of course, in an effort to fit in and to make friends. Despite his enormous size, Corey didn't stand out on his team the way Sam did on the basketball team. Therefore, Corey quickly became just another good player on an already-good football team. Corey didn't mind too much, though. He seemed perfectly content to drive home after the games in order to get up early the following morning to go fishing or hunting with his father.

Standing in the corner enjoying the revelry, Coach Cannon also heard everything his players discussed as they made plans for the weekend. He grinned. The talk about girls, hanging out and getting into a little trouble brought back memories of the Lazarus of some years ago when Cannon ruled the school and the town. Cannon still believed with every ounce of his being that his high school experience will live forever as the best four years of his life. He watched Roy carefully and called him over when the two made eye contact.

"Roy, that was a great game you played tonight."

Roy looked him in the eye, man to man, and shook his hand. "Thanks. It felt good."

"Roy, things are goin' too good for you to get in trouble this weekend. Don't do nothing stupid, alright? Use your head. Remember what we talked about in my office back when school started."

"I remember," Roy said as he returned to his locker. He gave his buddies a thumbs up and a smile and headed out the door. On his way out, Roy passed Principal Haskins making his way into the locker room. Principal Haskins patted Roy on the back as the two passed. From opposite sides of the locker room, Haskins and Cannon glanced first at Roy heading out the door then at one another; Haskins shrugged and Cannon replied with a grin and a shake of his head. Ready for a fitting ending to a memorable night, Roy made his way through the parking lot to his truck where Logan Russell sat on the hood and two giddy girls sat in the backseat of the extended cab. Logan and Roy jumped in the truck, cranked the radio and sped away from the stadium into the night.

Sunday afternoon Calvin Haskins, Patton McArthur and Tommy Cannon gathered for coffee and dessert in Mary's Kitchen. They met there to discuss the events of the weekend and to plan how they would proceed with things Monday morning. As the three men talked about Coach Lewis, about Logan and Roy and about the girls, a former player of Haskins' walked in and sat down next to Cannon and across from Haskins and McArthur. As he sat down he dropped a manila folder on the table, which caused several photographs from inside the folder to spill out between the coffee cups and the desert plates. Each of the three patrons grabbed at the photos and passed them back and forth looking closely at each. Martha noticed the meeting and tried to sneak a peek at what had captured everyone's attention at the table. It was no use, though; as the men saw her approaching they turned the photos face down before she reached the table. Martha refilled their coffees and left the bill on the table without saying a word. The four men stared silently at one another until she left and the tension lifted.

A call on the visitor's radio broke the silence. "Dispatch to Unit 2. Officer assistance needed for a 10-67 on Ranch Road 145 westbound one mile outside city limits. No injuries reported and no ambulance requested."

"Unit 2 to dispatch," he said as he stood and handed the photos to Haskins. "En route to 10-67."

"10-4, Unit 2," the scratchy voice replied over the radio. The officer made his way out of Mary's Kitchen and headed across the street where his cruiser was parked.

The three men sat and finished their coffee with little conversation. Finally, Haskins reached into his pocket and pulled out a twenty. He snatched the folder and tucked it beneath his arm. The men stood and the meeting adjourned. As they left Mary's Kitchen they said nothing to Martha on the way out, a sure sign to Martha that something was amiss. Martha had known these men long enough to recognize their sneaky and suspicious behavior. She wasn't sure exactly what was happening, but she had a bad feeling in her gut.

CHAPTER VIII

The girls had heard rumors all day long in the halls, in the cafeteria and in class about events of the weekend, about their team and teammates, and about possible repercussions. They endured hateful looks from cheerleaders, football players and even from a few teachers as rumors of foul play and questionable conduct circulated through the tiny school's rumor mill. By the end of the day, confused, upset and thoroughly distracted, the girls wanted answers. When Coach Lewis entered the locker room before practice, he found them more animated than ever before.

Rita sat on a stool pounding a basketball off the lockers and making an awful racket.

"I want somebody's butt for this one. Oooh, Cassie, they did you wrong girl! Brooklynne, you, too! Look, here's Roy's face!"

She pounded the basketball into the lockers again. The rest of the team applauded and chanted for Rita to do it again. Rita was more than happy to oblige.

Coach Lewis got everyone quiet and seated on the floor in front of him. When everyone settled down, he began the difficult process of debriefing his team. Though he knew most everyone in school had heard about the water tower, the boys leaving the girls on top of the tower and the spray paint, he gave the girls the facts, the real story as it actually happened. He told the girls about the photos of the graffiti and, after vehement denials from Brooklynne and Cassie, he assured them he believed they had nothing to do with the vandalism. As far as he knew, there would be no consequences for anyone, boys or girls.

From there, the coach moved on to the alleged schedule conflict and the untimely cancellation of the scrimmage against Cotton Center on Friday, the first and only chance they would have had to play against another team before the beginning of the regular season, which would be upon them in a matter of days. Understandably, the news upset and discouraged the girls. They had been looking forward to actually getting on the court against someone other than their own teammates. With only eight players, they couldn't run a full five-on-five scrimmage in practice; they were dying to get on the court against someone else. With the Cotton Center scrimmage cancelled, they would have to wait for Friona.

The season opener against Friona would be played at Friona as planned the following Tuesday. Hopefully, he explained, barring some unusual circumstance or act of God, the rest of the season would continue as scheduled. The girls rationalized that Friday's game actually didn't count anyway since it was just a scrimmage and they talked themselves into feeling better about the cancellation. Besides, they argued, with a home football game against the hated Lefors Pirates, nobody would even think about going to a gym to watch a girls basketball scrimmage anyway.

Coach Lewis walked to where Brooklynne sat and stood next to her with his hand on her shoulder. "I'm afraid I have more tough news for you guys. I've already spoken to Brooklynne about this, so she's not going to be surprised by what I'm about to tell you. Somehow, eligibility reports ran a week early this term and, unfortunately for the team, Brooklynne ended up on the wrong side of the minimum GPA.

Looks like Brooklynne's going to be out for four weeks until she gets her grades back up." He smiled down at Brooklynne. "And she *will* get her grades back up."

"Yes, sir. I will."

The girls looked at one another suspiciously and the wheels started turning. Finally, after a few moments of bewildered silence, Nairobi spoke up uncharacteristically.

"Coach, the graffiti, the scrimmage, the grade reports... You don't really think this is coincidence, do you?"

Nairobi's accusatory question expressed what her teammates suspected. Caught off-guard, Coach Lewis's non-response confirmed the girls' fears. One by one, heads dropped and no one said a word. With the girls' emotions now headed in a direction he wanted to avoid, he did his best to refocus his team.

"Look," he said, "we can either take the role of the victim and go through the rest of the season all woe-is-me or we can man-up and just play basketball."

"Girls can't *man-up*, coach," Brooklynne retorted.

"Oh, yes they can," Sam answered. "*We* can."

Autumn spoke up from behind the rest of the girls. "She's right, you know. We can keep being helpless little girls and keep taking this crap from everybody or we can start doing our own thing. I, for one, think we need to get over it and just play. What would those boys like more than anything but for us to give up? Mark my words: I'm not walking away from this team or this season."

Though MJ had been reluctant at first to buy into the team concept and Coach Lewis's system, her frustration had shifted over the last several weeks and she'd started to come around. She focused her rebellious attitude and her aggression not so much at Coach Lewis now but at the obnoxious boys, the haters, who seemed destined to make the girls' lives miserable. Both her teammates and Coach Lewis had noticed and they welcomed the shift in her attitude.

Suddenly, MJ stood up next to Autumn and slapped her on the back. "I'm with Autumn. Let's forget about everybody else and focus on us."

Coach Lewis pondered what MJ said. She was on the right track, perhaps a little misguided, but now thinking in the right direction. He then returned to his usual spot next to the white board and picked up a marker to get on with the business at hand. He wrote as he spoke.

"OK, then we're over it. Agreed? Good. Let's get down to business since we only have six practices left before our first game. With Brooklynne out, this is going to cause a lineup change."

MJ and Molly smiled discreetly as their minds filled with thoughts of how Brooklynne's absence would impact their status and roles on the team. Molly, especially, considered all the extra minutes she surely would pick up in Brooklynne's absence, probably as a starter. MJ all but drooled over the extra shots she would take with the other shooting guard off the floor and on the bench. The coach scribbled on the whiteboard: 1–Rosales, 2–Jasperson, 3–Griffin, 4–Whitaker, 5–Colter.

"With Brooklynne out, I'm plugging Autumn in the 3 spot. She's consistently been the most unselfish player on the perimeter and we'll need her to feed the post. Rita, obviously you'll keep running the show but you have to stay focused. Don't let your emotions get the best of you. Friona's guards will be all over you. Just handle their pressure and you'll be fine. MJ, keep working to get open and create your own space for shots. You're going to need to take some pressure off Sam when the defense starts doubling down on her, and you're going to need to help Rita get the ball up the floor. Take your shots, but only take the good shots. Don't take every shot. Nairobi, you're going to have to screen for Sam, a lot. Teams aren't going to let her stand there wide open without a fight. Also, Nairobi, you have to block out and grab every offensive rebound that comes anywhere close to you. We're taking all scoring pressure off of you. Use your other skills. Sam, we're gonna get you the ball, but you have to finish. If you score like I think you can, we're gonna cause some problems for teams. When they start doubling after the entry pass, kick it out to MJ then immediately get in position to block out."

MJ thought to herself that she didn't like the idea of taking only "good shots." MJ hadn't met a shot yet she didn't like. Besides, her dad always told her, "MJ, you miss one hundred percent of the shots you don't take. Pull the trigger early and often." Though she was mostly on board with his overall plan, MJ would just have to help her misguided coach see the error of his judgment and his game plan by taking advantage of every shot opportunity she got against Friona. A high shooting percentage and twenty or more points, she decided, certainly would change Coach Lewis's mind.

"Cassie and Molly, believe it or not you guys have maybe the toughest job. You have to know everything we're doing offensively and defensively at all times. If we get in foul trouble or if someone's hurt, you guys are going in and we can't miss a beat once you get in the mix. You could come off the bench at any moment and you have to be able to get in and get after it right away."

Cassie listened attentively, but wondered if she really could come off the bench and contribute without being a liability for the team. Still desperately needing both experience and confidence, she'd been asked to be prepared to step in at any time and keep the team's performance at the same level as before she entered the game. This seemed a tall order for an inexperienced freshman, she thought.

Molly, on the other hand, sat disgusted, arms crossed and eyes staring off into space. She tried hard to fight off tears that wanted to well up in her eyes. She couldn't possibly imagine how Coach Lewis could move Autumn ahead of her to a starting role. It shouldn't matter that the team needed a guard on the floor at the 3-spot and not a post. It wasn't fair. She thought about how much better she was than Autumn at shooting, at free throws, at practically everything. The fact that Coach Lewis was a young and inexperienced coach who simply didn't know any better didn't relieve any of her frustration. Just wait 'til her dad found out.

The coach and his team headed out to practice with the new lineup in place and the game plan fresh on their minds. The first practice after the rough weekend went as well as could be expected given the circumstances. MJ decided she'd have to wait and see how things went before she totally committed, but Molly seemed almost anxious to watch Coach Lewis's ideas about the new offensive scheme crash and burn. Though there were no confrontations, Coach Lewis found himself correcting and redirecting the two girls more often than necessary during the offensive part of practice. He had hoped MJ had turned the corner for good, but now he wasn't so sure. He was pleased, though, with Rita's go-get-'em attitude, Autumn's mistake-free play and Sam's ability to dominate everyone in practice, including Coach Lewis, who played defense against her during offensive drills. The team had only to maintain its focus for the remainder of the week, then hope for a restful, and uneventful, weekend before the first game of the season the following Tuesday night.

Campus-wide, the talk all week centered on the playoff game with Lefors. The players, the coaches, the parents, and the entire Longhorn community could deal with losing, or so they thought, as long as the loss didn't come at the hands of the Lefors Pirates. The Pirates, from clear on the other side of Amarillo, had halted Longhorn playoff runs before and the Longhorns never forgot wins and losses of days gone by. The consensus seemed to be that Lazarus had a pretty easy road through the bracket, for at least a few rounds, provided the Longhorns didn't fold and lose to Lefors. With so much riding on the game, the football players should have been more focused and intense than at any point in the season. That wasn't the case, though.

Roy Haskins knew the Sheriff's Department had gotten involved in the incident from the weekend. He wasn't sure how much anyone outside the locker room knew about Friday night, so he worried all week about teammates with loose lips. He knew the administration had been pretty rough with the girls on Monday. Roy had no sense of social injustice weighing on his mind about unfair treatment of the girls or their coach. Rather, what Roy Haskins feared most was that the wrath of his coaches and the administration might come crashing down on him. He feared their reaction not because of any perceived wrongdoing on his part. Instead, he knew they would be furious with him for creating distractions for his team that might jeopardize the Longhorns' chances against Lefors.

With his conscience weighed down by the fear of the unknown, Roy Haskins lacked his usual edge in practice all week. Roy's teammates, however, perceived his dull performances on the practice field as their collective inability to match Roy's skills. Dropped passes always fell because the receivers couldn't hang on to the ball. Routes that were run incorrectly resulted from miscommunications caused by receivers and missed blocks always seemed to be the responsibility of the other ten players. Roy stood alone as the one player who, at the end of each day's practice, knew the team had lost its edge solely because he had not performed up to his potential. And he knew why.

Coach Lewis sat patiently in the vinyl chair outside Haskins' office where he had waited for his interview only a few months earlier. Though the temperature outside had dropped considerably since the day of his interview, he found himself sweating no less on this particular morning than he had then. He sat clutching a duffle bag and tapping his foot against the leg of the chair. Gladys once again peered at him from behind her monitor. This time, though, she remained silent. Coach Lewis stared intently at Haskins' office and strained to hear what was being said behind the door. All he could make out were muffled voices whose volumes rose then dropped repeatedly. He cleared his thoughts then rehearsed over and over again in his mind the soliloquy he had prepared the night before. Haskins' door finally opened and a loud voice from inside the office called for the coach to join them right away.

The young coach stood, drew one last deep breath then marched into Haskins' office trying hard to look confident and unafraid. As he entered the office, the door slammed shut behind him. He turned to see the General move behind him and lean against the door. Seated in the office were Haskins, behind his desk, and Cannon leaning against the far wall. Against another wall stood a man Coach Lewis had never met but whom he knew to be Neill Frederickson, the superintendent. All eyes were on the coach as he entered. Coach Lewis cleared his throat and asked permission to speak.

As he unzipped the duffle bag he began, "Gentlemen, thanks for seeing me this morning on such short notice. I've been trying to decide whether or not to talk to you about this for some time. However, after some things happened this weekend I feel like I don't have any choice but to confront you about something."

He reached into his duffle bag and produced a letterman's jacket that read "Russell" across the back. He flippantly tossed it onto the desk in front of Principal Haskins. The four imposing figures glanced at the jacket then returned the glares to Coach Lewis. They appeared unconcerned with the letter jacket or anything Coach Lewis implied with it.

"From the minute I arrived here in Lazarus I've worked hard to try to build a respectable program, but I feel like I've had no support from anyone in this room. In fact, I often feel like you don't want me to be successful. I think your football and basketball players feel the same way, too, and their attitudes are simply a reflection of yours. My girls have been ridiculed for working hard. They've been mocked for having goals. They've been told by their peers and adults alike that they can't and won't accomplish anything this season but rather will embarrass themselves and the school simply by taking the court. They've had pranks pulled on them. They've had their belongings from their locker room tossed into the dumpster behind the cafeteria.

They've been taunted by other students, specifically the football and basketball players. They've been told by the cheerleaders that everyone in the school thinks the girls' team is a joke.

"Then, this weekend, one of your players and one of your players," he continued as he pointed to Cannon and to McArthur, "took two of my girls up on top of the water tower and left them there. Left them up there in the middle of the night. No warning. No reason. Left them there. This treatment has to stop or…"

The four men seethed with anger at the audacity of the rookie, the outsider, the pretty boy from the big city. Their blood boiled, their faces turned all shades of red and the veins protruded from beneath the skin on their necks and foreheads. Cannon gritted his teeth and fingered the pocket knife in his pocket. McArthur rubbed his knuckles in his palms and cracked his knuckles one at a time. Neill stood with his arms folded and scowled at Lewis. Haskins, though, jumped to his feet and, with both hands, threw everything off his desk and practically leapt across it so he could stand toe to toe with Coach Lewis. He pointed his finger at Lewis, poked him in the chest and pushed him so that Lewis fell backwards into a chair.

"You insolent little bastard. How dare you talk to us like this? If it weren't for us, you wouldn't even have a job right now. You come in here all high and mighty like you have it all figured out. Well, guess what. You don't know crap, son! You have no idea what kind of hornets' nest you've stirred up now. You little punk! You have no right. No right! You think your precious little girls are the innocent victims in all this? You couldn't be more wrong, boy! One of the little tramps gets knocked up last year and now not only is she back in school but you have her front and center with your team for all the other girls in school to see. Some example you've set for our other kids struggling to do the right thing! Then we have the issue of the other... girls on your team that won't leave Patton's and Tommy's players alone."

Haskins wheeled around and grabbed a manila folder from his chair behind the desk and threw it at Lewis who was still seated in the chair where he fell.

"Friday night, two of your girls dragged two boys up the water tank to do God knows what. When our boys wouldn't give in to 'em, your girls cursed 'em and hit 'em. Our boys, knowin' what's good for 'em, got off that tank fast as they could. Guess what your precious little angels did then! Go ahead, guess! Better yet, open that folder and see for yourself. Go ahead, boy, open that folder!"

Coach Lewis slowly looked away from Haskins who towered over him the way a bully stands over his victim on the playground after hitting him with an unexpected cheap shot. With trembling hands he opened the folder and discovered a stack of photographs inside. The photographs had been marked digitally with yesterday's date. The photos clearly pictured the water tower from a number of angles. In the first photo, spray-painted in large, pink letters across the side of the water tower's tank were the words "LONGHORN FOOTBALL SUCKS." He thumbed through the folder and looked at the next photo. In the same pink spray paint, "WE LOVE COACH LOUIS" appeared clearly on another section of the tank. The next photo showed yet more graffiti: "LADY LONGHORNS HOOPS."

"Go on, boy, say something. Don't get bashful on us now."

Stunned by what he saw, Coach Lewis found himself at a loss for words. He thumbed through the photos again trying to make sense of what he was seeing. Something seemed wrong. He stood atop the tank with the panic-stricken girls. They certainly were in no state of mind to spray-paint graffiti on the water tower. He continued through the photographs once more then it struck him. He pulled the photo of the "WE LOVE COACH LOUIS" graffiti and looked carefully at the spelling of his name. In his mind, this vindicated his girls but he knew the four men surrounding him wouldn't buy it. With a new sense of humility, he asked if he could keep the photos but Haskins seized them as violently as he had thrown them at him.

Though Coach Lewis felt a small sense of relief that his girls did not vandalize the water tower, that fact could not repair the damage Haskins had done to his ego and his psyche. Lewis sat with his chin on his chest and his eyes on the floor. Never in his life had he experienced such a humiliating and degrading tongue-lashing. Despondent and dejected, he wanted nothing more than to crawl out of the office. Self-doubt crept into his mind and gnawed at his sense of purpose, raising questions in his mind as to whether the good fight actually was worth fighting after all. Haskins, though, had not finished with him.

"Seems as though we have another couple of issues that've come up, too," Haskins began in a more subdued tone than he had taken a few moments earlier. "With the big playoff game coming up this Friday against Lefors, Tommy thought it would be a good idea for us to run our eligibility reports a week early so that if and when we win Friday night, no one can say we played academically ineligible players. When we ran the report, one of your girls, Brooklynne Meyers, failed to meet the eligibility requirements. She has two Fs and one D. Unfortunately, as I'm sure you know, that means she'll be out of commission for a while. Four weeks, to be exact. We'll check her eligibility again then."

"With all due respect, she had make-up tests and a project due this week so her grades would be up before the eligibility reports next week. She can't be expected to…"

Haskins cut him off. "Sorry, but she should have had her grades up anyway. Let's move on to the next issue. You have a scrimmage scheduled for Friday night against Cotton Center. Considering the importance of the game on Friday, we all feel that having a conflict on our athletic schedule will undermine what we're trying to accomplish here as an athletic department, as a school. We don't want to put our kids in a position where they have to choose between a football game and a girls basketball game. I'm sure you understand. We've already called Coach Rodriguez at Cotton Center and cancelled the scrimmage."

When he finished delivering the news, Haskins sat on the edge of his desk and folded his arms across his chest. Coach Lewis bit his tongue for once and sat quietly in his chair. Nothing he could have said would have been helpful so he sat and continued staring at the floor.

"Just so you know," Haskins added, "if Tommy wins Friday, we're cancelling next Friday's basketball game, too."

Coach Lewis knew the four sets of eyes staring at him were daring him to speak. He could feel the intensity of the situation weighing down on him, an almost impossible burden to bear on his young and inexperienced shoulders. His heart felt like it might pound its way out of his chest. Coach Lewis stood, nodded once at Haskins then turned and left the office without making eye contact with the others. He wandered back to his office as his stomach knotted and his head throbbed. He closed his office door behind him and sat at his desk.

The practices over the next few days were crucial to beginning the season on a positive note. He couldn't imagine how he'd tell the girls about the scrimmage and about Brooklynne and then have a week of productive practices. The girls, he felt sure, already were shaken by the events of the weekend. He knew Rita would be fighting mad at the boys and possibly unable to concentrate, a disastrous state of mind for a point guard. The point guard acted as the quarterback, as the extension of the coach on the court. Rita's ability to focus would be imperative. He suspected Cassie would be too emotionally fragile to have a good week of practice. With Brooklynne out, Cassie would have to provide quality minutes as a sub and that would be quite a challenge for her. Molly and MJ would be their usual selves, thinking only of their shot attempts and playing time; he hoped MJ would come full circle, but he couldn't be sure. Their attitudes almost surely would not change over the course of this week once he shared the tough news. Nairobi probably would be calm and relaxed as she always was. Nairobi seldom showed emotion. Autumn probably would be encouraging and optimistic as usual, though the stress of the weekend might take its toll even on her. Then there was Sam.

Sam had developed into the leader on the court and in the locker room. On the court, she showed the potential of being unstoppable if only her teammates could get her the ball consistently and if she could keep herself out of foul trouble. Coach Lewis knew the season rested on her ability to score and defend but he needed everyone, even Molly, on board. He had to find a way for Sam to have an intense week of practice but everyone, himself included, faced the prospect of being emotionally exhausted and practically ineffective before they spent the first minute on the court for the week. He scribbled and scratched in his notebook until the bell rang for first period.

The first Friday night in November felt unseasonably cold thanks to a north wind that blew in unexpectedly and chilled Bethany County. Nevertheless, the Longhorn faithful began their tailgating as always a few hours before kickoff and then, primed for action, they filed into the stadium. Red wool caps and red blankets showed as much school spirit as red t-shirts as far as the fans were concerned and the stadium was awash in red. Being a playoff game, photographers, sports writers and TV crews from Lubbock and even Amarillo descended upon Lazarus to document what Coach Cannon hoped would be a memorable event in the long and storied history of Lazarus football.

The Longhorns took to the gridiron like any other Friday night, to the deafening roar of a passionate home section and a belligerent, booing visitors' section. The energy in the stadium gave the players a little something extra in their steps and a little extra confidence in their minds. The energy drained from the home section quickly, however, when Roy Haskins' first pass of the game glanced off his receiver's fingertips and landed in the hands of a Lefors defensive back, who returned the interception along the sideline for a Pirate pick-six. As the defensive back streaked back upfield, Roy Haskins stood and watched, stunned. On the sidelines, his receiver consoled Roy and took responsibility for the interception; his offensive linemen took responsibility for the missed tackles. None of the Longhorns, including the coaches, allowed themselves to believe the mistake had been Roy's. But Roy knew. He'd suddenly been snapped into reality and he knew.

Roy's play improved over the course of the game, but Lazarus never caught Lefors. The boxscore in Saturday's paper, "Lefors 60, Lazarus 56," made the game seem like a tight, back-and-forth contest. In truth, though, Lefors never relinquished the lead after scoring on its first defensive series. Roy Haskins finished the game with seven touchdown passes and one lone interception. However, it was an interception that would plague Roy for years to come. After the game, the Lefors fans stormed the field and celebrated on the fifty-yard line, much to the chagrin of the Bethany County Sheriff's deputies and Texas State Police who tried to hold back the multitude. Amidst the ensuing chaos, a reporter from the *Lubbock Avalanche Journal* found Roy Haskins kneeling alone on the thirty-yard line, ironically the same general location from where he tossed the interception, and asked Roy to comment on the loss.

"I'm not sure I can explain what happened here tonight. I don't think it was supposed to happen this way. I'm not sure if I believe in destiny, but something sure made the ball bounce the way it did."

The reporter paused, anticipating something additional from Roy, something profound. Tears welled in Roy's eyes and spilled down through his eye black and created black streaks on his cheeks.

"I'm sorry. I don't know what else to say."

The loss to Lefors deeply affected Lazarus, the same way every last game of the season affected the small town when the season ended with a loss rather than a win. On such nights people traveled straight home after the game, shell-shocked, and then went straight to bed. Still feeling the collective punch in the gut on Saturday, people mostly stayed home. Those who did go out remained fairly subdued. Mary's Kitchen served almost no one and the customers who were there neither said much nor spent much. At First Church of Bethany on Sunday morning, the mood of the congregation bordered on gloomy, bleak and hopeless. The pastor even prayed a special prayer asking God to heal the hurt of the community. Judging by the mood of the town for the entire week that followed, God had little sympathy for those coping with losing a football game. As such, the weekend passed without event.

Like a small child after months of waiting for Christmas to arrive, Coach Lewis struggled to pass the time as he longed for his first basketball game to tip off on Tuesday night. For Coach Lewis, the weather couldn't have been more perfect for basketball. The weather, for someone who has never coached the sport, might seem irrelevant for the sport of basketball since games are played in gymnasiums. However, like most diehard basketball coaches, Coach Lewis longed for the weather to turn cold and mark the beginning of basketball season. For Coach Lewis, there were few feelings like walking from a warm gym into a cold parking lot, climbing aboard a warm bus and driving through the foreign countryside to a gym he'd never played in before. He always looked forward to climbing off the bus and standing on the pavement in the swirling, frigid wind as his players filed out single file and marched uniformly into the gym. He loved walking in out of the cold into a warm gym lobby where the aroma of popcorn and nachos wafted and the sounds of sneakers squeaking on a freshly-cleaned hardwood floor reverberated through the gymnasium. Basketball season had arrived.

As the bus warmed up in the parking lot behind the gym after school on Tuesday, the Lady Longhorns made their way from their locker room inside through the gym lobby and out to the parking lot where their ride to Friona awaited. The sun was on its way to setting on the horizon and its golden-orange rays washed over the team as they emerged from the gym. Coach Lewis sat in the driver's seat as the girls boarded in a single file line, brand new travel bags on their shoulders. Martha had dipped into her rainy day money to sponsor the team on behalf of Mary's Kitchen and had purchased gym bags for the girls. The girls had put up with Spartan conditions long enough, she'd said, and deserved something nice for a change. The bags weren't fancy but they were all the same and all new. Even Coach Lewis got a bag.

Bringing up the rear of the line, Summer Griffin carried the medical kit, the books, the stats notebook and the coach's shiny, white clipboard on which he could draw plays and formations using dry-erase markers. As she stepped up to the bus, she noticed out of the corner of her eye Roy Haskins sitting in the tailgate of his truck watching the girls board. Roy wore his letter jacket, mirrored aviator sunglasses and a green John Deere cap. She glanced up to her coach and he nodded once; she ran to Roy's truck, gear in tow.

"We're playing here on Friday. Are you and some of the guys coming to watch?"

Roy laughed out loud and looked away without making eye contact. Summer had her answer. She often asked herself why she still thought about Roy even though he treated her like a pariah, especially since her return to Lazarus High School, and even though he continued his antics with other girls. She wished secretly that Roy would disappear, either disappear or take an interest in her new life he had helped create. Disappointed but not surprised by his reaction to her question, Summer waved goodbye and jogged back to the bus for the half-hour trip to Friona.

The bus ride through the barren, dusty landscape of west Texas marked the beginning of the next phase of the team's journey, a journey with a destination fate had yet to reveal. The girls laughed and sang and, at least for a little while, forgot about the stress and angst of school, of boys and of life.

Upon arrival at the gym in Friona, the girls filed off the bus and headed into the visitors' locker room to change into their out-of-date uniforms of faded red, almost pink, with white trim. Both the gym and the girls' locker room back in Lazarus paled in comparison, even to Friona's modest but modern facilities. A freshly-refinished gym floor, new chairs for both home and visiting teams, brand new basketballs and both boys' and girls' athletic banners hanging from the ceiling served notice that not every town in Texas resembled Lazarus.

After changing into their uniforms, the girls took the floor and, just as they'd rehearsed, jumped right into their warm-up routine, which included various dribbling, passing and shooting drills they'd choreographed in practice the week before. Summer and Brooklynne sat on the visitors' bench and watched the Friona Lady Chieftains shoot their pregame layups and jump shots. Coach Lewis, trying not to look as nervous as he felt, stood near the scorer's table and made small talk with the Lady Chieftains' coach, an experienced female coach who'd been coaching successfully at Friona for years. As the referees called for captains to meet at mid-court, Sam for Lazarus and the shortest girl on the team for Friona, Coach Lewis shook hands with the opposing coach, took a deep breath and returned to his seat next to Brooklynne and Summer.

Seated in the stands behind the Lazarus girls' bench, a small eclectic group waited in anticipation. Sam's parents and brother sat next to Nairobi's parents in the first row behind the players. Behind them sat Rita's father. Next to him sat Martha, sans April. She'd left April with her neighbors, the Juarez family - "a godsend," Martha would say - as she had done so many times in the past and would again so many times in the coming months. One father apiece for MJ and Molly stood on the top row of the stands, each with a handheld electronic device complete with basketball statistics software. Leaning casually against the gym wall, Dee stood just past the end of the stands where he could watch action by himself. Dee shot Coach Lewis his signature reverse nod and flashed him an ear-to-ear good-luck smile. Noticeably absent were adults showing support for Cassie and Brooklynne. Across the gym sat almost a hundred Friona fans including parents, students, faculty and administrators, many of whom sported Friona Chieftains garb.

The girls racked their warm-up balls and circled around Coach Lewis in front of their bench. The girls reached their hands into the center of the huddle and awaited words of wisdom from their coach. Coach Lewis looked into the faces of each of his players then smiled. At once, his journey to this point in time flashed in his mind: the drive from Houston into the middle of nowhere; the intimidating interview; the shirts and skins football game with the football coaches; the first practice; the confrontation with Bill; the long hours in the heat of the Lazarus sun; the long hours of heat in the Lazarus gym; the confrontation with the four horsemen in Haskins' office. Coach Lewis focused on his girls and the ambient sounds of fans and officials faded to silence. *I've waited my whole life for this.*

"OK, here we go. Think back to the first days of practice when we stood out in the sun. Think about all the hours we've put in working on the press break, working on our offenses and defenses, working on free throws, working on our game plan. You know the game plan. Now it's time to execute. Above all, though, just compete. Have fun and compete. The rest will take care of itself." He put his hand on top of the pile of hands in the center of the huddle. "Remember, the strength of the pack is the wolf and the strength of the wolf is the pack. Longhorns on three! One! Two! Three!"

"Longhorns!" shouted the team as their hands flew up in unison and the huddle broke.

Molly joined Brooklynne, Cassie and Summer on the bench. Rita, MJ, Autumn, Nairobi and Sam hustled onto the court. They exchanged smiles with one another then bumped knuckles with the other team and took their positions for the opening tip of the season. Coach Lewis sat, then stood up, then knelt, then sat down again. The officials checked in with each coach, then with the scorer's table. The head official moved to center court for the jump ball to start the game.

As the ball floated upward in slow motion, all eyes followed it high into the air above the gym floor and watched the rotation of its dark seams and orange-leather panels. In the extended moment the ball hung in the air above Sam's outstretched fingertips and those of her significantly shorter opponent, the hopes of the Lady Longhorns floated upward with the ball. Sam tipped the basketball backward and the ball landed precariously in Autumn's hands. Autumn, for a brief second, held the ball as time stopped then started again. Autumn passed the ball ahead to a streaking MJ along the sideline and MJ raced to the basket for an easy layup. Coach Lewis exhaled and pumped his fist with delight. He couldn't have wished for a better start to the season.

Coach Lewis reviewed play after play in his mind as he made his way from the locker room across the length of the basketball court toward the exit doors. The Friona coached patted Coach Lewis as he passed in silence, head down and eyes focused on the stat sheet. Had his girls really made half the field goals Friona made? He felt critical eyes watching him from across the gym. In his mind he imagined what people were saying. He pushed the door open and waded out into the cold November night to wait for his girls to join him on the bus for the ride home.

As he sat alone on the cold bus he rehashed his post-game conversation with the girls in the locker room. He wondered if he had been too hard on MJ after the game. MJ had scored eighteen points but she took thirty shots, many of which she took with a defender's hand in her face. Part of him wondered if she hadn't been blatantly disobeying his instructions to get the ball inside to Sam, especially in the second half. It didn't help, of course, that both MJ's and Molly's dads yelled "Shot!" every time MJ touched the ball. He felt sure he was too tough on Rita for not settling down when she got into foul trouble. As he reflected on his conversations with Rita, he suspected he rattled her more than he settled her. "Give MJ the ball!" echoing through the gym from the top row of the bleachers didn't help things with Rita. Maybe, he wondered, he hadn't been hard enough on Autumn for not handling the defensive pressure better on the perimeter; she'd have to handle pressure better and cut down the turnovers. The same held true for Sam. Maybe he hadn't pushed her enough to handle the pressure of the free throw line or the physicality of aggressive double-teams down low. Sam scored twenty-two but, in his opinion, she should have scored thirty. A rapping on the bus door interrupted his meditation; he had come to the realization that much work needed to be done yet before the winning would start. Coach Lewis opened the door to find his team in street clothes standing in the cold.

"Coach, I'm riding home with my parents. See you tomorrow," said Nairobi as she turned and disappeared.

One by one, his players checked in and let Coach Lewis know they were riding back to town with their parents or friends instead of riding back to the school on the bus. The last girls to let him know were the Griffin girls. With Summer standing behind her, Autumn smiled at the loneliest man in Bethany County.

"We gotta start somewhere, Coach," Autumn said. "Now we know what we gotta work on. We're not riding the bus either, so we'll see you at school tomorrow."

Without saying a word, Coach Lewis closed the door of the bus and pulled out of the parking lot. He made his way back through Friona then turned right to head south on Highway 214 toward Lazarus. As he drove into the night, he wondered how many other coaches had felt this way. Then, he wondered how many felt this way after only one game. The desolate highway in front of him, lit only by the headlights of the bus, stretched ahead into disorienting darkness. Never in his life had eighteen miles seemed like such an unfathomable expanse. Ahead, he could see only a short distance. To either side the only thing visible was the faint glimmer of his headlights reflected in the barbed wire running from fence post to fence post. Exhausted and still in a fog, Coach Lewis pulled the bus into the empty parking lot at

Lazarus High School; he struggled to remember any part of the journey home from Friona. He sat alone in the bus and stared into the night searching the gloom for a glimmer of hope.

CHAPTER IX

For all the disappointment that followed the season opener against Friona, the elation and relief after the home win against Amherst seemed all the sweeter. Neither the Lady Longhorns nor Coach Lewis cared much that Amherst's team consisted mostly of awkward, unathletic underclassmen or that Amherst's coach sat in a slouch with his legs crossed virtually the entire game. For the Lady Longhorns, the win vindicated them and rewarded their hard work dating back seemingly forever. Few in Lazarus shared the joy, though, as the only fans in the gym from Lazarus were the same ones who had followed the girls to Friona.

Sam scored twenty-nine points and grabbed sixteen rebounds in the winning effort against the hapless Lady Bulldogs. MJ and Autumn each dished out nine assists, most of them to Sam. For MJ, the proverbial light came on as she realized in the first half that passing inside to Sam seemed like automatic points for the team and that she garnered as much attention and praise for assists as she did for points. MJ recognized later in the game that as her defender dropped down to help double-team Sam, as a direct result of the assists MJ distributed in the first half, that she could find wide-open looks at the basket. These wide-open looks allowed MJ to score seventeen points on seven-of-fifteen shooting, a much more efficient effort than against Friona. The rest of the team, too, got a glimpse of how the offensive plan could and should work when the individuals played selflessly, as a team. Molly, who played hardly any more minutes than Cassie but still had managed a couple of buckets and several rebounds, refused to get on board despite her team's new fervor.

With a new sense of confidence, the Lady Longhorns marched into the next week cautiously optimistic. While the practices following the opening loss had been tense and unproductive, the team showed up Saturday morning ready to work out hard. The enthusiasm carried through the weekend, through Monday's practice and into the night on Tuesday. Unfortunately for the Lady Longhorns, the Sudan Nettes lay in wait for the Lady Longhorns in a gym perennially known as one of the toughest west-Texas venues for visiting teams to play. The Sudan squads, boys and girls, had back to back games scheduled and the fans filled the gym early for both affairs.

Coach Lewis rallied his girls in the locker room before the game and encouraged them to ignore the Nettes' fancy white uniforms and knee-high black socks, the banners hanging from the rafters in the gym, the loud music and the rowdy fans. Play your game, he insisted. Handle the press, get the ball inside early and often and hustle after the loose balls. Somehow he got the girls fired up and ready to take on all comers. Shortly thereafter, though, under the delusion of a sense of false confidence, the Lazarus girls ran into a buzz saw in the opening minutes. Sam won the jump ball but Sudan stole the tip and rocketed down the court for a layup. The Nettes stole the inbound pass, went up hard for the easy bucket and scored again immediately. After falling behind 14-0, Coach Lewis, to no avail, called a timeout to settle his team.

Despite using all but one of his timeouts in the first half, Coach Lewis couldn't stop the bleeding. His girls trailed 42-15 at halftime. The situation didn't improve in the second half as MJ fouled out quickly and Rita found herself in foul trouble. Sam took the game on her shoulders and did everything in her power to carry the team. Despite her best efforts, the Nettes cruised to a 79-33 win. Sam finished with twenty-two of the team's meager point total. Frustrated and exhausted, the girls slumped onto the benches in the locker room after the game.

"At least we don't have to play them again until next year," Autumn said. "Right?"

The thrashing the girls took from Sudan deflated the rising hopes of the girls, their parents and their coach. The boys basketball team had begun the season at 3-0 behind the hustle of Logan Russell and their success did nothing to help the community's perception of the Lady Longhorns. The girls lacked the mental toughness to put aside the Sudan loss; self-doubt crept in during the week. They traveled to Hereford for the first tournament of the season and dropped their two games without making either game close.

As the losses added up, Autumn, Sam and Nairobi worked harder than ever to reverse the trend. They showed up early for practice and stayed late working on free throws, jump shots and post moves. They studied the stats with Coach Lewis. Brooklynne actually buckled down in an effort to pull up her grades and regain eligibility status. In the meantime, she practiced three-point shooting on one end of the court while the team practiced on the other. MJ, Cassie and Rita exhibited no change in behavior. Molly, however, withdrew from the team more and more. On the bench during games, she sat and pouted, arms crossed and eyes scanning the gym. During practices, Molly gave only partial effort and often questioned Coach Lewis in front of the girls both on the court and in the locker room.

The girls added yet another loss to their record in the first game of the following week. After the game, the girls filed into the eerily-quiet locker room with heads hung low. Their faces confirmed what everyone else told them day after day at school: the Lazarus girls never will amount to anything and the fight is useless. Before the girls had their uniforms off, Nairobi broke the silence with an uncharacteristic tirade. She called out every girl in the room by name.

"My daddy says we have to hold one another accountable and it's time we had some accountability on this team. Me, it's high time I quit being afraid of gettin' hit out there. I been playin' like a sissy girl. Rita, you gotta run this team, girl. You gotta fire us up and settle us down and quit worryin' about when someone's gonna do the same thing for you."

Wide-eyed and intense, Nairobi walked to each girl as she spoke and made each of them look her in the eye. It was a look none of the girls had seen before from Nairobi.

"MJ when you gonna quit shooting every time your daddy hollers at you to shoot it? Your daddy ain't the coach of this team. You got a coach already. Sam when are you gonna be the Sam-Colter-blue-chip-prospect-Miss-All-State-potential-post-player you have the potential to be? You could own these girls every night but you can't always sit back and wait for someone else to get the ball to you. Man up and be the Sam Colter God put you on this earth to be! Autumn, quit being so freaking nice all the time. Get a mean streak in you, girl, and bring some intensity with you. Cassie, you, too. You gotta get tougher and quit being scared all the time. You could be a lot better than you think but you gotta get outa' your self-pity. And Brooklynne, when you gonna quit flirting with the boys and pay attention to what we're doin'

177

out there? One of these days, when your grades are up where they're supposed to be, we gotta have you out there and ready to play."

Finally, she turned and pointed at Molly.

"You, girl, need to keep your mouth shut instead of runnin' your mouth all the time. If you put as much energy into gettin' better as you do into stirring stuff up, you'd be pretty good. Your blabberin' ain't helpful so shut up and play. Get *with* our team or get off!"

Every jaw in the locker room dropped.

"And you can tell your daddy I said it, too. He don't scare me none."

Nairobi grabbed her bag, flung open the door and stormed out into the gym. Still amazed, the girls sat staring at one another. Not knowing what to say, Coach Lewis followed Nairobi out of the locker room and left the girls alone. Rita wiped her eyes. MJ looked at Sam and hugged her. Autumn, smiling and crying, put her hands on Sam and MJ. Without saying a word, Brooklynne sat bewildered and watched the drama unfold. Molly, alone in her anger, lowered her head and strained her eyes upward to stare with fury at her teammates; she did not appreciate being called out, especially in front of everyone else. Autumn's eyes met Molly's and Molly jerked her head around away from Autumn's tender face. Autumn made her way over to Molly, knelt in front of her and placed her hand on Molly's.

"She's right, you know. Being mad at Coach isn't gonna fix anything. You're still part of the team, Molly, and we're gonna need you more than you know before this season's over. You have to be with us. We need you to be with us."

In years past, the Longhorns football team still had a game or two left on the schedule when December 2 rolled around. On this December 2, though, basketball was the only show in town. The small gathering of fans settled in for what was sure to be another Friday night blowout, this time at the hands of seventh-ranked Whiteface. The Lady Lopes rolled into Lazarus an hour or so before game time and had been goofing off in the gym since arriving. Their coach sat quietly on the visitors' bench listening to music by himself while the girls ran around the gym in their dazzling blue warmups, occasionally taking time to shoot a few jump shots or free throws. The Lady Longhorns, however, looked focused and ready to play. Nairobi's speech somehow had accomplished what Coach Lewis had been unable to thus far. The practices on Wednesday and Thursday were the best of the year and, with the exception of Molly, the girls seemed at last to be on the same page. Even MJ seemed to have turned the corner for good at this point. As the Lady Longhorns ran through their pregame warm-up routine, the basketball gods smiled on them. Shots fell from everywhere. The girls, with extra bounce in their steps, smiled while they concentrated and enjoyed the movement and flow of their drills. They high-fived and bumped fists after made shots. They clapped in unison after made free-throws. The Lazarus fans in the stands noticed something different that night, but no one, the players included, quite could put a finger on it.

The trash-talk from the tall, muscular Whiteface players began even before the opening jump ball, but the Lady Longhorns kept their composure. Even the visiting coach, with his gel-spiked hair, bulging biceps and thin waist, exuded an arrogance Coach Lewis hadn't experienced in a long, long time. The Lady Lopes, along with their coach, struck Coach Lewis as even cockier and more self-absorbed than the Lazarus football players. *Losing to this team will be unbearable, no matter how good they are,* Coach Lewis thought.

"Welcome to Lazarus," said the announcer over a public address system garbled with static. "The Lady Longhorns, coached by Gabe Lewis, with one win and five losses, welcome the Whiteface Lady Lopes, coached by Keith Britt, with a record of nine wins and no losses."

The raucous and rowdy fans from Whiteface cheered and overpowered the small rattle of applause from the home section of the quaint, vintage gym. Atop the bleachers, Calvin Haskins, Tommy Cannon, the General and Bill Merrick sat alongside Molly's father and MJ's father. MJ's father sat with his electronic stat counter and stylus in hand; Cannon held a yellow legal pad and a pen.

As the official tossed the ball upward, two things struck Coach Lewis. First, his team didn't seem nervous. He wasn't sure if a lack of nerves against a top-ten team was a good omen or not. Perhaps his girls should have been scared to even take the court. Second, the visiting team seemed distant and disconnected from the game at hand. The Lady Lopes looked lackadaisical and carefree as they joked and ran their mouths right up to the tipoff. If there existed a chink in the Whiteface armor, perhaps he had found it.

The ball bounced off Sam's hands and landed on the floor between MJ and Whiteface's best player, Jaimee Gillen, a returning All-State guard who had committed already to Texas Tech. MJ lunged for the ball as Gillen lowered her shoulder and cut MJ off. Only seconds into the game, Gillen had been charged with her first foul. To avoid being embarrassed, the girls from Lazarus knew they had to play harder than they had thus far in the season. To keep things even remotely close, the girls knew they needed to play a near-perfect game and get some lucky breaks along the way. Coach Lewis and his girls recognized Gillen's first foul and Gillen's second foul, a questionable charging call just moments later on the Lady Lopes' first possession, to be exactly the kind of breaks they would need throughout the game.

The Lazarus girls played inspired, nearly-flawless ball for the entire first half and went into the locker room at halftime trailing 26-23. Whiteface's star, Gillen, had picked up three fouls but remained in the game the entire half. Rita Rosales, though, had held the considerably taller and faster Gillen to only a handful of good shots and a respectable eleven points. MJ had connected on all four of her jump shots and had gotten the ball inside to Sam several times where Sam capitalized each time with a bucket. Enthusiastic and not wanting the first half to end, Coach Lewis and his girls met briefly to make minor adjustments before returning to the floor to shoot free throws and jump shots until the third period began. As Coach Lewis sat fidgeting with his clipboard and marker while his girls took shots from around the three-point line, the Lazarus parents sat quietly above him with collective breaths held, knowing better than to get their hopes up for a miracle in the second half. No one in the gym believed the Lady Longhorns could sustain this effort for sixteen more minutes.

Everyone in the gym figured wrong. As the Lady Lopes put extra pressure on MJ and Sam, Autumn and Nairobi picked up the slack and somehow kept pace with Whiteface. As the buzzer sounded at the end of the third period, though, Rita collided with Gillen while chasing down a rebound. Lost in the intensity of the contest, both players lifted elbows to fend off their opponent. The officials raced over, blew their whistles and called a double foul. Realizing that Rita had picked up her fourth foul, Coach Lewis hung his head. Coach Britt, realizing Gillen now had four fouls, too, went ballistic. Rather than addressing his girls in the timeout between periods, he charged the court and berated the official who made the call. The fans from Whiteface echoed Britt's frustrations and threw popcorn and empty cups onto the court. The officials escorted Britt back to the bench, issued him a warning and gave him the proverbial seatbelt. While he pouted and cursed under his breath, his Lady Lopes took the floor flustered and fuming.

After trading baskets in the opening seconds of the fourth period, the teams took turns making unproductive trips down the court. Gillen launched an ill-advised three over Cassie, subbed in to replace Rita on defense, and missed off the front of the rim. Cassie, who had turned and blocked out Gillen in textbook fashion, caught the rebound as the ball ricocheted to her off the iron. Without thinking, Cassie turned and sprinted to the other end of the court. She ran faster than she dribbled, though, and started to lose control of the ball as she crossed the free throw line. A fraction of a second before the ball flew from her hands, Gillen raced in behind her and jabbed at the ball to prevent a layup. Somewhere behind them a whistle blew. The official ran to midcourt, reported Gillen's number to the official scorer and informed Coach Britt that Gillen had five fouls and had to leave the floor.

At that, Britt stomped his feet and flailed his arms like a madman. He stepped onto the floor toward the official and the official, without hesitation, gave the coach a technical foul. The Whiteface fans jumped to their feet and shouted obscenities at the officiating crew. The Lazarus fans, for one brief second, chuckled at the scene then went back to holding their breath. Coach Britt, still screaming at no one in particular grabbed Gillen's jersey and flung her to the bench in disgust. Without thinking, he kicked over a cooler of Gatorade and turned to head toward the scorer's table where the officials worked to sort things out. One of the officials saw the coach approaching and ordered him back to his bench, but Britt ignored the instructions. As two of the officials stopped the coach's advance, the third official shrieked his whistle and issued a second technical foul as he made a violent "T" with his hands. The coach threw his clipboard onto the court and, leaving a trail of expletives hanging in the air behind him, stormed into the visitors' locker room, where he'd remain the rest of the game.

By this time, the Lazarus boys team had seated themselves in the stands waiting for their turn on the hardwood. Entertained, the boys heckled the coach and the opposing fans. Coach Lewis settled his team and drew a play on his clipboard while the officials decided on the order of free throws to be shot. Cassie shot the first two and buried both, pulling her team to within one point. The few fans in the gym rewarded her efforts with applause. Sam shot the next four technical foul free throws and buried three. Lazarus now led Whiteface by two. On the inbound pass, which Lazarus earned as a result of the technical fouls, the Lady Longhorns casually lined up beneath the Lady Lopes' basket, not the basket at which they were shooting in the second half, and the Lady Lopes followed. As the official handed the ball to Sam for the inbound pass from the sideline, MJ broke free from beneath the basket and raced the ninety-plus feet toward her own end of the floor. By the time the Lady Lopes knew they'd been had, Sam had already connected with MJ on a soft pass and MJ made an uncontested layup to put the Lady Longhorns up by four. Even Haskins and his cronies couldn't help smiling at the antics.

As the fourth period wound down, the Lady Lopes pulled even with Lazarus and the lead changed hands multiple times in the last two minutes. Even without Gillen and Coach Britt, the Lady Lopes were very good. The Lady Longhorns' play, fueled entirely by adrenaline and emotion at this point, kept the game close, though. With just under a minute left, however, Rita Rosales fouled out. Coach Lewis subbed in Cassie, then moved MJ to point guard and Autumn to the shooting guard position. One of the two free throws fell and Whiteface regained a one point lead.

For the next forty seconds, the teams traded baskets and lead changes. On what would be the last inbound pass of the game, Sam grabbed the ball after a go-ahead eighteen-foot jumper by Whiteface, stepped behind the baseline and looked for an open teammate. The Whiteface press had been intense but manageable all night until now. Now the press seemed unbreakable without Rita on the floor and Sam called the final Lazarus timeout. After a brief huddle and a tweak to the press break, the Lady Longhorns took the floor down by one point. Sam inbounded the ball to MJ who broke free after a hard but clean screen by Nairobi. Nairobi then pivoted and screened for Sam, who streaked down the hardwood. MJ, head up and eyes scanning the floor, weaved her way across midcourt and glanced at the clock: seven seconds. The Lazarus fans hadn't breathed in quite some time and they weren't about to take a breath now. MJ dribbled hard to the top of the key and passed the ball to Sam who broke open to the right side on the wing. She glanced up again: five seconds. Sam, instantly double-teamed, reversed the ball back to MJ at the top of the key. A defender rushed at MJ as she lifted her head, her shoulders and the ball for a shot. The defender, with arms extended and fingers stretching and grasping and reaching for the ball, left her feet to block the shot as MJ glanced toward the clock one final time: three seconds. MJ finished her head fake, took one dribble beneath the airborne defender and fired a pass to Cassie standing alone, unguarded, beneath the basket.

───────────

Calvin Haskins pulled his black, dust-covered pickup truck into the Dairy Queen parking lot, put the truck in park and idled his engine. He sipped his black coffee as the large toolbox in the bed of his pickup opened wide then slammed shut. The doors opened, letting in the cold air, Tommy Cannon, Bill Merrick, Patton McArthur and the ubiquitous red dust of west Texas. Each of the three new passengers wore a khaki shooting vest, sunglasses and a camouflage cap. With Johnny Cash playing softly through the truck's speakers, Haskins' pickup kicked up a rooster tail of dust as they pulled onto Ranch Road 145 and drove toward the Bethany County Shooting Range.

Chatter on the way to the shooting range centered on the usual. The men talked about the Dallas Cowboys and were they gonna make the playoffs this year, about Red Raider football and were they gonna contend in the Big 12 and go to a bowl game. They talked about Roy Haskins and was he gonna commit to Texas Tech or somewhere else, about next year's football schedule and would there be any changes. They talked about getting old and sore and they'd had enough of girls basketball and it wasn't even district yet and Thanksgiving was still almost two weeks away.

"I'm gonna name every one of them pigeons when they come off the trap," Haskins grumbled from the front seat. He held the steering wheel with his left hand and made a left-to-right sweeping motion above the dash with his right hand. "Gabe Lewis. Blam! That sorry lawyer from Houston stickin' her nose into our business. Blam!"

From the backseat Cannon interjected, "The whole town of Lefors. Blam! Blam!"

The four men chuckled at themselves as they pulled into the gravel parking lot of the shooting range. They ambled out of the truck and retrieved their shotguns and ammunition from the large metal box in the bed of Haskins' truck. Looking like soldiers in formation with their shotguns leaned against their shoulders, they made their way to the range and set up the trap for the clay pigeons. Carefully, each slid his shotgun from its gun case and filled his gun with bright red shells. They readied themselves to take out their frustrations on unsuspecting clay pigeons when they realized no one had brought the boxes of skeet from the truck. Haskins volunteered Tommy, the only one of the four without wrinkles or aching joints, to hike back up the trail to the parking lot to fetch the skeet.

The four enjoyed the freedom of the outdoors and sought refuge in the west Texas wilderness as often as possible; if they weren't shooting skeet, they were hunting deer or feral pigs. On the wide-open red earth with nothing above them but blue sky, an intense orange sun and an occasional wisp of a white cloud, free from nagging wives and kennel-blind parents, the four men of Lazarus could scratch and grunt, fart and belch, moan and groan and be themselves. There were no wins and no losses outside the city limits of Lazarus, no budgets, no kids making bad choices, no pressure from the superintendent or the school board. There were neither teachers nor coaches to hire or fire, only the wind and the dirt and the quiet and the horizon that stretched westward all the way to California. And, for a few hours, the soothing sound of shotgun blasts.

Blam! Blam! The double blast of a double barrel 12-gauge shotgun shattered the silence. For the entire afternoon, the four blasted away their stress and strife two clay pigeons at a time. When they ran out of shells, they collected their things and walked back to the truck to clean their weapons. As they sat on the lowered tailgate of Haskins' truck polishing the bluing of their barrels, Tommy Cannon noticed a distant plume of dust from a vehicle far off down the dirt road headed in their direction. The dust behind the vehicle shone as the sun backlit the dust cloud and gave it a phosphorescent glow. After several minutes, the big black vehicle, another four-wheel drive pickup, pulled into the parking lot and slowed to a stop across the lot from Haskins' truck. The gravel crunched beneath the giant off-road tires. Out of the drivers' side slid Rick Jasperson. The gunsmiths nodded to Rick and continued their task so as to finish before the waning sunlight disappeared.

"Can we help you, Rick?" Haskins spoke first.

"I hope you don't mind me catching up with you fellas out here. Calvin, your wife said you'd be here, so we drove out hopin' we'd find you."

Haskins looked over Rick's shoulder at the tinted windows of the black, jacked-up truck now covered with a thin coat of dust.

"Len Frost rode out here with me. Molly's here, too, and she'd like to say a few things. We need to talk about Gabe Lewis. It's pretty serious, fellas."

The four men seated on the tailgate exchanged glances then watched Rick Jasperson as he produced a piece of paper from his back pocket and unfolded it. They could see a list, a long list, written in black ink on the creased paper. Haskins, his gun now clean, slid his shotgun into its case and set it gently in the bed of the truck. He took his pocket knife out and pared his fingernails.

"We figured this'd be coming at some point. Go ahead, Rick."

Rick Jasperson held the paper with a firm grip and trembling hands. He cleared his throat and began the speech he'd practiced in front of the mirror in the bedroom of his doublewide trailer.

"First, I'm asking the administration to not standby and to do something and do something soon about Gabe Lewis. Lewis doesn't know enough about basketball to coach a varsity team and he never should've got the job in the first place. I don't know why you fellas hired him and I'd like an answer to that question. Even if he does know a little about the game, Lewis sure doesn't know how to use the talent on the team, in particular MJ's God-given talent for shooting a basketball. A talent, I might add, that none of the girls has like her. The guy just might ruin MJ's shot at playing college ball if somebody doesn't step in and put a stop to him before he does more damage.

"Second, that coach of yours started off all wrong by being too stubborn to listen to all the returning players about what would work, what wouldn't and who should get starting spots on the team. This ain't Houston, you know, and west Texas is a whole new ball game. That moron that's gonna ruin my daughter's shot turned everyone off with his big-city know-it-all arrogance and refusing to listen to an old timer like Bill Merrick. The girls haven't ever respected him because he spends too much time talking about journeys and destinations and philosophical crap and not enough about man to man defense.

"Finally, he pushes the girls too hard in practice. Bill's seen it with his own eyes and I have, too. In games, he's too demanding and frankly he's delusional about what the other girls on the team are capable of. Molly Frost would be glad to testify to everything I've said and she probably has lots more to add, too, that the girls haven't even told me about. I'd be much obliged if you guys would come to just one game and watch for yourselves so you can see what a train wreck the season's turning into. This has got to stop before it's too late. As a parent, it's well within my rights to demand you look into this and do something."

Haskins and the others listened to Jasperson's diatribe against Gabe Lewis. They nodded in agreement from time to time, shifted their weight, crossed their arms and noted every word. When Rick Jasperson finished, Tommy Cannon motioned for Molly to join them. She opened the truck door and jumped down into the gravel. Her oversized baggy sweatshirt and dusty brown cowboy boots hid most of her blue jeans.

"Understand you came here to talk about your coach."

"Yes, sir, Mr. Cannon. I'm here to talk for all the girls. We need a new coach and we'd like to have Coach Merrick back."

"Is that so?"

"Yes, sir. Coach Lewis is more interested in talking nonsense and seein' how many points Sam Colter can score than he is in letting other people play. None of the girls like him and we'd be fine with you getting a new coach for us."

Molly went on to describe Coach Lewis's unreasonable expectations of the team physically and in terms of goals he'd set for the season. He's put too much pressure on the team and he's made

189

everyone feel the pressure rather than just the talented girls, she explained. Everyone would agree he's played favorites all year and no one can believe he let the town tramp hang around with the team all season. Things were OK until he showed up and said he could make something of the girls in Lazarus.

Haskins, Cannon and McArthur asked Rick Jasperson and Molly leading questions so they'd get the answers they wanted to hear. Even though only two games into the young season the girls had one win and one loss, and even though last year's team didn't win a single game until December, all agreed the season wasn't sitting well with anyone and something had to be done. As much as they were ready to run him out of town, though, they needed to see things firsthand, in person; they needed to know just how bad things were going to get. What they didn't tell Rick Jasperson and Molly Frost, however, was that they knew going into the new school year just how bad the girls team would be and, honestly, they didn't really care. In fact, if Gabe Lewis had just kept his mouth shut without rocking the boat, a winless season would have been fine as long as he didn't draw unnecessary attention to himself or the program.

Haskins assured Rick and Molly the administration would make it to a home game at some point in the next few weeks. In turn, Rick, Len and Molly agreed to keep a running list of issues and problems with the team and to give that list to Haskins or Cannon whenever it might be useful. Rick helped Molly into the jacked up four-wheel drive and moments later the taillights disappeared around the bend and into the dusk. Haskins and the others could hear the crunching of the mud tires and the rumbling of the engine fade as the truck headed back toward Lazarus. Haskins and Cannon thought back to the day they hired Gabe Lewis and regretted their decision. The outsider they brought to Lazarus just months ago now threatened to shatter the peace and quiet of Lazarus. He needed to be dealt with soon.

For the next few weeks, as the Lady Longhorns endured a losing streak spanning four games, Rick Jasperson, Len Frost and Molly made frequent visits to Calvin Haskins after school, after practices and on Sundays. Each time, Calvin Haskins received more information about the dismal emotional state of the team and new accusations about Gabe Lewis being unfit to handle his role as coach of the team. Despite Haskins' request to speak to "all the other parents who feel the same way," Jasperson and Frost were the only two who offered information to the administration. Furthermore, Tommy Cannon and Patton McArthur received several anonymous letters during the same span of time in which Haskins visited secretly with Jasperson and the Frosts. The letters outlined the same information being conveyed to Haskins. Finally, after having been pressured into it, Haskins agreed to mark his calendar for Friday, December 2, the date of the next Lady Longhorns home game. Haskins agreed, too, to have former coach and basketball expert Bill Merrick on hand to offer his professional opinion on the team, the coach and the state of things, at least to the extent it could be perceived from the top row of the stands in the gym. Jasperson and the Frosts couldn't have picked a better game for the administration to attend as the Lady Longhorns would be hosting a top-ten powerhouse, the Lady Lopes of Whiteface.

As people trickled into the parking lot before the game against Whiteface, the football players milled about following their afternoon off-season workout in the weight room. Among those hanging around outside the gym admiring each other's biceps, Roy Haskins in particular called attention to himself because of the crowd gathered around him. Roy and the other players relished chances to show off their arms in public after a hard workout, even when the weather was too cold for normal people to stand around outside. Their sleeveless t-shirts accentuated their bulging shoulders and hard, thick arms with their biceps and triceps competing for attention. Autumn and Summer easily spotted Roy as Autumn pulled into the lot and found a parking space against the wall of the gym. Summer sighed, knowing she'd have to walk past Roy on the way into the gym, knowing he probably wouldn't look at her and knowing for certain that he wouldn't speak to her. Autumn put the truck in park and placed her hand on her sister's knee.

"It'll get easier eventually," Autumn said. "He can't be this heartless forever. He just thinks he's too cool to be mature right now. Come on, we got a game to play."

They climbed out of the silver and maroon truck and headed for the gym door. As they approached the crowd gathered around Roy, Autumn grabbed Summer's hand and pulled her along at a quickstep. The sisters passed Roy, who happened to be leaned against the wall with one foot on the ground and the other pulled up onto the bricks, without looking at him. Just as they entered the door, though, Summer glanced back over her shoulder. She had to know if Roy had even noticed her as she passed. She caught Roy staring directly at her through the mass of people around him. Roy didn't smile or wink or nod or acknowledge her in any way, but he was watching her. She shivered at Roy's dispassionate stare and followed Autumn into the gym.

No one could have predicted the way things would play out in the Lazarus gym that night. In fact, everyone present fully expected a rout, as the Lady Longhorns really had no business even being in the gym with the Whiteface Lady Lopes. Instead of a predictable rout, however, the fans were treated to an entirely unpredictable back-and-forth affair complete with technical fouls, players fouling out, ties, lead changes, unchecked emotion and, most importantly, a last-second drama that would unfold seemingly frame by frame.

The Whiteface fans, on their feet and screaming like banshees, raised their hands and grabbed at their heads as MJ pump-faked the Whiteface defender. The defender's momentum carried her forward as MJ slid by her with one purposeful dribble. The defender craned her neck, flailed her arms and stabbed at the ball as it flew in slow motion toward Cassie, who was standing unguarded on the block beneath the basket. As if connected somehow by a string, the arms of the parents behind the Lazarus bench flew upward in expectation as the heads of the Whiteface fans dropped in agony. Without flinching, Cassie extended her arms for her hands to meet the ball in flight. In one fluid motion she caught the ball, drop-stepped toward the basket and jumped. She raised her arms in textbook fashion, the ball balanced just so on her fingertips, and she saw from the corner of her eye a flash of blue crashing toward her. At the instant the ball left her fingers on its way toward the backboard, a Whiteface defender plowed into her and knocked her across the baseline and into the padding on the wall. For one brief, evanescent moment, no one took a breath. In a flash, the moment was gone. From the floor against the wall, Cassie heard the horn sound and heard the Lazarus players erupt in wild cheers as they danced about the court, a clear sign her last-second shot found its way off the backboard and through the rim. She rolled over to see her teammates running towards her, arms open wide and smiles even wider, eager to dog pile the freshman-turned-heroine. Coach Lewis, too, ran toward her with one hand in the air and Summer Griffin in tow with the other. Behind her teammates, blue jerseys collapsed to the floor. The Lady Longhorns had done the unimaginable.

Along the top row of the stands, Haskins and the others sat dumbfounded. They looked at one another, shrugged and said nothing. From the end of the row, someone mumbled, "I'll be damned."

Before the girls had a chance even to climb back to their feet, hip-hop music boomed over the sound system and the Lazarus boys basketball team began their traditional pregame sprint around the court. Everyone in the gym shouted and applauded for the boys as they took the floor. By the time the girls reached their bench to retrieve their water bottles, the boys had begun their layup drills. Still dancing with joy, the girls skipped through the gym to their locker room. Even Molly couldn't fight the urge to smile. They doused each other and Coach Lewis with their water bottles and basked in the joy of the moment.

Finally, when he had the girls settled enough to speak to them, Coach Lewis, with his shaggy, dripping hair hanging in his face, reminded the girls they had not reached their destination. They had, however, reached a significant milestone on their journey. He reminded them again of the proverb he often quoted in the heat of August: "Sometimes, the journey isn't about the destination; sometimes the journey is about the journey." Coach Lewis high-fived most of the girls, hugged Sam and Autumn and MJ and wished them all a happy weekend.

The following night Gabe Lewis decided to spend Saturday evening relaxing in Mary's Kitchen with a good book and a plate of baby back ribs, slaw and onion rings. Since the season had begun, he hadn't enjoyed much free time. Most week nights he spent grading papers and watching game film of upcoming opponents. In his lonely living room, Coach Lewis viewed and reviewed game film of the Lady Longhorns as well as game film of upcoming opponents. A type-A strategist, Coach Lewis always wanted a game plan to rehearse in practice before the next game. A night spent in relaxation at Mary's Kitchen would be a nice diversion, he hoped, from the stress of dealing with stubborn players, parents who proved even more stubborn and administrators who seemed to relish his struggles. However, there existed a part of Gabe Lewis that would have traded the quiet and relaxation for just a few congratulatory handshakes and pats on the back from Mary's Kitchen patrons for his accomplishment the night before. Gabe Lewis, ever the idealist, failed to realize, though, that few people outside those who witnessed the Whiteface game even knew or cared the girls had played, much less knew or cared about the final score or the fact it had been an improbable upset win for the Lady Longhorns.

As Martha set the oversized, white ceramic plate in front of Gabe Lewis, she slid a small sheet of paper under the edge of his plate. He thanked Martha for the food and glanced down at the paper. He picked it up and read the newspaper clipping with bemused delight: Whiteface Lady Lopes Drop Rare Road Game. Beneath the headline of the blurb from the Lubbock newspaper's Prep Sports section, three choppy sentences told the unlikely story of how the Lady Lopes managed to lose a game on the road to an unknown, unranked and severely overmatched Lazarus squad. The article mentioned Sam but none of the other girls on the team. *My first article.*

Gabe Lewis read the article three more times and memorized all three lines. As he did, he covered his mouth with his hand as he tried to hide his giddy delight. He knew exactly where he'd pin the article: on his bare, empty bulletin board hanging on the cinder block wall of his office. It would be the first of many such articles, he hoped, with each successive article providing more and more details about bigger and bigger milestones for the program. He tucked the clipping safely inside his book and proceeded with dinner, which he ate in its entirety without being disturbed by a single well-wisher or back-patter.

On the court, the Lady Longhorns followed the upset win over Whiteface with the most successful December in team history. What constituted the best December in Lazarus girls basketball history, however, would have been described in many other west-Texas towns as a major disappointment. The girls traveled to Dimmitt, where they won two and lost two in a weekend tournament. As a bonus, Sam and MJ each earned all-tournament honors in the effort.

After dropping the next game at Hale Center, Coach Lewis's girls won one and lost two games in the Whitharral Tournament. Despite good effort from the entire team, none of the girls earned tournament honors at Whitharral. Night after night, the girls trekked across west Texas on the dark and dusty roads in search of something positive, in search of the next milestone on their journey. On the road for the ninth consecutive game, while the Lazarus boys enjoyed a long homestand, the road-weary Lady Longhorns ran their losing streak to three games with a lackluster loss at Cotton Center.

The girls had scrounged a few victories; however, each loss weighed heavy on Coach Lewis even though he saw marked improvement from his team. He knew from his experiences thus far in Lazarus that most of the parents, and almost certainly the administration, cared more about wins than unquantifiable improvement.

Truth be told, over the course of the two weeks and nine games following the miracle against Whiteface, the girls had indeed begun to jell. While the improvement may have gone unnoticed by those in the stands, Coach Lewis noticed and so did most of the girls. Most of the team finally grasped the new offensive and defensive principles they'd been struggling with since August. Despite what the ornery parents alleged, all but one of the girls bought into the new system and the roles they were expected to play within the parameters of the system. Coach Lewis settled on a regular starting five with Cassie and Molly coming off the bench. Cassie responded well to the reserve role and made significant strides. The game-winning shot against Whiteface had been a Godsend for Cassie. Molly alone failed to improve or to find her place on the team. Brooklynne, still ineligible due to grades she couldn't manage to keep up, had yet to take the court in a single game; nevertheless, she worked every day at practice on three-point shooting. While there was no way to tell how Brooklynne would respond to her first games back after the Christmas break, assuming her grades improved, Brooklynne shot the ball well enough at practice to get Coach Lewis's attention. He had a sinking feeling he would need her in the lineup when district play began in January.

Off the court, the girls on the team managed to steer clear of trouble and controversy. Coach Lewis, on the other hand, remained at the center of the maelstrom stirred up by Rick Jasperson and Molly Frost, who were more than happy to provide embellished answers to any and all questions Haskins or Cannon asked about the team. Interestingly enough, no one involved in trying to keep Gabe Lewis in check really wanted Gabe Lewis fired; they wanted him forced to change his approach to the game and with the girls. Bill Merrick had already said he wouldn't coach the girls, even if Lewis quit, and Texas high school rules prevented someone not employed by the school from coaching a varsity team.

The fact the girls had won five games already made no difference to Rick Jasperson, Molly Frost, Calvin Haskins or anyone else determined to make life difficult for Gabe Lewis. In fact, no one in the Haskins and Jasperson bunch gave any credit to Lewis for winning the games he had won thus far. In their minds, the players won those five games while the coach lost the rest. They refused to consider what a terrific start this season would have been deemed in any of the years prior to this one. Relatively speaking, Gabe Lewis's success and what his future success with the girls would mean, caused the most consternation for his detractors. That Gabe Lewis experienced any amount of success, no matter how small or insignificant, validated what he'd been working toward all along. If Lewis's vision, plan and beliefs became validated somehow, by some stroke of luck or good fortune, the traditional Lazarus assumptions about its weaker, inferior citizens might appear suspect, thereby threatening the traditional, time-honored order of things.

A few of the girls realized before the Shallowater game, the last game before Christmas break, a win for the Lady Longhorns and a loss for the boys, who had been struggling of late, would send both teams into the break with the same number of wins. The boys team did not realize this, as it simply would be unthinkable for the teams to have the same number of wins at any point in any given season. Not that the Lazarus boys were world-beaters by anyone's standards, but no girls basketball team in Lazarus history had ever accomplished such a feat. The extra motivation of pulling even in the win column with the boys created enough extra adrenaline for Sam, Rita, MJ and Autumn to power the Lady Longhorns to yet another upset win at home, this time over the black and red Shallowater Fillies. Sam, who towered above even the Shallowater coach, scored a season-high and career-high forty-one points. Autumn and Rita each reached double digits in assists, while MJ turned in her best defensive effort of the season.

In the locker room after the game, Autumn summed up the team's wonder at heading into the break on a positive note. "Our sixth win! That's pretty amazing!" The water bottles came out again and showered everyone in the locker room, coach and statistician included. When the water bottles had been emptied, Autumn produced a large brown box from behind the bench and opened it with a smile. Autumn wished each player "Merry Christmas," told each "I love you," then distributed wet hugs and small tins of homemade chocolate chip cookies to everyone in the room. Coach Lewis took his tin and headed back to the gym to watch the boys play and to let the girls change clothes in the locker room. After taking a seat at the end of the bottom row of the stands, by himself, he opened his tin of cookies to have a snack. Inside he found a handmade, handwritten card. It read, "Be not weary in well doing. 2 Thessalonians 3:13. Coach - you're going to make a difference here. Love, Autumn." He smiled then finished the cookies while the Mustangs corralled the Longhorns.

CHAPTER X

Gabe Lewis tossed and turned and tried to cover his ears in the darkness of his bedroom. The noise would not go away. It persisted in his dreams like a siren passing by over and over, or a shrieking alarm sounding then going silent then sounding again, each time just out of reach. He snapped to attention, looked blindly around the room and listened for the uninvited, unwelcome sound. He heard it once more then tried to move from the dream world to the reality of the early morning hours in Lazarus, Texas. *My phone.*

He sat dumbfounded on the edge of his bed as he concentrated in his sleep-induced stupor to remember where he'd last left his phone. *No one calls at this time of night. Or is it morning?* His phone rang again as he glanced at the clock whose red digital numbers read 2:47. Gabe Lewis sat dazed on the edge of his bed then realized in a flash of clarity the late-night call finally had come, the late-night call he'd been able to avoid his whole life, the late-night call that makes knots in your stomach. His mother had told him once about the late-night call, the call that rips you from your sleep and makes you grimace at the thought of the news that inevitably, impolitely would follow a polite "hello." The phone rang again. In his moment of lucidity, the ring of the phone sounded somehow different. The ring sounded foreboding, menacing and ominous. He wiped his eyes and tried to gather his senses before answering. After searching in the dark for the sound of the ringing phone, Gabe Lewis stumbled through the shadows to the kitchen and found the phone near the sink. He flinched as it rang again.

Gabe Lewis held his breath, exhaled a long, slow breath, then answered the phone. After just a minute, maybe two, Gabe Lewis returned the phone to the counter near the sink and stood motionless, alone in the kitchen. He heard what the voice told him, but he couldn't bring himself to believe it. He reached out to touch the wall and feel his way under the cover of night back to the safety of his bed. As he did, the siren sounded again. He turned to reach for the phone. This time, however, the sound he heard was the unmistakable sound of an actual siren racing somewhere into the abysmal black of night. He swallowed hard and squeezed his eyes closed. He knew exactly where in the night the siren was racing and why.

When Gabe Lewis reached his bedroom, he curled into a fetal position at the foot of his bed and tried to hold off the nausea. The feeling washed over him in wretched waves. He closed his eyes as tight as he could and searched his mind for all the memories he could conjure: the smiles, the tears, the happiness, the sweat, the hugs, the silliness, the high-fives, but mostly the smiles. The evanescent images in his mind's eye vanished as quickly as they had appeared only to be replaced by black nothingness, devoid of thoughts or memories. He lay in silence, alone in the world and abandoned by reason.

Gabe Lewis struggled with what to do next. Part of him wanted to get dressed and go. Part of him rationalized staying at home, in bed, in the dark; he could offer no help, no assistance. He grabbed his jeans from the floor and pulled them on without leaving the bed. He decided he needed to call someone, but he didn't know whom to call. He picked up the closest shirt to the bed and pulled it over his head. He needed to let everyone know. On the other hand, it wasn't his information, really, to pass along. That information and the responsibility that went with it belonged to someone else, not to him. He grabbed his leather jacket from the back of a chair and pulled it on. He lay still and quiet, curled up like a baby, listening for the proverbial still, small voice to guide him.

As he lay sick and motionless in the darkness, unsure about what to do, a knock at his door gave him a start. Gabe Lewis went to the front door and fumbled with the lock. He opened the door and flipped on the porch light. On his porch stood Calvin Haskins. Haskins started to speak then looked at the coach who stood in the darkness of the living room fully dressed except for his bare feet. The young man returned a blank stare. Haskins looked different, as if something had dragged years of bitterness and anger out of him, but, with the bitterness and anger, something else had vanished too. His face was long, his eyes sad and tired. His bald head speckled with salt-and-pepper stubble. Haskins looked directly into Gabe Lewis's eyes, almost with a look of compassion, then nodded twice as he pursed his lips. Seeing that Gabe Lewis was dressed already, Calvin Haskins turned and walked back through the cold to his truck he'd left running in the driveway. Not knowing what else to do, Gabe Lewis slipped on his shoes, grabbed his keys and made his way to his Blazer.

Gabe Lewis sat in the driver's seat and stared ahead at nothing as he waited for the frigid engine to start. He didn't notice the cold but his Blazer did. The engine finally turned over and gave life to the instrument panel, the heater and the radio. Gabe Lewis reached and silenced the radio, put the Blazer in reverse and backed out into the road. As he put his vehicle in drive and crept forward in silence, he gripped the steering wheel and squeezed. *God, help me because I can't do this. I don't know what to do. I don't know what to say. I'm going to fall to pieces and be no good to anyone. This is not what I came here for. I did not sign up for this. Help.*

Gabe Lewis rolled to a stop at the stop sign. As he sat, he watched car after car driving west past his street. He knew where the cars were headed because there is no traffic at three in the morning in Lazarus. Gabe Lewis waited for the last of the caravan of slow-moving vehicles to pass and he pulled into the road behind the last of the passing vehicles. He could see a few miles down the road the dull glow of light reflecting off the black ceiling overhead and dozens of red taillights peering back at him. He shivered. After a mile or so of driving into the night, the cars ahead of him pulled over on the shoulder of the road. Gabe Lewis parked in the shoulder behind the car he was following and stepped out of his Blazer into the unknown.

Night fell on Lazarus early on the shortest day of the year. And on this night, the darkness would loom blacker, more disturbing than any night since the beginning of days in Lazarus. Though the darkness had been present for generations, it had grown deeper and more troubling in recent months. The shroud of darkness weighed heavily upon those beneath it. Its weight suffocated those who gasped for a glimpse of light. The more Lazarus struggled against it, the heavier and more repressive the shroud became. Eventually those beneath it would submit, against their will - the result of desperate fatigue.

On this night, beneath the starless black expanse above him, a man from Lazarus rocketed southbound from Friona along Highway 214. There were no stars, no moon, no light visible anywhere other than directly in front of him cast by the aging headlights of his truck. The grit and grime from his countless miles of travel lay thick and heavy over his headlights. The man from Lazarus barreled ahead at a speed far too great for his limited visibility. As he drove, he busied himself with thoughts neither of where he had been this night nor of his destination. Rather, the man's thoughts were of the great trouble he feared might descend upon him and his family in the coming days and weeks, suddenly and without warning.

Just days before, at the incessant prodding of his nagging wife, he visited his doctor for a routine check-up that had been many years overdue. The doctor poked and prodded at the man, assessed his vital signs and listened as the man described his habits, his routines, the things he consumed, the activities that occupied him when he wasn't working long, lonely hours in the trucking industry. All the while, the doctor watched, listened and took extensive notes. With wrinkled brow, the doctor ordered a battery of tests to further assess the man's condition.

The man underwent the tests, then sat alone in the small examination room for what seemed an eternity. The white lights reflected off the sterile white walls and cabinets and he squinted at the brightness. As he waited for the doctor's return, he cracked his knuckles, wrung his hands and fidgeted like a convicted criminal waiting for his sentence. He looked at his hands as he wrung them in his lap; the intensity of the light highlighted the blemishes and imperfections on his rough, calloused skin. The door opened without a sound and the doctor took a seat in front of him. He reached out and placed his hand on the man's knee.

RESURRECTING LAZARUS, TEXAS

The man remembered the doctor's words as if they had been recorded and played over and over again. As he sped into the night, the man pictured the scene in his mind as if he somehow were hovering above the examination room looking down on the conversation as it happened. The doctor leaned forward. He told the nervous man the tests and the examination revealed a serious, potentially life-threatening heart condition. As the man broke eye contact with the doctor and looked away, the doctor continued. The heart condition, though serious, could be reversed with a drastic course of action. The man's years of poor life choices and bad habits, hard living and wanton disregard for his own health had led to a hardening of the heart and the tissue surrounding it. Unless immediate measures were taken to reverse the effects of choices made through the years, the doctor explained, the heart could fail at any time, without warning. As the doctor talked, the man grew still and pale.

After the visit to the doctor, the man had returned to work straight away. He had climbed behind the wheel of his truck, cranked the diesel engine, and without calling his wife, he drove off toward his next deadline, his next scheduled delivery. That night in bed, he had lain still and quiet. He had ignored his wife's repeated inquiries about the checkup and insisted he seemed to the doctor to be in perfect health. Then, he had rolled over with his back to his wife and stared out the bedroom window at nothing in particular.

On this frozen December night as he drove from Friona, not a single star appeared in the sky to show him the way home. The man needed neither star nor compass, however, as he had driven this route hundreds of times in the dead of night. He imagined he could make the drive with his eyes closed or with his headlights off. The engine droned and the white lines in the middle of the two-lane highway blurred into one, pale white line. He whizzed past a blur on his right side, a road sign indicating to travelers the impending intersection of two roads ahead. The man from Lazarus had driven past the sign so many times before he failed to register the appearance of the sign on the side of the road as he passed.

For days, the man had wrestled with the cold, hard facts given him by the doctor. Faced with his own mortality, he fought off reality and replaced it with denial. He had nearly resolved to tell his wife the truth about his diagnosis when denial set in permanently. The doctor had embellished the seriousness of the condition and had exaggerated the prognosis. The man closed his eyes for an instant and tried to control his now-rapid breathing.

As the man from Lazarus opened his eyes and exhaled, his chest grew tight. He breathed in again, with some difficulty, and noticed a subtle ache in his neck and back. The long drive had taken its toll on him. The man had been gripping the steering wheel so tightly his fingers tingled. He released his right hand and flexed his fingers then did the same with his left. Again his chest tightened as he inhaled and exhaled. He shivered as droplets of sweat beaded on his neck and forehead and a twinge of nausea pulled at his stomach. A moment of panic swept over him then passed. He shook his head and refocused on the road ahead of him. The nausea struck again and caused him to tighten his stomach. As he did, his chest tightened again, though more severely and with some pain. The man sat up straighter and pulled at his shirt as the pressure and the pain intensified. The anxiety returned and intensified to an eerie sense of imminent doom. He shook his head once more to refocus but it was too late.

A flash of something metallic appeared without warning in the glow of his headlights. An instant, even in the slow motion of one's memory, after the flash of metal before him, he heard the grinding, gnarling, screeching slam of metal gnashing metal and he felt the pull of the seatbelt across his already-aching chest. A shower of glass covered his face, his hands and his lap. He pulled hard at the steering wheel and pounded on the brakes, but the mangled mass of metal was now driving him, with no headlights, into the dark. Sounds and smells swirled around him though he couldn't locate them in time or space. Tires exploded. Diesel fumes floated in his face. More glass shattered. Steel scraped and scratched against the cold, black asphalt. Gasoline fumes pushed the diesel fumes aside and burned his nose and lungs. Air brakes rattled and popped. Steel scraped again but more slowly, deliberately. A moment later, the mass of metal now at a standstill, the man sat leaning slightly to his left in the twisted cab of his truck suspended somewhere between vertical and horizontal, alone in the darkness with pain in every part of his body, the smell of gas and diesel all around him and the sound of an unimaginable silence in his ears.

Afraid to move yet afraid not to, the man felt the cab tipping to his left. The weight and momentum of his trailer twisted and rotated counterclockwise then rolled the cab of the truck to the left so it came to rest on the driver's side door. Still strapped into his seat, the man both sat and lay staring through the glassless windshield. When the cab tipped, he felt his flashlight fall from an overhead storage bin onto the driver's side glass near his head. With great effort, he reached downward across his body with his right arm and fumbled for the flashlight with his numb, bleeding fingers. He grasped the metal tube and struggled to depress the on/off button of the flashlight. The man pointed the dim beam ahead of him through the crushed windshield. After a gasp, he turned off the light and dropped it. He closed his eyes and wept.

The highway patrol car rolled to a stop on the shoulder of southbound Highway 214 a few yards from the edge of Ranch Road 145. He stepped out of the vehicle and pointed his flashlight at the green metal signpost protruding from the ground at the intersection of the two roads. He shook his head and cursed the darn kids who stole the stop sign again. As he walked back to his patrol car to report the missing sign to dispatch, the wind shifted and blew over him from the south. The wind carried with it the unpleasant and unmistakable smell of fuel, automotive fluids and burnt rubber. His heart sank as his nostrils filled with the smell he'd tried so hard to escape. Three years ago, the officer moved with his wife of thirty-nine years to west Texas from Austin to enjoy a simpler, slower-paced life with fewer drunk drivers, fewer arrests and fewer traffic accidents. Now just four months from retirement, the officer had been hopeful he'd reach retirement in uneventful fashion. The odor on the breeze told him otherwise.

The officer returned to his car and powered up his spotlight. The spotlight illuminated the black skid marks on the asphalt just ahead of his car. With the spotlight, the officer followed the skid marks south along the highway and into Ranch Road 145 where the black rubber tracks met a set of black skid marks coming from the west. The skid marks comingled then moved south across Ranch Road 145 along Highway 214. His stomach knotted as he moved the spotlight along the road following the skid marks. Finally the beam from the powerful spotlight caught a glint in the darkness. His hand trembling, the officer moved the beam upward and the shaft of light revealed the carnage he had feared he would find. The intense beam reflected off the brown liquid pooling in various places around the vehicles. The officer then scanned back and forth across the ground around the wreckage with the spotlight. Miscellaneous debris lay strewn about in the grass on the side of the road and on the asphalt from the site of the vehicles about a hundred yards ahead all the way back to Ranch Road 145, where the two sets of skid marks met. Lying in random places were books, a sneaker, a baseball cap, shreds of Christmas wrapping paper flapping in the breeze, a tattered backpack, sheets of white and yellow paper, a hair brush, CD cases and other unidentifiable pieces of memorabilia of someone's life. What appeared to be the bed of a pickup truck, mauled and twisted, had been tossed onto a barbed wire fence fifty feet from the road about halfway between the point of impact and the place where the vehicles had come to rest. The officer sighed, then slumped into the driver's seat of his cruiser. He radioed dispatch for all available law enforcement units, an ambulance, a MedEvac chopper, a fire and rescue crew equipped with the Jaws of Life, and the coroner.

As Gabe Lewis walked along Ranch Road 145 past what seemed like half the vehicles in Lazarus, the December wind assaulted his ears and his nose and dried out his eyes. He squinted to see clearly and held a hand to his ear as he strained to make sense of the muffled and muted noises he heard ahead. Blue light danced and whirled like a dervish somewhere up ahead. In the distance the unmistakable sound of a helicopter appeared, then grew louder and louder by the second. Far away in the night, more sirens seemed to be descending on the sleepy little town in which, at the moment at least, very few people were asleep.

Gabe Lewis could see the helicopter approaching and slowing just ahead. The whir of the engine and rotors drowned out every other sound, hypnotizing him. Watching and listening to the helicopter, he stumbled over something and fell to the ground. He turned and in the darkness noticed two people, barely visible, huddled together, leaned into one another, in the grass along the side of the road. They sobbed quietly as they rocked rhythmically back and forth. Carefully he stood to his feet and turned as the helicopter illuminated its searchlights. As the helicopter scoured the area with harsh light, a scene unfolded before Gabe Lewis's eyes he never would be able to put out of his mind.

As if a bomb had detonated in a crowd and scattered its victims, dozens and dozens of mourners stood, sat, knelt and lay prostrate in shock and disbelief along the sides of the road, against fence posts, in the ditches between the fence line and the road, against cars and in the beds of pickup trucks. As the searchlights moved about below the MedEvac chopper and lit the barren west Texas landscape, Gabe Lewis scanned the lighted areas for familiar faces. Everywhere he looked as he stumbled through the chaos there were sad eyes, red faces, bodies rocking with their knees pulled to their chests, hands on heads or faces buried on the shoulders of others. He walked along the road toward the crash site with his eyes flicking back and forth from people to wreckage and back to people. Instinctively he reached down with his hands and touched shoulders as he passed those sitting and crouching below him.

Emergency response vehicles arrived on the scene sporadically and worked to light the area with flares and headlights and spotlights, to establish a perimeter and to move onlookers away from the crash site so the helicopter could land. After a few moments, the helicopter landed just up the highway and killed its engines. As the rotors slowed to a standstill and the engine grew silent, the only audible sounds were the cracking and barking of the radios and walkie-talkies and the sniffling, stammering and weeping of the mourners. Rescue workers descended like ants upon the truck using the Jaws of Life to pry apart the cab of the jack-knifed eighteen-wheeler and somehow extricate a person from the mangled mess of metal. The array of lights around them backlit the steam of their breath each time they exhaled. After several minutes, they pulled a body from the cab, loaded the limp figure onto a stretcher and carried it to the helicopter whose rotors had begun to turn again. The helicopter ascended into the night sky and vanished in less than a minute.

With the MedEvac chopper gone, the only light left at the grisly scene was a strange mix of red and blue police or rescue vehicle lights, spotlights from the highway patrol cars, orange flares, red taillights and white headlights, all of which now seemed to shine in every direction. Suddenly, the red and blue lights along with the spotlights went out and officers stepped in front of several headlights as if to prevent some of the light from reaching the wreckage. A lone ambulance backed into empty space at the crash site, idled for several moments while rescue workers and officers stood near the back of the ambulance, then it drove slowly away with neither siren sounding nor emergency lights flashing.

Gabe Lewis ambled through the dry, knee-high grass along the side of the road toward a huddled mass of something familiar. In the scant artificial light, he noticed several girls wearing a hodge-podge of red. Indeed a few in the jumble of girls wore Lazarus sweatshirts or pieces of Lady Longhorns basketball warm-ups. There in front of him, in the frozen darkness of the early morning hours sat several of his shell-shocked players. He knew they needed him right now but he wondered if, in fact, he might need them more.

When Coach Lewis reached the spot where they were crouched on the cold, hard ground, he knelt behind them and placed his hands on the shoulders of two of his girls. Which two, he didn't know until they turned toward him. Molly turned first, her face blotched and her eyes puffy and bloodshot. MJ turned next, still crying and on the verge of hyperventilating. Simultaneously, they grabbed their coach and sobbed into his jacket. Cassie turned around and, upon seeing him, broke down as she shuffled over to him. Brooklynne, too, fell to pieces and moved over to be part of the huddled mass of mourners.

Coach Lewis did his best to comfort the girls, though he said not a word. In the distance, through the long hair blowing across his face, Coach Lewis saw Sam and Corey Colter, arms around one another, making their way toward the team. They fell to the ground with the other girls and wept. Coach Lewis lost track of time and space sitting there with his girls. His mind had wandered a million places, though it never left Lazarus. Maybe they stayed there for hours or for only a few, brief moments.

Through tears, someone asked if he would take them to her house. Coach Lewis didn't know what else to do so he stood and extended his hand.

Coach Lewis led his girls along the road, hand in hand like a kindergarten class on a field trip, to his Blazer; they all piled inside, leaned on one another and held hands. Coach Lewis did a U-turn and drove back through town the long way because the wreckage had not yet been cleared from the highway. After several minutes, he pulled into the driveway in front of the doublewide trailer and parked between a highway patrol car and the Sheriff's car. Other cars sat scattered about. All the lights were on inside the trailer. He didn't know where else to go or what do with his girls.

With his team behind him, Coach Lewis climbed the steps and stood before the door silent and scared. *God, please help me because I don't think...* The door opened and Summer Griffin stood in the doorway, clearly in shock. She looked first at her coach, then at the girls behind them before disappearing back into the trailer without saying a word. Coach Lewis stepped with great care through the door into the living room of the trailer. People milled about everywhere in the small space – law enforcement officers with notepads and coffee cups, the preacher from Greater New Life Church, Calvin Haskins, and an unfamiliar man in a suit – yet an eerie silence hung in the air. On an old, green sofa Martha sat clutching a handkerchief in one hand and a worn, red Bible in the other. She reclined helplessly and pitifully against Elijah Washington and stared with empty eyes across the room at the Christmas tree in the corner. Summer stood like a sad statue in the middle of the room and watched her team fill the miserable space around her.

The girls, once again sobbing and joined now by Nairobi, took Summer's hand and pulled her down the hall to Autumn's room. As Summer moved away from the living room and walked down the short hall she turned and looked over her shoulder first at her coach then at Martha. Summer's eyes welled with tears then the well overflowed as she disappeared into Autumn's bedroom with her teammates. Gabe Lewis, unsure of what to do, turned and walked to the sofa where Martha sat, wilted and lifeless. He knelt in front of Martha and put his hand on hers, the one holding the Bible. Martha's eyes met his and she fell forward and wept on his shoulder. Gabe Lewis didn't know how long he had knelt holding and consoling Martha but his knees and back ached and his soaked shirt clung to his chest and back beneath his jacket.

After a while, Calvin Haskins and the Reverend Washington helped Martha to her feet and escorted her down the hall where they helped her into her bed. When they returned to the living room, they found Gabe Lewis sitting on the sofa holding a picture frame in his hand. Beneath the glass lay a team photo taken on picture day back in the fall. He used the sleeve of his jacket to wipe away the smudges on the glass created earlier undoubtedly by someone's discarded tears. He returned it to the coffee table next to the sofa and stood to find Calvin Haskins standing before him. Without saying a word and without really making direct eye contact, Haskins put his hand on the young man's shoulder and shook his head. Haskins moved on and the Reverend Washington placed both hands on the young coach's shoulders. The preacher leaned down and whispered into the coach's ear that he should go be with his girls because they needed him now. The Reverend pulled Gabe Lewis in tight against his chest and patted him on the back before pointing him down the hall. He pulled away from the Reverend and noticed the meager Christmas tree standing in the corner of the living room near one of the windows. The tree looked sad with the lights hanging on the tree without any twinkle; no one had thought to plug in the lights tonight.

Coach Lewis forced his heavy feet to lumber down the hall one cumbersome step at a time and stopped just outside the room into which the girls had disappeared. He turned and leaned back against the wall next to the bedroom door. With his hands on his head, Coach Lewis took a deep breath and exhaled. Reluctantly, he knocked on the door. The door swung open and the lamplight from the room spilled into the hallway and splashed against the wood-paneled walls. Coach Lewis walked in and forced a half-smile for his girls. He put his hand on Summer's head and slid down the side of the bed to a seated position on the carpet next to her. On the floor of Autumn's bedroom, Coach Lewis sat with his girls, held their hands, and let them lean on his shoulders and cry until they could cry no more. The girls took turns asking questions, most of which he couldn't answer. They exchanged stories, looked at pictures, laughed some more, cried again, then sat in uncomfortable silence. One by one, the girls fell asleep exhausted by the emotional strain of the night's events.

As Coach Lewis untangled himself and climbed to his feet, he noticed for the first time the details of the bedroom. Simple furnishings filled the small room: a white, cast iron double bed with a faded pink comforter, a small vanity and stool, a chest-of-drawers that matched neither the bed nor the vanity, a tall lamp with a frilly, pink lampshade. Tucked between the mirror and the frame of the vanity hung photos of Autumn's teammates and a photo of Autumn with Martha, Summer and April. In the corner of the bedroom sat a box of small Christmas bags much like the ones she'd made for the team, each bag filled with cookies and each bag with a name tag and a curly red ribbon.

Coach Lewis made his way back down the hall toward the living room. As he approached Summer's room, he heard April tossing and turning in her baby bed. He tiptoed the rest of the way. By now, the officers had gone home to their families. Corey Colter and Calvin Haskins sat slumped and asleep on the sofa. Coach Lewis let himself out the front door into the cold.

A faint hint of golden sunlight appeared on the horizon, so Coach Lewis walked through the trailer park and sat down on a rickety picnic table to watch the sunrise. He zipped his jacket and waited. He focused on the eastern horizon and let his mind float away. He didn't notice the Reverend who had walked up behind him. The Reverend placed his large, dark hand on Coach Lewis's shoulder then sat down with him on the picnic table. As the two anticipated the imminent sunrise, a cold gust blew in and swirled around them, picking up a few dried leaves then tossing them aside. The menacing wind brought with it the bitter chill of winter.

CHAPTER XI

The garland and poinsettias decorating the Greater New Life Church seemed out of place, irreverent even. On any other Christmas Eve, the Greater New Life Church would have been abuzz with the excitement and hope of a joyful Christmas Eve service, a service complete with Christmas carols, the Nativity Story, and children dressed in their Sunday best waiting to enjoy hot chocolate and cider after the service. On this Christmas Eve, a gloomy, overcast Monday, the casket at the front of the church, along with the myriad wreaths of sympathy flowers, sucked the life and the joy out of the occasion. The candles in the center of each decorative garland seated uncomfortably in each window sill of the church remained unlit. The Christmas tree in the baptistery stood at solemn attention without twinkling or sparkling or spreading cheer. The Church Decoration Committee felt it would be insensitive and in poor taste to get too showy with the decorations in light of the family's loss and bereavement.

Coach Lewis arrived about an hour before the start of the service, as Martha and Summer had requested, and found them surrounded by the rest of the team on the front pew. As he took a deep breath and tried not to look at the casket, now draped in Autumn's red #20 Lady Longhorns jersey, he made his way to the front of the church. He gritted his teeth as he knelt in front of Summer and Martha and took their hands in his. The girls and Martha surrounded Coach Lewis and sobbed as he focused on a random spot on the wall at the back of the church. He had somehow made it through the night of the accident without crying. He had held it together through the grief counselors' community-wide assembly at the Lazarus High School gym on Saturday, the day after the accident, as well as through dinner at Martha's home after the assembly. He'd managed to call his parents and tell them, too, without shedding a single tear. He had maintained his composure while he stood with Martha and Summer in the receiving line at the visitation on Sunday night and while he sat outside in the church parking lot afterward with Summer, Sam and Cassie. Somehow, Coach Lewis convinced himself he had to be strong, had to be the pillar, for everyone else around him. His team, Martha and even the other kids at school all needed him to be rock-solid, to be unflappable, to keep it together no matter what. So far he'd succeeded and he was determined to make it through the Christmas Eve ordeal without showing a crack or a falter.

As each girl leaned on him and cried, Coach Lewis held and consoled her for as long as she needed. Though his legs and back ached from kneeling and squatting, his position allowed him to watch the people pour in the back of the church and fill the pews. The teachers and coaches from school arrived one by one, most arm-in-arm with a significant other. Scores of students entered in groups of three or four, some of whom Coach Lewis recognized and some who looked unfamiliar. Behind many of the students, most of whom were sullen and quiet, trailed adults who presumably were their parents. Dozens and dozens of people Coach Lewis did not know but recognized took seats all over the sanctuary and dozens more he'd never seen before also made their way into the pews. Haskins, Cannon, McArthur and Merrick, along with their wives, slipped in and took their places in the back of the sanctuary where Neill Frederickson had saved seats for them.

A full twenty minutes before the beginning of the service, Reverend Washington and his deacons scurried to get chairs placed along the inside and the outside of the aisles as the people of Lazarus continued to pour into the church in droves. Just moments before noon, the church could hold no more people. People lined the side walls and back walls of the sanctuary, filled the pews and the overflow chairs, packed the foyer and huddled together outside the foyer on the front steps in the blustery cold.

As he made his way to the pulpit to begin, Reverend Washington placed his hand on Martha's shoulder and told her he'd never seen half this many people in the church at one time in all the years he'd been in Lazarus. Reverend Washington patted Coach Lewis on the shoulder, nodded to the organist and stepped up to the pulpit, which hid behind a depressing veil of flowers.

Coach Lewis sat on the front left pew with Martha and Summer to his left. The rest of the team filled the pew to Summer's left. Under other circumstances the pew would not have held so many people. As the service began, Coach Lewis scooted far back into the pew and leaned forward, resting his elbows on his knees and his chin on his folded hands. He stared straight ahead at a wreath of white lilies; he couldn't quite read the card on the wreath from this distance but a few feet closer and the writing would have been legible. The organ music, the prayers, the photos in the slide show, the pastor's message seemed to flow past Coach Lewis like the landscape during a long drive along a west-Texas highway at dusk. He imagined one day he'd regret not knowing what had been said, but staring at the lilies and the card

219

required his full concentration. Occasionally his concentration lapsed, though, when Martha trembled or when Summer squeezed his hand or when someone behind him broke down. The lilies looked almost too beautiful to be real.

Coach Lewis stood, helped Martha and Summer to their feet, then turned to watch the deacons carry the casket down the aisle toward the back door. The front rows then emptied and followed the casket out into the dark December day. Hundreds of eyes, wet and grief-stricken, showered the procession with sympathetic stares.

At the gravesite behind the church, hundreds of mourners filled and surrounded the small cemetery. The Greater New Life Church cemetery held none of the important or influential people of Lazarus but rather the meek, the salt of the earth and the forgotten. Many of those who had come to pay respects on this day had never seen the small cemetery hidden away behind the rustic structure. Packed in close together to shield one another from the frigid air, the mourners shivered and shuddered as they gazed at the casket-gray sky overhead. The biting wind blew hard across the wide open, ranging landscape and pierced the coats and shawls and sweaters of those standing graveside. The bitter cold overcame many of the mourners forcing them to lower their heads and shield their teary eyes from the blustery gusts.

Reverend Washington recited the 23rd Psalm then motioned for Nairobi to join him. He removed his overcoat and slipped it over Nairobi's shoulders. Nairobi wiped her eyes with both hands, bowed her head and slowed her breathing. For just a moment the wind died. Nairobi grabbed Reverend Washington's hand, lifted her head and sang.

Nairobi, with a slight tremble, quaking with soul and sorrow, lifted her voice to heaven, which seemed infinitely far away.

One by one heads lifted to seek the source, to find the voice.

With each of Nairobi's beautifully sad notes, her breath hung frozen in the air. She reached with her other hand and grabbed the hand of the person standing next to her.

Someone else grabbed a hand nearby, then someone else, then another. Fingers interwoven, palm against palm, black and white, young and old. Someone else, another and another and another holding hands, sharing sorrow, taking comfort, giving and finding strength.

As Nairobi continued, the floodgate of emotions burst for many gathered in the cemetery and the crowd found themselves swept away in a deluge of tears. Nairobi somehow forged ahead, maintaining her composure until the very end. At the end though, her voice cracked and she labored to produce the last lines of her lament. With the final words of her refrain, Nairobi could contain her emotions no longer; she turned and buried her head in Reverend Washington's chest as he pulled her close.

Summer and the rest of the team huddled together for a group hug before going their separate ways for the day. As the group hug ended, Sam squinted through her tears and scanned the sad faces of the crowd, looking for no one in particular. Near the back edge of those gathered graveside, Sam saw Principal Haskins with Mrs. Haskins pulled close with one arm. Sam leaned slightly then raised up on her toes to be sure. She was sure. Beneath Principal Haskins' other arm stood his favorite grandson, Roy, red-faced and visibly shaken. Roy's eyes did not meet hers; they were fixated somewhere else. Sam followed his gaze to Summer, who stood looking back expectantly at Roy. Sam looked again at Roy. He shook his head in slow motion and he mouthed something to Summer. Sam couldn't be sure but it seemed like he said, "I'm so sorry."

Finally, the last of the visitors shuffled past the casket to say a final goodbye, caressing the casket with their fingertips or placing a hand on the cold, gray veneer. The crowd returned to their cars and trucks then to their quiet homes.

On this Christmas Eve there would be no celebrations in Lazarus, no joyous homecomings, no merriment, no happiness, no hope. The people of Lazarus once thought they knew no hope when their football dreams had been dashed. Now, though, the town truly understood its view of reality had been skewed. Now, the town truly understood how it felt to have the life drained from the community. Autumn Griffin died and so, too, had Lazarus. Autumn Griffin lay dead in the cemetery behind Greater New Life Church and Lazarus lay dead all around it. That day, so many wept. Young and old, friends and strangers, black and white, men and women wept. The angels wept. Jesus wept. Coach Gabe Lewis, though, with his eyes on the lilies, shed not a single tear.

———————

A standing room only crowd, fully debriefed but wholly in shock, went their separate and solemn ways following a two-hour assembly in the gymnasium. Grief counselors from as far away as Lubbock and Amarillo rushed to the tiny cowtown to help students and parents alike make some sense of the tragic accident. All but a few Lazarus High

School students, the entire faculty and several hundred grief-stricken citizens listened, cried, shared, questioned and cried some more during the assembly. When the last of the grieving students and assisting counselors had left the campus, Tommy Cannon, Calvin Haskins and Patton McArthur made their way through the quiet buildings to the solace of Haskins' office.

"Of course it's terrible, Tommy, but that's all the more reason for my boys not to go," the General offered. "They go to that funeral and their heads are gonna be all messed up. How're we supposed to keep clear heads the rest of the season if they actually go? We have the tournament here next Friday and Saturday and we need to have our heads on straight if we're gonna have a good showing. It's bad enough just having to deal with it."

Tommy Cannon sat with Patton McArthur on one side of the desk as Calvin Haskins sat on the other side and stared at them with a vacant look.

"We'll send flowers from the boys. That would be a very respectable gesture on our part. I'll even pay for it myself."

"General, I have to confess," said Tommy, "I don't really know what to do here. This has put a damper on the holidays for the whole town and probably on the next few months for the school, too. And I see what you mean about messing with their heads but... I don't know. At least your boys can get back on the court again."

The General scratched his head and sighed, "Fine. I'll let the boys make up their own minds about this but I can't imagine they'll want to go. Those girls don't even like my boys so they sure as heck won't be looking to the boys for any comfort." After pausing for a moment, he continued, "Well, I reckon *we* all need to go even if our boys don't. As for us, it would look awful bad if we weren't at the funeral. Right?"

Tommy Cannon nodded.

"You know, fellas," Tommy said, "Bill mentioned to me during the assembly that our gut reaction about canceling the girls' season would be a good idea. He didn't seem to think the girls or the coach will have the mental toughness to handle the grind from here on out under these circumstances or will even want to play anymore this season. 'Cut your losses,' he said, 'and regroup next year when things have settled down. It's too much to expect from these girls. Their hearts are broke so why go addin' insult to injury, so to speak?'"

Haskins leaned back in his chair, crossed his arms and closed his eyes. After a momentary pause, he sat back up, leaned forward on his desk and said, "If we do this, are we sure we're doing the right thing here?" For some reason unknown to Haskins, Roy seemed to be struggling with the accident more than he would have expected, even considering Roy had known the family for a long time. According to Haskins' son, Cal Jr., who found himself at a complete loss about how to handle the tragedy at home, Roy had been virtually inconsolable since the accident. Haskins noticed Roy just moments ago in the assembly, too, clearly more despondent than the others around him. Roy's brooding and withdrawn behavior weighed on Haskins' mind and tugged at heartstrings that hadn't been stirred in many, many years.

Tommy leaned forward.

"Since when did you give a rip about those girls or that team? Besides, it's all but done. I agree with what Merrick said so I've already called the Farwell coach and that one's done. He's a buddy of mine and he understood. Said he didn't really want his girls competing against a team like this anyway. A sympathy case, you know. He said it was a no win situation for either team. His girls would feel sorry for our girls and wouldn't play hard, or play well, and his fans wouldn't want to be depressed sitting in the stands feeling sorry for a team they're kicking the crap out of anyway."

Haskins took a deep breath and answered, "Maybe you're right. Maybe Bill's right about the kids not handling all this. I don't know if I could have at that age. Come to think of it, I've never dealt with anything like this even at my age now. Maybe they do just need some down time. There's always next season for them, right?"

"I'll help you make the rest of the calls to the district teams after Christmas," the General offered, winking at Haskins' observations. "The rest of the coaches will understand, too. They'll probably appreciate it."

Tommy Cannon reached into his pocket for his keys and nodded in agreement. He headed out the door then turned back to say, "I'll break the news to Lewis next week once we're on the other side of the funeral and Christmas. Talk about bad timing, huh?" As Cannon made his way to his vehicle, he noticed Coach Lewis's Blazer still parked in the mostly empty parking lot. He figured the young coach was working in his office trying to keep his mind occupied with anything other than the current state of affairs in Lazarus. Cannon could have gone to see Coach Lewis. Instead, Tommy Cannon climbed into his truck, tuned the radio to the Christmas music station out of Lubbock and made his way home through the frozen Lazarus landscape.

In his small office in the gym, Coach Lewis sat at his desk looking at the remaining schedule. The first game back after the holidays against Farwell lay just two weeks ahead. As the last non-district game on the schedule, Coach Lewis knew the Farwell game would be a good one to get everyone's legs back under them and to regain their composure before district play, which was set to begin just days after the Farwell game. Based on the box scores in the papers over the last two weeks, Farwell might just be a team the Lady Longhorns could steal a win from and then, perhaps, the girls would regain some confidence.

Coach Lewis sat and looked out his door into the silent, empty gym. He could hear the swirling winds outside whistling past the gym windows and rattling the windows in their vintage frames. He scribbled starting lineups on his notepad as he worked to sort out a lineup without Autumn Griffin. A realization dawned on him: winning not only with one less player but also with crushed spirits would be terribly difficult and entirely different than the challenges he'd faced thus far. He gritted his teeth then tossed his pencil across the office in frustration.

To add to his sudden feeling of gloom and doom, the visitation loomed just a day away with Autumn's funeral the day after that, on Christmas Eve of all days. His thoughts wandered away from basketball as he imagined the subdued if not spoiled Christmas gatherings around town, especially for the Griffins and for the other players' families as well. He thought about the Griffins – Martha with one less child in her home, Summer with no sister and the baby with no aunt. He thought about the Colters and what an unpleasant welcome to Lazarus this turned out to be for them. Coach Lewis's heart ached for all his girls and their families.

He closed his notebook, placed it in a desk drawer and closed the drawer as he thought about how the "most wonderful time of the year" had, in a matter of one unforgettable night, turned into the most awful time in most people's lives in Lazarus. Tired, disheartened, and overwhelmed, Coach Lewis drove home and crawled into bed where he lay in solitude for the next twenty-four hours.

Lazarus lay hushed and still and dark for days. The streets remained almost empty, the houses quiet, the Christmas lights conspicuously not illuminated. The entire town lay in dread of the tribulation waiting in the hours and days ahead. The early nightfall of the shortened days and the bitter cold only added to the feeling of despair that gripped the town. Though everyone in Lazarus planned to attend the visitation and the funeral, selfishly, no one wanted to go. It just didn't seem right to bury a child on the eve of the celebration of the birth of another.

Nevertheless, the hours and minutes crept by and the visitation came and went with its awkward receiving line and countless uncomfortable statements like "I'm so sorry" all night long intended to make the grieving family somehow feel better temporarily in their time of very permanent loss. Christmas Eve, the day of the funeral, finally arrived. Hundreds of mourners and well-wishers mustered the resolve to brave the elements and pack the Greater New Life Church for the noon service. The people of Lazarus filled the church and the overflow spilled out into the cold that Christmas Eve day in west Texas. After the Reverend Washington delivered to the mourning masses a message of hope and redemption, the throng made its way to the cemetery behind the church where Autumn's family returned her body to the earth and said goodbye to their sister and friend.

After the services, many people lingered and exchanged handshakes and embraces. Others, heads hung low, made their way to their vehicles, returning home to try to salvage what was left of the Christmas holidays. Roy Haskins, though, headed for his truck, climbed in and sped away from the church parking lot, leaving a spray of dust and gravel behind him. Haskins glanced toward Cal Jr., who returned a helpless shrug. Haskins understood Roy's grief, but something about Roy's behavior had been gnawing at him over the last several days. All the way home, Haskins drummed his fingers on the steering wheel and ground his teeth as he worried about Roy. At home, he sat in his recliner wringing his hands and refusing to eat. The worry had become almost too much.

Just before dark, the phone rang. Haskins answered and heard Cal Jr. on the line shaken and upset. Roy hadn't returned home from the funeral and none of Roy's friends had seen him since he left the church. Haskins told his son to calm down, call the sheriff and wait at home in case Roy returned. "I think I know where to find him," he said as he hung up with his son. He grabbed his coat and headed to the driveway.

Haskins raced out of his driveway and around the outskirts of Lazarus. He knew that Roy and his buddies, and more often than not their female companions, too, hung out at the gravel pit a few miles outside of town. He also knew, at least according to the word on the street, Roy spent at least one infamous night with Summer Griffin in the bed of his truck at the gravel pit. There seemed to Haskins a pretty good chance Roy would be there now if, in fact, Roy wasn't with any of his friends.

As Haskins made his way along the dirt road from the main highway to the gravel pit, the last of the waning daylight disappeared. Though he hardly could see in the dark light of dusk, he scanned the road ahead, as well as the ditches alongside, for any sign of Roy's truck. Finally he reached the gravel pit, skidded to a halt and jumped out of his truck with his flashlight in hand. Haskins scanned the horizon with the light but Roy's truck appeared to be nowhere in sight. Haskins frantically walked along hundreds of yards of the gravel pit's shifty and unstable ledge panning the horizon with the flashlight. Somewhere in the darkness, though, he heard a faint sound like music floating up from the gravel pit below. He shuffled even closer to the edge and shone his light into the deep, dark pit. There at the bottom, some thirty feet below and at the end of a steep incline from where Haskins stood, Roy's truck rested in total darkness. With the beam focused on the bed of the truck Haskins saw Roy lying motionless in the bed, feet dangling down over the lowered tailgate, with a glistening object resting next to him reflecting the flashlight's probing beam.

Haskins scooted down the incline into the pit toward the truck. Gravel slid and shifted beneath his feet as he made his way down toward Roy and the truck. As he descended, a plume of dust floated upward and reflected the light of the flashlight creating an eerie, glowing cloud that seemed to follow Haskins to the bottom of the pit. As he reached the bottom and made his way across the crunching gravel, the pungent odor of whiskey and vomit wafted toward Haskins' nose. When he reached the truck he shook Roy, called out his name and shone the flashlight in his face. With slurred speech, Roy lifted his head and responded, "Grampa, ith that you?"

"It's me, buddy," Haskins answered with a sigh of relief. "Looks like you've gotten yourself into a pretty good mess here."

"Grampa, you hab no idea," Roy answered in slow motion then flopped his forehead down onto his arm in woe-is-me fashion. "No idea, 'tall."

"Roy, let's see if we can't drag you out of this big ol' pit you got yourself into. We need to get you home, son, and get you cleaned up. Your folks are worried to death about you. Sounds like we got a lot of talking to do."

Haskins reached in and dragged his grandson out of the vomit that had pooled in the bedliner of his truck. He sat Roy up, pulled off his own coat and wrapped it around his grandson, who still had on the Sunday clothes he had worn to the funeral. Haskins picked up the green, half-empty Cutty Sark bottle, took a whiff and poured the rest into the gravel below. For nearly half an hour Haskins practically dragged Roy up the incline, out of the gravel pit and, finally, onto level ground where they made their way back toward the headlights of Haskins' truck.

After he reached the truck and piled the slumped figure into the front seat of the warm, still-running vehicle, Haskins bent over and leaned on his knees trying to catch his breath. After finally catching his breath, he wiped the sweat from his bald head, climbed in and drove back towards town thankful that Lazarus would not have to bury a second young person in less than a week.

CHAPTER XII

Just one week and one day after the funeral, the Longhorn boys basketball team tipped off the opening game of the annual Longhorn New Year's Tournament, a round-robin tournament with its first game always on New Year's Day. The General wanted to be sure his boys had adequate gym time in the days prior to the first game, though there were no high-profile teams scheduled to appear, so he had the team in the gym the first Monday after Christmas, on New Year's Eve. As holiday basketball tournaments go, the Longhorn New Year's Tournament probably deserved a rating somewhere between weak and lousy. The Longhorns, more specifically Coach Patton McArthur, liked hosting a tournament full of cupcake teams. He wanted his boys full of confidence and bravado coming off the holidays and heading into district play. Nevertheless, the General wanted practice time and that meant Dee had to leave his family during his Christmas vacation to get the gym ready for practice.

Dee always arrived early and wet-mopped the hardwood before the General's boys took the floor, even for practice. The General had been known to throw a fit if the gym floor didn't shine and if the players' shoes didn't squeak on it. Even so, Dee never complained about the General's demands or anyone else's. In fact, Dee poured himself into everything he did at Lazarus High School because he took an unusual amount of pride in keeping the facilities in top shape for the kids, "his kids" as he liked to say. There were plenty of people around who considered Dee "the help," but Dee never let on that he knew.

Nevertheless, Dee had a smile, a handshake, and a "yes, sir" or "yes, ma'am" for everyone.

The students at Lazarus adored Dee, especially the athletes. He never missed home games, he drove the bus to some away games and he always wished the players good luck during the school day when he saw them. There was just something cool about Dee, too. Years ago Dee injured his back and the injury made Dee walk with a slight hitch in his gait. As a result, when Dee walked, he looked cool, confident and full of swagger. The students loved Dee so much they all pitched in a few years back and bought Dee a new car. Dee wore out his truck hauling things around for the school and his old truck practically fell apart in the parking lot one afternoon. Autumn Griffin, as a freshman, came up with the idea for everyone to contribute to the "Dee's New Wheels" fund. When the covert fundraising drive was over, the students, faculty and coaches had raised enough to buy Dee an old Impala, which they tricked out with black tint, a mean metallic green paint job, and twenty-inch chrome spinners. Aside from the kids at Lazarus High School, Dee loved his green machine more than anything in the world.

Dee had almost finished wet-mopping as the basketball boys trickled into the gym. The normally boisterous group of boys seemed more reserved than usual as they traipsed down the sideline to their locker room. As Dee watched the crew file in, he noticed someone else had slipped in with a few of the boys. He leaned his mop against the bleachers and made his way over to Summer, who stood just past the baseline. She looked tired and very pale.

"Summer," Dee said, "I'm so glad to see you." He went straight to her and gave her a big hug. She received the hug but didn't reciprocate.

"Hey, Dee."

"Summer," he began and waited for her to make eye contact with him. "I know I can't say anything to make you feel any better right now, but I'm gonna say something anyway. I'm so sorry about your sister. My heart's been broken wide open ever since I heard. I sure did think a lot of her. She was one-of-a-kind, you know."

"Thanks, Dee." She looked as if she were trying to smile but didn't have the energy. "Hey, Dee, I was wondering if you could let me into the locker room so I can get..."

Dee noticed she was about to break down so he took his keys out of his pocket with one hand, grabbed her hand with his other, and led her toward the girls' locker room. After several minutes Summer exited the locker room only to find Bradley Banks and Tucker Munson, two of the non-starting basketball players, waiting for her. Looking awkward and timid, the duo fidgeted and stared at their feet. Tucker finally broke the silence.

"Uh, Summer," he began then finally looked up at her. "We just wanted to say we're sorry about your sister and all."

"Yeah, we're real sorry," Bradley added. Bradley's solemn face confirmed his sincerity.

Tucker went on. "We're sorry about the team, too. For the record, we don't think it's fair. Pretty much none of us think it's fair."

"What are you talking about, about the team? What's not fair?"

It didn't take long for Summer, as upset as she was, to round up the rest of the team. Less than an hour after Summer left the gym, she sat in a booth at Mary's Kitchen with Nairobi, Cassie and Molly, crammed into her side of the booth while Sam, MJ and Rita packed into the other. Mary's Kitchen had been closed since the day after the accident and the place filled up only partially on this day; a re-opening of sorts but also the first day of business Martha had not made it into work in years. Customers filled perhaps half the seats in the diner, but the mood remained somber and subdued. The customers ordered and ate with little or no small talk or conversation with the waitress or with one another. The noise level, usually pretty high due to the relaxed, down-home atmosphere, remained eerily hushed. The jukebox hadn't been turned on so there happened to be no blues or classic country playing to drown out the silence.

The girls, especially Summer, needed the company more than they realized. The girls hugged one another at least twice, some three times, and cried plenty of tears as they entered the diner and headed to the booth for the impromptu team meeting. Brooklynne, to no one's surprise, arrived last. She was red-faced and crying before she ever reached the booth; in fact, her neck seemed remarkably red too, and she was scratching her neck and her ribs almost obsessively. After the hugs and kisses and tears, Brooklynne used her hips to scoot Rita in toward the middle of the booth, plopped down and asked what all the fuss was about.

"I heard something today at the gym that you guys aren't going to like," Summer began. "Bradley and Tucker heard from a couple of the other guys that Coach Cannon decided to cancel the rest of your season."

"What do you mean 'cancel'?" Sam interjected. "And it's *our season*, not *your season*."

Summer mustered a smile for Sam. For a split second, the rest of the girls, too, grinned at Sam, amused by the sweetness of her comment. When the split second had passed and the girls fully realized what Summer had just said, grimaces and scowls replaced the grins. Rita grabbed a handful of napkins and started shredding them with her hands.

"OK, *our* season," Summer agreed. "So, I said you guys wouldn't like it. Apparently, the powers that be have come to some sort of an agreement that we *girls* need some… recovery time." Summer drew a deep breath then forced herself to continue the story. "They're worried about us not handling things well, getting back in the saddle before we're ready, and all that jazz. Sorry to be the bearer of bad news, but I knew you'd all wanna know right away."

After she'd delivered the news, Summer somehow felt guilty for being a downer when she knew her friends already were struggling to get over their melancholy. In Summer's mind, she was adding to her friends' grief and stress. According to Summer's convoluted logic, her family, by virtue of Autumn's death, had caused enough trouble for her friends; she hated to pour salt in their freshly opened and rather significant wounds.

Speechless, the girls looked at one another. As they pondered what Summer told them, myriad thoughts raced through their minds. Rita pushed Brooklynne out of the booth, stomped outside to the sidewalk and yelled at no one in particular. Brooklynne, caught off-guard by Rita's reaction, wondered silently if anyone other than the governor even had the power to do something like cancel a basketball season. MJ, Nairobi and Cassie thought about how sad the whole situation had become – first losing Autumn, then having the season taken away from them because no one had confidence in their ability to deal.

Completely unexpectedly, Molly broke down and sobbed. Her teammates had never seen a display like this from Molly, even at the funeral. They comforted her and asked what had suddenly set her off. Molly fought back the tears then poured her heart out right there in the middle of Mary's Kitchen.

"I've been so selfish for so long. Sam, I've been jealous of you and I couldn't stand that you came in and took my spot. I always knew you were better. I mean, it's not rocket science, but I couldn't ever come to grips with it. And my dad kept telling me how Coach was ruining my season and my year and how messed up things were. He even took me to talk to Principal Haskins about getting rid of Coach. I can't believe I did that. I'm so ashamed to admit this, but I didn't actually know how good things were. It wasn't until Autumn died that I realized what messed up actually looks like. I've been horrible to every one of you and I'm so sorry. I promise, if we figure this thing out, I'm in. Until the end, I'm in."

Molly's confession set off her teammates' emotions and the whole group of them cried together for a while. Sam killed the mournful mood when she pounded her fist on the table.

Sam's grief turned to anger and frustration as her thoughts returned to what Summer had just told the rest of the girls. Sam thought about her opportunity to play college ball being dashed by some group of people who didn't really know her and who, as far as she could tell, had no concern for her future. Sam also thought about how far the group of girls had come as a team and how much farther they possibly could go and how that, too, might be crushed by a bunch of old men who didn't care if the girls ever returned to the court. At first, Sam felt helpless. Then she remembered something Coach Lewis told the team back in the days of practicing outside in the sweltering heat. "Ladies, if you want equality," Coach had warned them, "you better be prepared to fight for it and take it by force. If you aren't prepared to fight for it then you should be prepared to do without."

Sam pounded her fist on the table. Suddenly Sam had everyone's attention.

The girls wiped their faces with a dispenser full of napkins, ordered Cokes and fries and listened to Sam explain what they were going to do next. After listening to Sam, they were all on board, even Molly. They got their game plan in order, mopped up the last dab of ketchup with the last few fries in the basket, and headed out to find their coach. If anyone could help now, it would be Coach Lewis. The girls knew he'd fight for them and, with a little luck, he might even convince the higher-ups to change their minds and let the girls play.

On the way out the door, Rita noticed a red rash around Brooklynne's neck and behind her ears; through all the drama at the booth, Brooklynne had been pawing at her sides and her neck incessantly. When Rita asked her what was up, Brooklynne rolled her eyes and whispered, "Come on. I'll explain in the truck. Kind of embarrassing. Real embarrassing, actually." Rita knew Brooklynne well enough to know the story would be a good one.

The girls followed Sam in a makeshift caravan of cars and trucks from Mary's Kitchen to Coach Lewis's house. The knock at the door and the familiar, friendly faces standing outside made his day, if only temporarily. Having needed their company more than he realized, he welcomed a chance to visit with his girls. He hoped they, too, were looking for some company. The girls needed to talk but not about their feelings or about the accident. Despite the chill in the air, the coach and his girls sat down on the steps outside and Sam explained everything, including her plan.

"You're sure about this? There's no way it's just a rumor?"

"We're positive," Summer said. "The boys on the team told me, and I got a text from... I got a text about it, too."

Just as Sam suspected, the news fired up their coach. He rubbed his face some then disappeared into his house. A moment later he reemerged with his jacket and his keys. As he scampered down the steps he told the girls to fall in line behind him because he had a pretty good idea where to find Coach Cannon, Principal Haskins and whoever else was in on this conspiracy. When they reached the school parking lot, they recognized Coach Cannon's truck and pulled into the parking spaces next to it. Everyone jumped out as soon as the cars were parked and practically raced Coach Lewis to the doors. Wisely the young coach stopped the girls and sent them back to their vehicles to wait for him.

"I got this."

With that, Coach Lewis flung open the door and headed through the field house to Tommy Cannon's office.

A while later when Coach Lewis opened the field house door and exited toward his waiting team. With his air of confidence obviously gone and his shoulders hung low, Coach Lewis looked toward his girls and, with a grim face, shook his head. By the time he reached the cars, several of the girls had tears streaking their faces. He told them simply to go home and he'd see them in a few days back at school. Without further conversation or eye contact, Coach Lewis climbed into his Blazer and sat.

He looked straight ahead and waited for the girls to leave. After several minutes when they finally did, he leaned his head forward on the steering wheel and stared aimlessly at the dirty floor mat beneath his feet. If the first confrontation with Cannon had been uncomfortable, this one registered somewhere in the neighborhood of dreadful, almost as bad as the dressing down he'd gotten from Haskins about the water tower. Though he believed with every fiber of his being that Cannon was not only making the wrong decision but also abusing his power, he knew the situation lay beyond his own control now. The season would be cut short, though he probably would be allowed to finish the year if he kept quiet and kept to his classroom. As for next year, Coach Lewis felt pretty certain everyone in Lazarus would be just fine with his seeking employment elsewhere.

Martha sat alone on her green sofa and stared at the half-finished cup of coffee that had been sitting on her coffee table for hours. Autumn had made the cup for Martha years ago. First grade? Maybe second? Why hadn't she kept more of the little knick-knacks her girls had made for her through the years? She stared at the coffee cup and didn't move even though she heard the persistent knocking at the door. Finally, a voice from outside called her name.

"Martha? I need to know if you're in there. I'm coming inside in another minute."

She recognized Calvin's voice but she didn't want to talk to him.

"Martha. Are you there?"

The knocking and calling continued but Martha remained planted on her sofa. Autumn had loved to sleep on the sofa when the girls would come by for a sleepover. She always gave up her bed and volunteered to sleep on the lumpy green sofa. That was so like her.

The screen door creaked and the door knob jiggled a bit. The door opened and Calvin Haskins stepped inside. He looked around the room a bit and saw Martha sitting quietly on the sofa in the dimly-lit room. The lights were off so he asked Martha rhetorically if she minded a little light. He flipped the switch and turned on the overhead light. In the corner he saw the Christmas tree standing over a small pile of unopened presents. "Do you mind?" he asked as he knelt and plugged in the Christmas lights. "That's better, don't you think?" Calvin walked over and sat next to Martha. Without saying a word, the two of them sat on the couch for a while listening to the silence and staring at the coffee cup with the tiny handprints beneath the shiny glazed finish.

Calvin eventually broke the silence and asked, "Is Summer here, too?"

"She's with the girls."

"OK, that's good. That's real good. I think she needs them right now."

Martha said nothing.

"Listen, Martha, things have been tough over at my place here lately. Not like here, I know, but pretty tough. I didn't want to come over unannounced, but you didn't answer your phone. I got worried."

When he realized she wasn't going to respond, he scooted to the edge of the sofa, turned back to Martha and reached out. He touched her under the chin and gently turned her face to his.

"Martha, I've got some things I need to say to you and some things we need to talk about. I understand if you don't want to hear it, and I'll leave if you tell me to. But I want you to know I'm here to do the right thing for once."

A single tear appeared in her eye and trickled down the wrinkles etched on her cheek.

"Go on."

Tommy Cannon sat in his office splicing together pieces of Roy Haskins highlight film for the latest handful of colleges who had inquired about the eleventh-grade gunslinger. Louisiana Tech, Kansas and the University of New Mexico were the larger schools now on the hunt for Haskins, though Hardin-Simmons University, Mississippi College and Mount Union also showed significant interest. If Cannon were the betting type, he'd put his money on Haskins' signing with the Red Raiders. As he weighed Haskins' options, a pounding knock at the door interrupted his concentration. Before Cannon could say "Come in," the door flew open and Coach Lewis stormed into the office.

"Is it true about the rest of the games? You really cancelled them? All of them?"

"That's the plan," he replied without looking away from the DVD monitor.

"You can't do that," he said as he slammed the door behind him.

"Sure I can. Especially if it's what's best for those girls."

Coach Lewis's hands trembled as he walked over to Cannon's desk and leaned forward on the desk. The veins in his neck protruded and pulsed under his collar.

"Don't even pretend. That's the biggest load of..."

Cannon jumped to his feet, leaned forward from behind the desk and moved his face in so close to Lewis he could smell coffee on Lewis's breath.

"To tell the truth, I'm surprised you didn't play the sympathy card and send your girls in here to whine and cry all over my office."

"To tell the truth?" he barked back at Cannon. "When's the last time you told me the truth about anything at this God-forsaken school? You haven't been honest with me yet about one single thing."

"OK, here's the truth. Your team is terrible and you're in so far over your head you don't have a clue how bad it really is. On top of that, your team is a black hole for revenue. You're a parasite in this athletic department. Nobody comes to your games so we get no gate revenue whatsoever. You had five district home games left on your schedule. That's ten officials plus five gate workers plus clock and books for five games, not to mention electricity and janitorial. And that's only for home games. Who do you think pays for gas for the bus for away games? Not your girls. By canceling the season I'm saving the athletic department almost enough for an entire team set of new football jerseys *and* pants for next season."

They stood nose to nose across Cannon's desk and stared one another down, breathing heavily and grinding their teeth. Coach Lewis felt his chin and jaw quivering and he prayed Cannon didn't notice; he figured Cannon could smell fear.

"You hired me to coach these girls, not to balance your budget. Besides, it's not the job of the girls basketball team to make money."

Cannon poked his finger in Coach Lewis's chest and pushed him backward. Coach Lewis couldn't believe how hard Cannon had pushed him with just his finger.

Tommy Cannon lowered his voice and said, "You're talking way above your pay grade now and you're way out of line. You want to stay on this payroll the rest of the year, I suggest you shut your know-it-all holier-than-thou big-city pretty-boy mouth and keep the rest of your opinions to yourself. Get out of my office."

Unsure what to do next, Coach Lewis sighed, turned around and plodded out of Cannon's office. He sent the girls away with no explanation. The girls could surmise, though, by his languid expression how his conversation had gone with Coach Cannon or Principal Haskins or whomever he had confronted. Completely and utterly defeated, he sat in his vehicle with his head laid forward on the steering wheel. He didn't see the devastated looks on the girls' faces as they drove away in complete disbelief. Nor did he see Haskins pull into the parking lot then go into the field house with another, smaller person at his side.

Still sitting in his Blazer wallowing in self-pity some time later, Coach Lewis nearly jumped out of his seat when a rap at his driver's side window snapped him back into the here and now. Haskins stood outside the Blazer motioning for Coach Lewis to roll down his window. Coach Lewis complied. He could tell by the look on Haskins' face that Haskins meant business.

"My office. 8:00 a.m. tomorrow." As if for effect, Haskins stood staring at Coach Lewis for several seconds longer then shook his head. With that, Haskins returned to his truck, then he and his passenger drove away from Lazarus High School.

Coach Lewis pulled into the parking lot, coffee in hand, at exactly 7:45 a.m. for his 8:00 meeting. "Early is on time and on time is late," someone once told him and the phrase had become words he lived by. As early as he was, though, Coach Cannon had beaten him here and, judging by the empty truck parked in Cannon's normal spot, Cannon had already gone in to wait in Haskins' office. As he shifted his Blazer into park, he saw movement in his rearview mirror. He turned and looked over his shoulder through the partially frosted, partially defrosted rear windshield and saw two familiar vehicles pull in and then park alongside him. He couldn't help but smile as Sam, Summer, Rita, Nairobi and Cassie climbed out of the two trucks and piled into his Blazer. Sam jumped in the front passenger seat and the other four stuffed themselves into his backseat.

"Fancy meeting you here, Coach." Sam gave him a big smile and friendly slug in the shoulder. Sam packed a wallop and he nearly spilled his coffee in his lap. "Careful with that coffee, Coach, or we'll have us another coffee lawsuit in the papers."

Coach Lewis returned Sam's smile then spun to greet the girls in the back.

"What are you guys doing here? How'd you know I would be here?"

"Word travels fast around here," Nairobi said.

Summer added, "We kind of heard things might not have gone too well yesterday and that's why this meeting got called. We just wanted to let you know how much we appreciate you trying to help. We don't want you getting in trouble or anything."

"Even if things don't get fixed, it's OK. Thanks for trying anyway," Cassie chimed in.

He didn't know how to respond, so he went back to his coffee.

Rita offered her thoughts. "Coach, we know you said we gotta fight sometimes and we know you tried yesterday, but we figure sometimes the fight's just too big for us. Maybe it's time we bow out of this one, huh? Even if we don't get to play again, we can all still hang out or something."

"You guys don't worry about me. Anyway, maybe something will happen this morning."

Coach Lewis hadn't gotten the sentence out of his mouth when another vehicle, a dusty black extra-cab truck, rolled into the lot and pulled in on the other side of Cannon's.

"There's Principal Haskins," Cassie observed as Haskins opened the door and stepped out, his shiny bald head appearing over the top of Cannon's truck. "He's got someone with him."

All eyes focused in Haskins' direction, waiting to see who else had been summoned to the meeting. As Haskins walked toward the front of his truck and stepped onto the sidewalk, a small head bobbed up and down just out of sight then appeared at Haskins' side.

Coach Lewis dropped his head as he realized who it was. "What's Martha doing here?" he said to no one in particular. "Hasn't she been through enough already?"

Summer reached forward and put a consoling hand on her coach's shoulder. She saw someone else, shook her coach by the shoulder, then broke the silence with, "Oh. My. God. Roy's here, too."

Roy, with his hands in the pockets of his unmistakable letter jacket, stepped around the front of the trucks and walked behind Haskins and Martha. Martha, bundled up inside a calf-length charcoal-gray coat with her hair pulled up beneath a scarf, appeared but a frail and fragile thing next to Roy and Principal Haskins. The girls and their coach, crammed into the tiny Blazer like circus clowns, watched the odd trio disappear into the building as Principal Haskins warmed his hands with his breath and held the door open with his foot for Martha and Roy.

"Well," said Coach Lewis as he killed the ignition, "this ought to be interesting. You guys should probably head on back home now, don't you think?"

Rita, without hesitation, responded, "Yea, whatever, coach. We ain't going nowhere."

"I had a feeling you'd say that. You do have to get out of my car, though."

As they opened the doors and poured out into the cold, Sam tried to ease the tension a little more.

"Car? I always wondered if this was a car or a truck. Thanks for clearing that up for me."

The young coach's biggest fans retreated to their own vehicles and gave him a final good luck thumbs up as he turned back over his shoulder one last time before heading inside to face the music.

As he made his way down the sparsely lit hallway, he thought back to the day he had arrived in Lazarus and sat in the sweltering lobby with

Gladys while he waited for his interview with Haskins and Cannon. He couldn't help but wonder… if he had known in August what would transpire during his first months on the job, would he have taken the job anyway or would he have turned around and driven back to Houston as fast as his Blazer would carry him? He felt pretty sure the question would be answered in the next several minutes. He bit his lip and walked into the lobby where he found Martha sitting alone. She didn't look up as he walked over and sat down next to her. She reached over with a cold, sinewy hand and touched his wrist.

"How are you holding up, Coach?"

"Shouldn't I be asking you that question?"

"Me, I suppose I'm gonna make it. Can't say I'm looking forward to this little pow-wow this morning, though."

"That makes two of us. I'm so sorry you got dragged into this. You shouldn't be here, you know."

"Well, Calvin came to see me yesterday."

Coach Lewis took her hand in his and squeezed gently. He looked up at her face for the first time since he entered the room. Martha's face startled him. Her eyes appeared deep set and the poor lighting in the room cast heavy, dark shadows over her eyes and cheeks. Her wrinkles seemed more prominent than he'd remembered and her skin looked strangely pallid, almost ashen. Martha had aged ten, maybe twenty years, since the accident. He hadn't noticed so much at the funeral but certainly he could see it now.

Haskins appeared in his doorway and motioned for the two of them to join him inside. In a softer-than-usual tone he said, "Why don't you two come on in?"

Haskins pulled the door behind them and took his seat behind his desk where he leaned forward with his elbows on his desk and his hands folded together. Martha took the seat next to Roy, who neither looked up nor acknowledged that anyone else had entered the room. Coach Lewis sat next to Martha on the other side of her from Roy. Across the office, Coach Cannon leaned back against a countertop with his legs crossed. Cannon held a football in his hands, then tossed it upward in a spiral and caught it. Though he didn't say a word, he tossed it up again and again while staring straight through Coach Lewis. After a few suffocating moments of palpable tension, Haskins broke the silence.

"Martha, Tommy, Coach. Roy and I've been doing a lot of talking the last few days and he... well, he asked me yesterday if he could have the chance to say a few things to you, all of you... things that've been weighing pretty heavy on him. Roy, you ready, son?"

Roy stood and made a gesture to Coach Cannon and Cannon tossed him the football. Roy caught it, looked around the room then sat down on the edge of his grandfather's desk.

"Sorry, I kind of think better when I have the ball in my hands. Especially when I'm nervous." He gripped the football and passed it back and forth from one hand to another. To no one in particular, he continued. "I'll be honest. I've been struggling an awful lot with everything that's been happening lately. I haven't ever had anybody close to me die before. Only my great-grandmother and I only saw her a few times - really even before I was old enough to know her very good. Grandpa and I have talked a lot and that's helped, but this thing's got me pretty shook up.

"Autumn's... um, accident... put a lot of things into perspective for me. I used to think I had it all figured out and I knew what was important. Football. Pleasing certain people. Getting scholarships. Getting girls. My buddies. Sometimes in that order, sometimes not. I just ain't so sure anymore. I think I had some things out of whack on my list of what's really important, what's supposed to matter. I'm not sure how my head got screwed up before, but I have a few ideas." He cut a glance at Cannon out of the corner of his eyes. "I'm not saying I got anything figured out completely now, but I'm pretty sure I feel terrible that it took something like this to get my attention and make me try to focus. Anyone who knows me will tell you I won't usually admit when I'm hurting, no matter how bad it gets, but let me tell you I've been messed up since that night. I've never felt anything like this before and I still don't know how to sort this out.

"Coach," he said turning to Cannon, "you've been telling us to 'man up' and 'keep our emotions in check' and 'be strong' and a whole lot of other pretty worthless clichés like that. It's not helping any and I ain't the only one that thinks so. No disrespect, Coach, but I don't think you know to handle this any better than the rest of us do. So you should stop pretending."

Roy set the football down on the desk behind him.

"Coach Lewis, I know we don't know each other real well, but I have a few things I need to say to you. Ever since you showed up around here most of the guys have been making fun of you, laughing at you. At first there were lots of reasons: your car, your shaggy hair and your expensive city clothes, you coaching the girls. I don't know exactly what you told the girls when y'all started working out, but word on the street is you said they deserved attention and respect and the same things that everybody else gets around here. Crazy thing is, they started to believe it. Coach, don't get me wrong. I'm not gonna stand here and pretend I like watching girls play basketball because I don't. It's about the most boring thing ever. But here's what I'm trying to say. Me and all the guys have been pretty hard on you and the girls from day one. Same goes for the basketball team and the football players had a lot to do with that. We're the ones that tagged the water tower and made it look like the girls. We did some other stuff, too, probably things you don't even know about. But bottom line is, I'm sorry. I'm so, so sorry."

Now standing in front of Coach Lewis, Roy tried to keep his composure and "stay strong" and "keep his emotions in check" as Coach Lewis stood, shook his hand then embraced him and patted him on the back. Roy reciprocated then backed out of the embrace; Coach Lewis sat back down and grabbed Martha's hand again.

"Miss Martha," Roy said as he knelt in front of her on one knee. He didn't look at her face but rather hung his head and stared at the floor. Tears welled in Roy's eyes and rolled off his cheeks onto the cold, dirty linoleum below. "I need to say some things to you, too, and they won't be easy for me to say or for you to hear. As much as you could've hated me all this time for what happened with me and Summer, and then the way I haven't really been around for her and April, somehow you haven't. Autumn would tell me you'd say, 'Kill him with kindness and he'll come around. He's a nice boy, but he just needs to grow up a little more ' Miss Martha, I don't know what made you say that but..."

Roy's breathing grew erratic and labored as he tried to keep going. Martha reached out and took his hand in hers to calm him but Roy still couldn't bring himself to look at her.

"As awful as me and the guys were to all the girls on the basketball team, including your Summer and Autumn, y'all never would give in and just hate me or tell me to jump off a cliff. To be honest, I don't know who actually had more faith in me, you or Autumn. That kind of brings me to what I've been trying to tell you this whole time. The night...see, there's two things, really, about that night you need to know.

"First, and no one outside this room knows this, but Autumn was with me that night. We had been together just a few minutes before... you know. Not 'been together,' not like that, but we were talking. Out at the gravel pit. She'd been bugging the heck out of me for weeks to just give her thirty minutes to talk to me about Summer and April and being a man and doing the right thing. I finally gave in and we talked. She was pretty convincing and I think maybe she got my head spinning a little. We had our first long talk the night before, actually. I made her meet me at the gravel pit because I knew it would be private and dark and I didn't want anybody to see us together. I know that's terrible, but it's true. And I'm so ashamed of that. I really am. I actually called her the next day to meet me out there again that night, the night of the accident. I wanted to give her some money to give Summer to help out a little. Still kind of cowardly, I know, but as she said, I was 'making some progress and some's better than none.' If I hadn't called her and asked...

Martha squeezed his hand. A tear dripped from her cheek onto their hands in her lap.

"The second thing is this. The intersection where it happened… A while back, a bunch of us partied after a football game and… Oh, God, I'm so sorry. We stole some stop signs, and…"

Martha leaned forward and put her head on his.

"Shhh, now, darling. You know what the police report said. That fellow's heart gave out. You know that."

"But what if we hadn't taken that one? Maybe he would have been able to…"

Martha, emotions no longer in check and tears cascading over the bags under her eyes, slid forward out of the chair and knelt on the floor in front Roy. Roy wept. Martha put her fingers under Roy's chin and gently lifted his face to hers. As his red, teary eyes met hers, Martha touched her fingers to his lips. With her other hand she pulled a tissue from inside her coat pocket and wiped his cheeks dry. She leaned forward, kissed him on the forehead and pulled him into an embrace. She whispered into his ear and, with that, Roy buried his face on her shoulder and sobbed until the shoulder of her wool coat grew dark with his tears. What she said, neither Martha nor Roy ever repeated.

Behind the desk, Haskins sat with his face buried in hands, also sobbing, a broken man. As he had agreed the day before with Roy, he hadn't interrupted, no matter what. Roy had insisted it was time for him to be a man and, as hard as it was to sit and listen, Haskins held up his end of the deal. During Roy's monologue, Cannon had turned and faced the bulletin board, pretending to read the old newspaper clippings thumb-tacked to the board. Coach Lewis sat in disbelief, shell-shocked by all he'd heard and the display of emotion he'd just witnessed, but still unsure about the upcoming district games not to mention his own future at Lazarus High School. In light of what he'd just seen play out, he felt terribly guilty for even thinking about basketball games and his job.

After a pregnant, awkward silence, Cannon excused himself then returned with a cup of coffee. Roy then excused himself and returned to find everyone stoic and statue-like, seated or standing in the same places and positions as when he left. Everyone in the room knew there was one issue left to discuss but no one wanted to be the first to break the silence. Coach Lewis wrestled with what to do next and finally convinced himself to speak up. He looked up and noticed that Haskins, Martha and Roy each were staring expectantly at Cannon, who had returned to browsing the bulletin board. Coach Lewis joined in and the weight of the collective stares finally pulled Coach Cannon away from the faded memories tacked on the bulletin board. Cannon turned and discovered all eyes on focused on him.

"That was a very emotional speech, Roy, and we all appreciate your honesty, but guys, this is not a good idea on any level. I think we all know that."

"Speak for yourself," Martha rebutted.

Roy followed suit.

"You can't hold all this against the girls, Coach. I think they actually need this. Maybe we all do."

Cannon crossed his arms in defiance and clenched his jaw. He exchanged silent, steely stares with each person in the office then turned back to stare at the wall. Finally, Cannon turned to Haskins, who had been quiet for a very long time. Cannon and Haskins stared at one another then Haskins stood and walked over to Cannon. He placed his right arm on Cannon's shoulder, leaned in and whispered, "Fine. Then *you* explain this to Martha. *You* explain this to Summer.

And *you* explain this to all the girls. And their parents. By yourself."
Haskins patted Cannon on the shoulder, motioned for Roy and Martha
to follow him, then left, leaving the two coaches sitting alone in the
office.

Cannon picked up the football from Haskins' desk, turned back to
the bulletin board and said, "Looks like you got what you wanted,
Lewis. When you've made a mess of all this in a few weeks, I'm gonna
remind everybody that this is exactly what you wanted, against my
better judgment. Credit where credit is due. Remember that."

Coach Lewis wanted to smile, to grin, to show enthusiasm
somehow, but he figured a display of emotion probably wouldn't sit
well with Cannon at the moment and he'd been on the receiving end of
Cannon's wrath one too many times already. Without saying a word,
he stood and headed back to the parking lot where he knew his girls
waited anxiously for the news.

Walking down the dark hallway lit only by the mid-morning
sunlight filtering in through the glass doors at the end of the hall, he
noticed again the trophies and plaques lining the hall. He was reminded
again of his slim chance of success by the conspicuous absence of girls'
hardware on the shelves of the trophy cases. As he reached the glass
double doors leading outside, he could contain his emotions no longer.
He flung the doors open and practically skipped back to his Blazer
grinning ear to ear.

He thought about the question he'd asked himself earlier. Feeling
now like he had a second shot at a coaching life, Coach Lewis answered
his own question by telling himself he'd take all the lumps and bumps
again if given the choice. Then his mind drifted suddenly to Autumn.
He felt foolish and stupid for thinking about his own struggles. He

changed his mind and decided he wouldn't do any of it over again, ever, and he'd never have picked up a whistle, and he'd never have driven to Lazarus in the first place, if he could go back and prevent all the pain and loss everyone else had to deal with since he had arrived. He suddenly felt numb, despite the good news.

Back in the parking lot, Coach Lewis delivered the good tidings to the girls even though his heart remained heavy. The girls then scattered to parts unknown, excited and somehow hopeful once again. Coach Lewis, on the other hand, took a long drive to sort things out and to try to clear his head.

When Cannon was sure Lewis and the girls had left the parking lot, he climbed into his truck, turned the key in the ignition then reached for his cell phone in the glove compartment. He thumbed through his contacts then dialed.

"Hey, buddy, what's going on in Nazareth these days? Good Christmas? Kind of weird around here. Exactly. Listen, we've had some developments here you're gonna want to know about. Got a minute to talk?"

CHAPTER XIII

Gabe Lewis settled into his favorite booth and ran his hand over the vinyl seat. He'd been in there to eat a half-dozen times since the diner reopened. As odd as it was to him, something about Mary's Kitchen made him feel at home, at ease. The sound of the country music over the speakers, the smell of the cooking grease wafting from the fryers, the chicken fried steak and gravy, even the sound of the old fashioned cash register opening and closing made Gabe feel safe and secure.

Martha's return to work full time helped move the diner back toward a feeling of normalcy though the general mood in the place still remained somewhat somber, certainly a reflection of the pathos of the entire community. Well-wishers occasionally stopped by to grab pie and coffee and to leave Martha kind words written on their receipts, but things weren't like they were before. Without Autumn's smiling face around the place, Mary's Kitchen never would be exactly the same again. Gabe knew it, and he knew he would never be the same, either. He'd been naïve to think he'd bounce back quickly and easily from losing Autumn, much the same way he'd been naïve to think he could waltz into Bethany County and change things that had been part of life there for generations. The greenhorn coach had been just as foolish to believe his girls would play inspired basketball and win games on inspiration, emotion and adrenaline alone. Just three games into the ten-game district schedule and he found himself revisiting the question of whether he would sign up for this again if given the chance. As he swirled his brown gravy into his mashed potatoes, the Reverend Brother Elijah Washington slid into the booth across the table from him.

"Mind if I join you?"

"Not at all. Glad for the company, sir, to be honest."

"I noticed. I've been sitting over there watching you and you've done nothing but play with your food. Seems like you're a million miles away, Coach. Still carrying the weight of the world on your shoulders, huh? Nairobi mentioned to me that she's worried about you."

"Worried about me? No need. Really, I'm doing fine." He avoided eye contact as he tried to dodge Reverend Washington's question.

"Is that so?" the pastor asked with a bit of chuckle.

"Yes, sir. Really." He could feel the pastor's all-seeing eyes staring into his soul and he suddenly felt uncomfortable. "Actually, I'm kind of tired, I guess. Emotionally. I thought things would be better by now."

"How so?"

"Well, the girls are still kind of like zombies right now. On the court, I mean. They seem to get through the days fine, but there's no fire in their bellies once they hit the gym. I guess I thought the gym would be the one place they could leave behind all their problems and their grief. You know, the 'check your emotions at the door' kind of stuff coaches always tell their players. I thought basketball and the whole team thing would be cathartic for them. And for me. I guess it might be more so if we were winning instead of getting killed... bad choice of words. Sorry. Instead of getting pounded every time we get on the floor."

The Reverend Brother Washington shifted into pastoral mode and let the young man share his heart. He waved over the waitress and ordered two cups of coffee but never let his attention wander from Coach Lewis.

"This is what I don't get," Coach Lewis continued. "Our first two practices back after, you know, were kind of rough. I figured they would be. But even though we felt like we didn't quite have our legs back under us and we didn't quite have much intensity during the practices, we thought playing that first game back against Kress would be really liberating. We should've been able to compete with them."

Coach Lewis ran his fingers through his shaggy blond hair and exhaled in frustration.

"I spent hours coming up with the pregame speech about playing for Autumn and her memory. I was fired up. The girls were all crying and I thought we were all ready to take on the world coming out of the locker room. When Sam won the opening tip, I remember thinking we were about to write our own fairy tale ending to the season. Then Sam came down with the ball, threw a weak pass down court to MJ that got picked off, and we got layed-up at the other end. Things never got any better after that. We were down thirty at the half, they dropped back in a zone and we pretty much went through the motions the rest of the game."

"That's what I heard," answered the pastor. "Must have been tough for the girls to look out on the court or down the bench or across the locker room and not see that #20 jersey and that blond ponytail bobbing up and down."

"I imagine it was. I internalized that loss pretty bad. The way I figured it, I didn't have them prepared emotionally or physically for that first game back. Thinking back on it, I didn't coach hard enough during the game. You know, I've been thinking and I've come to the conclusion I let those girls down."

"How so?"

"Because it was my job to have them ready."

The Reverend shifted in his seat, his large body obviously uncomfortable in the booth.

"Now, Coach, you're being a little hard on yourself, don't you think?"

Coach Lewis ignored the question and went on.

"I really believed winning the next game would fix things and take their minds off everything. I pushed them hard in practice and coached even harder in the second game against Happy. Kind of ironic, huh?"

"What is?" he asked as he leaned forward and put his large, crossed arms on the edge of the table between them.

"A bunch of depressed girls in a depressed little town losing a basketball game, the first district game at home, to a team from Happy, Texas. I couldn't make that up. At some point during the second half when things were out of reach for us, I found myself wondering if Lazarus would ever be happy again, if the town would ever come back to life. I also remember thinking just after tip-off that the gym and the handful of people in the gym seemed as dead the town has seemed lately. Are we ever gonna shake this?"

Coach Lewis meant the question to be rhetorical and carried on before the pastor had a chance to respond.

"Going into the Silverton game, Sam got pretty fired up in the locker room and made a big pregame speech. She went off during the game and completely dominated, but it was like she was taking on the whole team by herself. Silverton couldn't stop Sam, but they knew she couldn't beat the team by herself so they just let Sam wear herself out. Great game for her but now we're sitting at 0-3. So much for our fairy-tale ending, huh?"

"OK, Coach, let's take a look at this," he said without looking up. He scribbled on a card as he spoke. "You just lost one of your players so you're dealing with a team that has lost a friend and you're one basketball player short. You have another player out for personal health reasons. That means you're down to six girls and only three of them have any talent, at all. Nairobi told me way back when you first showed up on the scene that you preached over and over about the journey and the destination. Sometimes when I'm struggling, Coach, I go back and reread my own sermons. I often wonder when I revisit old sermons if God didn't somehow have me write those sermons just for me."

The Reverend Brother Washington stood, grabbed both checks from the table, then slid the card on which he'd been writing across the table. He shook the coach's hand, gave him a "Good luck tonight" nod and headed to the cash register. Coach Lewis flipped over the card and read the handwritten note: "He gives strength to the weary and increases the power of the weak. Even youths grow tired and weary, and young men (and young women!) stumble and fall; but those who hope in the Lord will renew their strength. Deliverance will come. – E. Washington."

The shocks and the suspension system, being entirely worn out, transferred the energy of every bump and pothole on the west-Texas highway through the bottom of the bus, through the seats and into the tired bodies of the Lady Longhorns. One of the windows on the bus remained stuck in the down position and the open window had been covered up with the taped-together front and back of someone's chemistry textbook. Neither the heater nor the radio worked. The wipers worked occasionally, even when they were turned off. Nevertheless, the girls once again scored this bus for an away game.

"We always get stuck with the short bus," Molly said. "We get treated like retards and the boys get a big bus. Something about that ain't right."

MJ replied, "You know, you say that every time we take this bus. It's getting old."

"The bus or my comments about it?"

MJ smiled, realizing Molly only wanted to ease the tension.

Cassie spoke up from the front of the bus, "Sam, you were awesome tonight. Maybe next game we'll give you some more help."

"I shouldn't have picked up that last foul," Sam answered as she pounded the back of the seat. "We can't afford anyone fouling out now. Down two people, we need all hands on deck. I'll do better next time."

"Cassie's right, Sam," said Nairobi. She scooted up two seats to slide in next to Sam. "You did your part. We just all came out flat. Not what I expected after the way we came out of the locker room, you know?"

"You know what else?"

"What, Sam?"

"This little bitty seat wasn't built for two big ol' tall people like us."

Everyone chuckled, even though they had to force themselves. The girls all had the same thing on their minds but nobody wanted, or knew quite how, to address it or even bring up the subject. The Lady Kangaroos of Kress were a beatable team; on any other night the Lady Longhorns had as good a shot at beating them as they did any team on the schedule. The Lady Kangaroos had graduated their post players last year and no one moved up to replace them. Sam and Nairobi should have owned the Roos on both ends of the floor, but it didn't happen. Sam indeed did her part despite looking and feeling uninspired. Nairobi, like the rest of the team, showed up in body only; none of the rest of the team really showed up ready to play.

Sam turned to MJ and said, "MJ, what happened to that jumper?"

"Good question. Didn't make the trip with me, I guess. My dad's gonna kill me."

"I'm not talking about it not going in. I'm talking about where'd it go? You took four shots then quit shooting, like you were afraid or something. They were pounding me down low and you were wide open outside. I've never seen you not shoot those before."

MJ shrugged it off, but Brooklynne chimed in for her.

"When I get back on the court, I'm gonna be deadly from out there. All I've been doing since I've been out is shooting threes."

Molly slugged Brooklynne on the shoulder and said, "Whatever!"

Rather uncharacteristically, Rita hardly said a word all the way home from Kress. She'd had perhaps the worst game of the lot with more fouls and turnovers than points and assists combined. Perhaps no one's surprise, Summer sat in silence the entire trip. For her, what happened on the court mattered little. Rather, Autumn's conspicuous absence from the spot in the seat next to her kept her mind a million miles away the whole night. She didn't even smile when the opposing coach made a trip over to the Lazarus bench to give her a card signed by all the Lady Kangaroos; she'd looked at the floor and taken it from the coach with only a muttered "Thanks." The girls realized Summer had drifted off, but gave her space.

The chatter settled down as the evening grew late and cold and as the girls bundled themselves in their blankets and jackets. The uncomfortable bus ride back finally came to a grinding halt when the short bus lurched into what should have been its final resting place behind the gym back at Lazarus High school. The girls each told Coach Lewis "good night" as they exited and headed to the frosted-over vehicles waiting for them in the parking lot. To each, he replied, "Be careful going home. See you tomorrow." To each, he said that, except for Brooklynne.

"Brooklynne," he said. "Can you hang back for a minute? I have a question for you."

Brooklynne's stomach tightened into a knot; she knew exactly what he wanted. Brooklynne started the season on the ineligible list and finally got her grades back up at semester. Unfortunately, another far more embarrassing situation landed her on the bench yet again just as her grades had peaked in the C range. She'd put the word out that she got into poison ivy or poison oak over the Christmas holidays. That was the official story intended to keep her out of trouble. It was not, however, the truth.

"Brooklynne, I hate to ask this but I think I need to because I'm getting conflicting stories."

Her eyes went straight to the frozen ground beneath her feet.

"You told me the rash you have all over you came from poison oak or something you picked up at your dad's deer lease over the holidays."

"Yes, sir," she affirmed in a tentative, whispered voice.

"Word on the street is something entirely different. Something about insulation."

Brooklynne kept quiet as her cheeks turned Longhorn red.

"I'd like you tell me the truth, please. You're not in trouble and I'm not your parent but I feel like you owe me the truth."

"Yes, sir. It's real embarrassing, though. Promise you won't repeat this?"

"Well, if neither you're health nor your safety is at risk, I can promise not to say anything."

"No, sir. It's nothing like that."

"OK, then. Go ahead."

Brooklynne drew a deep breath, covered her face with her hands and began.

"Well, I was with my boyfriend, you know, Kenny Buckley. We were at Kenny's house the day after the funeral and his parents were gone. Anyway, we were in his barn and it was really cold and we wanted to, um, hang out some, together... You know how in the movies the actors are always rolling around in the hay and getting' frisky? Well, the hay was really smelly and pokey and kind of damp, but the insulation in the top of his barn was all soft and dry."

Coach Lewis put up his hand and turned his head.

"OK, I appreciate your honesty but I think we can stop there. I'm pretty sure I get the idea and that's probably way too much information."

"Promise you won't tell anyone? I know everybody thinks I'm dumb already and they're probably right but if everybody finds that out they'll never forget about it and never let me forget, either. Promise?"

"Believe me. Not a word. Thanks for telling me... I think. Be careful going home, Brooklynne."

"Good night, Coach" she said as she headed away from the bus.

Coach Lewis called out after her, "Hey, Brooklynne."

She paused and looked over her shoulder at him as she fumbled in her gym bag for her keys.

"You're a sweet kid. And you're not dumb."

Brooklynne turned back and started walking again. A grin, a genuine smile, in fact, appeared on her itchy red face and it stayed there the rest of the night.

The Lady Longhorns looked forward to being back in their own gym after traveling to Kress for their first district game. The last two home games for the girls, and in fact the only two home games of the past month, resulted in a solid win over Shallowater and a miraculous, if not unforgettable, win over Whiteface. The girls knew they'd need more magic, though, if they were to have a chance against Happy. The Cowgirls of Happy had rolled into town to wrangle the Lady Longhorns of Lazarus and the irony was not lost on Coach Lewis.

If the Lady Longhorns were glad to be playing at home, the Cowgirls were anything but happy to be next on the schedule for Lazarus. They knew the hour-and-a-half bus ride would be miserable.

They knew they would have to put up with heckling and jeers, usually from the boys basketball team just before they take the court, usually something to the effect of, "Let us make you Happy Cowgirls." However, the Cowgirls knew long before they set out on the drive from Happy through Tulia, Nazareth, and Dimmitt to Lazarus that the Lady Longhorns were not to be feared. What the Cowgirls feared most manifested itself as they exited the bus and entered the gym early Friday evening: that the somber atmosphere in Lazarus would suck the joy and the life right out of them. Everyone in and around Bethany County had heard about the accident and about the basketball team. The story had been run on the news in Lubbock and had been printed in most of the newspapers within a sixty-mile radius.

A few of the Cowgirls wondered to themselves as they got off the bus if they were early or even in the right place because so few cars were parked at the school. Things didn't improve for the Cowgirls as they entered the gym, expecting the aroma of freshly popped popcorn, warm nacho cheese and roasting hot dogs to greet them in the lobby. What they found instead was a lobby with the concession stand closed, a gym with no warm-up music playing, and the thud thud thud of only a few basketballs bouncing on the gym floor. As they wandered into the quiet gym, a man greeted them, pointed them in the direction of the visitors' locker room then disappeared into an office.

Inside the office sat the General with his legs propped up on his desk and Coach Cannon across the desk from him. Bill Merrick stood in the corner of the office next to the door through which he had just come after pointing the Cowgirls to their locker room.

Merrick chuckled. "Should've seen those poor girls. They looked like they wanted to be here even less than our girls do. Rotten for them to have to drive all this way for no competition against a bunch of numb kids who probably don't even want to be playing. Tommy, why'd you let Haskins talk you into this anyway?"

The General shifted his gaze from Merrick to Cannon.

"They kind of had me in a pinch. I already told you that. Just drop it. That's not something I want to talk about. Anyway, run down to the concession stand and grab an armful of drinks, a few bags of chips and maybe a candy bar apiece. Here's my key to get in. I told the Booster Club just to come for the boys' game since we wouldn't have much draw for the girls' game. Hustle and get back in here before the game gets started."

Bill Merrick made his way through the gym along the sideline and never once looked up. He never saw the six Lady Longhorns attempting warm-ups on one end nor the twelve athletic Cowgirls running precision drills on the other end. He missed Coach Lewis, who was sitting at the far end of the Lady Longhorns' bench next to Brooklynne who still looked like she had contracted some rare, tropical disease. He missed Dee standing in his usual spot, leaning on his push-broom and quietly supporting the girls as he had all season long. He heard but never looked up to see the hundred or so fans who had made the trip from Happy all the way to the Lazarus visitors' section to cheer the Cowgirls to certain victory. He completely missed the fifteen or so parents and other interested persons sitting behind the Lady Longhorns' bench waiting for tipoff. Bill Merrick also failed to notice perhaps the two most conspicuous Longhorn supporters seated by themselves on the top row of the bleachers, leaned back against the cold metal of the gym wall: Calvin Haskins and Roy Haskins.

Bill Merrick returned from the concession stand loaded for bear, but didn't feel the weight of the stares of the hungry basketball fans in the bleachers whose envious eyes followed him from baseline to baseline. He disappeared into the General's office where the three men waited until the girls' game finished and the warm up time for the boys' game arrived. The three passed the time telling old gridiron war stories, eating contraband from the concession stand and watching game film of the Happy Cowboys basketball team that would take the court shortly after the Cowgirls made quick work of the girls from Lazarus.

While the team put forth a poor overall effort, Sam turned in a dominant performance, outscoring every other player in the gym that night, and both Cassie and MJ made strides. As Coach Lewis had always told them, though, every player has to play hard every minute of every period. It simply didn't happen against Happy, despite intense practices during the week, and the scoreboard reflected it. The Cowgirls proved that good teams really don't take into account the emotional state of their opponents when executing a game plan; the Cowgirls doled out no sympathy, just a good old fashioned whipping.

Cannon, Merrick and the General found themselves nonplussed by the downer atmosphere in the gym upon exiting the General's office. Neither Cannon, nor Merrick nor the General anticipated any carryover of the doldrums from the girls' game to the boys' game. That, at least, happened to be their explanation for the quiet, detached and distant fans scattered throughout the gym. The numb Longhorn fans sat idly by and never invested themselves emotionally in the basketball game. Despite there being scores more Longhorn fans for the boys' game, the energy level never moved beyond the depressing, lifeless level of the earlier game. In reality, the general mood of the

Lazarus fans that night reflected the emotional state of the entire town, not just the few people gathered to watch the girls earlier. Though most people in Lazarus kept telling themselves that time heals all things, the lingering mood of the town offered no evidence that the cliché was in fact true.

The following Tuesday, the Lady Longhorns climbed on the short bus yet again to ride off toward the horizon and play in another desolate Texas locale. This road trip, eighty-five miles down the road with one right turn, took the girls to Silverton to face the beatable Lady Owls. The Lady Owls were better-than-average at best but they had no answer for Sam and Nairobi, at least on paper. Nairobi flailed her way into foul trouble early on so the burden fell on Sam to do all the work. Through it all, Coach Lewis managed to coach his best game yet and to get within a basket with just under a minute left on the clock. Nairobi had already fouled out so when Rita fouled out, too, late in the game, the Lady Longhorns found themselves playing one player short: four-on-five basketball. The Lady Owls won by three points.

After the game, the girls made their way back to the bus with some hope stemming from their improved play, yet some despair at the prospect of being winless through three district games. As they exited the gym, Coach Lewis made a point to speak to each of his players, to tell them he was proud of them, and to encourage them to be proud of their gutsy performance. When the last of the girls headed away from the gym to climb aboard, Coach Lewis found himself standing alone in the dark with three other men. He squinted and recognized them to be Molly's father, MJ's father and Nairobi's father.

Jasperson broke the silence and spoke for the group.

"Coach, that was a close one there tonight. Just about pulled that one out. Nice job." He paused for a moment and fumbled in his pockets with his keys and his change. "Coach, we've been talking amongst ourselves all season, but especially since we all came back after the accident and since you convinced everybody to let the girls play. Not too sure how you did that, by the way. We'd heard it was all a done deal. Anyway, we weren't too sure you were doing the right thing by putting our girls back out there, truth be told. But we think you made the right call."

Jasperson withdrew his hand from his pocket and extended it toward Coach Lewis.

"Coach, I know we all hadn't always seen eye to eye, me and you in particular, but I think you're a genuine guy. A nice guy. We've been watching how you handle our girls and, well, we're pretty thankful for you now, actually. Anyway, we're behind you, Coach. Rest of the way."

Coach Lewis shook Jasperson's hand, then Frost's, almost unbelievably, then Whitaker's, then the three dads walked away and left the coach alone in the dark. Dumbstruck by what just transpired, Coach Lewis stood there momentarily then noticed a figure walking back toward him. It was Whitaker.

"Coach," he said in sort of a whisper, "I never had a problem with you. Nairobi and me, we always liked you."

Whitaker gave the coach a huge toothy smile, patted Coach Lewis on the shoulder and followed the other dads back into the dark.

When Coach Lewis arrived at the gym to begin the usual pre-game preparations, he found the parking lot already occupied by a number of vehicles he recognized. Before heading into the gym, he checked his clothes one last time for any signs of leftover chicken fried steak, mashed potatoes or gravy that might have fallen into his lap at Mary's Kitchen just a little while earlier. Coach Lewis knew clichés often were tired, worn out and overused, but he couldn't help thinking "now or never" about the impending game with the Hart Lady Longhorns in a few hours. This was the most beatable team in the district and his girls couldn't afford to let this one slip away if they were to salvage any part of the season.

Inside, the gym lay silent except for the incessant hum of the lights overhead. Coach Lewis stood on the baseline near his office and daydreamed about full bleachers, rabid fans, and a scoreboard with more points for the home team than for the visitors. He heard in his mind the squeak of basketball shoes on the freshly refinished playing surface, the pop of the nets as the ball found its way home over and over. *Maybe next year*, he thought as the daydream, pleasant as it was, evaporated as quickly as it had appeared in his mind.

At the other end of the gym, sitting in the second row of the bleachers, were two figures. He could tell from the letterman jacket that one of the figures was Roy Haskins. Coach Lewis leaned his head to the side just a bit and was able to make out Summer's face just over Roy's shoulder. Coach Lewis then noticed Dee mopping in the other corner of the gym. Dee paused for a moment, motioned subtly across the gym toward Summer and Roy, then winked and smiled at Coach Lewis. Coach Lewis smiled back and let himself into his office. As he set his clipboard down on his desk, he realized the vehicles in the parking lot indicated more girls were here but they certainly weren't warming up in the gym yet; he decided to check the locker room.

271

Coach Lewis knocked on the locker room door, always cautious about the private space that belonged to the girls. He knew the girls were inside because he could hear them mulling around and talking in low voices. After a moment, Rita opened the door a few inches and pressed her puffy, tear-stained face to the crack. She smiled just a little and opened the door for him.

Inside Coach Lewis found his girls seated in a circle on the floor already dressed in their uniforms save one important part. Each of the girls had her basketball shoes in her lap and had a magic marker in her hand. Sam stood and greeted her coach with a smile, then grabbed a stool for him to sit on. He followed her lead, sat and watched the girls without saying a word. Something had come over the girls. They seemed different, quiet, focused. All had been crying, some still let tears slide down their cheeks as they worked, though they seemed not unhappy but rather calm, at ease. Coach Lewis reached down and picked up the basketball shoe lying closest to him, Cassie's, and examined it. On the heel of her left shoe, on the small field of white leather just above the rubber of the sole, Cassie had written in black permanent marker "20," Autumn's jersey number. Cassie noticed her coach for the first time and handed him her other shoe. Where she had written "20" on her left shoe, Cassie had drawn a simple smiley face on her right shoe with tiny hearts where the eyes should have been. Coach Lewis pondered it for a moment then looked to Cassie.

"She was always smiling, you know? Always."

"Yep, you're right," he said. "Always smiling."

Coach Lewis handed the shoes back to Cassie, then took note of the jumbled pile of shoes in the center of the circle of socked feet on the locker room floor. Each pair had "20" on the left shoe, but had something different written or drawn on the right shoe. One shoe bore a musical note, another a cross, another the words "miss you," another a basketball, another the letters "BF," another a sun and the last a heart. The girls picked up random shoes one at a time, examined them thoughtfully then passed them around for everyone else to see and hold.

Rita interrupted the hush that had fallen over the girls. "Coach, we've been here talking for a while and we think we've got our heads on straight. We got a lot cleared up and figured out. See, we've been goin' at this all wrong. We've been trying so hard, not wanting to mess up, trying not to get beat. We remembered some really smart guy told us one time a long time ago to quit tryin' not to lose but to play to win instead. I think that's what we've been doing here since the accident – tryin' to not let this thing beat us. We know now we gotta' play to beat this thing instead of the other way around. Right, *chicas*?"

The girls applauded and laughed in approval.

"Are we still talking about basketball here?"

"You tell us, coach."

"Sounds like there's not much else for me to say."

"You," said MJ as she jumped to her feet and pointed at Coach Lewis, "will see a different team out there tonight."

Sam stood and added, "It don't matter to us how many people are there or not. We're playing anyway with all we got. We don't care what everybody else says or does anymore. We control what we can control and let the chips fall where they may."

Nairobi tossed her "20" shoe at Coach Lewis and chimed in. "And Autumn's still a part of this team, in case you're wondering. We've all been tiptoeing around this like it was some kinda ghost haunting us, but it is what it is and we owe it to Autumn to keep going and keep pushing."

"Well, then," said Coach Lewis, "let's get this new team laced up, warmed up and ready to play. See you on the court in five for warm-ups."

As he left the locker room, he poked his head back in before the door shut completely. He looked briefly at each of his girls, making eye contact with each. "I love you guys... and I wouldn't trade you guys for any team anywhere. I mean that."

Cassie grinned ear to ear and answered, "We know, Coach."

"And when I say 'guys,' you know I really mean..."

Sam interrupted with, "We know that, too. Get out of here," then tossed a basketball at the door as a playful exclamation point.

As the team warmed up and went through the drills as best they could with only six players, and with Brooklynne sitting on the bench next to her coach hopefully for the final time of the season, the team looked different. The girls smiled but with intensity, not giddiness. They cut hard, they snapped their passes back and forth, they moved with purpose. When the referee tossed the ball for the opening jump ball, hardly anything looked or felt different throughout the rest of the gym. Two dozen Lady Longhorn supporters sat scattered behind the home team bench, and even Dee had propped his push-broom in the corner and joined the fans in the stands. Roughly two or three times as many fans made the trip to watch the other Lady Longhorns, the ones from Hart. Coach Lewis overanalyzed the Longhorns versus the Longhorns. *We've been playing against ourselves a lot lately and here we are doing it again. Maybe we get it right tonight.*

Get it right, they did. By the end of the first period, Lazarus looked like a team possessed as they threatened to win this one going away. Sam already had a double-double with rebounds and points. Rita had five steals, a handful of assists and no turnovers. No one had gotten into foul trouble. Every player had logged quality minutes. Granted, Hart hardly counted as a formidable opponent, but the girls from Lazarus could not have cared any less nor performed any better.

The emotions and the adrenaline faded some after halftime, but the team still turned in one of its best performances of the season, behind only the miracle game against Whiteface and the upset of Shallowater. At the sound of the final buzzer, the girls rushed their coach and they embraced one another in relief. Behind the bench, an unfamiliar sound rolled down the bleachers and washed over the team. They turned to see their parents and a couple of their friends standing and applauding, something the girls hadn't seen in quite some time. They shook hands with their opponents at mid-court then raced to the locker room.

Once inside, the girls danced around delirious with joy and exhaustion. Just as Coach Lewis quieted his team, the door opened and Summer strolled in, clipboard and stats in hand. She tugged on her coach's shirt and told him she had something he had to see. She handed him the clipboard and he read over the stat sheet, three times. The girls picked up on the boyish wonder now apparent on their coach's face. Finally, after a moment of silent wonder, the girls shrugged their shoulders and looked at him with wide eyes. Coach Lewis motioned for the girls to take a seat; his eyes still searched the clipboard in his hand.

"Ladies, I've got some interesting news for you. I have to watch the game film to verify this but…" He took the pencil from summer and double-checked her math again. "Looks like Sam did something pretty unusual tonight."

"Yea," Sam piped up. "I didn't foul out for a change!"

Everyone laughed and high-fived Sam.

"Well, that, too. More remarkable, though, Sam got a quadruple double tonight."

Leave it to Brooklynne to weigh in with her profundity. "What the heck is that, Coach?" Sounds like a Dairy Queen combo meal."

From across the locker room, a basketball sailed and ricocheted off Brooklynne's head as the girls rolled with laughter.

"It's when a player hits double digits in four different statistical categories," he explained. "Points, rebounds, you know. Anyway, here's Sam's line for tonight. Thirty-two points, seventeen rebounds, eleven assists and ten blocked shots. Sam, that's unbelievable."

The girls whooped and hollered and piled on top of Sam.

"I don't know if you guys understand, but statistically this almost never happens. If I remember right, I think only about four guys have ever done this in the NBA in the last thirty-five years or so. Hardly any more in college… maybe five or six. Sam, congratulations. You need to let this sink in for a while. Here's the great thing, Sam: nobody can ever take this away from you. Here's the great thing for the rest of you guys, too: Sam couldn't have done this without great team play from all of you. I'm so, so proud of you. All of you. You have twenty-four hours to celebrate and enjoy this one because we've got to get to work since we're headed to Nazareth next. Let's go see everyone outside waiting for you."

When the girls emerged from the locker room, the fans had made their way down from the bleachers and had posted themselves outside the locker room. They greeted the girls like the team had just won a huge game. There were hugs and handshakes and smiles all around. Coach Lewis made his way out of the huddle and eased down the sideline, but not before Martha grabbed his arm and stopped him.

"Nice one, coach," was all she said, and she nodded at him once, but her eyes twinkled just for a second and made Coach Lewis wonder if she might not be coming back around.

Coach Lewis smiled and reciprocated the nod in appreciation, then headed to his office to review the film and call the score in to the newspaper. As he made his way past mid-court where Cannon stood with his arms crossed talking to the General, he stopped just long enough to whisper to the two men, "Sam just dropped a quadruple double on that team."

Without hesitation, Cannon turned and said, "That team's terrible; talk to me when she does something meaningful against a real team," then returned to his conversation with the General.

Rounding out the first half of the district schedule for Lazarus were the Nazareth Swiftettes. Nazareth, or Naz in some circles, had been a perennial powerhouse in small school girls basketball in Texas. The Swiftettes had won numerous state titles and they boasted a trophy case full of various hardware from the best tournaments all over the state. The team had even been featured once on ESPN. The place had developed a reputation as a girls basketball machine, producing great team after great team. The team waiting for Lazarus to roll into town wouldn't go down in history as one of the great Nazareth teams, but the girls from Nazareth already had won twenty-four games in the season with six games yet to be played. The girls were fast, well-coached, well-disciplined and known state-wide for their killer instinct. When the Swiftettes found an opponent down for the count, they pushed harder to make sure the opponent had no chance of getting back up. The Swiftettes were a team no one wanted to play. Unfortunately, Lazarus had no choice.

The night of the game, the Lady Longhorns emerged from the locker room to find a packed gym with two dozen Swiftette fans for every one Lazarus fan. The atmosphere bordered on pandemonium. The Nazareth fans had come to watch a public beating and they expected nothing less. The tall, lanky coach, who visited with Coach Cannon at mid-court for nearly half an hour and talked about old times before the game, never glanced a single time at the seven girls warming up in front of his bench. Likewise, the Swiftettes paid no attention to the ragtag unit at the other end of the floor. In the minds of nearly everyone in the gym, the outcome of this game had long since been decided.

As far as Coach Lewis could see, he had two things going for him as he headed into this impossible game. First, he had momentum. While one game does not momentum make, the girls had been improving ever so slightly over the last few games and that had to count for something. Second, the Lady Longhorns had a secret weapon: Brooklynne. The secret weapon was so secret that even Coach Lewis had no idea what to expect. He couldn't wait to find out, though.

The ball sailed high above the gym floor for the opening tip, and the home team lived up to the hype right away. The Swiftettes' point guard, a University of Texas signee named Whitney Huff, stole the opening tip right out of Rita's hands, took two dribbles and made a rocket pass to her teammate who slashed to the basket for an easy layup. Immediately, the Swiftettes went into a relentless full-court, in-your-face, man-to-man press; the Naz press far exceeded what the guys had done against the girls back in the early preseason scrimmage that cost the boys the gym. The home team quickly stole Molly's inbounds pass, drove toward the basket then kicked the ball back outside for a quick, uncontested three-pointer. Back into the press they went, pushing and shoving on all four Lady Longhorns who scrambled frantically trying to get open for the inbounds pass. Nadine Collier, the tall, scrawny post assigned to Sam, pounded her elbows into Sam's ribs as the two jockeyed for position. Just before the baseline official whistled Lazarus for a five second violation, he blew the whistle and charged Sam's defender with a foul. The action resumed. Molly threw the ball away again on the inbounds pass and Huff rifled the ball effortlessly across the court to an unguarded player in the corner who buried a second three in less than ten seconds. Frustrated, Sam called a time out and the Longhorns sulked as they retreated to the safety of their bench.

Down 8-0 less than a minute into the game, Coach Lewis sat his players on the bench to calm them down. He drew up their press break on his clipboard to remind everyone where they should be and what they should do to advance the ball up the court. Finally, on a hunch, he subbed in Brooklynne for Molly, who seemed flustered.

Coming out of the time out, the Lady Longhorns perfectly executed the press break, moved the ball up the floor and pressured the defense. Rita kicked the ball out to Brooklynne on the perimeter. As

Brooklynne's defender closed on her, she dumped the ball down low to Sam. With a head fake and powerful drop-step, Sam got the bucket and drew a quick foul on the scrawny girl assigned to shut down Sam. Collier, who stood as tall as Sam at about 6'3" tall, gave up about thirty pounds to Sam, so she stood very little chance of matching up with Sam all night. Sam knew it and Coach Lewis knew it. Collier would figure it out later. Sam sank the free throw and the action resumed.

By the end of the first half, the Lady Longhorns had managed to hang around and trailed by only four points. The Swiftettes pounded each of the players throughout the first two periods every chance they got. The officials let the girls play and blew the whistle only for the most egregious fouls. Nairobi had provided valuable support for Sam down low, Rita and MJ had handled the ball well with few turnovers despite the intense pressure of the Nazareth defense, and Cassie had come up with a few nice defensive plays to prevent easy baskets here and there. The biggest surprise, though, came in the form of four three-pointers and four assists from the one and only Brooklynne Meyers. Brooklynne had been telling everyone for weeks she'd been practicing her three-point shooting, but everyone had dismissed her without a second thought.

When the second half resumed, electricity filled the air. No one expected the visiting team to keep the score respectable, but now the Lady Longhorns looked poised to stay competitive for the entire game. The Swiftettes got the ball first and they walked the ball down court slowly and methodically where the Lady Longhorns waited to engage them. Huff dribbled to the wing and flung the ball inside to Collier. Sam bellied up to her with a hand in her back and waited for Collier to make her move. Skinny little Nadine Collier faked left then swung around to the right leading with her elbow. Her bony elbow connected squarely with Sam's nose, then she drop-stepped and scored an easy bucket while Sam lay on the ground below her.

Coach Lewis ran onto the floor calling for a timeout with his arms flailing about. Sam's teammates gathered around as Coach Lewis and Summer helped Sam to her feet. Sam held a towel to her face and put pressure on her nose. Despite the pressure, the white towel bloomed red as she made her way back to the bench where her father and an athletic trainer from Nazareth waited for her. Play continued while the trainer iced Sam's nose and managed to stop the bleeding. Coach Lewis knew his girls had no chance at all unless Sam got back in the game and got back in soon. His girls were playing hard, but they were no match for the Swiftettes without Sam.

Finally, with just a few minutes left in the third period and Nazareth leading by thirteen points, Sam re-entered the game. She returned with a vengeance. Sam's determination fueled her to four points and two blocked shots in the waning moments of the third. After three periods, the Lady Longhorns trailed by nine points; the possession arrow indicated Longhorns' ball when the final period began.

Inspired by Sam's beastly return to the game, the girls from Lazarus began the fourth period playing like they were possessed. They ran faster, leaped higher and banged harder than they should have been able to under their own strength. Memories of Whiteface flashed in their minds as they chipped away at the Swiftettes' lead. With five minutes remaining and Lazarus trailing by only five points, the Nazareth coach called a timeout and made a substitution. Play resumed and the Swiftettes went right at Sam. First, Collier attacked Sam down low. She got the basket but failed to draw a foul. The next time down the floor, after a timely three-pointer from MJ that cut the lead to just four points, the Swiftettes attacked Sam again. Nairobi slid in to help on defense but Collier managed to catch Sam in the stomach with an elbow as she went up for a basket down low in the paint. Collier missed, but grabbed her own rebound and passed it out of traffic to the hands of Huff, who was slashing to the basket from the three-point line. Sam slid in to take a charge and Huff barreled into Sam with a horrific smack. A sickening thud sounded as both players fell limp to the wood beneath their feet.

The official on the baseline stepped in with no hesitation and charged Huff with an offensive foul. As the official ran to center court to report the foul, the Nazareth coach erupted in a violent fit of profanity, flying water bottles, kicked-over chairs and yet more profanity. Knowing the coach had a tendency to put on a show for the fans, the official ignored his tantrum and waved both coaches to the lane, where all the players had gathered to help their respective teammates up from the floor. Coaches and officials waded into the throng gathered at the site of the collision and sent the players back to their benches so the trainer and coaches could attend to the fallen players.

The Nazareth coach grabbed Huff's jersey, pulled her up and pointed in the direction of the bench. He waved to someone in the stands then bent down over Sam and Coach Lewis kneeling at her side. Momentarily a gentleman from the stands appeared at the coach's side.

"I'm a doctor," the newcomer said. "Stay down, Lazarus. Let me have a look at you. How do you feel?"

Sam tried to sit up as she said, "I'm good. Just had the wind knocked out of me. It's all good."

The gentleman who claimed to be a doctor pushed on Sam's shoulder and made her lie back again. He took a small penlight from his pocket and shined it first in Sam's right eye, then her left, then back and forth again.

"Doc, I'm OK. Let's get this game going again." Sam pushed his hand away and sat up.

The doctor motioned to the trainer with a "make the call" gesture then turned to the official. He explained to the official in complicated medical jargon that Sam should be made to lie back down immediately, placed on a hard stretcher, immobilized and transported to the nearest emergency room without delay. Sam protested with an obscenity or two of her own. Sam's family had joined the group by this time and they stood by, quietly concerned, and trying decide whether to listen to Sam or to the doctor. Sam made eye contact with her dad and he understood that she was fine, ready to play, and more than a little agitated. Samuel Colter tried to wave off the officials and the doctor so he could help Sam to her feet. At that moment yet another man, who introduced himself as the Nazareth Athletic Director, stepped in and addressed Coach Lewis and the officials. The AD made it clear that the game would not proceed with the injured player in the game, that the doctor had ordered an immediate evacuation of the injured player to an emergency room, on a stretcher, and over his dead body would anything other than those two things happen in the next few minutes.

With that, the doctor and the trainer loaded Sam onto the stretcher and carried her out the door at the end of the gym. Sam's parents and Corey followed close behind, bewildered by all that had just transpired. The girls watched in terror as their one shot at beating Nazareth disappeared from sight on a stretcher. Coach Lewis did his best to regroup and calm his players but it was no use. As he tried to calm his girls, the thought struck him that the fans in the bleachers seemed far more rowdy and disinterested, almost disrespectful, than any he had ever seen when a player was down on the court; they certainly weren't helping the already-tense situation. All he could do was shake his head in disbelief. The shell-shocked girls from Lazarus finished the game but endured a fourth-period Swiftette onslaught that resulted in a twenty-two point Nazareth win, not to mention an unhealthy dose of trash-talking from the Swiftettes players and fans after the game.

Disappointed and heartbroken, the girls collected their things, loaded the short bus and drove to Dimmitt, where Sam had been taken, the only nearby town with an after-hours emergency clinic. When they arrived, the girls found Sam sitting alone on the tailgate of her father's truck in the clinic parking lot.

Before anyone could ask the obvious question, Sam explained, "They looked at me in there like I was crazy. The trainer and the doctor dropped me off then split. The doctor on duty in there checked me out and just shook his head. The doc said there wasn't nothing in the world wrong with me and no doctor worth his salt woulda' sent me to an emergency room. Coach, we got..."

Coach Lewis cut her off. "Yep, it appears we did."

CHAPTER XIV

As much as he wanted to deny it, Logan Russell felt the tide turning. He'd heard all about the dirty trick Nazareth pulled at the girls' game but, much to his chagrin, he'd sensed people beginning to empathize with the girls for a change rather than laughing at them or gossiping about them. Logan resented the Lady Longhorns, both as a team and as individuals. He hadn't forgotten about losing the gym to the girls and their obnoxious coach back in the preseason. He resented not only the way the girls had made strides this season but also the possibility that they might, somehow, finish the season with almost as many wins as the boys basketball team. He loathed the attention the girls seemed to be garnering suddenly. Nor had Logan forgotten the water tower. Not helping matters was the way he had been reamed by his parents, by his coach and by the school administration recently for his spray-paint stunt with Roy on the water tower after the girls got dragged down; he also had caught hell for stranding the girls up there in the first place. He thought they'd gotten away with the brilliant prank until Roy went soft and rolled over on him. Between Roy's selling out and the recent chatter about the girls, Logan found himself in a funk. The order of things around school and around town had been upset, according to Logan, and it was time to put things back as they should be.

"Ah, come on. You have to admit that was pure genius. I never heard of that before but believe me, I'm gonna file that one away and use it one day when I'm coaching."

Corey Colter found Logan's comment less than amusing. Corey knew firsthand how devastated Sam and the girls were after Nazareth. He pushed the weights off his chest five more times to complete his set then sat up straight on the bench. Logan, standing behind him as a spotter, continued running his mouth about how brilliant the Nazareth coach was and how he couldn't believe Naz had actually pulled it off. Roy stood quietly off to the side curling dumbbells and watching the reflection of his biceps flexing and contracting; he pretended not to pay attention but he heard the entire conversation. Roy debated whether or not he should get involved and interrupt Logan's fun. He took note of the irritation on Corey's face, though, and opted to stay quiet, leaving Logan's fate in Corey's large, angry hands.

Logan turned to face the mirror that covered the entire wall of the weight room of the field house. It was no secret that he prided himself on his Abercrombie good looks. He balled his hands into fists, extended his arms toward the floor, tensing his "guns" hard to make his triceps bulge, and examined the ripples of his chiseled arms and shoulders.

"I don't know why everyone's getting so worked up about all this," Logan continued. "Naz would've won anyway. It was just…"

Before Logan could finish his sentence, Corey suddenly rushed Logan from behind and crushed him against the mirrored wall. Corey's right forearm pressed against the back of Logan's neck and held his face against the smooth glass while Corey's body leaned into Logan's back keeping him pinned helpless and defenseless against the mirror.

The mirror flexed and threatened to crack and shatter under the pressure of the impact. Logan wriggled between the mirrored wall and Corey's body and struggled for a breath. Logan realized Corey wasn't fooling around. As the rest of the football players circled up to watch the sideshow, cheering and cajoling the two in the process, Corey leaned in and put his lips near Logan's ear.

"Listen, you piece of crap, that's my sister that happened to. I think you've said about enough. I'm tired of listening to you run your mouth all the time like you own this place." After a brief pause for effect, Corey pressed harder and finished his message to Logan. "You keep it up and I promise you I'll beat the hell out of you and not think twice about doin' it, either."

From across the field house Coach Cannon heard the ruckus and emerged from his office. By the time Cannon forced his way through the mob, Corey had released Logan and the two stood chest to chest, bowed up like two main event prize fighters waiting for the opening bell. Logan may have had the body of Adonis but he gave up several inches and forty pounds to Corey. Cannon stepped between the two and managed to shove them apart. Corey's gaze remained fixed on Logan as Logan backed away and slipped out the back door of the field house. Cannon sent Corey to the locker room to cool off, then sent everyone else back to their stations to finish their workouts. On the way back to his office, Cannon grabbed Roy's shirt and pulled him into a corner. Roy knew the look on Cannon's face all too well.

"Son, you gonna stand there and watch two of your buddies go at it like that? What's the matter with you? You're supposed to be a leader and you're standing off to the side watching the show like every other knucklehead in here. Step up and be a real man for a change and stop being like everyone else. You're special, son, so you better start acting like it! Seriously, are you ever gonna lead this bunch of idiots or are you gonna keep standing around waiting for someone else to take over for you?"

For a split second, Roy debated engaging his coach, arguing with him about how Logan was being a jerk and Corey was doing the right thing. He desperately wanted to point out the irony of Cannon's last statement. Instead, Roy gritted his teeth and said nothing as Cannon pushed him aside and walked away mumbling under his breath something about pansies and wusses and real men. Coach Cannon returned to his office and slammed the door behind him. The football team and the rest of the guys working out stood silent, not sure what to do or say. A few of the guys had been chuckling amongst themselves about the Nazareth incident just moments ago, mostly because they wanted Logan's approval. They weren't pleased that the girls had taken the loss because of the trickery but they, too, thought the Nazareth plan was clever in an evil-genius sort of way. Word had spread through school like wildfire earlier in the day but, to the surprise of many, there had been fewer cruel remarks than usual. The guys left in the field house considered Corey's agitated state and decided they'd keep their thoughts to themselves for the rest of the afternoon, or at least until after they'd finished their workout and Corey had left the building.

Roy made his way back to the rack of free weights and resumed his workout. With each press of the dumbbells above his head, he replayed Coach Cannon's comments in his mind. He imagined himself standing up to Cannon and saying, "It's about time someone around here showed *you* what a real man is." Roy finished his workout. His arms and legs felt like jelly and his head throbbed. Without showering or saying a word to his teammates, Roy grabbed his things from his locker and set out to find Corey and keep him out of trouble.

Coach Lewis strolled into Mary's Kitchen out of the cold, dry wind that blew without ceasing down Main Street during the winter months. He found his way to his favorite booth and slid in with his hands still warming in the pockets of his city-slicker leather jacket. He shook out his shaggy blond hair and waited to be served. Lost in the Hank Williams tune floating above the din of the customers and the kitchen noises, Coach Lewis didn't see Martha sidle up to his booth.

"Cold's downright nasty this afternoon," she said. Martha's voice startled her customer. He sat up straight, a little embarrassed and afraid he had jumped conspicuously at her voice. "Shouldn't you be at practice? It's still kind of early yet."

"Yes, ma'am, pretty cold. It doesn't get this cold in Houston." Coach Lewis pulled his hands from his pockets, blew into them then placed them on the table. "The girls played their hearts out last night and they're pretty tired today. We shot a few baskets then I gave them the rest of the afternoon off. No need to…" He almost let the word *kill* slip from his lips but caught himself. "…wear them out at this point."

"That was good of you," Martha said as she placed her hand on his shoulder. "Interested in the special tonight?"

"Actually," he chuckled, "You know what I want? A cheeseburger, onion rings and a Diet Dr. Pepper."

"Comfort food, huh?"

"Maybe so. Just sounds good right now."

"You're funny, Coach. How do you stay so skinny? One of these days eating like this is gonna catch up with you. You know that, right?"

"That's what the Diet DP is for."

Martha returned a few minutes later with his drink. As she set the fizzing beverage in front of him, she slid across the red vinyl until she sat directly across from Coach Lewis. After a moment of awkward silence followed by a deep sigh, Martha opened up.

"You know, Coach, this has been so hard. On Summer. On me. On the whole town. It's like this whole place died when she did. I've been here a long time but I've never seen the people here affected this way. Kids, adults, everybody. Just devastated.

"Not too many days after the funeral, Summer had some of the girls over. We all sat around on Autumn's bed in our pajamas talking and crying with each other 'til all hours of the morning. Mostly it was good. I was trying to be strong for Summer, and for the others, and I was explaining how life was going to have to go on. It was just going to have to."

Martha's eyes suddenly became red-rimmed and cavernous. She fidgeted with her apron in her lap and looked down, away from Coach Lewis's eyes. Coach Lewis leaned forward trying to pick her soft voice out of the hodge-podge of other sounds that surrounded them.

"After watching the girls' hearts get broken again last night... Coach, it's like there's a curse on us now that won't lift. Like some kind of shroud that just keeps us... buried... in our own grief. I don't see us snapping out of it or breaking the cycle. Do you?"

"Yes, ma'am, I do. With all my heart, I do."

Coach Lewis got out of his seat and slid in next to Martha, put his arm around her and pulled her in close. It was all he could think to do.

"Coach, maybe if you had gotten here sooner. I don't know." She wrung her tired, withered hands in her lap. "If you had gotten this team sooner, had a chance to make your mark here sooner with the girls, with everyone else, maybe we wouldn't be talking about this now. I can't help but wonder what things would be like now if you'd gotten here sooner than you did."

He didn't know what to say.

"Coach, I reckon it's about time I tell you a story. After you hear it, maybe you'll have a better idea why all this is so difficult for me to watch, all the drama with the team and with Summer and Roy and the baby. You up for a story?"

"Sure."

"You see, Coach, we seem to be stuck in a cycle here. A cycle we can't seem to break. How come you've never asked about why the girls lived with me all this time? Didn't you ever wonder?"

"Honestly, sure. But it's not any of my business. You don't have to…"

"Let me take you back a long, long time ago to when I was just a girl, not much older than Summer is now or Autumn would've been. Like so many other girls in town, I fell for a big, strapping football player. Oh, he was handsome, and a smooth talker. I thought he'd fallen for me, too. So off we went one weekend night after a dance, out to a quiet little place in the moonlight he said he picked out just for us. I don't have to do the math for you but it wasn't long before I was all alone with a child on the way and my parents as ashamed as they could be.

"They sent me out to Colorado to stay with an aunt for a few months. They expected me to come back by myself but I surprised them when I showed up with a bundle in my arms. Well, they wouldn't even let me back in my own house. No problem, I told them. I'd just go find you know who and we'd settle down and everything would be fine. Much to my surprise, you know who had moved on to someone else and wanted nothing to do with me.

"My sister, Mary, felt sorry for me and she let me stay with her. Together we raised my daughter, Ruby, and we made a pretty good life for ourselves. Mary and her husband, me and Ruby. Well, Ruby grew up to be quite a looker and she liked the boys as much as they liked her, I suppose. As much I tried to steer her right, she was a free spirit none of us could tame.

"After high school, she worked at the diner for a while with me. At this point, I'd gotten our own little place for just the two of us and I thought things were going to be OK. Well, that is 'til a rodeo rolled through town one weekend and she met the love of her life. Off she went with that cowboy without even saying goodbye. Every once in a while I'd get a postcard from Colorado or Wyoming or Oklahoma but she never called or came back home. One Saturday morning years later, I answered a knock at my door and there stood Ruby with two little ones, one in each arm.

"What's a mother gonna do? Of course I took her in, cleaned the three of them up and fed 'em real good. Later we got the two little ones tucked in for the night and the two of us just sat and talked. Finally, she said she was tired and she was going to bed and she'd see me in the morning. Well, the next morning she was gone and the two little ones were still curled up on a palette on the floor in the guest room right where we left them the night before.

"Fast forward fourteen years and here we are. As I was saying, judging by what I see happening now, things haven't changed any and I don't see the cycle breaking. So, I ask you again, Coach. Do you?"

———————

Life for Coach Lewis began to feel a little different the morning after the Nazareth game. When he arrived to school that morning and went to the workroom to check his mailbox, Gladys, from behind her giant computer monitor, slipped him a hand-written note scribbled on the back of a tardy slip. The message said simply, "Eddie Freeman – high school sports – *Lubbock Avalanche-Journal*," followed by a couple of phone numbers. Coach Lewis couldn't imagine what this could be about. He folded the note, shoved it in his back pocket and headed straight for his office in the gym.

After a few rings, a voice on the other end of the line said, "Sports desk."

"Uh, yes, this Gabe Lewis from Lazarus High School calling for Eddie Freeman."

"Who?"

"Gabe Lewis, from Lazarus High School."

"Got it. Looking for Freeman? Let me see if I can find him."

After a few moments' wait, a new voice came on the line.

"Coach, this is Eddie Freeman from the *Avalanche-Journal* down here in Lubbock. Thanks so much for calling back." Without taking a breath, the voice kept going. "So, listen, I won't keep you long. First, let me say I'm sorry about your player back before the holidays. I know that's probably put a real damper on things for you this season."

Coach Lewis tried to accept the condolences but the voice on the phone cut him off and kept going without missing a beat.

"I picked up your little story a while back about that quadruple double, see, so I've been keeping an eye on the boxscores. Looks like that kid of yours is tearing it up right now. So, listen, here's the deal. There might be an interesting little story here if you guys can manage to land in the playoffs, so I'm going to keep an eye on things and see how everything shakes out down there in Lazarus. Not trying to add any pressure, you understand, just saying with the loss of the player, and all, plus the fact that no news but football ever comes out of Lazarus, there might be some kind of human interest story here that some of my readers may find to be worth following. That's all. So, listen, I'll be in touch in a few weeks and we'll see where we are. Hey, now, thanks for your time, coach, and you have yourself a good morning."

With a click, Eddie Freeman from the *Lubbock Avalanche-Journal* sports desk hung up the phone and left Coach Lewis wondering what just happened. He replayed the conversation in his mind a few times and realized that, yes, a sports reporter showed some interest in doing a story, maybe. *If* they made the playoffs. He rubbed his face with his hands and sat quietly for a moment. *Great*, he told himself. *No pressure*. He decided then and there not to tell the girls.

Life for the Lady Longhorns began to feel a little different the morning after the Nazareth game, almost as if the proverbial new day finally had dawned for them. As soon as they got to school, they could tell things were a little different. Not changed entirely, just different by a few degrees, subtly changed somehow. While the girls never had to endure ridicule at the hands of the general population at school, they certainly never garnered any amount of positive attention for their efforts on the court. Cheerleaders neither decorated the girls' lockers or their locker room nor made cookies or goodie bags for the girls on game days. The school marquee never advertised the girls' games. The school newspaper never featured the team, their scores or even their photos; in fact, the newspaper staff never even took photos at their games. The red and white hallways of the school featured no posters or flyers urging fans to pack the gym for upcoming Lady Longhorns events. As far as most of the high school was concerned, the girls basketball team might as well not have existed.

The accident had changed that sentiment to some degree but purely on a human level. Everyone in school knew Autumn and grieved the tragedy of her passing. In a town and school as small as Lazarus, such grieving couldn't be avoided. The students and teachers shared their condolences with Summer and Martha as best they could and, to some extent, even to the girls on the team simply because everyone realized Autumn's teammates had suffered a loss on a level deeper than their own. Mostly, though, the accident brought a hush over the school, a subdued and somber atmosphere that showed no signs of dissipating anytime soon.

The day after Nazareth, for the first time ever, a handful of students made subtle gestures of kindness and support, offered words of encouragement, to several of the girls. The understated but sincere "heard about the game" and "sorry about last night" and "sucks what happened to y'all" utterances in the parking lot and in the hallways between classes marked a change for Lazarus. The comments remained few and far between, but they were there. The table in the cafeteria farthest from the hot lunch line door where most of the girls usually ate lunch together never attracted any amount of attention from the other cafeteria patrons until that day. A few of the boys from the basketball team and even a few football players gave the girls a collective nod, the universally understood expression for "good effort." Several of the teachers encouraged the girls, patted them on their backs and bumped knuckles with them as they entered or exited classrooms or as they passed in the hallways. Principal Haskins even made a point to drop by the gym after school to address the girls before practice and to encourage them to "fight the good fight."

All things considered, the girls had a good day and enjoyed the pleasant surprise of a little empathy and positive attention. The drama of the night before and the late return from Nazareth, however, left the girls physically tired and emotionally drained. Coach Lewis, showing signs of maturing as a coach, recognized the lethargy in the first few drills of practice and decided to go easy on the team rather than pressing them and pushing them. After a round of shooting drills and a walk-through of some new inbounds plays for the second half of the district schedule, Coach Lewis circled the girls at center court and sat with them on the giant red longhorn painted at the center of the gym floor.

Though his heart didn't want to accept the truth, Coach Lewis's mind had almost come to terms with the fact that the girls' season had been all but wrapped up the night before in Nazareth. The top three teams from each district advanced to the playoffs and he understood that finishing the first half of the district schedule with one win and four losses put his team in a precarious position. How many wins would they need to finish in the top three? How many teams would have to pull an upset here or there to give the Lady Longhorns the help they needed in terms of other teams' wins and losses? What would be the odds of winning the games they had to win even to be in a position to get help from other teams? Things looked pretty grim and everyone reclining on the high-gloss gym floor knew it.

The day had been surprisingly encouraging for Coach Lewis, too, but he had no way to know the girls received the same small tokens of appreciation and acknowledgement as he. He argued with himself throughout the day about the approach to take with the girls. Part of him wanted to believe some small glimmer of hope still existed for salvaging the season. At the same time, though, part of him wanted to congratulate the girls for giving it "the ol' college try," give them the old standby "there's always next year" speech, and just let them have as much no-pressure fun as possible the rest of the way.

Unable to decide which route to take, Coach Lewis opted for Plan C, a stall tactic. He reminded them of how hard they'd worked all year, how they'd bonded and become a family through and in spite of the adversity along the way, that the focus early on in the season had been on the journey and not the destination, and, perhaps most importantly, without question Autumn would want them to keep fighting for her and for themselves. The last comment, after he made it, hung in his mind and pricked his conscience. Did he really mean it or was it just a cheap and shameless attempt to appeal to the girls' emotions? He wasn't sure. Coach Lewis told the girls to go home and get some rest. As for Coach Lewis, he resolved to find the biggest cheeseburger and the greasiest onion rings he could find to get him through the night and he knew just where to find them.

The girls stayed behind at the gym after Coach Lewis left. They hung out on the gym floor and reflected on the season; basketball was

297

only part of the conversation. They talked about what a crybaby Cassie had been at the beginning of the season and how she'd almost quit. They talked about how Sam had turned into a basketball monster in recent weeks and they speculated as to which college would offer her the biggest scholarship. They remarked at how MJ and Molly had come around and warmed to the other girls and, much to everyone's surprise, to Coach Lewis. They laughed at a long list of Brooklynne anecdotes and marveled at how valuable she had become on the court since her return. They ragged Rita that her temper hadn't improved at all over the course of the season. They interrogated Summer about recent developments with Roy and inquired in jest about a wedding date. They teased Nairobi and asked if she was headed to Nashville to start a singing career when the season was over.

As would be expected, the topic of their conversation shifted at last to Autumn. Though the loss of their friend and teammate weighed on them still, the girls managed for the first time to talk about Autumn without becoming overly emotional, to remember her, to compare stories and to laugh at things they remembered. Taking turns, the girls shared stories, forgotten stories from the past which, at the time, were nothing more than passing moments but now bubbled back to the surface as cherished memories. What struck them most in the quiet of the empty gym was how many very different memories each of them had of Autumn, yet how each girl seemed to remember Autumn the same way: kind, silly, positive, hopelessly romantic, encouraging, selfless.

The whole time the girls had been lying around beneath the buzzing lights overhead, Sam had been flat on her back shooting a basketball, one-handed, straight up toward the ceiling and catching the ball with one hand as it fell back down. Occasionally she switched hands then switched back again. Finally, after the girls were talked out, MJ dared Sam to shoot the ball backward from where she lay on the floor near center court. If Sam scored, MJ said, she'd get up and practice for the next hour. If Sam missed the shot, MJ added, Sam would have to run twenty down-and-backs. The rest of the girls jumped to their feet and said they'd take the bet, too. They circled round Sam and chanted her name. *Sam! Sam! Sam! Sam!* Flat on her back, Sam spun herself around toward the basket, arched her back, took aim and Cassie grabbed the basketball from her hand. Showing wisdom beyond her years, Cassie explained that no matter what happened, make or miss, everyone would participate; it was neither a question nor a suggestion. After a brief pause, the girls each nodded their assent. Cassie gave the ball back to Sam. Sam pressed her heels into the floor, took aim once more then let the ball fly.

When the girls were done, they sprawled wherever they fell, lungs burning in the cool air and muscles aching from the exertion. Physically, they were spent. Emotionally, though, they were almost giddy. With no coach, no coaching, no instruction, and no game plan, the girls became a team. That afternoon in the Lazarus High School gym, the girls dedicated themselves to fighting the good fight and finishing the race. Destination be damned, they would resume the journey. They vowed to one another, for themselves and for the memory of Autumn, to enjoy the journey come what may. They determined to rejoice in the destination when they arrived, no matter when or where the journey ended. For the Lady Longhorns of Lazarus, Texas, it finally clicked. The girls never told anyone about what happened that cold Wednesday afternoon in the gym, less than twenty-four hours after Nazareth broke their hearts.

With the first half of district play complete, the Lady Longhorns were set to host the Kress Lady Kangaroos on Friday night. The district teams now would repeat the first half of the district schedule but with home and away games reversed. The Lady Kangaroos had hosted Lazarus for the first district game just a few weeks earlier. It had been the first game back on the court for the girls after the accident. The numb, lifeless performance by the Lady Longhorns had resulted predictably in a convincing loss. With the girls coming off a heartbreaking defeat earlier in the week, no one expected a different outcome from the rematch – no one except for the Lady Longhorns, that is.

In round two of the Lady Kangaroos versus the Lady Longhorns, the Lazarus girls played poor hosts and ran away with the game early in the second half. By the time the final buzzer sounded, every Lazarus player had scored; Sam finished just shy of a triple-double and Rita had notched a career-high in steals and assists. The few fans present rewarded the girls' efforts with cheers and applause. The applause, however, soon was drowned out by the boys' warm-up music pumping electronica rave music at a ridiculous volume over the speakers hanging high above the gym floor. Unfazed, the girls danced briefly on the longhorn painted at center court and celebrated their long-overdue win. As the two boys' teams took the floor for stretching and pregame warm-up drills, the girls skipped and floated back to their locker room where Dee stood by to high-five each of them as they entered.

The girls' performance against Kress astonished Coach Lewis. Kress hadn't been playing too well since their early win over Lazarus, according to the box scores and the scouting reports he'd collected, but Coach Lewis still anticipated a fight to the finish with the Roos. One thing he'd always been taught, though, is that a win is a win is a win. He knew better than to dwell on his surprise at how well his girls managed their opponents, so in his mind he filed away the win and focused his attention on building up the girls and reaffirming their efforts. He praised his girls for great team play and applauded both Sam's and Rita's individual accomplishments. He congratulated his team for playing to win and being aggressive, but he cautioned them about overconfidence. The Happy Cowgirls on the road, he warned, certainly will be a far different experience from the Lady Kangaroos.

Nairobi responded with a simple, confident statement. "We'll be ready, Coach."

Nairobi had been absolutely right. The Lazarus Lady Longhorns were ready. After a great Monday practice, the girls were focused and highly motivated, if not driven. They filed off the short bus into the cold, poorly-lit parking lot in Happy nearly two hours after they had left Lazarus but the ride seemed to have none of the usual anesthetic effects on the girls. They strolled into the small, old gym, each girl confident and with a bounce in her step. They surveyed the court, glanced up at the banners hanging from the rafters overhead, and made their way to the visitors' locker room to get changed. When the girls emerged from the locker room for pre-game warm-up drills, they moved efficiently, with purpose and precision. Their eyes, slightly squinted, moved quickly from player to player, to the ball and back again, without wandering or searching about in the stands. They were ready to play.

301

As the Happy coach watched the visiting Lady Longhorns run through their precision passing and shooting drills, he knew something had changed. He remembered the somber bunch of girls from their last meeting and he remembered how his girls had pounded the lethargic, uninspired team. He had a funny feeling he'd somehow have his hands full on this night. Nevertheless, he had a plan to clamp down on Sam since she had outscored everyone on the court during their last meeting.

From the first Lazarus possession, the Happy Cowgirls double-teamed Sam and didn't let her touch the ball a single time the entire first period on offense. The Cowgirls' plan worked to perfection. Coach Lewis's girls knew, though, that double-teaming requires someone to be left open or unguarded. Not recognizing Brooklynne, the Cowgirls chose to leave the newcomer unguarded. Brooklynne made them pay dearly as she quickly dropped four threes on the unsuspecting Cowgirls. After playing even in the first period, the Happy coach made the decision to stick with his game plan in the second period, too. Again, Sam struggled to get any touches on the ball and again Brooklynne, planted in the corner outside the three-point line, made the Cowgirls pay. As a result, Lazarus took a slim lead into halftime.

Coach Lewis figured the Cowgirls would abandon the double-teaming scheme in the second half so he spent halftime sorting out plans to get Sam the ball as often as possible. Much to his chagrin in third period, though, the stubborn opposing coach kept the double-team on Sam and shifted his best perimeter defender to Brooklynne. The Cowgirls' coach had no way of knowing that Brooklynne never had the ability to create space or to create her own shot. Brooklynne's gift lay in her ability to hit wide-open shots. When Rita and MJ realized the coach's lapse in judgment, they almost laughed out loud. For the entire third period, Rita and MJ had their way with the Cowgirls, slashing through the lane, often drawing contact in the process. For the Cowgirls, the wheels were coming off and the home team needed a new plan to stop the bleeding.

Lazarus inbounded the ball to begin the final period of play with a comfortable thirteen-point lead. As Rita walked the ball down the floor where her teammates waited on offense, she noticed the Cowgirls had dropped into man to man defense. No more double teaming Sam. Sam, who also recognized the defensive adjustment, immediately posted up hard on the right block. Rita cleared the right side of the court, dribbled to the wing and fed Sam down low. Sam turned and squared up to the rim, gave her defender a vicious head fake then drop stepped to the basket. She easily made the shot and drew a foul from her overmatched defender who went for the fake, left the floor and came down on top of Sam as she shot. Sam sank the free throw and, for all intents and purposes, she sank the Cowgirls, too. Rita and Sam went to work again on the next possession and Sam again "got the hoop and the harm," as she liked to say after a big play. After Sam again sank her free throw, the Happy Coach planted himself on the bench where he stayed, disgusted and quiet, the rest of the game. The Lady Longhorns won going away as Brooklynne, Rita, MJ and even Sam ended up in double figures; despite being held scoreless for three periods, Sam still managed sixteen points for the game.

In the locker room after the game, Coach Lewis had so much to say, he hardly knew where to begin.

"Wow! Where'd that come from? Seriously, that was a heck of a game. I could talk some about rebounds we missed and free throws we should've made, but let's focus on some really positive things to take away from this one."

He made his way around the locker room and high-fived the girls as he spoke, being sure each of them saw how proud he was of her effort.

"Those guys didn't know what hit 'em out there tonight. Brooklynne – amazing job. You never cease to amaze me. Rita and MJ – great decision making and great teamwork. Sam – way to hang in there and keep working on both ends of the floor even when you weren't getting rewarded offensively. The rest of you guys – way to hang in there on defense, nice job staying out of foul trouble, being ready to sub in and out so much. Nairobi, you said you guys would be ready. You weren't kidding!"

Rita interrupted before Coach Lewis got too wound up and too wordy, "So, how 'bout them playoffs?"

"Whoa, now, wait just a minute. Let's not get ahead of ourselves here," Coach Lewis cautioned. His smile dissipated and he suddenly seemed all too intense and focused. "We only have three district wins. We only have three games left."

"So how many more do we need?" MJ asked.

"My best guess is we need six district wins to guarantee a playoff appearance. Everyone else is looking up at Naz right now. You have to think Happy, Silverton and even Kress all have a legit shot at finishing two and three."

"And us?" asked Cassie.

He drew a deep breath and thought about how best to answer the question. He had a hunch but he neither wanted to give his girls false hope nor dash the glimmer of hope they had after two straight wins. "Honestly…" All eyes were locked on his. The girls shifted in their seats, slid forward a little, leaned in, and waited expectantly for the good news. "I have no idea."

The collective sigh said that wasn't what they wanted to hear.

"Look," he said, "we're on a roll, but we can't lose touch with reality. Let's see what happens when we get Silverton at home, then we'll talk. I can tell you this, though. Not to put any undue pressure on you but… Without a win at home against Silverton, you can pretty much count on needing to buy a ticket if you're interested in a playoff game."

In the wee hours of Friday night, technically Saturday morning, the buses rolled back into Lazarus from a split decision in Happy. Gradually, all the basketball players unloaded from the two buses and shuffled sleepily toward their cars and trucks, or to where their parents waited sleepily in their vehicles with their heaters blowing on high. A few minutes later, as Summer emerged from the gym where she and Coach Lewis had been putting away the bag of balls, the water bottles, the training kit, the clipboard, the game book and the stats, she noticed a shadowy figure lurking as if it were waiting for her in the parking lot. She could just make out the red vest and white sleeves of a letter jacket. Though it could have been one of any number of athletes sporting a letter jacket, Summer allowed herself to hope it might be one specific Lazarus football player. Keeping an eye on the figure, Summer went to Sam, her ride home on this particular night, and sent Sam away, hopeful that the stranger in the shadows would be her ride home. As she made her way toward the specter, she noticed Roy's truck parked on the other side of the parking lot with a few other vehicles. Her heart pounded with anticipation. A moment later, Roy stepped casually from the shadow and into the glow of the flickering floodlight, which turned the white in his jacket to a dingy yellowish-orange.

"It's cold out here. Want to climb in my truck for a few minutes?"

Without waiting for a response, Roy ambled to his truck, climbed in and cranked the cold, sluggish engine. A moment later, the passenger door opened and Summer climbed in next to Roy. Roy sat with one hand on the steering wheel and the other held out in front of the heater vents waiting for the cold air to blow hot. Summer sat awkwardly with her hands in her lap. As they sat and waited for the truck to warm up, vehicles intermittently chugged to life around the parking lot and crept off into the night.

After a few minutes of silence, Roy commented on the CD playing in his truck. Roy's comments then led to a lighthearted debate about which Pat Green album each liked best. Roy insisted on *Wave on Wave* but Summer stood her ground for *Three Days*. They agreed, though, his old stuff would always be his best. From there they moved on to random topics: what prom might be like this year, what colleges had most recently sent letters to Roy, who was working in Mary's Kitchen instead of Autumn, how long Coach Lewis would stay in Lazarus after the school year, whether the softball team would make this year, did Roy's truck need new tires. Finally, Roy could stall no longer and the conversation took a serious turn.

"I know I can't really say anything to make you feel any better, Summer. I wish I could. You know how sorry I am about everything, right?"

"Martha told me everything you said to her and that's enough. Even if Autumn were still around there's still another conversation I'd want us to have, you know. About you and me, and about you and April."

"I figured you'd get around to that."

"Roy, come spend one afternoon with April. You can come over this Sunday afternoon, after church."

After Roy failed to respond, Summer continued.

"An hour, Roy. Please? Roy, for what it's worth, I still want you to be in our lives. Always have. But if you don't get on board soon, Roy, I don't know if I always will."

"I'm sorry I've been such a jerk to you all this time. I know you probably can't forgive me, but…"

"I already have, Roy," she interrupted. "Please? Sunday afternoon?"

Roy slid over toward her and put his hand on her knee, gently, though, and not like he was up to his same old tricks. A tear formed in Summer's eye and trickled down her cheek as she closed her eyes and placed her hand on his. Suddenly, a door slammed just outside Roy's truck, headlights flashed on and an engine roared to life. After a few revs of the engine, the truck next to Roy's screamed backward out of the parking space, skidded to a brief stop, then growled away, kicking up a spray of gravel as it left.

"What was that all about?" Summer asked as she looked over her shoulder and watched the taillights disappear in a hurry.

307

"I don't know but it can't be good. That was Corey's truck."

Roy pulled his hand away and jumped out of the driver's seat to try to catch a final glimpse of the truck. Summer, too, piled out into the cold.

"I have no idea what got into him or where he's headed in such a hurry," Roy said as he gave a half-shrug.

On the ground near where Corey's truck had been parked, something caught Summer's eye as it reflected the faintest bit of light coming from inside Roy's truck. She reached down, collected a wadded piece of paper, then turned around and uncrumpled it in the dim light.

"Oh my God, Roy. I know where he's going."

She handed Roy the piece of paper across the seat.

"Get in. We've got to stop him."

Corey sped away from the school and barreled along the dark roads leading out of town. His hands held the steering wheel in a death grip and his ears throbbed with the pounding of the music booming from the speakers. With complete abandon, Corey ran two stop signs and demolished every speed limit before he careened off one of the main roads and onto the dirt road that led toward the gravel pit. Corey made the final turn with a powerslide that flung gravel in a monstrous rooster tail behind him as he made the ninety-degree turn onto a dark, washboard dirt road. He pushed harder on the accelerator and rocketed toward his final destination. His heart boomed in his chest and his head throbbed as an adrenaline-and-testosterone cocktail coursed through his veins. Ahead of him he could see red taillights and the glow of headlights. Corey drove straight at the taillights then stood on the brakes to bring his truck to a sliding, grinding halt. He threw the gearshift into park, flew from the truck and scanned the darkness.

"Took you long enough to get here. Ready to get your butt kicked?"

Corey recognized the voice but couldn't locate its source. He stepped around in front of his truck and looked in every direction, squinting and trying to find someone in the murky haze created by headlights reflecting off the dust in the air. Suddenly a dark silhouette dashed into the beam of Corey's headlights and plowed into Corey so hard he fell backward against the hood of his truck. His assailant's arms were locked tight and he felt what must have been a knee pound into his side over and over. Corey struggled and fought and managed at last to break his assailant's grip. Corey grabbed the fellow's arm, twisted it and threw the attacker to the ground with a loud grunt. The gravel crunched as the figure faceplanted on the dusty ground.

"Logan, what the hell's wrong with you man? You keep this up and I'll-"

Logan grabbed a large stick he found on the ground as he struggled to stand back up. As Corey spoke, Logan lunged with the stick and struck Corey square in the gut, causing Corey to gasp and wheeze as he exhaled. Logan climbed to his feet and squinted into the high beams of Corey's truck as Corey leaned against the hood between the headlights. Any other time, Logan would have been no match for Corey. Corey stood a few inches taller than Logan, at about six feet four inches, and outweighed him by many pounds. Logan, leaner and quicker than Corey, could not overcome Corey's adrenaline-fueled raw strength. As Logan struggled to get his bearings on his target, Corey flung himself forward and wrestled the stick away from Logan. He swung at Logan several times, landing one or two swings in Logan's chest and cheek and one crunching blow on Logan's nose. Logan fought back and landed a few good shots of his own before the two tumbled to the ground like grappling wrestlers.

"Ever since you showed up around here, I knew I didn't like you," Logan said as they rolled back and forth in the gravel grasping and grabbing at each other's faces and necks. "Did you think you could run your mouth about me without me finding out?"

"If you'd mind your own business and lay off my sister and her friends like I warned you to," Corey grunted, "I wouldn't be telling everyone what a coward you are."

The two struggled and rolled ever closer to the edge of the pit, though neither could see the ledge.

"It's time someone taught you a lesson about knowing your place when you're new in town," Logan screamed in Corey's ear.

Logan grabbed a handful of gravel and dirt and ground it into Corey's face. At that, Corey let out a ferocious yell, rolled over and flung Logan off him. He clambered to his feet and quickly wiped the dirt and grime from his eyes, anticipating another blitz from Logan. With his hands up in a defensive position, he looked first left then right but Logan was nowhere to be seen. Corey listened but he couldn't hear gravel crunching anywhere. Finally Corey realized he was standing only a few feet from the edge of the gravel pit. He couldn't see down into it on this moonless night so he had no idea how far down the slope extended to the bottom of the pit; in some places the bottom of the pit lay only a few yards beneath the edge while other parts of the pit lay nearly thirty feet below the ledge.

Somewhere down below, Logan sat up with a groan and rubbed his head. He tasted the blood mixed with dirt that flowed from his nose down over his lips. He felt along his forehead and tried to assess the damage. At least one gash now spread across his forehead and it, too, seemed to be seeping blood. Logan couldn't quite understand what had happened. He'd lured Corey into an unfamiliar place and had gotten a good jump on him. He'd had the perfect opportunity to teach the big sister-loving oaf how things were gonna be here in Lazarus, but somehow he'd blown it. He'd had all he could take of Corey talking up the girls, hating on the basketball players and the football players who'd been stirring things up and keeping things interesting for the last few months. He'd really blown a gasket when he'd heard that Corey said he must be impotent to keep picking on girls all the time and he ought to pick on someone for once who could fight him back. That's all the motivation he'd needed to make his move and get the out-of-towner out here in the middle of nowhere and beat him senseless. He just couldn't grasp how things had gone so wrong so fast.

Logan looked around, then up and could see only the glow of the headlights fifteen or twenty feet above him. He felt blindly along the ground for the stick he'd lost in the struggle. When he found it, he'd climb up and finish this. His hands moved over empty cans, some discharged shells and then, finally, something far better than the stick he'd used moments earlier. Logan moved his hands slowly over the heavy piece of metal. He could tell by the raised ridges running horizontally around the metal rod that he'd found a piece of iron rebar.

Logan closed his eyes to let his eyes adjust to the complete darkness. A few seconds later, he opened his eyes and made his way as quietly as he could up the slope toward the headlights. Determined to teach Corey a lesson once and for all, Logan reached the top and pulled himself over the ledge. His ribs and his head throbbed as he exerted himself. Logan stood, hunched over slightly, with the rebar in his hands like a club. He saw a figure move just beyond the beam of the headlight. Logan raised the bar above his head, yelled out to Corey and started to charge. Just as he began his rush toward the figure, a second figure appeared next to the first.

"Logan," called the voice. "It's over, man. Don't do it."

Logan stopped in his tracks, bent over and breathing hard. His chest heaved and his eyes squinted in the bright light.

"Roy," Logan mumbled despondently. He dropped the rebar and plopped himself down into a seated position between Corey's truck and the edge of the pit. He hadn't realized until now how intense the pain was throughout his body. He looked back up where the two figures stood staring back at him. Without warning, out of the blackness beyond the headlight beam, a third, much smaller figure appeared and stood between the other two.

CHAPTER XV

The girls already were changing into their uniforms in the locker room when the Swiftettes entered the gym. Coach Lewis sat alone next to Summer on the two end chairs of the home team bench, not actually a bench but rather a row of red and white chairs. He felt a gust of cold February air rush past his face, and he knew the visiting team had just opened the gym door to come inside. Led by their coach, the girls followed militarily in a single file line. Each girl wore intimidating black warm-ups and carried a black bag with her name and number on it. Each wore a black headband with her number stitched onto it. Some of the girls' heads bobbed and rocked in time with the pulsing music pumping through the tiny white wires into their earphones.

The Nazareth coach peeled out of the line and cut across the gym floor to where Tommy Cannon waited in the corner of the gym. Whitney Huff led her teammates the rest of the way to the visitors' bench. Her face stoic, she led the line of girls past Coach Lewis without so much as a sideways glance. The rest of the Swiftettes followed suit and marched with a singular purpose. Coach Lewis recognized the look of intensity on the faces of the Swiftettes. Their eyes were straight ahead, their jaws set, their chins held just a little higher than usual. The Lady Longhorns had gotten their attention when they played in Nazareth a few weeks earlier. Judging by the looks of the Swiftettes, the Lady Longhorns would not catch them off-guard this evening.

The Swiftettes dropped their bags near the visitors' bench and made their way to the center of the gym. They sat in a large circle around center court, right on top of the massive longhorn painted there, and began their light stretching. Without saying a word, the Swiftettes stretched, then hopped up and ran some warm-up sprints back and forth, sideline to sideline. After a few trips back and forth, they collected their things and disappeared into the visitors' locker room. Coach Lewis felt a sense of relief that his girls hadn't seen the display he'd just observed. The small glimmer of hope he had about coming out on top in this contest all but vanished. He felt knots twisting in his stomach. He did not want this to be the last game of the season. With the weight of the world back on his shoulders and a sense of desperation swelling inside him, he grabbed his clipboard and plodded to the locker room to ready his troops for battle.

The Lady Longhorns soon emerged from the locker room ready to burst with excitement and anticipation. Somehow, it had all come down to this. What had begun as a nightmare season for the girls now had the potential to be a dream season. The odds of making the playoffs were slim, but there existed a chance. And, as Coach Lewis encouraged them in the locker room, as long as there is a chance… For perhaps the first time ever in Lazarus, a girls basketball game against Nazareth actually meant something. For the boys, however, the game later in the evening would mean nothing except perhaps an opportunity for Logan Russell to pad his stats and shore up all-district honors; after the girls game, the boys would wrap up district play with a paltry four wins, an overall poor showing even for a school whose exuberance clearly was reserved for football.

The Lady Longhorns began their pregame shooting and passing drills and, as they were instructed, they focused only on their end of the court. Even though they all wanted to steal glances at the Swiftettes running through drills ninety or so feet away, they resisted temptation. The one minute buzzer sounded. They returned to the bench and huddled up for their pregame cheer. They piled their hands in the center of the huddle, one on top of another, ready to do their cheer but Coach Lewis interrupted them with one final thought. "No matter what happens out here tonight, remember that I love you guys. No regrets. Play your hearts out like you'll never have the chance to play together again. You can recover from being tired, from being hurt, from being banged around. You'll never recover from regretting not giving it everything you've got. No regrets. Here we go, 'No regrets!' on three!"

On the end of the third row of the stands sat Martha. She had been doing better of late, more good days than bad at this point. Her mere presence in the stands sent the message to those who saw her that healing will come. Standing next to her were the Reverend Washington and Nairobi's father. Seated behind her were Calvin Haskins, Bill Merrick and even Neill Frederickson, the superintendent. Below Martha sat the Colter family; Martha found herself constantly scooting a little to the left or a little to the right to be able to see around their massive frames. Jasperson and Frost occupied their usual place along the top row where they could best see the action to keep stats for their girls. As both teams warmed up with the usual drills, Martha overheard bits of a conversation behind her.

Neill Frederickson, perhaps making small talk or perhaps genuinely interested, asked, "So, do the girls have even a prayer tonight?"

Bill Merrick answered without hesitation, "Nope. None at all."

"Why do you say that, Bill?" Haskins retorted. "They gave Naz all they could handle at their place and, heck, the way they've been playing, who knows, right?"

"No, sir, Calvin. Not a prayer. You see the look in those girls' eyes? They're here on a mission tonight."

"Well, that'd be a shame, I suppose," Frederickson said. "You guys reckon we did the right thing letting 'em play after all?"

Simultaneously Haskins and Merrick answered, "Yes," and "No," respectively. They glanced at each other and shook their heads. Ever since the decision was made to let the girls play, the two old friends had been somewhat at odds. Haskins knew perhaps better than anyone what the girls had endured and overcome in the last few months. Bill Merrick, on the other hand, knew without a doubt how the season would end and he knew tonight's loss would leave a bitter taste in everyone's mouth. Everyone'd gotten themselves all worked up for nothing, he'd argued.

Martha could bite her tongue no longer. She turned back and gave the three an impish grin as she said, "Well, now, gentlemen, I expect to hear the three of you cheering for the young ladies tonight all the same." She patted Coach Merrick on the knee, then returned her gaze back to the court. The official was just about ready to toss the ball to begin the game.

Samuel Colter leaned back and said to Martha, "Well... here we go." Martha put a consoling hand on his shoulder. She knew the Colter family probably had a great deal riding on this game, almost certainly the last game of Sam's high school career. Sam still had been neither heavily recruited nor signed yet, and the entire family seemed on edge about Sam's college options. Samuel reached up across his chest and placed his hand on Martha's.

The official stepped in between Sam Colter and Nadine Collier at center court, ready to get the game underway. The two players made eye contact, then focused on the ball. The official bounced the ball a few times on the floor, held it firmly between his two hands, and deliberately brought the ball upward to toss it high into the air. The ball seemed to rotate in slow motion as it floated upward to its zenith. As the ball reached the highest point in its trajectory, Sam and Nadine exploded up from the floor, each with an outstretched arm, and extended their fingers upward, each hoping to be the first to touch the ball and gain control for her team. Each wanted desperately to win the tip, and the game, but for far different reasons.

Nazareth had the district title already locked up with seven district wins and no losses so on paper the game meant nothing. However, Nadine Collier, like the rest of her teammates and indeed her entire small town, wanted to send a message that the near miss in Nazareth was a fluke. For Sam and her teammates, however, this game meant everything. This game would serve as a milestone in a long and difficult journey; either the journey ended here tonight or, by divine providence, perhaps, the game propelled the Lady Longhorns into the playoffs against all odds. Furthermore, and perhaps adding to the drama of it all, the Lady Longhorns wanted and needed to avenge not just the loss but also the foul play in Lazarus. Sam, in particular, needed to right the wrong.

The official tossed the ball perfectly. The ball floated high above everyone and hung suspended in midair, just out of reach of the two sets of grasping fingers, for what seemed an eternity.

Mary's Kitchen didn't serve chicken spaghetti and garlic bread very often. In fact, the kitchen actually buttered huge, thick pieces of Texas toast and generously sprinkled garlic salt on them; there was no French bread or other such loaves to be had in Lazarus. In light of the big game later that evening, though, Martha figured spaghetti would be better for the girls than chicken fried steak or fried chicken or Salisbury steak or fried chicken tenders. As Martha set the plates of spaghetti down on the table in front of the girls, she made an observation that caught the girls completely off-guard.

"Well, ladies, it looks like we've got ourselves a little winning streak going here."

All at once the girls froze for a moment to consider. They looked around at each other in disbelief.

"That's only two games," Brooklynne deduced.

Martha smiled and patted Brooklynne on the head as she said, "I didn't say it was a big streak, but it's a winning streak nonetheless. Beating Kress and Happy does count as a win streak. Now, if we can knock off Silverton, we'll just run that streak to three games." She passed out the rest of the plates as a waitress brought them out of the kitchen. "I sure am proud of you, ladies. It does my heart good to see you getting on with things."

"Sure was nice of Principal Haskins to give us lunch off-campus today," Cassie said to no one in particular between mouthfuls of pasta. "How'd we manage that? He used to only do that for the football team."

Martha just smiled and winked at a few of the girls as they looked to her for an answer. Rather than elaborating, she asked, "How're you ladies feeling about the game tonight?"

Uncharacteristically, Molly spoke up, "I think we'll take 'em tonight. Last time we finished the game with only four players on the court, at their place, and we only lost by three. We won't let that happen tonight."

"Nope, not in our gym," MJ added.

"And not on my watch," said Sam.

The girls chuckled a bit and dove into their spaghetti. Martha stood and smiled, content that she could just watch the girls be girls again for a change. Martha had been so thankful for the girls in recent weeks. She knew how much Summer missed her sister. She'd heard Summer crying in her room many nights since the accident. Summer may have been a stalwart in public, but behind closed doors she hurt terribly and wept often. Martha always welcomed the girls to her modest home whenever they could drop by to see Summer, to do homework or to play with April. The friendships meant the world to Summer. Just months before, Summer had been a pariah but she now felt she belonged, that she had a place, that she had a group in which she felt safe.

Nairobi noticed Martha hovering over the table. She reached and took Martha's hand as she invited Martha to join them for the meal.

"Tell you the truth, I don't mind if I do."

About the time the girls were cleaning their plates with the last few pieces of garlic bread, an older couple shuffled toward them from the other side of the dining area. As the couple approached, hand in hand like newlyweds, the gentleman paused near where the girls were seated. He wore dusty blue overalls, a heavy work coat and a vintage red cap emblazoned with an "L" that probably used to be white.

"What time do you ladies play tonight?" he asked.

For the second time in the same meal, everyone at the table simultaneously stopped what they were doing mid-chew and mid-sentence. The girls turned to see who had stopped to ask the question. After a moment of awkward silence and conspicuous staring, Summer told him they played at five. He wished them luck and said he'd try to get by tonight if the cold didn't make his joints ache too much. The old gentleman released his wife's hand and made his way to the cash register to settle his bill. His wife, hunched over and frail, remained with the girls.

"I used to play basketball, too, you know. That was ages ago." Her eyes twinkled for just an instant.

"Were you good?" Brooklynne inquired.

"I *was* pretty good, sweetie, but things were a lot different in my day. I bet you didn't know it, but when I played all the girls wore skirts. And they only let us play on half the court."

"No way!" The girls couldn't believe it. They'd never heard anything like this before.

"Know what else?" She leaned in a little closer and slid her glasses down her nose so she could look over the top of the frames at the girls. She looked around to be sure neither her husband nor anyone else could hear her. She whispered, "They wouldn't let us jump either."

Sam asked what everyone else was thinking, "What the heck?"

"Afraid jumping would shake up our ovaries and foul things up in here," she said with a sly grin as she patted her belly.

The girls roared with laughter and fell all over one another. They couldn't believe what they'd just heard.

"Now, I want you girls to win tonight, you hear? And jump up and down all you want. You won't hurt a thing."

With that, she smiled at the girls and shuffled off to meet her husband at the exit.

The Lady Longhorns had finished their informal pregame stretching and warm-up drills and had returned to the locker room for Coach Lewis to go over the last minute details. He circled the girls and reminded them what happened in Silverton in the previous game against the Lady Owls. Nairobi and Sam should have dominated, but Nairobi had been in foul trouble. Rita fouled out, leaving the team without its point guard. Others, too, fouled so much that the Lady Longhorns ended the game with only four players on the floor. This could not happen again, especially at home. The game plan for tonight, he reminded them, would be slow, conservative and methodical. Plenty of zone and no man-to-man. Plenty of help side defense and nobody getting isolated one on one. No stupid fouls. Good positions for rebounds, especially on the offensive end. The girls were focused and ready to play. They were just about to break when Summer burst through the locker room door. She hustled to Coach Lewis's side and whispered something in his ear. Coach Lewis nodded and sent her back to the bench to make sure things were in order. The team huddled, cheered and headed out to the gym for their run-in and pregame passing and shooting drills.

Coach Lewis went over the game plan in his head once more, reviewed the stats from the last game against Silverton then exited the locker room. He opened the door half-way then paused. Summer had been right. There were more people in the stands tonight than there had been at any Lady Longhorns home game this season. The stands were far from full, but the difference was noticeable. As always, the girls' parents were well represented. The usual school administrators were there. But there were dozens of people he had never noticed at a girls' game before. Some he recognized as teachers, some as Lazarus High School students, some as parents of students. Coach Lewis took a deep breath and exhaled with a sense of satisfaction.

To the delight of everyone in the home section of the gym, the game plan for Silverton worked to perfection. After a slow start by both teams, the first period ended in a tie; however, only Cassie had picked up a foul. In the second period, Sam hit some big shots down low and Brooklynne sank some pivotal threes from the corner to give Lazarus an eight-point lead going into halftime. In the third period, Silverton came out feeling aggressive and ready to press full court, but Rita and MJ went to work and shredded their press; after conceding an 8-0 run, Silverton called a time out and dropped back into a zone. Sam and Brooklynne went to work again, playing a deadly inside out game that put Lazarus ahead by an unbelievable nineteen points at the end of three periods of play.

Despite believing the game was well in hand, Coach Lewis sent the starters back onto the floor to begin the fourth period. He looked down the bench past Summer and saw Molly and Cassie completely into the action, cheering their teammates with towels waving and fists pumping. It made him happy to see how far those two had come since the beginning of the journey: Cassie in terms of confidence, ability and maturity, and Molly in terms of attitude. Coach Lewis called a time out and subbed in the two reserves for Rita and Sam. Coach Lewis wanted these two to get some rest, but he also wanted Nairobi to get some work on her own down low and Cassie and Molly to get plenty of touches on the ball. As Rita and Sam came off the court together, an unusual thing happened. A number of the fans stood and applauded. Their praise clearly was intended for the two girls and the entire team noticed.

"Uh, *chica*, what's going on in here?"

"I have no idea," Sam said as she scanned the stands, "but I have to admit I like it. A lot."

They high-fived, embraced quickly and returned to the bench where they cheered for their teammates with as much energy as they had expended on the court. The Silverton coach, seeing the two starters head to the bench, went back to his press and prompted his girls to pick up their intensity. The Lady Owls gained a little ground, but they never moved within striking distance of the Lady Longhorns. To the delight of the hometown fans, Lazarus finished the game and won by fifteen, the team's third win in a row. As the girls danced off the court back to the locker room, a few of them noticed the couple from Mary's Kitchen sitting on the first row. Still in his overalls and

323

coat, the gentleman tipped his cap to the girls as they passed. His wife, sitting next to him and holding his hand once again, smiled and winked.

In the locker room, MJ got everyone quiet as Coach Lewis and Summer made their way into the frenzy of ecstatic players.

"OK, Coach, everyone wants to know."

"Wants to know what?" He was baffled.

"Can we talk about the playoffs now? You said 'let's get a win against Silverton and…'"

He put his hands up defensively and interrupted her.

"I changed my mind. I don't think it's a good idea to start talking playoffs yet. That's only four district wins. We'll need six."

"Yea, but we got Hart, Coach," MJ fired back. "We already beat 'em once. They got nothing on us now."

The girls whooped and high-fived each other, but Coach Lewis calmed them back down.

"First, of all teams, *we* cannot afford to take anyone for granted. Even Hart. We have to take one game at a time. Let's just take care of Hart and then we'll talk. I promise."

The girls were disappointed. They wanted to talk about playoffs. For the first time ever, the Lazarus girls had a shot at the playoffs and they wanted to explore that possibility more.

"Go enjoy this win over the weekend but whatever you do, don't let it go to your heads. Get plenty of rest and be ready for practice Monday. You know," he continued after a slight pause, "this is some journey we've been on, huh?"

"Don't get all sappy on us, Coach," Sam said as she threw her warm-ups at him. "It ain't over yet."

Coach Lewis exited the locker room full of pride. He grabbed a Diet Dr. Pepper and some nachos from the concession stand, which happened to be open and enjoying a booming business during the girls game for a change, and retired to the stands where he watched the Silverton Owls prey upon the faltering Lazarus Longhorns.

On Sunday evening, Coach Lewis sat in his favorite booth at Mary's Kitchen and reviewed the week ahead: Hart, away on Tuesday, then Nazareth, at home on Friday. He was glad the schedule had worked out this way. First, at least on paper, the girls shouldn't have any trouble against Hart; they'd handled them once already. Second, he and the girls needed the practice time to prepare for Nazareth. Against his better judgment, he decided to look past Hart and start preparations for the Nazareth game. Monday would be devoted to ball-handling and shooting drills, to knock off any rust the girls may have accumulated over the weekend, and to the Nazareth game plan. As he worked his way through his cheeseburger basket and onion rings, he scribbled and scratched notes, drew up a few new inbounds plays, reviewed the stats from the last contest and scribbled some more.

In the locker room before the Hart game, Coach Lewis reminded the team about Sam's quadruple double the last time these two teams met. Clearly, the defensive focus would be on Sam tonight for the *other* Lady Longhorns and the rest of the team would have to take advantage of opportunities to score whenever possible. His gamble paid off later that evening as the Lady Longhorns of Lazarus left the Hart High School gymnasium with their fourth win in a row. Hart indeed had come out ready to clamp down on Sam, but Nairobi had a breakout game and notched a double-double in the process. Rita also had a field day dishing assists to open girls, MJ being one of them, who had no trouble draining the open shots created by double-teams on Sam. There were more Lazarus fans in the gym at Hart than anyone could have expected and the girls fed off their energy all night long. Also in the gym that night, though, were two men seated on the top row of the stands next to Coach Cannon. Coach Lewis wouldn't have recognized the two if he had seen them, but he certainly would have recognized their jackets to be the distinctive blue and gold of Nazareth.

The day of the showdown finally arrived after two days of intense practice, nervous waiting and endless planning and scheming from Coach Lewis. A few of the parents, namely Jasperson and Frost, along with Coach Cannon, sat in the stands and watched practice on Wednesday and Thursday as the girls finalized the game plan for Friday night. When the girls arrived at school on Friday, much to their surprise they discovered red and white ribbons and cute little "Good Luck!" signs taped to their lockers. *Another first*, they thought. The kind gesture from the cheerleading squad helped ease the tension of the day. The teachers offered words of encouragement and several promised to be at the game. Principal Haskins even surprised the girls with another off-campus lunch privilege so they could eat lunch together at Mary's Kitchen again. The positive energy felt foreign to the girls but they basked in the unprecedented attention.

Across town later that afternoon, Martha put the finishing touches on a handmade sign, turned out the lights and hung her sign on the door of Mary's Kitchen on her way out. The sign read, "WHAT ARE YOU DOING HERE? YOU SHOULD BE AT THE GYM. SEE

YOU AFTER THE GAMES. – MARTHA" Martha arrived at the gym a little early, as usual, and discovered a surprising number of vehicles already in the parking lot. Sure, many of the cars and trucks sported blue and gold paint on the windows and Nazareth stickers on the back bumpers and back windows, but there were plenty she recognized as local, but hadn't seen before at a girls' game. She thought to herself how much she wished Autumn could see how the tide had begun to turn.

Inside the gym, electricity filled the air as the teams prepared for tipoff. The Nazareth fans, overflowing the visitors' section, filled the gym with raucous cheers and obnoxious racket. The Lazarus fans, still outnumbered by the visitors, worked hard to let the girls know that the Naz faithful weren't the only ones ready for a big game. The perennial powerhouse versus the flash-in-the-pan had morphed into a main event somehow, and the gym brimmed with excitement.

As the ball came down from its peak, Sam got her fingers on it first. She tipped it back to MJ, who then hit Rita streaking down the left sideline. The crowd roared as Rita received the perfect pass, put the ball on the floor and attacked the basket. The crowd then gasped in horror as Whitney Huff, a streak of blue jersey, raced in at a hard angle from the right side to cut off Rita's layup attempt; Huff swiped at the ball but collided with Rita and sent her spinning and flailing to the floor where she skidded past the baseline and came to rest against the wall of the gym. A hush fell over the entire gym.

As the Swiftettes nonchalantly made their way back toward their bench, Coach Lewis, Summer and the rest of the Lady Longhorns rushed to see about their fallen player. The officials reported the foul on Huff to the scorer's table, ordered the teams to the lane and waited to see if Rita could shoot her free throws. Rita hobbled to the free throw line and grimaced as she set her feet; she clearly had all her weight on her left foot while her right foot hung lifelessly like the leg of an injured animal. Rita sank her first free throw, then her second. The Swiftettes quickly grabbed the ball, inbounded it and raced down the court for any easy five-on-four layup. Rita had dropped to the floor holding her ankle and spewing a stream of caustic Spanish expletives. Coach Lewis called a time out, helped Rita to the bench and subbed in Cassie. Rita's night was finished.

The electricity never returned that night. The girls from Nazareth had come ready to play and to send a message. The Swiftettes pressed relentlessly full-court and the Lady Longhorns had no chance at advancing the ball against the press while their point guard sat on the bench with a bag of ice on her ballooning ankle. Coach Lewis tried everything in his playbook, everything in his bag of tricks, but to no avail. Even when his girls broke the press and advanced the ball, the Swiftettes seemed ready for every play Lazarus ran. Nazareth had an answer for everything offensively and defensively. As the game went on, he could feel the journey winding to a close and the season slipping away. The girls, too, realized early on that on this night they were outmatched and outmanned. As such, the devastating blow that surely would have come with the loss of a close game was softened by the gradual realization that they were playing out their final minutes of the season. Coming out of the locker room for the second half, the Lady Longhorns huddled and decided to play hard, finish strong and go down fighting.

Once the game was out of hand early in the third period, Coach Lewis struggled to maintain his concentration. Several times in the second half, he found himself thinking back to various points throughout the season. He remembered winning the gym from the boys, stunning Whiteface, walking along the road amongst the mourners the night of the accident. Somehow winning his last four games in a row seemed a lifetime ago. Coach Lewis finally snapped back to reality when he realized his team had retreated to the bench and the official was trying to tell him his girls had just used their final timeout.

MJ had grabbed his clipboard and huddled everyone around her. Using one of Coach Lewis's markers, she scribbled some X's and O's and lines on the clipboard then handed it back to Summer. Coach Lewis was baffled. His girls were down thirty-five points late in the fourth period, even though they were playing as hard as if the game were tied, yet someone had called a timeout that seemingly would serve only to prolong the agony. Before MJ could rejoin the others, he grabbed her by the arm and asked her what the heck they were doing?

"Just watch," she said. She winked, gave her coach a mischievous smile, then scampered back to the far end of the court where her teammates had set up to inbound the ball against the Nazareth full-court press.

Coach Lewis looked past the scorer's table and the visiting bench to the far baseline, past where the Naz coach stood griping at his players for some misstep or for some mishandled pass. The official handed Sam the ball. Sam slapped the ball, triggering the beginning of the set play, and her four teammates broke sharply in four different directions. MJ darted up the sideline nearest the Nazareth bench and Sam fired the ball toward her. At the last second, though, MJ cut back toward the baseline away from where the ball had been thrown.

Clearly, it appeared, the timeout had resulted in a miscommunication rather than an effective strategy. If MJ had not cut when she did, she would have received a perfect pass from Sam right in front of the Nazareth bench. Instead, the missile Sam had launched from the baseline struck the Nazareth coach squarely in the side of his head and careened up toward the rafters. The ball struck with such force and took the coach by such surprise that he dropped his clipboard and fell forward onto two of his seated players; the three of them, chairs and all, toppled over backwards. Coach Lewis bit his lip to maintain his composure as the crowd erupted, the home section with cheers and laughter and the visitors' section with obscenities and protests.

When the final buzzer sounded, Nazareth showboated on the longhorn at center court as the Lady Longhorns made their way to the locker room. The Lazarus fans stood and applauded the girls for their effort as the team walked past. With tears in their eyes, the girls scanned the crowd and smiled, waved or blew kisses to their friends, family, teachers and other well-wishers. It hadn't ended the way they had hoped, but the stands were full of people, some smiling back at them and some crying, but applauding them nonetheless. Somewhere in the stands, Coach Cannon stood and rubbed his hands back and forth as if washing his hands after a job well done. As he made his way down through the cheering fans in the stands, he mumbled under his breath, "Well, that takes care of that."

With their arms around one another, the girls piled into the locker room and collapsed into a heap on the floor. No one said a word. To be sure, they were sad, but they weren't despondent. They had somehow figured out along the way that losing a game and even ending a season with a disappointing loss were just bumps in the road they would move past. These disappointments were nothing compared to losing Autumn, and everything needed to be kept in perspective along the way; as badly as Sam had wanted to make the playoffs, she had been the one reminding her teammates of this for weeks.

The girls grabbed Summer, dragged her into the middle of the pile and surrounded her. Alone together, they embraced and cried and laughed all at once. What a journey it had been. Though none verbalized it, they all desperately wished Autumn could have been with them the rest of the way to see how things had started to change. A few minutes later Coach Lewis joined them in the locker room where he just sat and watched his girls. After several minutes, the emotions wore off and the girls tried to compose themselves.

Coach Lewis got their attention, ready to give the final locker room postgame speech he had hoped he wouldn't have to deliver tonight. As he began, though, a knock at the door interrupted him and MJ's dad poked his head into the locker room.

"Coach, there's a guy out here wants to talk to the team. Says his name is Freeman and that it's important."

"He's a reporter from Lubbock," Coach Lewis responded in an irritated tone. "I don't think we have anything to say to him. Tell him to call me tomorrow."

"Coach, he's pretty insistent. He says you need to hear what he has to say."

Coach Lewis looked at the girls and they shrugged dispassionately.

"Fine, send him in, I guess."

A moment later a short, skinny little fellow wearing black nerd glasses on his nose and a handful of media-passes and IDs around his neck slipped into the locker room.

NATHAN BARBER

As he extended his hand to Coach Lewis, he said to the group, "So, ladies, my name is Eddie Freeman and I'm from the *Avalanche-Journal* down in Lubbock. See, I've been kind of following you guys for a few weeks, just watching to see how things would turn out for you since the accident and the big games that Sam has had, and I figured there might be a story here. So, listen, I'm sorry about how things turned out tonight. That's a tough one to lose, especially to a team like that. Anyway, that's not what I came in here to tell you, really. See, I just got off the phone with the desk down in Lubbock. Scores are starting to roll in from the girls' games all over. So, here's the deal. Kress beat Silverton tonight. Maybe fifteen minutes ago."

He waited for a response, but the girls stared blankly at him. He could see the wheels turning in Coach Lewis's head, though.

"Kress beat Silverton," he repeated. "So Silverton finished with four wins. They're out."

The girls' expressions told him it still hadn't registered yet.

"Listen, Nazareth won the district. Happy takes second place with five wins and a tie-breaker. So your five wins puts you in third." He could see the reality finally dawning on the girls. "You're in."

332

CHAPTER XVI

The Lady Longhorns and Coach Lewis wrapped up Thursday's practice, which was actually more like a final walkthrough and shootaround, and headed quickly across campus to the media room in the high school. When they arrived, their front-row, reserved seats were the only chairs left in the large room, so they grabbed the VIP seats. All the girls' parents were there waiting for them, even Cassie's mother and Brooklynne's parents; Martha had made some pretty persuasive phone calls to make that happen. Martha, the Reverend Washington, and other supporters from Greater New Life had claimed pretty good seats. A few other students, a handful of teachers and a few friends sat in the remaining seats. Cannon, Haskins, the General, Frederickson and a few others stood against the wall in the back of the room. Dee stood along a side wall next to Corey Colter, Roy and Summer; for the first time since the accident, Summer seemed genuinely happy and relaxed standing next to Roy. It was hard not to notice her wearing his letter jacket, which was three sizes too large, but suited her nonetheless. Once the girls were seated, someone flipped a switch and the big screen lowered slowly from inside the ceiling.

"OK," came a voice from the back of the room, "everyone quiet. Here it comes."

The room fell silent as the lights flicked off and the projector illuminated the room an eerie blue. After a brief moment of a blue screen, the screen came to life.

The pulsing ESPN-style music crescendos and the giant, red TWSR logo spins in from the left side and lands on top of the outline of the state of Texas centered in the middle of a white background. The logo, the state's outline and the music fade away and the scene changes suddenly to a beautiful sunrise over a barren landscape. Rich oranges, brilliant golds, intense reds and soft pinks fill the sky just over the horizon while deep blues and purple begin to emerge at the top of the scene. The camera slowly pans the horizon and finally stops when an attractive blond female reporter appears on the screen standing to the left of a road sign that reads "Welcome to Lazarus." White letters scroll across the bottom of the screen: VICTORIA AVERY, Texas Weekly Sports Report. After the sun dramatically peeks out over the horizon from somewhere off-camera and shimmers in her blond hair, Victoria begins her report. Half-way through her opening, the live shot changes and becomes a series of still images with a voice-over. The screen fills first with the Lazarus football field, then with the trophy case full of football trophies and memorabilia, then finally with a still image of the empty Lazarus gymnasium. Golden rays of sunshine pierce the darkness of the gym in a shaft that enters through a window and magically illuminates the longhorn at center court.

"A new day is dawning here in the football-crazy town of Lazarus, Texas. For a town whose revered football team usually is the only major media story, not to mention the only topic of conversation in the diner and around the water cooler, this has been an unusual winter."

The team photo of the Lady Longhorns from picture day fills the screen.

"The Lady Longhorns basketball team, which historically has experienced little success on the court, suddenly has become a hot topic here in Lazarus."

The photo changes to a couple of video sound bites featuring Victoria Avery holding a microphone as Lazarus citizens respond to a question.

With Mary's Kitchen in the background, an older gentleman in overalls and an old red cap speaks nervously into a microphone as he tries to decide if he should look at the camera or at Victoria. Letters scroll onto the screen: ERNEST STEWART, Lifelong Lazarus resident.

"We're just real proud of our girls. They've been through a lot here lately, you know, and they've worked real hard to just keep going," he says like a proud grandfather.

The clips fades out and a new one fades in.

With Lazarus High School in the background, Neill Frederickson, wearing a white shirt and a red tie dotted with tiny white Longhorn logos, speaks directly into the microphone while maintaining eye contact with Victoria. Letters scroll onto the screen: NEILL FREDERICKSON, Superintendent, Lazarus Independent School District.

"After what happened here, for these girls to respond the way they have, and to have this kind of success... they've really accomplished something."

The team photo reappears on the screen. Most of the screen becomes opaque except for a circular area first around Coach Lewis and then around Sam Colter.

"The Lady Longhorns' season began this year like many others. However, with an enthusiastic new coach and a talented move-in, the Lady Longhorns seemed like they might be on the verge of turning around a long-suffering program."

The screen fills with a printed copy of the Lady Longhorns schedule; the camera pans from top to bottom showing handwritten scores next to each of their games.

"The Lady Longhorns seemed on the right track, having recorded six wins on the season heading into Christmas break and with one of those wins a shocking upset of the Whiteface Lady Lopes. The Lady Longhorns earned their sixth win in their final game before Christmas, and the holidays, at that point, looked pretty promising for the program trying desperately to earn some respect both in the world of Texas basketball and, perhaps more importantly, in their hometown... where football always has been king."

The screen fades to black.

"Then, tragically, just four days before Christmas, the Lady Longhorns' senior guard and sister of the team's manager, Autumn Griffin, died in a violent automobile accident just outside the city limits."

First one image of the wreckage appears on the screen, then another, then finally an image appears showing items from Autumn's truck scattered about in the grass and blowing against the fence on the side of the road at the scene of the accident.

"To the tiny west-Texas community, it seemed that when Autumn died that cold, December night, a big part of the town died with her."

Video of Calvin Haskins replaces the depressing accident scene image. Haskins is seated in his office and he's holding a basketball in his hands. Letters scroll across the screen: CALVIN HASKINS, Principal, Lazarus High School.

"I've been here my whole life and I hadn't ever experienced anything like this town losing Autumn. That kinda thing doesn't happen around here so, really, none of us knew what to do, or how to act. It was like the life just went right of this place. And you know, it's not just about the death itself. I think it's just as much about what dies inside of us when something like that happens," Haskins says, making eye contact with neither Victoria nor the camera.

The Haskins video fades out and video of Victoria Avery, standing in front of Lazarus High School, fades in; the camera zooms gently until Victoria nearly fills the screen.

"Facing the daunting task of coping with the tragedy off the court, the school administration faced an excruciating decision about how to handle the loss on the court."

Victoria begins walking toward the gym and the camera follows.

"After days of heated and gut-wrenching deliberation, the administration rendered a heartbreaking decision: they would cancel the remaining games on the Lady Longhorns' schedule in order to give the girls a chance to grieve the loss of their fallen teammate."

Victoria reaches the gym, opens the door and walks quietly through the lobby and into the gym where she stops at center court; the camera follows.

"Then, in a sudden, if not miraculous, turn of events, the administration announced that the Lady Longhorns' district games would not be cancelled after all and the season would continue as scheduled."

Suddenly, as Victoria pauses, several loud clicks echo through the gym and the rows of lights overhead pop and buzz to life, slowly filling the gym with light.

"The mood of the girls, as one might imagine, changed from devastation to elation when they heard the news. They had been issued a new lease on life and they were determined to make the most of it."

The image of the Lady Longhorns' schedule reappears on the screen, with only the district games visible, and the camera pans again top to bottom. As before, the scores for the games are handwritten on the schedule. Victoria Avery's voice returns.

"After the Lady Longhorns opened district play with three consecutive losses, the administration, the parents and perhaps even some of the players began to wonder if finishing the season really would be in anyone's best interest. The Lady Longhorns won their next game, though, momentarily renewing hope, then dropped a disappointing, close game filled with controversy and heightened emotions to perennial powerhouse and district rival Nazareth. Just when those closest to the team expected a total collapse from the girls, something quite remarkable happened."

The schedule fades away and the image of a newspaper article from the *Lubbock Avalanche-Journal* appears. The title of the article reads, "Small-Town Team Reaches Milestone Despite Tragedy." Victoria's voice continues while the article remains on the screen.

"The Lady Longhorns, on the verge of declaring the entire season an utter disaster, rattled off four consecutive wins. With a little help on the final night of district play, the unlikely Cinderellas found themselves in third place in district and in the playoffs for the first time in school history."

The video transitions to a scene in the gym on the basketball court. Victoria is standing at center court with the Lady Longhorns running drills near the basket behind her. Standing with her are a few of the players. Letters scroll across the screen: SAM COLTER, RITA ROSALES AND BROOKLYNNE MEYERS, Lazarus Lady Longhorns.

"With five district wins and just eleven wins on the season, the Lady Longhorns of Lazarus, Texas, earned the dubious honor of being the team in the 1A-Division 2 playoffs with the fewest wins this season. If you ask the girls, though, they'll insist they weren't discouraged by that statistic one bit. As they will tell you, they were just thrilled to be in the playoffs at all."

Victoria hands the microphone to Sam. Rita smirks and winks at Sam while Brooklynne stares wide-eyed into the camera.

"No, ma'am. We didn't care about having the fewest wins of anybody. After all we'd been through and how hard we'd all played, we were just happy to still have one more game. Who knew, huh? We're still just trying to enjoy our journey, to be honest with you."

Rita reached up and pulled the microphone down so she could speak.

"We all just wish Autumn could've been with us all along. We're all a lot tighter now than we used to be and we're just sorry she can't see how it is now. Nobody in this town will ever forget this season. That's for sure. We miss you, Autumn!"

The girls wave at the camera and mouth the words "Hi mom" as the camera zooms in on Victoria. Trying hard not to let the impending tears streak her makeup, Victoria Avery continues.

"An amazing story, indeed. But where and how does this magical story end? Will there be a storybook ending in Austin, Texas? Or will there be more heartbreak and disappointment in the future for these amazing young women and their courageous town of Lazarus, Texas? The Lady Longhorns, to a player, assure me that no matter how this story ends, it will be a bittersweet combination of tragedy and triumph, and their only sadness will be for their friend, teammate and sister, Autumn Griffin."

The screen fades to black and "20" appears in the middle of the screen in white-trimmed red numerals. Three seconds later, the screen fades completely to black.

———

Martha slid into the booth next to Coach Lewis as the girls wrapped up their pregame meal of chicken spaghetti, salad and Texas toast garlic bread; Principal Haskins had granted off-campus lunch privileges again for the day of the playoff game against Texline since they'd be leaving school early anyway for the three-and-a-half hour trek north. As he was so focused on the notes and scouting report on the table in front of him next to his half-eaten chicken spaghetti, Coach Lewis hardly noticed Martha seated next to him until she spoke.

"How many times have you been over all that?"

"A hundred, maybe? I don't know. A lot."

"Coach, I'm sure you're ready," she said as she placed her aging hand on his. "How are you?"

"Scared to death, if I'm being honest. We're going to have our hands full tonight. We've got a torturous bus ride ahead. The girls seem too relaxed. Texline is really good and they've got a legit D-1 stud we've got to manage. The list goes on and on. My stomach is in knots."

"I'm sure it is. Are you exhausted yet? I have to confess. I'm exhausted."

"Actually, I am. I thought I was the only one feeling it. The girls and I have talked about it a lot during practice this week. On some level, we don't ever want this season to end and we just want to keep playing forever. It's like, if we can keep playing then all these memories, the time we spent with Autumn, the time we spent with each other, all will be fresh and right there with us. On the other hand, we're all spent, physically, emotionally. Every time we take the court, all the emotions get stirred up again and, on some level, we relive the last few months all over again. I'm not sure how much we have left in the tank. Does that make any sense at all?"

"Actually," Martha said, "perfect sense."

Martha stood and discreetly wiped a tear from her eye with her apron.

"Coach, go grab yourself a Diet Dr. Pepper and a couple of those homemade cookies by the register for the drive up. You be careful now and I'll see you up there later tonight. We're awful proud of you, you know."

"Who?" he asked as she walked away.

Over her shoulder she turned and answered, "Everyone."

A few moments later, Coach Lewis climbed aboard the short bus with his Dr. Pepper and cookies to go. His girls had already loaded and, giddy with excitement, they waited for their coach. When he boarded the bus, the girls whistled at him and teased him with catcalls. They'd never seen him wear a tie before. He got everyone's attention then addressed them one last time before heading north to Texline, another small west-Texas town, this one located directly on the New Mexico border and just south of the Oklahoma border.

"Alright, this is what we've waited for and worked for all season long," he began. "Ninety-six teams and one dream. Remember, all the first-place teams have a bye in the first round so don't be surprised to see other schools in the stands scouting tonight. After the first round games are done, sixty-four will be left in the second round, thirty-two after that, and so on. As always, the final four play in Austin on the big stage, front and center for the whole state to see. I figure we already beat one in a million odds so what's one in ninety-six, right?"

The girls cheered their approval.

"OK, as we're driving up this afternoon, I want you to go back over the game plan that we've worked on all week in your mind. Visualize the film we've seen of these guys. Visualize yourselves playing the perfect game. Remember, the big kid will be the best post player we've seen all season. She's fast, athletic and she can leap out of the gym. She's blocked nearly two hundred shots this year so don't forget about that. Guards and forwards, think about how we're going to attack offensively; Sam and Nairobi, think about how you'll defend her. Everything we do tonight offensively and defensively centers on number 00, Maryann Sparks. OK, then. It's going to be a long ride, so get comfortable and try to relax."

He plopped into the driver's seat and started the engine.

"Alright, let's go do this."

The road-weary Lady Longhorns arrived in Texline a little early to allow them ample time to stretch their legs and loosen up before game time. As they unloaded into the empty parking lot outside the gym, they realized the temperature seemed much lower than it had been in Lazarus; the cold didn't help with their stiff muscles. A custodian in a threadbare Texline Tornadoes letter jacket met them at the door and let them into the old gym. Once inside, the Lady Longhorns laced up their basketball shoes and ran some drills in an empty, silent gym; the Lady Tornadoes were nowhere to be seen. The girls finished their drills, and then retreated to their tiny, unwelcoming locker room to change into their uniforms, go over the game plan once more and wait for game time.

As they waited in the confines of the cold, cinder block locker room, they heard activity buzzing on the other side of the door. They heard people milling around in the gym and bustling about in the stands. They heard cheers and a round of applause, apparently signaling the emergence of the Lady Tornadoes from their locker room. They heard the squeak of basketball shoes for a few minutes as the home team stretched and ran about the court. Coach Lewis cracked the door to peek out at the clock and steal a glance at the Lady Tornadoes as they hustled back to their locker room, probably for their last-minute instructions. He shut the door then huddled his girls for yet another last-minute pep talk and his own final set of instructions.

Suddenly, hip-hop music blared in the gym and the crowd went wild; the home team had just left their locker room and had done their run-in. Coach Lewis decided to wait no longer.

"OK, this is it. No more pep talks. We all know what to do. It's time to get after these guys."

Coach Lewis flung open the door and his Lady Longhorns, bouncing on the balls of their feet with excitement, streamed out of the locker room and into the gym for their run-in and pregame warm-up drills. He drew a final, deep breath then stepped halfway out. Standing just outside the door blocking his way, however, stood Calvin Haskins. Haskins motioned for Coach Lewis to step back into the locker room then followed the young coach inside.

"Coach Lewis," he began, betraying no emotion, "before we get started I want you to know something. I can't say I ever liked you all that much. You came strutting in here from the big city a little too big for your britches, son."

Coach Lewis stood speechless. *This is not what I need to hear before my first, and perhaps my last, playoff game.*

"You still got some growing up to do and you still need to figure out your place around here. Having said that, though, Coach, I want you to know there's a hell of a lot of good people out there that drove an awful long way to support your girls tonight. What y'all have been through... What we've all been through, really, the last several months... Everyone was just torn up after Autumn died and for a while there I was beginning to think this town would never recover. Somehow, son, your girls have breathed some new life into everyone. Your girls have got some fight in 'em that none of us ever knew was there. I think there's real joy and real life starting to return to Lazarus.

Anyway, I say all that just to let you know we're all pulling for you and the girls. No matter what happens out there tonight, son, it's been some ride."

With that, Calvin Haskins gave Coach Lewis a manly pat on the shoulder, walked out of the locker room and climbed into the stands. As Coach Lewis drew a deep breath and headed for the visitors' bench, he glanced up into the stands and froze. He hardly could believe the scene before him. He continued on toward his bench and strolled almost confidently across the court, fighting off a ridiculous grin that seemed determined to fix itself on his face. As the music faded away, he became fully aware of the volume of the rowdy fans across the court. The atmosphere was just as intense as he imagined it would be.

"Coach," Sam practically yelled at him as she grabbed him by the shoulders, "we may have a problem. You see how many girls they have? They didn't have that many on the video."

Coach Lewis turned and counted the girls seated on and standing around the home bench. He wrinkled his brow and counted again. The game film he'd seen indicated Texline would have only nine girls and really would play only seven of them. To his disbelief, he counted sixteen girls of all shapes and sizes dressed out in slick white uniforms with maroon and black trim.

"That must be every girl in this town," Brooklynne said as she stared past the scorer's table.

"Something else is weird, too, Coach," Summer added. "Where's Sparks? She's listed in the scorebook but we haven't seen her yet. Didn't she warm up with the rest of the team?"

Coach Lewis hadn't noticed when he peeked out earlier, but indeed big #00 was nowhere to be seen. He turned back to his team and shrugged. Without warning, the crowd erupted and the entire Lady Longhorns team craned their necks to locate the cause of the ruckus. At the far end of the gym, behind the home bench, Maryann Sparks exited the locker room and entered the gym.

Nairobi turned to Coach Lewis and said, not at all trying to hide her excitement, "Sparks is on crutches! She's not even in uniform!"

"Now what, Coach?" asked Rita, who happened to still be nursing a sore and swollen ankle. "Our whole plan revolved around her."

Coach Lewis thought about it a moment as he watched Sparks hobble to the bench.

"Get the ball in to Sam. Period," he said as he turned back to his team. "Everyone got that? The ball goes in to Sam. They've got nobody to cover Sam."

Moments later, Sam easily won the jump ball to begin the game and she tipped the ball behind her directly into Rita's hands. With the Texline guards swarming everywhere, Rita patiently advanced the ball down the floor. Beneath the basket, Sam had posted up hard against a skinny little Lady Tornado; it looked as though Sam was going to have a field day. Rita cleared Brooklynne out of the corner, dribbled out to the wing and easily passed the ball inside to Sam. Sam gave her defender a signature head fake, spun and made her move to the rim; she expected an easy basket. As Sam moved to the rim, though, her defender along with the next two closest defenders collapsed onto Sam, hacking and flailing at the ball. Sam's teammates heard the aggressive slaps on Sam's arms from across the gym. The referee blew his whistle, reported the foul and set Sam on the free throw line.

Coach Lewis screamed for a time out as he jumped up and down and signaled to the closest official. The official awarded Lazarus the time out and the Lady Longhorns jogged back to the bench wondering amongst themselves why their coach had burned a valuable time out just a few seconds into the game. When they reached their bench, Coach Lewis grabbed Sam's arm and inspected the fifteen or so little red marks left by defenders' slapping fingers.

"You get it?"

His girls just looked at him.

"Do you see what's happening? Hack-a-Shaq. It makes perfect sense."

They stared back at him without saying a word.

"On the video we watched, they had nine players, counting Sparks. Without Sparks, though, they'd be screwed trying to defend Sam. Unless… Unless they put a whole army in uniform to foul Sam every time she takes a shot. They have sixteen girls suited up. Theoretically, that's sixty-four fouls to give without a single player fouling out. They could dole out another eleven fouls and still have five players left. They're probably going to sub in and out like line changes in a hockey game, too, so the players on the floor are always fresh and their best offensive players don't end up in foul trouble."

As he explained, the gravity of the situation dawned on the girls. MJ spoke up.

"So they're gonna press us all night, trap the guards like they did on the video, then they're gonna clobber Sam every time she touches the ball?"

"Wow," Brooklynne added, "that's genius."

All eyes turned to Sam.

"Give me the ball. I can handle as many fouls as they can throw at me. We'll win this thing at the free throw line one shot at a time. I shoot free throws way better than Shaq ever did."

Just like that, Sam put her team on her shoulders, fully intending to carry them all night. Each trip down, the Lazarus guards worked against the press and Texline's relentless traps to get the ball inside to Sam knowing the defenders were going to collapse onto her and foul her repeatedly and aggressively. Each time the defenders fouled Sam, the Lazarus fans grew more and more irritated. They berated the officials and told them to take control of the game. They hissed at the Texline fans. They derided the Texline coach. Unfortunately, the incessant roar of the Lazarus crowd did not have the desired effect. The Lady Tornadoes seemed to feed off the noise and the commotion and their game plan soon took its toll on Sam and the Lady Longhorns. After one period of play, the Lady Longhorns trudged back to their bench down by seven points.

Sam, Nairobi, Brooklynne, MJ and Rita plopped down in their seats as Summer, Molly and Cassie handed out cups of water. Rita drained her cup then turned to massage her ankle, hoping no one would notice. MJ grabbed her cup and threw it against the wall behind her. Nearly on the verge of tears from the abuse, Sam just hung her head and rubbed the red, puffy and scratched skin on her arms. Coach Lewis tried to focus his team and calm them down.

"Coach," Sam said quietly, "this is way worse than I thought. They're killing me. I think they'll do the same thing to Nairobi even if I screen for her and try to help her get open down low for some shots. I was wrong, Coach. I don't think I can do this all night."

Nairobi patted Sam on the back and said, "Let's try it a few times anyway. Let me take some of those blows and give you a break." Sam nodded in agreement.

Brooklynne spoke up next, also frustrated. "And I can't get my shots off. Those guards are everywhere."

The rest of the girls griped and complained, too, already frustrated and off their game. Coach Lewis hadn't anticipated such a rough go of it with Sparks on the bench. His mind raced against the clock to think of something brilliant to say before the buzzer sounded for the second period but nothing brilliant came to him. He settled for predictable.

"OK, Sam and Nairobi, you guys will have to shoulder the load together. Cassie, get in there for Brooklynne and see if you have any luck driving to the basket as they rotate to trap. Molly, you be ready to relieve Cassie or MJ. Rita, you're doing a great job handling the press. Just keep that ball back where they can't get it. We all have to stay calm and focused. Let's make 'em pay for all these cheap shots they're dishing out. Here we go. Longhorns on three!"

The Lady Tornadoes delivered more of the same as the second period got underway. In less than a minute of game play, Texline put Nairobi on the line three times. Nairobi cracked under the pressure; she made just two of her six free throw attempts. On the other end of the floor, the Texline guards got hot and drained three consecutive three-pointers. The lead grew to eleven and the energy of the Longhorn fans waned. Dejected, the girls from Lazarus felt the game slipping away.

Determined to right the ship after the third three-pointer, Sam quickly inbounded the ball to Rita, who raced down the court with her mind set on attacking the basket and taking a layup. To no one's surprise, the white-clad Lady Tornadoes raced to the basket and crushed Rita as she left the floor for her shot. Reminiscent of the last game, Rita crashed to the floor and skidded to a stop far away from where she got fouled. Incensed, the Lazarus fans erupted and called for the officials to give the Lady Tornadoes a flagrant foul. Coach Lewis, too, flew from his place on the bench and stepped onto the court to give the officials a piece of his mind. While one official reported the foul under the basket, another official made a "T" with his hands, shrieked his whistle and charged Coach Lewis with a technical foul. The wheels were coming off in a hurry. Coach Lewis called another time out to compose himself and his team.

When his team reached the bench, he immediately noticed Rita's ankle swelling to the point he thought it might pop like a balloon.

"Rita," he said as he put his hand on her shoulder, "get some ice on that ankle. I'm afraid you're done."

Normally, Rita would have uttered a stream of expletives, probably in Spanish, but Rita was broken. She pulled a towel over her head and sobbed. She couldn't stomach the thought of her season ending this way.

Coach Lewis got all his players seated on the bench and knelt in front of them with his back to the chanting crowd across the court. The girls' faces said they had just about reached their limit. Perhaps all the stress of the season, of losing Autumn, of fighting so hard through district, had taken its toll. Perhaps the girls were spent. Suddenly, Molly jumped up and pointed across the gym.

"Roy's here!"

Summer wondered what had possessed Roy to drive all the way to Texline. She stood without thinking and looked his direction. He flashed Summer a quick thumbs up then disappeared briefly behind the far end of the bleachers. After a moment, he reappeared. When he did, Summer stammered, "Oh. My. God. He's got company." She tapped Coach Lewis on the shoulder then covered her mouth in astonishment. As Coach Lewis turned to glance over his shoulder, the rest of the Lady Longhorns stood and watched, dumbfounded. Rita pulled the towel off her head and dropped it to the floor.

Across the court at the far end of the gym, the Lazarus Longhorns football team filed past Roy, who seemed to be directing traffic. They marched along the sideline for the entire length of the court and lined up shoulder to shoulder on the floor in front of the first row of the stands. The intimidating line stretched from one baseline to the other and made the Texline fans feel as though their town had just been invaded by hostile forces. The entire group wore the unmistakable red and white Lazarus letterman jackets, the ones that matched the one Summer had on at that very moment. One by one, they put their hands together, slowly at first and then with more energy, until the applause reached a deafening crescendo. Like sheet lightning before an impending storm, the energy from their applause coursed through the stands and the rest of the Lazarus fans rose to their feet. The very fans who had nearly given up hope just moments earlier roared with excitement and showered praise on their team battling on the court below. The energy from the stands billowed onto the court and flowed across to the other side where it washed over the girls.

"Is this really happening?" Cassie asked no one in particular.

Summer put her arm around Cassie and answered, "I'd give anything for Autumn to see this."

Cassie leaned her head over and whispered in Summer's ear, "I bet she can."

Suddenly reenergized, the girls bounced up and down as they huddled up. In a minute's time, the Lady Longhorns went from feeling utter desperation to eerie invincibility.

"After Brooklynne makes these free throws for Rita," Sam interjected before they headed back onto the court, "let's get a stop and get the ball back. Then give me the freaking ball next time down. And the next. And the next. I didn't work my butt off all season long to get sent packing by a bunch of little midgets!"

To the delight of the Lazarus crowd, Brooklynne drained both free throws for Rita, who sat with her shoe off and a bag of ice taped to her grapefruit-sized ankle. The Lady Longhorns took Sam's words to heart and did just what Sam instructed. They battled on defense then found a way to feed the ball in to Sam on offense. Sam gritted her teeth, braced for the fouls then went to the line. She didn't miss a free throw the rest of the half and at halftime Lazarus trailed by only four.

After halftime, the Lady Tornadoes stuck to their game plan and continued the brutal assault on Sam down low. As minutes ticked away in the third period, the home team's players started fouling out of the game at a rate of about one per minute. As their opponents' numbers dwindled, the Lady Longhorns smelled blood and, from somewhere deep inside, a killer instinct surfaced in the girls from Lazarus. The football players, too, smelled blood and focused their attention on the Lady Tornadoes. They heckled the home team mercilessly, taunted Texline's coach and mooed repeatedly at the Texline cheerleaders. With the help of their newly expanded cheering section, the Lady Longhorns were turning the tables on the home team. After a series of dramatic lead changes in the third period, the visiting team pulled away for good in the fourth.

When the final buzzer sounded, the Texline players retreated to their bench where they sobbed and pouted and sat with their faces buried in their hands. Sam and her teammates, though, raced to center court where they embraced and fell into a pile right on top of the giant black and maroon tornado painted in the middle of the court. The stands emptied in a flash. The Texline fans made their way out of the gym to get away as quickly as possible from the obnoxious out-of-towners, while the applauding Lazarus fans spilled onto the court and surrounded the battle-weary but victorious Lady Longhorns.

Near the scorer's table, the stunned coaches met and shook hands before making their way in opposite directions to their respective teams. Coach Lewis paused a moment to take in the scene. The scoreboard read "Texline 46 Visitor 61." The last of the maroon-and-black-clad fans streamed out of the gym shaking their heads. In the center of the basketball court, the pile of girls disappeared behind a wall of red and white letter jackets and a throng of other fans trying to congratulate the girls. All the Lazarus fans, regardless of where they stood, continued their applause. Many had tears in their eyes. Coach Lewis caught a brief glimpse of Sam's parents hanging onto one another in the stands – going thirty-one of thirty-six from the line and finishing with forty-one points and nineteen rebounds after being mauled the entire game, Sam had turned in one of the gutsiest performances he'd ever witnessed. He scanned the chaos on the floor. To his surprise and delight, he saw Roy and Summer in an emotional embrace with Martha weeping joyfully close by. He saw the Reverend Washington pointing and looking upward. The court had become a mosh pit of revelers hugging and high-fiving one another. Even the football players, who patted the girls on the backs and bumped knuckles with them, seemed genuinely thrilled. Coach Lewis photographed the scene in his mind's eye for posterity and wished with all his heart the journey could end like this.

There formed a perfect storm that night in Texline. On any other night, the Lady Longhorns probably would have been eliminated from the playoffs, their unforgettable season complete. Some people chalked it up to pure chance, others to providence, others to fate and still others attributed the outcome to Autumn's being the angel on the shoulder of her team. With Maryann Sparks out, with Roy and his guys leading the cheers, with Sam hell-bent on winning at all costs, the Lady Longhorns defied all odds and advanced to the field of sixty-four.

As if the evening weren't fortuitous enough already for the girls from Lazarus, there happened to be in the stands that night assistant coaches from several colleges. Although they had been in Texline to scout Maryann Sparks, they stayed to watch the big kid from Lazarus, Sam Colter. Though the coaches weren't ready to sign Sam after her performance against a horde of inferior defenders, they were intrigued enough by her gutsy performance to add her next game against the Shamrock Lady Irish to their calendars. After the game, Calvin Haskins handed Coach Lewis a small stack of business cards from the scouts along with the scouts' requests for Sam's highlight film. Coach Lewis flipped through the cards: Texas Tech, Oklahoma, Texas, New Mexico, and Baylor. Sam and her dad both cried when Coach Lewis shared the news.

"Any idea which lucky school gets Sam Colter?"

"You know, Coach," Sam said through her tears, "I'm thinking I might look pretty good in green and gold."

"Congratulations!" Coach Lewis shook Mr. Colter's hand then embraced Sam. "Baylor couldn't be getting a better kid," Coach Lewis added.

Early the next morning, Coach Lewis's phone rang and woke him from his much-needed Saturday morning slumber; on the line was Eddie Freeman down in Lubbock at the *Avalanche-Observer*. Eddie apologized for the early call, but he had a long list of coaches to talk to today. Eddie explained that although he hadn't been in Texline last night, he'd sent an intern to the game to snap some photos and take some notes and it sounded like a heck of a game. He went on to explain that he'd added the Shamrock game to his calendar, not to attend himself, of course, because it happened to be so far away, but he'd send his intern again. Eddie wished Coach Lewis good luck and, oh by the way, a friend of his at the Texas Weekly Sports Report had been following the team lately and would be interested in doing a little TV piece if the girls could somehow find a way to knock off Shamrock.

CHAPTER XVII

Before Sam broke her huddle at the top of the key and stepped back to the free throw line, she reminded her teammates, "After I make this, we need the ball or a foul! Find your girl, get on her and get us a steal or a foul! This is it, ladies! Right here, right now."

As Sam stepped to the free throw line, her knees wobbled from exhaustion and sweat dripped from her forehead. In front of her on the left side of the lane stood two black-clad Lady Tigers with MJ in between, and in front of her on the right side of the lane stood two Lady Tigers with Nairobi in between. Behind Sam, Rita and Cassie clung to the opposing point guard who danced around near center court trying to shake her unwanted company. The official reminded the girls the next shot was live. All six of the girls between Sam and the rim took their positions, all determined to come down with the rebound in the unlikely event that Sam missed. They tensed their fatigued muscles, leaned in toward the center of the lane and waited for Sam's free throw.

About halfway up the uncomfortable gold bleacher seats of the Amarillo High School gymnasium, some ten rows above the rest of the

Lazarus crowd, Calvin Haskins stood with Tommy Cannon, Bill Merrick and Patton McArthur. As Sam stepped to the free throw line far below and waited for the official to bounce the ball to her, Haskins leaned in toward his three companions. He asked them a question and elbowed Cannon, then realized they hadn't heard him because of the roar of the crowd.

He elbowed Cannon again and yelled, "Still standing by your prediction?"

"Absolutely."

"How 'bout you?" he yelled as he reached across Cannon and prodded the other two.

With their arms crossed, they glared at Haskins and returned their gaze to the basketball court far below. On the court, the official gave inaudible instructions to the girls around the lane then sent the basketball to Sam with a perfect bounce. Sam caught the ball, spun it backwards in her hand and bounced it on the floor three times, just as she did before every free throw she shot. She brought the ball upward into her shooting position as she exhaled and bent her knees, all in one smooth motion.

The fans from Lazarus grew suddenly quiet as they inhaled almost in unison and held their collective breath. The fans from Groom, on the other hand, squeezed out every decibel they could muster while they stomped their feet and clapped their hands violently. The fans gathering elsewhere around the gym for the next game also stood transfixed, unable to tear their eyes away from the unfolding drama. On both benches, the players sat on the edges of their chairs and clenched the hands of the players and managers seated next to them. The coach from Groom stood with her arms crossed and her weight shifted onto one hip while she tapped her toe. Coach Lewis looked slightly less calm with his hands on head and his fingers buried somewhere in his hair. Behind the scorer's table, Victoria Avery sat with her camera man, unsure at this point which direction to head after the game for the first interview.

Somewhere in the black and gold bleachers of the modern, large-capacity gym sat Martha. She could no longer bear to watch. The game had been too intense, too stressful. With her eyes closed and her hands folded in her lap, she sat still and quiet in the midst of the insanity around her. *These girls have endured so much*, she kept thinking to herself, *more than anyone deserves*.

Sam bent her knees and pushed against the floor through her heels and through her legs. Her body straightened, her arms moved upward and out in front of her toward the rim, her wrists flicked forward and the energy flowed through her fingertips into the ball, carrying it forward precisely fifteen feet in a beautiful, slow-motion, arcing trajectory. The seams on the ball rotated backwards as the ball floated toward its destination. For a brief moment after she released the ball, Sam knew without a doubt it was one of the most beautiful shots ever to leave her fingertips: the perfect spin, the perfect velocity, the perfect arc. Beautiful.

———

Coach Lewis sat behind his desk in the solitude of the empty gym. With the boys no longer practicing basketball, the gym became almost too quiet each afternoon shortly after the girls finished their practice. They'd had another exceptional practice, due almost certainly to the momentum they'd picked up from the back to back wins over Texline and Shamrock. Most teams he'd been around tended to practice and play uninspired basketball after a huge emotional win. After two emotional wins, though, his girls showed no signs of coming out flat. Furthermore, they were playing anything but uninspired basketball. With the #20 and other items drawn in marker on their shoes, not to mention the new black shoelaces they added after the Shamrock win, the girls couldn't help but be inspired each time they headed onto the court.

Coach Lewis reflected on the win against the Shamrock Lady Irish, a team the Lady Longhorns had no business competing against, and replayed the final few minutes of the game in his mind. The girls took the floor with a swagger he hadn't seen before. Their attitude seemed to reflect both a feeling of invincibility and a "nothing to lose" sense of abandon. The Lady Irish, in their dazzling white uniforms with bright green numbers and trim, never knew what hit them. He felt sure Shamrock regarded the Lazarus win over Texline as a fluke – in truth it probably was – and Lazarus, therefore, was a team that could be overlooked. He knew in his gut Shamrock hadn't anticipated either Rita playing hurt or Sam being effective after the beating she took at Texline. The eyes of the Lady Irish surely were focused on the Groom Lady Tigers, one of the favorites to make the state tournament from Region 1. Coach Lewis couldn't help but chuckle as he mentally replayed Brooklynne's threes falling like rain on the frustrated Lady Irish guards in the final minutes just as the home team began to cut into the lead of the overachieving Lady Longhorns. Despite the two great practices since the Shamrock win, he couldn't imagine how his girls could play any better than they had played against Shamrock. He also couldn't imagine beating Groom unless his team played a perfect game.

"Coach?" Summer's voice interrupted his train of thought. "I brought you something."

Summer walked in and sat in one of the old chairs across the desk from her coach. She reached across the desk and handed him an envelope. He reached in and pulled out two newspaper articles. His eyes scanned the articles then he opened his desk drawer in search of pushpins.

"I thought those might look good on your little cork board up there on your wall."

"I think you're right," he said. "Someone mentioned the article about us beating Shamrock, but I hadn't been able to get my hands on a copy yet. I had no idea about this other. Thanks. These are great."

Coach Lewis mounted the first article, "Lazarus Girls Bring Bad Luck to Lady Irish," then mounted the next one right alongside, "Groom Pounces on Nazareth Swiftettes." That particular Nazareth loss and playoff exit made him almost as pleased as the fact that his girls had won and advanced.

"No problem."

"You know, I think that jacket suits you."

Summer's eyes twinkled and the slightest smile appeared.

"Things are looking up, huh?"

"Well," she said as her smile grew just a bit, "we're talking, at least. That's something. He's spent some time with April, too, and he's never done that 'til now."

"I hope things keep getting better for you."

"Speaking of getting better, I just want to say thanks for all you've done for us here in our messed up little cowtown. Even though all the girls still don't tell you, you've made things better for us. We all love you, you know. Even Molly." She wanted to look away. "We'd all miss you."

He tilted his head just a little and looked into Summer's eyes. He could see her eyes misting just a bit and he could sense that she didn't want to look directly at him.

"Hey, now, Summer, you're talking like you're saying 'goodbye.' What's that all about?"

She hesitated a moment and turned away to look at something else.

"I heard you're probably getting in your truck, and driving as far and as fast you can as soon as the season's over and that you won't even look back in your rearview mirror at us on the way out of town."

"What? First of all, don't go getting all sentimental on me like the season's over because it isn't. Second..."

"Coach Cannon says it is. Over."

"He told you that?

"He told Roy and Roy told me."

Anger burned inside Coach Lewis, but he took a deep breath and clinched his fists to keep his emotions in check.

"Well, we'll just have to see."

They sat for a moment in awkward silence then Coach Lewis stood and moved around in front of the desk. He sat down on the edge and looked deep into Summer's sad eyes.

"I've been meaning to thank you for something. The other night at Texline and then again at Shamrock. Roy and the football players..."

"Coach, you're thanking the wrong person. Corey Colter had more to do with it than me."

"So, what's the story?"

"I wanted to know the same thing," she answered. She turned away from him trying to hide the tear she wiped from her eye. "The guys still don't give a hoot about girls basketball, really. But, Corey convinced Roy and Roy convinced his guys that even if girls basketball was lame, the girls on the team were Lazarus girls. And since they're Lazarus girls, the least they could do was show up and pull for 'em because they're from Lazarus. Corey and Roy also said they owed it to me, 'because of Autumn.'"

"Well, tell them we appreciate it more than they can imagine."

A swell of emotion overtook Summer and, sobbing, she fell into the empty chair near Coach Lewis. Unsure of what to do, he put a hand on her shoulder and let her cry.

Martha sat the four big plates on the table one at a time. Haskins took the first and passed it to Tommy Cannon, the next he passed to Patton McArthur. Bill Merrick took his from Martha then Haskins did the same. The heaping mounds of chicken spaghetti took the men by surprise; they had expected chicken fried steak and mashed potatoes as their Blue Plate Specials. They stared at their plates then glanced at one another with raised eyebrows. Despite their best attempts to be discreet, Martha noticed; she, on the other hand, showed no discretion as she flashed them a subtle but mischievous grin. She handed out their sweet teas and returned to the kitchen.

"OK, gentleman, let's not beat around the bush. I'll get right to it," Haskins began in his best Principal Haskins voice. "Neill called this morning. I know this is short notice but y'all need to cancel your plans for tomorrow night. Listen, fine by me if you throw Neill under the bus on this one with your wives since it was his call."

The General wasted no time in expressing his disgust.

"You gotta' be kidding me. He wants us to go all the way to Amarillo for that stupid game?"

Cannon asked, "Did you even put up a fight or did you just roll over?"

"Tommy, I've known you a long time and I'm telling you to tread lightly here. He's my boss and he played the boss card. He also reminded me that I'm your boss, all of you, and that I'm to play my boss card with you. Like it or not, we're all going to Amarillo."

The other three sat and picked the celery out of their spaghetti without saying a word. Their silence spoke volumes.

"Listen," Haskins said almost in a whisper, "Frederickson's got a good point. These kids are the town's sweethearts all of a sudden... and, you know, that's not so bad. Anyway, we need to be seen there. All of us. Everybody I talked to is driving up. The whole town's shutting down and heading north tomorrow. That includes us. Besides, it's the right thing to do."

"They're gonna get drummed, just so you know," Cannon popped back.

Merrick added, "No chance they'll even get within twenty. Maybe thirty."

"Maybe you're right," Haskins seemed to concede. "And maybe you're not."

The General continued, "Why're you acting like they even have a prayer up there tomorrow? What's got into you, Calvin? Groom killed

363

Nazareth. What do you think's gonna happen to our girls? They're gonna get embarrassed. One positive, I suppose, is we all get to watch that know-it-all pretty boy finally get put in his place."

At that, Cannon and Merrick lifted their glasses of sweet tea to McArthur for a toast. Haskins just stewed. After a few moments more with no conversation, Haskins stood up and threw his napkin on the table.

"You bunch of sore losers! I swear you're like menopausal old women! I'm not asking you to dress up in skirts and tote pom-poms up there, but by God we're all going! We pull out tomorrow at 3:00 sharp!"

As Haskins slid out of the booth, he bumped the table and spilled two glasses of tea, most of which ran straight off the edge and into Bill Merrick's lap. Merrick jumped to his feet, banged the table accidentally and let slip a few choice words. When he looked up from wiping his lap with his napkin, he noticed that all eyes in Mary's Kitchen were staring back at him.

As the Lady Longhorns unloaded the bus in the parking lot of Amarillo High School, Sam turned to the group and said, "You know, if I hadn't moved to Lazarus, this is where I'd have been playing this year. This is my old school. The Amarillo Sandies. I think I like Longhorns better."

"The Sandies? *Chica*, that's totally lame!" Rita replied.

"And," Sam added, "they didn't make the playoffs this year."

The girls trekked across the huge parking lot, made their way out of the blustery wind into the warm gym, and located the locker room marked by a sign that read "Lazarus Lady Longhorns – Visitors." Sam had explained to them on the way through the parking lot that the school's enrollment hovered somewhere near 2000 students. The rest of the girls couldn't imagine going to a school with more than twice as many students as their entire hometown population. But a student body of 2000 students hardly compared to some of the schools in Houston, Dallas and San Antonio, Coach Lewis added.

Inside the locker room, the girls stared in wonder at the spacious accommodations. The locker room never would be considered luxurious, but there must have been fifty huge lockers. There were six long benches running the length of the lockers along each wall, a huge whiteboard mounted on wall beneath a TV/DVD combo hanging from the ceiling, dirty clothes hampers, ball racks and more. Through a door in the back corner, the girls could see a row of shower stalls, each with its own black and gold curtain.

The girls sprawled out all over the locker room; they stretched out on the benches, sat against the lockers and piled onto two sofas MJ had discovered through another door. Coach Lewis went to the white board and jotted some diagrams, some quick-hitter plays, the Groom lineup and a few other things on the board in red marker. Unlike his girls who seemed far too relaxed and just happy to be there, Coach Lewis felt like he needed to be doing something. He told the girls to change into their red uniforms and left the locker room to explore the gym.

Coach Lewis gazed out onto the basketball court where his girls once again would be playing for their lives. His eyes moved from the high, black and gold bleachers on either side of the court to the retractable basketball goals already hoisted up near the ceiling to the huge black "A" on the court outlined in gold with "SANDIES" written beneath it in gold lettering. He studied the beautiful, new, bright gold pads hanging on the walls just past the baselines at either end of the court. His eyes shifted then to large photos of the players hanging on the walls, boys on one wall and girls on the other. He made a mental note to look into that idea. Above him, the gym ceiling seemed a hundred feet above the court and a sophisticated scoreboard hung down from the ceiling. He figured this would be as nice a place as any to play a big game.

As much as he liked the new gym, though, he still preferred the old, quaint, intimate gyms built decades ago for small-town basketball played by skinny kids in short shorts and Chuck Taylors. The dark wood floors, wooden bleachers right on top of the court, tight quarters that turned even modest crowds into standing-room-only crowds. Had he been asked a year ago which he'd prefer, he would have said big, bright and modern, but after a season travelling the back roads of west Texas to play in small-town gyms, he'd take the old gyms any day.

"You must be Coach Lewis, from Lazarus?"

Coach Lewis turned to find a tall, thin woman in her mid-thirties standing behind him. She wore black warm-ups with white trim and a pouncing tiger on the chest, and expensive looking cross-trainers; her outfit matched those worn by the twelve big, athletic-looking girls lined up behind her single file and carrying black duffle bags.

"I'm Coach Holland, from Groom," she said as she extended her hand.

Coach Lewis shook her hand but he couldn't take his eyes off the basketball machine that had filed in behind her. Across the board, they were bigger than he anticipated and they looked like they could be a small college team.

"Listen, Coach, we wanted say how much we admire your kids. We know your story and understand your kids have been through a lot. Sounds like you're one of the good guys. Anyway, we're proud of your kids and just wanted to let you know. It'll be an honor to go toe to toe with you guys today."

Coach Lewis nodded and thanked her. Then, one by one the girls filed by him, shook his hand and said something along the lines of "good luck" or "have a good game" on the way to the other locker room. He stood there flabbergasted, unsure of what to say next.

Before she walked off with her team, Coach Holland turned back to Coach Lewis and said with a smile, "Now, Coach, you guys take it easy on us out there tonight."

His heart sank and his stomach knotted. She had just given him the kiss of death. Although he hadn't coached as long as plenty of other coaches, he'd been around the game long enough to know that innocent little phrase actually had a hidden meaning. That ostensibly polite and jovial phrase happened to be coach-speak for, "No hard feelings, but we're about to kick your butts and there's nothing you can do to stop it." As polite and classy as Coach Holland and the Lady Tigers of Groom seemed, they were here for one reason and one reason only: to win and win big.

Back in the locker room, Coach Lewis decided to go over the game plan again with the girls before the initial stretching and shooting they would do to loosen up. The girls circled around him and faced the white board he'd covered with all sorts of coaching jargon and basketball hieroglyphics. He moved quickly and abruptly from one point to the next, then lost his train of thought momentarily, and then suddenly got back on track again. When he turned back to his girls to see if he'd lost them in his almost-frantic run-through, the sight caught him completely off-guard. The girls seemed perfectly relaxed and, in fact, sat smiling up at him as if they'd done this a hundred times.

"Coach," MJ asked with a grin, "are you nervous?"

"Are you?"

"No fair, Coach," said Molly, "we asked you first."

"A coaching textbook probably would tell me to tell you that I'm not," he said as he drew a deep breath. "But that wouldn't be the honest truth. I'm not going to lie to you. I'm a little nervous."

"Why are you afraid, Coach?" Cassie wanted to know.

"Not afraid, not scared. I'm just a little nervous, that's all. There's a difference. I just want everything to go well for you guys, for all of us. There's going to be a lot of people out there," he said as he pointed out toward the gym, "who've driven a long way to watch you play. You guys have inspired more than a few people in this ornery old town of ours and now they're pulling for you. I just want…"

Sam interrupted him. "I think we know, Coach. And it's gonna be fine. We're ready. A hundred percent. We're gonna give everybody what they came for tonight." The intensity in her eyes said she was serious.

"Is that so?"

Sam just nodded.

"Well, then," he said as he motioned for everyone to huddle up around him, "what are we waiting for?"

From the opening tip, the Groom Lady Tigers and the Lazarus Lady Longhorns went to war. No shot went uncontested. No rebound hit the hardwood before someone snatched it from the air. No inbounds pass went undefended. Though Groom played every game this way, Lazarus had yet to play a game at this level of intensity. Nevertheless, the two sides battled as if the physicality were commonplace. Fouls were hard but clean. Banging under the basket was brutal and often breathtaking. Regardless of who won or lost the contest, all the participants would be bruised and aching the next day. The two sides battled on undeterred.

At the end of the first period, the stunned Groom squad led Lazarus by only three points. However, the Lady Longhorns drew first blood in the second period on a long, ill-advised three-pointer from Brooklynne to tie the score. The lead changed dramatically several times during the second after each team made small runs and took turns at the free-throw line. Then, as the seconds ticked away and the second period gave way to half-time, the point guard from Groom launched a ridiculous circus shot from well beyond half court. The ball somehow found its way to the goal and bounced high off the rim as the buzzer sounded, then dropped straight down through the center of the hoop for an improbable three points. The Lady Tigers leapt and roared with excitement and their fans erupted in applause as the hands-down favorites took a slim two-point lead into the locker room at the half. The Lady Longhorns, undaunted by the miraculous bucket at the end of the half, hustled off the court to the other locker room encouraged by the thunderous ovation from the Lazarus faithful.

During halftime, Coach Lewis fed off the girls' intensity and remained completely focused. No longer did he seem like the frightened rookie coach the girls observed before the game. His nervousness had been replaced with steely determination and optimism. He encouraged his troops and praised their effort. He diagrammed a few things on the white board and offered a few suggestions to fortify the defense in the second half. He then diagrammed a few quick-hitter plays he hoped would bolster the attack and put the Groom defense on their heels. He rallied his girls, stirred them with more fiery encouragement, then marched them quickly back out to the court for the final showdown.

As the second half resumed, the speed of the game picked up considerably. Groom decided to run the outmanned Lady Longhorns and wear down both the starters and reserves by pressing and trapping on defense and by running a fast break on offense. Coach Lewis brilliantly rotated his players in and out of the action. It didn't seem to matter who he put in the lineup in support of Sam, Rita and MJ; all the girls played at a level they'd never reached before. The third period wound down in a flurry of traded baskets on quick shots at both ends of the court. With the score unbelievably tied after three periods of play, the two unlikely foes, showing signs of fatigue for the first time, slogged to their respective benches to hydrate for the final round.

Like two prize fighters determined to win or die trying, the teams returned to the floor a minute later for what would be the most remarkable eight minutes of basketball that anyone in the Amarillo High School gym had seen in years. Before they inbounded the ball, Sam, Rita, MJ, Nairobi and Brooklynne met at center court. Sam said something audible only to the other four in the huddle. They hugged briefly, Sam glanced up into the stands in the direction of Martha, and the five girls took their places to run their favorite inbounds play. Sam inbounded the ball to Nairobi, who quickly dumped the ball off to MJ. MJ pivoted and fired the ball down the floor to Sam, who had just been freed by a wicked double-screen from Brooklynne and Rita. Sam caught the ball, dribbled once and went up for a layup, the only uncontested layup of the entire contest. The noise from the crowd reached a deafening level as the Lady Longhorns regained the lead.

For the next six minutes, as both teams made numerous trips to the free throw line following hard foul after hard foul, neither team managed to find a way to hang on to the lead. As the momentum swung back and forth like a pendulum, the excitement drove the entire crowd into a frenzy. The Groom fans proved intimidating, but Roy and the football players matched every decibel the Tiger fans mustered. Though the pressure mounted with each possession and free throw, the shooters for both teams seemed entirely incapable of missing; free throw after free throw rattled home.

With just under two minutes left, the better of Groom's two post players bit on one of Sam's vicious head fakes. The defender left her feet and came down flailing on top of Sam as Sam went up for her shot. Sam powered the ball upward and off the backboard in spite of the foul, and the ball found its way into the basket. The official signaled for the shot to count, then signaled to Coach Holland that her player, now with five fouls, had thirty seconds to leave the floor. After Groom's substitution, the official sent Sam to the line where she completed the three-point play and gave her team a two-point lead.

The Groom guards inbounded the ball and raced down the court hoping to beat the Lady Longhorns to the other end of the court. In a flash of white, the point guard dribbled hard to the top of the key as the Lady Longhorns scrambled to get into position. When she reached the top of the key, she slashed into the lane and drew the red-clad defenders into the lane with her. Instead of pulling up for a point-blank jumper in front of the rim, the guard slung the ball over her head into the corner to her left where Groom's three-point specialist had spotted up for a shot. The on-target pass landed perfectly in the hands of the waiting shooter. MJ cut hard when the guard made the pass, then darted back out toward the shooter who had begun her shooting motion already. In her rush to contest the shot, MJ stumbled, lost her balance and fell headlong into the guard a split second before she released the ball. The two tumbled in an alternating red and white jumble out of bounds and landed against the wall. The crowd let out a single, horrified gasp at the sight of the two competitors crashing to the ground. The Groom fans turned to berate the Lazarus fans, but suddenly erupted in ecstatic cheering and applause. MJ looked over her shoulder and saw her teammates on the floor with their hands on their heads. The Lady Tigers high-fived one another and walked toward the lane where they seemed to be setting up for the impending free-throw. MJ knew immediately the guard she just tackled somehow had managed to drain the three. MJ then saw the official headed her direction with his arm out and all five fingers extended. She had just coughed up the lead for her team and fouled out of the game in one fell swoop. Dejected and disgusted with herself, MJ made her way to the bench where Coach Lewis and Summer tried to console her.

Coach Lewis subbed Molly into the game for MJ, then shouted some nearly-inaudible instructions to his team. As the Groom guard drained her free-throw with cool confidence and extended her team's lead to two points, the crowd ratcheted the racket in the gym to a new level of loud. Sam swiftly inbounded the ball to Rita, who zigzagged her way down the court against intense pressure from the Groom point guard. Rita stole a glance at the game clock above and saw that there were just thirty-six ticks of the clock left in regulation. She spun past her defender and drove into the lane, drawing defenders just as the Lady Tigers had done on the last possession. Rita spotted Brooklynne breaking to the corner and she fired a pass to where she knew Brooklynne would be a split-second later. Brooklynne caught the pass just inside the three-point line, jumped and released the long jumper in one fluid, flawless motion. Everyone on the floor stopped momentarily and watched as the ball floated first up then back down in a rainbow-shaped arc and dropped through the hoop to tie the score with less than thirty seconds left.

Before the ball hit the floor, Coach Lewis called a time-out and motioned for his girls to hustle off the court to grab some water and get some instructions. He thought briefly about subbing in Cassie for Nairobi to add some speed, but changed his mind hoping Nairobi could come down with a rebound in the event of a missed shot. As Summer handed out water bottles to her exhausted teammates, Coach Lewis huddled his team and looked at each one of his girls before he spoke.

"What an incredible game! You've played thirty one and a half minutes of incredible basketball and you've given a thirty-win team all they can handle. I know you're exhausted and your muscles probably hurt like never before. But I need you to give me thirty more seconds." He paused and pointed up to the stands where the Lazarus faithful were screaming themselves hoarse. "I need you to give them thirty more seconds. Play these last thirty seconds as if you love this game more than life itself and may never have another chance to play again. Make these thirty seconds count. Now, on the floor, expect them to try to draw contact by driving to the basket. Whatever you do, do not give up an uncontested layup and if you foul them, do not let your girl get off her shot. Here we go, thirty more seconds! Let's finish this!"

Groom inbounded the ball and, rather than racing the Lady Longhorns to the other end of the court, the guard walked the ball toward their basket. Rita pressured her but didn't dare go for the steal and risk a foul. Rita dropped back a little and the guard reached the top of the key with twenty seconds left on the clock. The guard jabbed at Rita with her foot like she was going to drive past, causing Rita to step back just a bit, but then the guard pulled back suddenly leaving just enough space between Rita and her for a quick shot. The guard stepped back to be sure she was behind the three-point line and sailed a long three over Rita's outstretched arms. With fifteen seconds on the clock, Groom regained the lead and went on defense with a three-point cushion.

Sam immediately inbounded the ball to Molly, who whipped it right back to Sam. Sam took everyone by surprise as she faked a pass to Rita then took off with the ball herself. Sam caught her defender completely off-guard and got a few steps on her as she dribbled awkwardly toward her goal. Sam drove hard to the right side of the basket, picked up her dribble for a layup and got clobbered from behind as she released the ball for her layup with nine seconds left on the clock. Sam crashed to the floor and the ball hit the underside of the rim. Though Coach Lewis and the Lazarus fans went ballistic, the official declined to charge Groom with a flagrant foul. The big, brawny girl who had taken Sam out just seconds earlier reached down and helped Sam to her feet.

Every muscle in Sam's body screamed at her as she lumbered to the free-throw line for her first attempt. She heaved the ball toward the rim where it bounced around a few times before finally falling into the basket. Sam had cut Groom's lead to two points. Sam stepped back and called her teammates to her. In the quick huddle, she put her hand out without saying a word and her teammates responded in kind. They looked around the huddle at one another, smiled and nodded just as the official squawked at them to step back into position. Before Sam broke her huddle at the top of the key and stepped back to the free throw line, she reminded her teammates, "After I make this, we need the ball or a foul! Find your girl, get on her and get us a steal or a foul! This is it, ladies! Right here, right now."

Sam bent her knees and pushed against the floor through her heels and through her legs. Her body straightened, her arms moved upward and out in front of her toward the rim, her wrists flicked forward and the last ounce of her energy flowed through her fingertips into the ball, carrying it forward precisely fifteen feet in a beautiful, slow-motion, arcing trajectory. The seams on the ball rotated backwards as the ball floated toward its destination. For a brief moment after she released the ball, Sam knew without a doubt it was one of the most beautiful shots ever to leave her fingertips: the perfect spin, the perfect velocity, the perfect arc. Beautiful.

The Lady Tigers knew Lazarus would be looking for a steal or a foul immediately, so they spread themselves across the court as wide as possible with a player at center court, a player in the lane and a player standing near each sideline. The Lady Tiger inbounding the ball from the baseline quickly fired a pass toward Rita's girl. The ball drifted just past Rita's outstretched fingertips. Nairobi and Molly closed in quickly, but the guard dished the ball off to her teammate before Nairobi and Molly could get there to foul her. The Lady Tiger, now with possession of the ball and no defender on her at all, turned toward the opposite end of the floor and took off. Sam and Brooklynne gave chase but they both were several steps behind her. As the white uniform seemed to pull away from her pursuers, Sam dove toward it and reached for anything she could grab: ball, uniform, shoelaces, anything. As Sam hit the ground with a thud, the buzzer shrieked as the final second vanished from the clock on the scoreboard far overhead.

The Lady Tigers collapsed on the floor, exhausted from the Herculean effort needed to fend off the lowly Lady Longhorns from Lazarus. The Lady Tigers looked around at one another and smiled finally, satisfied that they had survived and advanced. Suddenly, though, they became aware of the pandemonium around them.

The Lazarus fans poured out of the stands and onto the court below. With their mouths agape and their hands on their heads, the girls from Groom watched the Lady Longhorns pile on their big post player still sprawled on the floor after the final play. They watched in awe as the Lazarus fans pushed their way past security and surrounded the Lady Longhorns on the court. One of the Lady Tigers on the bench said to her coach, "But they didn't win. We did." Seemingly the entire town of Lazarus, except a few stubborn souls still sitting high up in the stands, danced and cheered and embraced the girls and one another as if they'd just won the biggest game of their lives. High overhead, a voice over the loudspeakers urged fans to please clear the floor, please clear the floor.

Coach Lewis waded into the fray. He knew his girls were somewhere in the middle of the chaos but he couldn't get to them. People ran to him, patted him on the back, rubbed his head, embraced him, and said, "Way to go, Coach," "That was unbelievable, Coach," and "We couldn't be prouder." Even the guys in Lazarus letter jackets congratulated him as he passed by them in the multitude. He pushed his way through the pulsing, chanting mob on the floor but he couldn't seem to make any headway.

In the midst of the scrum, he made eye contact with Nairobi's parents, who were dancing and cheering but crying all the same. He saw Gladys, Dee and some of the teachers from school, all of whom looked overwhelmed with a mix of emotions. The fans pulled him this way and that and hugged and congratulated him. He was sure he'd appreciate it all later, but he wanted to get to his girls. Finally, with the fans cheering uncontrollably, the Groom fans looking down on them in bewilderment and the agitated voice above still urging the fans to clear the floor, he broke through the jubilant mass of bodies and found his girls piled on top of one another on the floor. They were laughing and crying and hugging one another almost triumphantly. Exhausted, he sank to the floor to just watch, to soak it all in, and to commit this scene to memory.

On the other side of the pile, Victoria Avery emerged from the wall of bodies with her cameraman in tow. The crazy celebration had taken a toll on both her makeup and her perfectly-coiffed hair. Victoria dragged her cameraman over to the girls and prompted him to start filming. She straightened her hair as best she could and grabbed Sam by the shoulder. As Sam turned to find Victoria and a camera invading her space, she smiled at Victoria through her tears.

"Sam, may I have just a word with you? You look like you're taking this pretty hard. This must be just devastating for you, for your team and even for your entire town. There were so many people who had so much hope in your team, so much riding on tonight's game. This must be incredibly difficult for you."

She practically shoved the microphone in Sam's face.

"What? You really don't get it at all, do you?" Sam asked with a hoarse, raspy voice.

"I'm sorry?" Victoria responded.

"I said you don't get it. At all. We just played the game of our lives. The best game we've ever played, against an unbelievable opponent. Isn't that enough? After all we've been through this year, losing our friend and almost losing our season, look around right now," Sam said as she looked all around her with teary eyes, "look around at what we've won."

EPILOGUE

The dingy light from the old fluorescent bulbs overhead seeped out into the long-vacant gym and disappeared in the darkness. All the girls and their families had gone home; Coach Lewis sat alone in his office in the pre-dawn hours. In his hands, he held a basketball. On the way out of the gym in Amarillo, Molly had snatched the game ball from the rack and tucked it away in her duffle bag. The ball had been signed by each of the girls and marked with the date. Summer had even added to the mish-mash of names on the ball Autumn's name along with her jersey number, 20. He turned the ball slowly in his hands. Below the signatures and the date, one of the girls had written, "Sometimes the journey is not about the destination – sometimes the journey is about the journey. Lazarus Lady Longhorns – 13 wins!" Over and over Coach Lewis turned the ball in his hands, read the names one by one, and read the one-sentence story of their unforgettable season. And wept.

Lazarus Lady Longhorns Basketball Schedule

Nov-11	Friona	AWAY
Nov-14	Amherst	HOME
Nov-18	Sudan	AWAY
Nov-20-22	Hereford Tournament	AWAY
Nov-25	Bovina	AWAY
Dec-2	Whiteface	HOME
Dec-4-6	Dimmitt Tournament	AWAY
Dec-9	Hale Center	AWAY
Dec-11-13	Whitharral Tournament	AWAY
Dec-16	Cotton Center	AWAY
Dec-19	Shallowater	HOME
Jan-6	Farwell	AWAY
Jan-9	*Kress	AWAY
Jan-13	*Happy	HOME
Jan-16	*Silverton	AWAY
Jan-20	*Hart	AWAY
Jan-23	*Nazareth	AWAY
Jan-27	*Kress	HOME
Jan-30	*Happy	AWAY
Feb-3	*Silverton	HOME
Feb-6	*Hart	AWAY
Feb-10	*Nazareth	HOME

*denotes district games

Lazarus Lady Longhorns basketball
Gabe Lewis – Head Coach   Tommy Cannon – Athletic Director

ACKNOWLEDGEMENTS

Thanks first and foremost to God, for being in the redemption business. Thank you, Christy, for encouraging me to complete this project. A huge thanks to Shannon Owen, editor-extraordinaire, for your guidance and direction. For making the cover photo possible, thanks to Jennifer Allison, a.k.a. Monsey, for the uniforms, and thanks to Margaret Hartman, for wearing them. Thanks to all my numerous beta readers for your input, feedback and assistance in making this make sense.

ABOUT THE AUTHOR

Prior to writing *Resurrecting Lazarus, Texas*, Nathan Barber penned more than a dozen books, including his most recent release *The Complete Idiot's Guide to European History, 2e*. A lifelong educator and former basketball coach, Barber lives with his family in Houston, Texas, where he continues to write.

CPSIA information can be obtained at www.ICGtesting.com
Printed in the USA
LVOW05s1448070813

346784LV00002B/129/P